PRAISE FOR THE NOVELS OF THE NIGHTSIDE

Something from the Nightside

"The book is a fast, fun little roller coaster of a story—and its track runs through neighborhoods that make the Twilight Zone look like Mayberry. Simon Green's Nightside is a macabre and thoroughly entertaining world that makes a bizarre and gleefully dangerous backdrop for a quick-moving tale. Fun stuff!"
—Jim Butcher, author of The Dresden Files and *Proven Guilty*

"A riveting start to what could be a long and extremely addictive series. No one delivers sharp, crackling dialogue better than Green. No one whisks readers away to more terrifying adventures or more bewildering locales. Sure, it's dangerous, but you're going to follow him unquestioningly into the Nightside." —*Black Gate Magazine*

"Cross *The X-Files* with *The Twilight Zone,* add a pinch of *The Outer Limits* and a dash of *Eerie, Indiana,* and one might have a glimmer of an idea what the Nightside is like . . . Simon R. Green has written a fascinating little gem that makes people want to walk on the wild side and visit his extraordinary world." —*BookBrowser*

Agents of Light and Darkness

"I really enjoyed Green's first John Taylor novel and the second one is even better. The usual private eye stuff—with a bizarre kick."
—*Chronicle*

"The Nightside novels are a great blending of Lovecraft and Holmes . . . an action-packed thriller, a delightful private eye investigative fantasy tale." —*Midwest Book Review*

"If you like your noir pitch-black, then return to the Nightside."
—*University City Review*

continued . . .

Nightingale's Lament

"Great urban fantasy . . . [An] incredible world . . . John is in top-gun form."   —*BookBrowser*

"Filled with supernatural creatures of various sorts, the action leavened by occasional bits of dry humor, the Taylor series has proven to be a welcome break from the endless quasi-medieval intrigues that dominate contemporary fantasy."   —*Chronicle*

"Strong horror fantasy."   —*The Best Reviews*

"John Taylor . . . work[s] in a place that's like the bastard offspring of *The Twilight Zone* and every dark, rainy city of the night described by Raymond Chandler . . . Green cleverly keeps background mysteries boiling along, enriching the backdrop of his world . . . Taylor is a fascinating blend of types. He's a private eye from the Sam Spade school . . . People and objects from science fiction, horror, fantasy, and every other literary genre mix and meet [in the Nightside], resembling a demented and evil version of Toontown or an outpost of Hell itself . . . [It's] a rich, fascinating place, truly a setting that is memorable long after the book is closed. The Nightside is a place no sensible person would ever want to visit—but which a reader will savor time after time. *Nightingale's Lament* is an excellent addition to Green's impressive and diverse body of work. Fans of modern urban or dark fantasy, such as Jim Butcher's Harry Dresden novels, will be rewarded by picking up this book."   —*SFRevu*

"Imagine if you will a darker version of Neil Gaiman's *Neverwhere* and its setting, London Below. Now further imagine that in this place, the Nightside, all the dimensions, all the times drift together . . . Simon writes some of the coolest narrative I've ever read . . . So much fun to read . . . *Nightingale's Lament* has everything I like in an urban fantasy novel—an interesting and very cool protagonist, snappy dialogue, loads of violence, a smidgen of sex, weird characters, a bit of a mystery, and a pacing that never lets up. Add in that John Taylor is evolving— yes, evolving—as a character and you have a series that goes on for years to come. Call it dark fantasy, call it urban fantasy, call it horror if you want—just read it."   —*Green Man Review*

"[An] incredible world." —*Paranormal Romance Reviews*

"[The] strong characterization of a complicated hero is one of the qualities that makes Green's series effective. He deftly balances his hero's turmoil as he fights the darkness both within and without. With dark humor and psychological horror he rivals urban horror writers such as Jim Butcher and Christopher Golden; Laurell Hamilton fans should enjoy this series as well." —*Romantic Times*

Hex and the City

"[Green's] style is unique, stylized, and addictive . . . urban fantasy with a splatterpunk attitude, a noir sensibility, a pulp sense of style, and a horror undercoating." —*Green Man Review*

"The Nightside saga takes a huge leap forward . . . It's a big, turbulent stew but Green is a master chef . . . A terrific read." —*SFRevu*

"Totally enjoyable . . . Take a vacation into the Nightside . . . just try not to get lost in it . . . All the elements of a classic PI story . . . Green is a natural storyteller with a wonderful imagination. Think Mickey Spillane writing episodes of *Millennium*." —*CrimeSpree*

Paths Not Taken

"Fans of the Nightside series will enjoy the journey into the past of London's underworld." —*Booklist*

"A fantastic fantasy . . . The story line is action-packed . . . fabulous." —*Midwest Book Review*

"Green's storytelling is engaging, as always, and his gift for worldbuilding is still going strong. Glimpses of the Nightside's past are compelling, and the Wild Hunt will have you unconsciously holding your breath." —*Purple Pens*

A WALK ON THE NIGHTSIDE

SIMON R. GREEN

ACE BOOKS, NEW YORK

THE BERKLEY PUBLISHING GROUP
Published by the Penguin Group
Penguin Group (USA) Inc.
375 Hudson Street, New York, New York 10014, USA
Penguin Group (Canada), 90 Eglinton Avenue East, Suite 700, Toronto, Ontario M4P 2Y3, Canada
(a division of Pearson Penguin Canada Inc.)
Penguin Books Ltd., 80 Strand, London WC2R 0RL, England
Penguin Group Ireland, 25 St. Stephen's Green, Dublin 2, Ireland (a division of Penguin Books Ltd.)
Penguin Group (Australia), 250 Camberwell Road, Camberwell, Victoria 3124, Australia
(a division of Pearson Australia Group Pty. Ltd.)
Penguin Books India Pvt. Ltd., 11 Community Centre, Panchsheel Park, New Delhi—
110 017, India
Penguin Group (NZ), cnr Airborne and Rosedale Roads, Albany, Auckland 1310, New Zealand
(a division of Pearson New Zealand Ltd.)
Penguin Books (South Africa) (Pty.) Ltd., 24 Sturdee Avenue, Rosebank, Johannesburg 2196, South
Africa

Penguin Books Ltd., Registered Offices: 80 Strand, London WC2R 0RL, England

PRINTING HISTORY
Something from the Nightside: Ace mass-market edition / June 2003
Agents of Light and Darkness: Ace mass-market edition / November 2003
Nightingale's Lament: Ace mass-market edition / May 2004
Ace trade paperback omnibus edition / September 2006

Library of Congress Cataloging-in-Publication Data

Green, Simon R., 1955–
    A walk on the nightside / Simon R. Green.
      p. cm.
      Contents: Something from the nightside—Agents of light and darkness—Nightingale's lament.
      ISBN 0-441-01448-8 (trade pbk.)
      1. Taylor, John (Fictitious character)—Fiction. 2. Private investigators—England—London—
Fiction. 3. London (England)—Fiction. I. Title.

    PR6107.R44W35 2006
    823'.914—dc22   2006042853

PRINTED IN THE UNITED STATES OF AMERICA

10 9 8 7 6 5 4 3 2 1

CONTENTS

SOMETHING
FROM THE
NIGHTSIDE

ONE

Money Comes Walking In

Private eyes come in all shapes and sizes, and none of them look like television stars. Some do insurance work, some hang around cheap hotels with camcorders hoping to get evidence for divorce cases, and damn few ever get to investigate complicated murder mysteries. Some chase things that don't exist, or shouldn't. Me, I find things. Sometimes I'd rather not find them, but that comes with the territory.

The flaking sign on the door in those days said *Taylor Investigations*. I'm Taylor. Tall, dark and not particularly handsome. I bear the scars of old cases proudly, and I never let down a client. Provided they've paid at least some cash up front.

My office back then was cosy, if you were feeling charitable, cramped if you weren't. I spent a lot of time there. It beat having a life. It was a low-rent office in a low-rent area. All the businesses with any sense were moving out, making more room for those of us who operated in the greyer areas of the legal and illegal. Even the rats were just passing through, on their way to somewhere more civilised. My neighbours were a dentist and an accountant, both of them struck off, both of whom made more money than I did.

It was raining hard the night Joanna Barrett came to see me. The kind of cold, driving, pitiless rain that makes you glad to be safe and dry indoors. I should have taken that as an omen, but I've never been very good at picking up on hints. It was late, well past the point where the day starts edging into evening, and everyone else in the building had gone home. I was still sitting behind my desk, half-watching the portable television with its sound turned down, while the man on the phone yelled in my ear. He wanted money, the fool. I made sympathetic noises in all the right places, waiting for him to get tired and go away, and then my ears pricked up as I heard footsteps in the hall outside, heading for my door. Steady, unhurried . . . and a woman. Interesting. Women always make the best clients. They say they want information, but mostly what they really want is revenge; and they aren't mean when it comes to paying for what they want. What they need. Hell hath no fury; and I should know.

The footsteps stopped outside my door, and a tall shadow studied the bullet hole in the frosted-glass window. I really should have got that seen to, but it made such a great conversation piece. Clients like a touch of romance and danger when they're hiring a private detective, even if they only want some papers served. The door opened, and she walked in. A tall good-looking blonde who reeked of money and class, looking immediately out of place amid the battered furniture and cracked-plaster walls of my office.

Her clothes had the quiet elegance and style that shrieks of serious money, and when she spoke my name her voice had an aristocratic edge that could cut glass. Either she'd been to all the very best boarding and finishing schools, or she'd spent a hell of a lot on elocution lessons. She was perhaps a little too slender, with a raw-boned face and minimal make-up that meant she would always be handsome rather than pretty. From the way she stood, the way she held herself, it was obvious she was a control freak, and the set of her perfectly made-up mouth showed she was used to being obeyed. I notice things like that. It's my job. I gave her my best unimpressed nod and gestured for her to take a seat on the only other chair, on the opposite side of my desk. She sat down without taking out a handkerchief to clean the seat first, and I gave her extra points for bravery. I watched her look around my office, while the voice in the phone at my ear grew ever more hysterical, demanding money with menaces. Very specific menaces. Her face was studiously calm, even blank, but as I glanced around my office, it was only too easy to see it as she saw it.

A battered desk, with only a few token papers in the in and out trays, a fourth-hand filing cabinet, and a rickety couch pushed back against the wall. Rumpled blankets and a dented pillow on the couch showed someone had been sleeping on it regularly. The single window behind my desk had bars on the outside, and the glass rattled loosely in its frame as the wind goosed it. The scuffed carpet had holes, the portable television on my desk was black and white, and the only note of colour on my walls was a give-away girlie calendar. Old delivery pizza boxes stood stacked in one corner. It didn't take a genius to work out this wasn't just an office. Someone lived here. It was also patently obvious that this wasn't the office of someone on his way up.

I'd chosen to live in the real world, for what seemed like good reasons at the time, but it had never been easy.

I suddenly decided I'd had enough of the voice on the telephone. "Look," I said, in that calm reasonable tone that if done properly can drive people absolutely batshit, "if I had the money I'd pay you, but I don't have the money. So you'll just have to take a number and get in line. You are of course welcome to try suing, in which case I can recommend a neighbour of mine who's a lawyer. He needs the work, so he won't laugh in your face when you tell him who you're trying to get money out of. However, if you'd care to be patient just a little longer, it's possible a whole lot of money just walked in . . . You know, hysteria like that can't be good for your blood pressure. I recommend deep breathing and visits to the seaside. I always find the sea very soothing. I'll get back to you. Eventually."

I put the phone down firmly and smiled politely at my visitor. She didn't smile back. I just knew we were going to get along. She looked pointedly at the murmuring television on my desk, and I turned it off.

"It's company," I said calmly. "Much like a dog, but with the added advantage that you don't have to take it for walks."

"Don't you ever go home?" Her tone made it clear she was asking for information, not because she cared.

"I am currently in between homes. Big, empty, expensive things. Besides, I like it here. Everything's within reach, and nobody bothers me when the day's over. Usually."

"I know it's late. I didn't want to be seen coming here."

"I can understand that."

She sniffed briefly. "You have a hole in your office door, Mr. Taylor."

I nodded. "Moths."

The corners of her dark red mouth turned down, and for a moment I thought she was going to get up and leave. I have that effect on people. But she controlled herself and gave me her best intimidating glare.

"I'm Joanna Barrett."

I nodded, non-commitally. "You say that like it should mean something to me."

"To anyone else, it would," she said, just a little acidly. "But then, I don't suppose you read the business pages, do you?"

"Not unless someone pays me to. Am I to take it you're rich?"

"Extremely."

I grinned. "The very best kind of client. What can I do for you?"

She shifted slightly in her chair, clutching her oversized white leather handbag protectively to her. She didn't want to be here, talking to the likes of me. No doubt usually she had people to take care of such unpleasant tasks for her. But something was eating at her. Something personal. Something she couldn't trust to anyone else. She needed me. I could tell. Hell, I was already counting the money.

"I have need of a private investigator," she said abruptly. "You were . . . recommended to me."

I nodded, understandingly. "Then you've already tried the police, and all the big private agencies, and none of them were able to help you. Which means your problem isn't one of the usual ones."

She nodded stiffly. "They let me down. All of them. Took my money and gave me nothing but excuses. Bastards. So I called in every favour I was owed, pulled every string I had, and eventually someone gave me your name. I understand you find people."

"I can find anyone or anything, if the price is right. It's a gift. I'm dogged and determined and a whole bunch of other things that begin with *d*, and I never give up as long as the cheques keep coming. But, I don't do insurance work, I don't do divorces, and I don't solve crimes. Hell, I wouldn't know a clue if I fell over it. I just find things. Whether they want to be found or not."

Joanna Barrett gave me her best icy disapproving look. "I don't like being lectured."

I smiled easily. "All part of the service."

"And I don't care for your attitude."

"Not many do."

She seriously considered leaving again. I watched her struggle with herself, my face calm and relaxed. Someone like her wouldn't have come this far unless she was really desperate.

"My daughter is . . . missing," she said finally, reluctantly. "I want you to find her for me."

She produced an eight-by-ten glossy photo from her oversized bag, and skimmed it across the table towards me with an angry flick of her hand. I studied the photo without touching it. A head and shoulders shot of a scowling teenager stared sullenly back at me, narrowed eyes peering past a rat's nest of long blonde hair. She would have been pretty if she hadn't been frowning so hard. She looked like she had a mad on for the whole damned world, and it would have been a sucker who bet on the world. In other words, every inch her mother's daughter.

"Her name is Catherine, Mr. Taylor." Joanna Barrett's voice was suddenly quieter, more subdued. "Only answers to Cathy, when she answers at all. She's fifteen, going on sixteen, and I want her found."

I nodded. We were on familiar territory so far. "How long has she been gone?"

"Just over a month." She paused, and then added reluctantly, "This time."

I nodded again. It helps me look thoughtful. "Anything happen recently to upset your daughter?"

"There was an argument. Nothing we haven't said before, God knows. I don't know why she runs away. She's had everything she ever wanted. Everything."

She dug in her bag again and came out with cigarettes and lighter. The cigarettes were French, the lighter was gold with a monogram. I raised my rates accordingly. She lit a cigarette with a steady hand, and then scattered nervous little puffs of smoke across my office. People shouldn't smoke in situations like this. It's far too revealing. I pushed across my single ash-tray, the one shaped like a lung, and studied the photo again. I wasn't immediately worried about Cathy Barrett. She looked like she could take care of herself, and anybody else stupid enough to bother her. I decided it was time to start asking some obvious questions.

"How about Catherine's father? How does your daughter get on with him?"

"She doesn't. He walked out on us when she was two. Only decent thing the selfish bastard ever did for us. His lawyers got him access, but he hardly ever takes advantage of it. I still have to chase him for maintenance money. Not that we need it, of course, but it's the principle of the thing. And before you ask, no; there's never been any problems with drugs, alcohol, money, or unsuitable boyfriends. I've seen to that. I've always protected her, and I've never once raised a hand to her. She's just a sullen, ungrateful little bitch."

For a moment something glistened in her eyes that might have been tears, but the moment passed. I leaned back in my chair, as though considering what I'd been told, but it all looked pretty straight forward to me. Tracking a runaway wasn't much of a case, but as it happened I was short on cases and cash, and there were bills that need paying. Urgently. It hadn't been a good year—not for a long time. I leaned forward, resting my elbows on my desk, putting on my serious, committed face.

"So, Mrs. Barrett, essentially what we have here is a poor little rich girl who thinks she has everything but love. Probably begging for spare change down in the Underground, eating left-overs and stale bread, sleeping on park benches; hanging out with all the wrong sorts and kidding herself it's all one big adventure. Living life in the raw, with the real people. Secure in the knowledge that once again she's managed to secure her mother's full attention. I wouldn't worry about her too much. She'll come home, once it starts getting cold at nights."

Joanna Barrett was already shaking her expensively coiffured head. "Not this time. I've had experienced people looking for her for weeks now, and no-one's been able to find a trace of her. None of her previous . . . associates have seen anything of her, even with the more than generous rewards I've been offering. It's as though she's vanished off the face of the earth. I've always been able to locate her before. My people have contacts everywhere. But this time, all I have for my efforts is a name I don't recognise. A name, given to me by the same person who supplied me with your name. He said I'd find my daughter . . . in the Nightside."

A cold hand clutched at my heart as I sat up straight. I should have known. I should have known the past never leaves you alone, no matter how far you run from it. I looked her straight in the eye. "What do you know about the Nightside?"

She didn't flinch, but she looked like she wanted to. I can sound dangerous when I have to. She covered her lapse by grinding out her half-finished cigarette in my ash-tray, concentrating on doing the job properly so she wouldn't have to look at me for a while.

"Nothing," she said finally. "Not a damned thing. I'd never heard the name before, and the few of my people who recognised it . . . wouldn't talk to me about it. When I pressed them, they quit, just walked out on me. Walked away from more money than they'd ever made in their life before, rather than discuss the Nightside. They looked at me as though I was . . . sick, just for wanting to discuss it."

"I'm not surprised." My voice was calm again, though still serious, and she looked at me again. I chose my words carefully. "The Nightside is the secret, hidden, dark heart of the city. London's evil twin. It's where the really wild things are. If your daughter's found her way there, she's in real trouble."

"That's why I've come to you," said Joanna. "I understand you operate in the Nightside."

"No. Not for a long time. I ran away, and I vowed I'd never go back. It's a bad place."

She smiled, back on familiar ground again. "I'm prepared to be very generous, Mr. Taylor. How much do you want?"

I considered the matter. How much, to go back into the Nightside? How much is your soul worth? Your sanity? Your self-respect? But work had been hard to come by for some time now, and I needed the money. There were bad people in this part of London too, and I owed some of them a lot more than was healthy. I considered the matter. Shouldn't be that difficult, finding a teenage runaway. A quick in-and-out job. Probably in and gone before anyone even knew I was there. If I was lucky. I looked at Joanna Barrett and doubled what I had been going to ask her.

"I charge a grand a day, plus expenses."

"That's a lot of money," she said, automatically.

"How much is your daughter worth?"

She nodded briskly, acknowledging the point. She didn't really care what I charged. People like me would always be chump change to people like her.

"Find my daughter, Mr. Taylor. Whatever it takes."

"No problem."

"And bring her back to me."

"If that's what she wants. I won't drag her home against her will. I'm not in the kidnapping business."

It was her turn to lean forward now. Her turn to try and look dangerous. Her gaze was flat and hard, and her words could have been chipped out of ice.

"When you take my money, you do as I say. You find that spoilt little cow, you drag her out of whatever mess she's got herself into this time, and you bring her home to me. Then, and only then, will you get paid. Is that clear?"

I just sat there and smiled at her, entirely unimpressed. I'd seen a lot scarier than her, in my time. And compared to what was waiting for me back in the Nightside, her anger and implied threats were nothing. Besides, I was her last chance, and both of us knew it. No-one ever comes to me first, and it had nothing to do with what I charge. I have an earned reputation for doing things my own way, for tracking down the truth whatever it takes, and to hell with whoever gets hurt in the process. Including, sometimes, my clients. They always say they want the truth, the whole truth and nothing but the truth, but few of them really mean it. Not when a little white lie can be so much more comforting. But I don't deal in lies. Which is why I've never made the kind of money that would allow me to move in Mrs. Barrett's circles. People only come to me when they've tried absolutely everything else, including prayer and fortune-tellers. There was no-one else left for Joanna Barrett to turn to. She tried to stare me down for a while, and couldn't. She seemed to find that reassuring. She rummaged in her bag again, took out a completed cheque, and tossed it onto my desk. Apparently it was time for plan B.

"Fifty thousand pounds, Mr. Taylor. There will be another cheque just like it, when this is all over."

I kept a straight face, but inside I was grinning broadly. For a hundred grand, I'd find the crew of the *Marie Celeste*. It almost made going back into the Nightside worthwhile. Almost.

"There is . . . a condition."

I smiled. "I thought there might be."

"I'm going with you."

I sat up straight again. "No. No way. No way in Hell."

"Mr. Taylor . . ."

"You don't know what you're asking . . ."

"She's been gone over a month! She's never been gone this long before. Anything could have happened to her by now. I have to be there . . . when you find her."

I shook my head, but I already knew I was going to lose this one. I've always been a soft touch where family is concerned. It's what comes of never having known one. Joanna still wouldn't cry, but her eyes were bright and shining, and for the first time her voice was unsteady.

"Please." She didn't look comfortable saying the word, but she said it anyway. Not for herself, but for her daughter. "I have to come with you. I have to know. I can't just sit at home any more, waiting for the phone to ring. You know the Nightside. Take me there."

We stared at each other for a while, both of us perhaps seeing a little more of the other than we were used to showing the world. And in the end I nodded, as we both knew I would. But for her sake, I tried one more time to make her see reason.

"Let me tell you about the Nightside, Joanna. They call London the Smoke, and everyone knows there's no smoke without fire. The Nightside is a square mile of narrow streets and back alleys in the centre of city, linking slums and tenements that were old when the last century was new. That's if you believe the official maps. In practice, the Nightside is much bigger than that, as though space itself has reluctantly expanded to fit in all the darkness and evil and generally strange stuff that has set up home there. There are those who say the Nightside is actually bigger than the city that surrounds it, these days. Which says something very disturbing about human nature and appetites, if you think about it. Not to mention inhuman appetites. The Nightside has always been a cosmopolitan kind of place.

"It's always night in the Nightside. It's always three o'clock in the morning, and the dawn never comes. People are always coming and going, drawn by needs that dare not speak their names, searching for pleasures and services unforgivable in the sane, daylight world. You can buy or sell anything in the Nightside, and no-one asks questions. No-one cares. There's a nightclub, where you can pay to see a fallen angel forever burning inside a pentacle drawn in baby's blood. Or a decapitated goat's head, that can tell the future in enigmatic verses of perfect iambic pentameter. There's a room where silence is caged, and colours are forbidden, and another where a dead nun will show you her stigmata, for the right price. She didn't rise again, after all, but she'll still let you stick your fingers in the blood-caked holes, if you want.

"Everything you ever feared or dreamed of is running loose somewhere in the shifting streets of the Nightside, or waiting patiently for you in the expensive private rooms of patrons-only clubs. You can find anything in the Nightside, if it doesn't find you first. It's a sick, magical, dangerous place. You still want to go there?"

"You're lecturing me again."

"Answer the question."

"How could such a place exist, right here in the heart of London, without everyone knowing?"

"It exists because it has always existed, and it stays a secret because the powers that be, the real powers, want it that way. You could die there. I could die there, and I know my way around. Or at least, I did. I haven't been back in years. Still want to do this?"

"I'll go wherever my daughter is," Joanna said firmly. "We haven't always been . . . as close as I would have liked, but I'll go into Hell itself to get her back."

I smiled at her then, and there was little humour in that smile. "You may have to, Joanna. You might very well have to."

TWO

Getting There

My name is John Taylor. Everyone in the Nightside knows that name.

I'd been living an ordinary life in the ordinary world, and as a reward no-one had tried to kill me in ages. I liked being anonymous. It took the pressure off. The pressure of recognition, of expectations and destiny. And no; I don't feel like explaining any of that just yet. I hit thirty a few months ago, but found it hard to give a damn. When you've been through as much bad fortune as I have in my time, you learn not to sweat the small stuff. But even the small problems of an everyday world can mount up, and so there I was, going back again, back to the Nightside, despite all my better judgment. I left the Nightside five years ago, fleeing imminent death and the betrayal of friends, and swore through blood-flecked lips that I'd never go back, no matter what. I should have remembered; God does so love to make a man break a promise.

God, or Someone.

I was going back to a place where everyone knew me, or thought they did. I could have been a contender, if I'd cared enough. Or perhaps I cared too much, about all the little people I'd have had to step on, to get there. To tell the truth, which I try very hard not to do in public, I never was all that ambitious. And I was never what you'd call a joiner. So I went my own way, watched my own back, and tried to live by my own definition of honour. That I screwed up so badly wasn't all my fault. I saw myself as a knight-errant . . . but the damsel in distress stabbed me in the back, my sword shattered on the dragon's hide, and my grail turned out to be the bottom of a whiskey bottle. I was going back, to old faces and old haunts and old hurts; and all I could do was hope it would be worth it.

There was no point in hoping not to be noticed. John Taylor is a name to conjure with, in the Nightside. Five years' exile wouldn't have changed that. Not that any of them ever knew the real me, of course. Ask about me in a dozen different places, and you'd get a dozen different answers. I've been called a warlock and a magus, a con man and a trickster, and an honest rogue. They're all wrong, of course. I'd never let anyone get that close. I've been a hero to some, a villain to others, and pretty much everything in between. I can do a few things, beside finding people, some of them quite impressive. When I ask a question, people usually answer. I used to be a dangerous man, even for the Nightside; but that was five years ago. Before the fates broke me, on the wheel of love. I didn't know if I still had it in me to be really dangerous, but I thought so. It's like knocking someone off a bike with a baseball bat; you never really lose the knack.

I've never carried a gun. I've never felt the need.

My father drank himself to death. He never got over finding out his wife wasn't human. I never knew her at all. People on my street took it in turns to look after me, with varying amounts of reluctance and attention, with the result that I never really felt at home anywhere. I have a lot of questions about myself, and I'm still looking for answers. Which is perhaps why I ended up as a private investigator. There's a certain comfort to be had in finding the answers to other people's problems, if you can't solve your own. I wear a long white trench coat when I'm working. Partly because it's expected of me, partly because it's practical, mostly because it establishes an expected image behind which I can conceal the real me. I like to keep people wrong-footed. And I never let anyone get close, any more. As much for their protection as mine.

I sleep alone, I eat everything that's bad for me, and I take care of my own laundry. When I remember. It's important to me to feel self-sufficient. Not dependent on anyone. I have bad luck with women, but I'd be the first to admit it's mostly my fault. Despite my life I'm still a Romantic, with all the problems that brings. My closest female friend is a bounty hunter, who operates exclusively in the Nightside. She tried to kill me once. I don't bear a grudge. It was just business.

I drink too much, and mostly I don't care. I value its numbing qualities. There's a lot I prefer not to remember.

And now, thanks to Joanna Barrett and her errant daughter, I was heading back into Hell. Back into a place where people have been trying to kill me for as long as I remember, for reasons I've never understood. Back into the only place where I ever feel really alive. I'm more than just another private detective, in the Nightside. It was one of the reasons why I left. I didn't like what I was becoming.

But as I headed down into the Underground system below London's streets, with Joanna Barrett in tow, damn if it didn't feel like coming home.

● ● ●

It didn't matter which station or line I chose. All routes lead to the Nightside. And the whole point of the Underground is that every rail station looks the same. The same tiled walls, the same ugly machines, the overly bright lights and the oversized movie and advertising posters. The dusty vending machines, that only tourists are dumb enough to actually expect to get something out of. The homeless, sitting or lying in their nests of filthy blankets, begging for spare change, or just glad to be away from the elements for a while. And, of course, the endless tramp of hurrying feet. Of shoppers, commuters, tourists, businessmen, and media types, always in a hurry to be somewhere else. London hasn't quite reached saturation point yet, like Tokyo, where they have to employ people to forcibly squeeze the last few travellers into a carriage, so the doors will close; but we're getting there.

Joanna stuck close to me as I led the way through the tunnels. It was clear she didn't care for her surroundings, or the crowds. No doubt she was used to better things, like stretch limousines with a uniformed chauffeur and chilled champagne always at the ready. I tried not to smile as I led her through the crush of the crowds. Turned out she didn't carry change on her, so I ended up having to pay for tickets for both of us. I even had to show her how to work the machines with her ticket.

The escalators were all working for once, and we made our way deeper into the system. I took turnings at random, trusting to my old instincts to guide me, until finally I spotted the sign I was looking for. It was written in a language only those in the know would even recognise, let alone understand. Enochian, in case you're interested. An artificial language, created long ago for mortals to talk with angels, though I only ever met one person who knew how to pronounce it correctly. I grabbed Joanna by the arm and hustled her into the side tunnel underneath the sign. She jerked her arm free angrily, but allowed me to urge her through the door marked *Maintenance*. Her protests stopped abruptly as she found herself in what appeared to be a closet, half-full of scarecrows in British Rail uniforms. Don't ask. I pulled the door shut behind us, and there was a blessed moment of peace as the door separated us from the roar of the crowds. There was a phone on the wall. I picked it up. There was no dialling tone. I spoke a single word into the receiver.

"*Nightside.*"

I put the phone back and looked expectantly at the wall. Joanna looked at me, mystified. And then the dull grey wall split in two, from top to bottom, both sides grinding apart in a steady shuddering movement, to form a long narrow tunnel. The bare walls of the tunnel were bloodred, like an opened wound, and the sourceless light was dim and smoky. It smelled of ancient corrupt perfumes and crushed flowers. A murmur of many voices came from within the tunnel, rising and falling. Snatches of music faded in and out, like so many competing radio signals. Somewhere a cloister bell was ringing, a lost and lonely, doleful sound.

"You expect me to go into *that*?" said Joanna, finding her voice at last. "It looks like the road to Hell!"

"Close," I said calmly. "It's the way to the Nightside. Trust me; this part of the journey is quite safe."

"It feels *bad*," Joanna said quietly, staring fascinated into the tunnel, like a bird at a snake. "It feels . . . unnatural."

"Oh, it's all of that. But it's the best way to get to your daughter. If you can't handle this, turn back now. It's only going to get worse."

Her head came up, and her mouth firmed. "You lead the way."

"Of course."

I stepped forward into the tunnel, and Joanna was right there behind me. And so we left the everyday world behind.

We emerged from the connecting tunnel onto a station platform that at first glance was no different than what you'd expect. Joanna took a deep breath of relief. I didn't say anything. It was better for her to notice things for herself. The wall closed silently behind us as I led Joanna down the platform. It was five years since I'd last been here, but nothing had really changed. The cream-tiled walls were spattered here and there with old dried bloodstains, deep gouges that might have been clawmarks, and all kinds of graffiti. As usual, someone had spelt Cthulhu wrongly.

On the curving wall opposite the platform, the list of destinations hadn't changed. *Shadows Fall. Nightside. Haceldama. Street of the Gods.* The posters were still strange, disturbing, like scenes from dreams best forgotten. Famous faces advertised films and places and services of the kind normally only discussed in whispers. The people crowding the platform were a sight in themselves, and I enjoyed Joanna's reactions. It was clear she would have liked to stop and stare open-mouthed, but she was damned if she'd give me the satisfaction. So she stumbled on, wide eyes darting from one unexpected sight to the next.

Here and there buskers were playing unfamiliar tunes, their caps on the floor before them, holding coins from all kinds of places, some of which no longer existed, and a few that never had. One man sang a thirteenth-century ballad of unrequited love in plain-chant Latin, while not far away another sang Bob Dylan verses backwards, accompanying himself on air guitar. The guitar was slightly out of tune. I dropped a few coins into both their caps. Never know when you might need a little extra credit in the karma department.

Further down the platform, a stooped neanderthal in a smart business suit was talking animatedly with a bored-looking dwarf in full Nazi SS uniform. A noble from Queen Elizabeth I's court, complete with ruff and slashed silks, was chatting amiably with a gorgeous six-foot transvestite in full chorus girl outfit, and it was hard to tell which of them looked more extreme. A woman in futuristic space armour and a nude man covered in tattoos and splashes of woad were eating things on sticks that were still wriggling. Joanna had come to a full stop by now. I tapped her on the shoulder, and she all but jumped out of her skin.

"Try not to be a tourist," I said dryly.

"What . . ." She had to stop and try again. "What is this place? Where have you brought me? And who the hell are these people?"

I shrugged. "This is the quickest way to the Nightside. There are others. Some official, some not. Anyone can walk down the wrong street, open the wrong door, and end up in the Nightside. Most of them don't last long, though. London and the Nightside have rubbed up against each other for so long now that the barriers are getting dangerously thin. Someday they'll all come crashing down, and all the poisons in the Nightside will come spilling out; but I plan to be safely dead and in my grave by then. However, this is still the safest way."

"And these people?"

"Just people, going about their lives. You're seeing a part of the world most of you never get to know about. The underside, the hidden paths, walked by secret people on secret business, pursuing goals and missions we can only guess at. There are more worlds than we know, or would wish to know, and most of them send people through the Nightside sooner or later. You can meet all sorts here, in the Underground, and never know harm as long as the ancient Truce holds. Everyone comes to the Nightside. Myths and legends, travellers and explorers, visitors from higher or lower dimensions. Immortals. Death-walkers. Psychonauts. Try not to stare."

I led her down the platform, and it was a mark of how shaken she was that she didn't have a single comment to make. She didn't even object to my holding her arm again. Without looking round, without interrupting their conversations or in any way acknowledging my presence, the people ahead of us moved back out of the way to let us pass. A few made the sign of the cross when they thought I wasn't looking, and older warding signs against evil. It seemed I hadn't been forgotten after all. A vicar in a shabby grey cloak, with a pristine white collar and a grey blindfold over his eyes, was hawking his wares before us, a much-travelled suitcase open at his feet.

"Crow's feet!" he yelled, in a harsh, strident voice. "Holy water! Hexes! Wooden stakes and silver bullets! You know you need them! Don't come crying to me if you end up limping home with someone else's spleen instead of your own!"

He broke off as Joanna and I approached. He sniffed the air suspiciously, cocking his great blind head to one side. His fingers worked busily at a rosary made from human fingerbones. He stepped forward suddenly to block our way and stabbed an accusing finger at me.

"John Taylor!" he snapped, almost spitting out the words. "Damnation's child! Demonspawn and Abomination! Bane of all the Chosen! Avaunt! Avaunt!"

"Hello, Pew," I said easily. "Good to bump into you again. Still working the old act, I see. How's business?"

"Oh, not too bad thanks, John." Pew smiled vaguely in my direction, putting aside his official Voice for the moment. "My wares are like travel insurance; no-one ever really believes they'll need it, until it's too late. *It can't happen to me,* they whine. But of course, in the Nightside it can, and it will. Suddenly and violently and usually quite horribly too. I'm saving lives here, if they'd only pay attention, the fools. So; what are you doing back here, John? I thought you had more sense. You know the Nightside isn't good for you."

"I'm working a case. Don't worry; I won't be stopping."

"That's what they all say," growled Pew, shifting his broad shoulders uneasily inside his threadbare cloak. "Still, we all do what we have to, I suppose. Who are you looking for this time?"

"Just a runaway. Teenager called Catherine Barrett. Don't suppose the name means anything to you?"

"No. But then, I'm pretty much out of the loop these days, by my own choice. Hard times are coming . . . word of advice, boy. I hear things, bad things. Something new has come into the Nightside. And people have been mentioning your name again. Watch your back, boy. If anyone's going to kill you, I'd much rather it was me."

He turned away abruptly and took up his piercing cry again. There's no-one closer, more like family, than old enemies.

The platform shook, there was a blast of approaching air, and a train roared into the station and slowed to a stop—a long shining silver bullet of a train, with no windows anywhere. The carriages were solid tubes of steel, with only the heavily reinforced doors standing out against their shimmering perfection. The doors hissed open, and people poured in and out. I was ready to take Joanna by the arm again, but it wasn't necessary. She strode into the carriage before her without hesitating, her head held high. I followed her in and sat down beside her.

The carriage was almost empty, for which I was grateful. I've never liked being crowded. All kinds of things can hide in a crowd. The man sitting opposite us was reading a Russian newspaper with great concentration. The date below the masthead was from a week in the future. Further down the immaculately clean carriage sat a young woman kitted out in full Punk regalia, right down to the multiple face piercings and fierce green mohawk rising up from her shaved head. She was reading an oversized leather-bound Holy Bible. The pages appeared to be blank, but the white on white of her unblinking eyes marked her as a graduate of the Deep School, and I knew that for her and her alone, the pages were full of awful wisdom.

Joanna was looking around the carriage, and I tried to see it through her eyes. The complete lack of windows made it feel more like a cell than a conveyance, and the strong smell of disinfectant reminded me irresistibly of a dentist's surgery. There was no map anywhere. People who took this train knew where they were going.

"Why aren't there any windows?" said Joanna, after a while.

"Because you don't want to see what's outside," I said. "We have to travel through strange, harsh, places to reach the Nightside. Dangerous and unnatural places, that would blast the sight from your eyes and the reason from your mind. Or so I'm told. I've never felt like peeking."

"What about the driver? Doesn't he have to see where he's going?"

"I'm not convinced there is a driver," I said thoughtfully. "I don't know anyone who's ever seen one. I think the trains have been running this route for so long now that they're quite capable of running themselves."

"You mean there's no-one human at the controls?"

"Probably better that way. Humans are so limited." I smiled at her shocked face. "Sorry you came yet?"

"No."

"Don't worry. You will be."

And that was when something from outside crashed against the side of the carriage opposite us, throwing the Russian to the floor. He carefully gathered up his paper and went to sit further down. The heavy metal wall dented inwards, slowly yielding under the determined assault from outside. The Punk girl didn't look up from her Bible, though she was silently mouthing the words now. The dents in the metal deepened, and one whole section bowed ominously inwards under unimaginable pressure. Joanna sank back in her seat.

"Take it easy," I said reassuringly. "It can't get in. The train is protected."

She looked at me just a little wildly. Culture shock. I'd seen it before. "Protected?" she said finally.

"Old pacts, agreements; trust me, you really don't want to know the details. Especially if you've eaten recently."

Outside the carriage, something roared with thwarted rage. It didn't sound at all human. The sound fell slowly away, retreating down the length of the carriage as the train left it behind. The metal wall unhurriedly resumed its original shape, the dents disappearing one by one. And then something, or a series of somethings, ran along the side of the carriage and up onto the roof. Light, hasty, pitterpattering fast, moving in unison, like so many huge insects. The carriage lights flickered briefly. It sounded like there was a whole crowd of them up on the roof, scuttling back and forth. Voices came floating down to us, shrill and high and mixed together, like the same voice speaking in harmony with itself. There was a faint metallic buzz in the elongated vowel sounds that sent a shiver down my spine. The Brittle Sisters of the Hive were on the prowl again.

"Come out, come out, whatever you are," said the chorus of a single voice. "Come out, and play with us. Or let us in, let us in, and we will play with you till you can't stand it anymore. We want to stir our sticky fingers in your gene pool, and sculpt your wombs with our living scalpels . . ."

"Make them shut up," Joanna said tightly. "I can't stand their voices. It's like they're scratching at my brain, trying to get in."

I looked at the Russian and the Punk, but they were resolutely minding their own business. I looked up at the roof of the carriage.

"Go away and stop bothering us," I said firmly. "There is nothing for you here, by terms of Treaty and sacrifice."

"Who dares address us so?" said the many voices in one, almost drowned out by the constant clattering of their taloned feet on the steel roof.

"This is John Taylor," I said clearly. "Don't make me have to come up there."

There was a long pause. They were all very still, until eventually the inhuman chorus said "Then farewell, sweet prince, and do not forget us when you come into your kingdom."

A scurrying of insect feet and they were all gone, and the train rocked on its way in silence. The Russian and the Punk looked at me, and then looked quickly away before I could meet their gaze. Joanna was looking at me too. Her gaze was steady, but her voice couldn't quite manage it.

"They knew you. What did they mean?"

"I don't know," I said. "I've never known. That's always been my problem. There are a great many mysteries in the Nightside, and much against my will, I'm one of them."

No-one else had anything to say, all the way to the Nightside.

THREE

Neon Noir

We came up out of the Underground like souls emerging from the underworld, with chattering throngs of people surging endlessly past in both directions. The train was already long gone, hurrying off as though glad to be leaving. The slow-moving escalators were packed with new travellers and supplicants, all carefully not looking at each other. No-one wanted to draw attention to themselves until they'd got their bearings. The few cold-eyed souls who looked openly about them were the predators and chickenhawks, picking out their prey for later. No-one looked openly at me, but there were a hell of a lot of sidelong glances, and not a few whispers. So much for a quiet visit. The only thing that moves faster than the speed of light is gossip in the Nightside.

Still, the crowd was much as I remembered. Boys, girls, and a few others, all looking for a good time. Business as usual on the dark side of the city. Up on the street, they spilled out of the train station, sniffing freedom and opportunities on the crisp air, and scattered into the endless night, hot on the trail of their own salvations and damnations. Joanna stumbled to a halt inside a dozen paces; wide-eyed, shell-shocked, transfixed by the wonders and strangeness of a whole new world.

This vibrant new city was almost overpoweringly alive; all fever-bright colours and jet-black shadows, welcoming and embracing, frightening and intimidating, seductive and hateful, all at once. Bright neon gleamed everywhere, sharp and gaudy, shiny as shop-soiled tinsel; an endless come-on to suckers and victims and all the lonely souls. Enticing signs beckoned the unwary into all kinds of clubs, promising dark delights and unfamiliar pleasures, drinking and dancing with strangers in smoke-filled rooms, the thrill that never ends, life in the fast lane with no crash barriers anywhere. Sex licked its lips and cocked a hip. It was all dangerous as Hell and twice as much fun.

Damn, it was good to be back.

People surged up and down the street, in all their many variations, from the unnatural to the unlikely, all of them intent on their own pursuits, while the roar of traffic never stopped. Every vehicle moved at great speed, stopping for nothing, in stark and noisy contrast to the packed city streets of everyday London, where the general speed of traffic hasn't changed much in centuries; thanks to the appalling congestion it still averages out at around ten miles an hour. No matter how important you think you are. Though at least these days the streets stink of petrol fumes rather than horse shit.

You can't step in petrol fumes.

Many of the sleek and gleaming vehicles darting through the Nightside had to be new to Joanna; shapes and sizes and even concepts that had never known the light of day; some of them powered from sources best not thought about too much, if you wanted to sleep at night. Taxis that ran on debased holy water, limousines that ran on fresh blood, ambulances that ran on distilled suffering. You can turn a profit from anything, in the Nightside. I had to take Joanna by the arm as she drifted unrealisingly too close to the edge of the pavement.

"Careful!" I said loudly in her ear. "Some of those things aren't really cars. And some of them are hungry."

But she wasn't listening to me. She'd looked up at the sky, and her up-turned face was full of wonder and awe. I smiled, and looked up too. Deep deep black, the sky, falling away forever, blazing with the light of thousands and thousands of stars, far more than you'd ever seen above any earthly city, dominated by a full moon a dozen times larger than the poor pallid thing Joanna was used to seeing. I've never been sure whether the moon really is bigger in the Nightside, or whether it's just *closer*. Maybe someday someone with serious money will hire me to find out.

I looked back at Joanna, but she was still clearly struggling to find her equilibrium, so I just stood there and looked mildly about me. It had been five years, after all. But it all seemed much as I remembered it. The same quietly desperate people, hurrying down the same rain-slicked streets, heading eagerly into the same old honey traps. Or perhaps I was just being cynical. There were wonders and marvels to be found in the Nightside, sights and glories to be savoured and clutched to your heart forever; you just had to look that little bit harder to find them, that was all. The Nightside is really just like any other major city, only amplified, intensified, like the city streets we walk in dreams and nightmares.

There was a kiosk beside the station entrance selling racks of shrink-wrapped T-shirts. I studied some of the legends on the shirtfronts. *Good boys go to Heaven, bad boys go to the Nightside. My mother took thalidomine, and all I got was this lousy hammer toe.* And the perennial *Michael Jackson died for our sins.* I snorted quietly. The usual tourist stuff. Joanna turned suddenly to look at me, her mouth snapping shut as though she'd only just realised it was hanging open.

"Welcome to the Nightside," I said, smiling. "Abandon all taste, ye who enter here."

"It's night," she said numbly. "What happened to the rest of the day? It was only just starting to get dark when we left."

"I told you; it's always night here. People come here for the things they can't find anywhere else; and a lot of those things can only thrive in the dark."

She shook her head slowly. "We're really not in Kansas any more, are we? Guess I'll just have to try and keep an open mind."

"Oh, I wouldn't do that," I said solemnly. "You never know what might walk in."

She gave me a hard look. "I can never tell when you're joking."

"Neither can I sometimes, in the Nightside. It's that kind of place. Life, death and reality are all flexible concepts here."

A street gang came whooping and hollering down the street towards us, shouldering people out of their way, and playfully pushing some out into the road to dodge the traffic, which didn't even bother with horns, let alone slowing down. The gang members laughed and elbowed each other and drank heavily from bottles they passed back and forth between them. They were loud and obnoxious and loving every minute of it, and the threat of sudden violence hung about them like bad body odour. There were thirteen of them, wearing polished leathers and hanging chains, with bright tribal colours on their faces. Their teeth came to sharp points, and they wore strap-on devil's horns on their foreheads. They came roaring and swaggering down the street, swearing nastily at anyone who didn't get out of their way fast enough and looking eagerly round for some trouble to get into. Preferably the kind where someone got hurt.

And then one of them spotted Joanna, recognising her immediately as a newcomer. Easy target, money on the hoof, and a woman as well. He clued in his brothers, and they surged forward, moving with a purpose. I stepped forward, out of the shadows, and put myself between them and Joanna. The gang lurched to a sudden halt, and I could hear my name on their lips. Their hands were quickly full of knives, long slender blades gleaming sullenly in the neon light. I smiled at the gang, and some of them started backing away. I let my smile widen, and the gang turned abruptly and walked away. Mostly, I felt relieved. I hadn't been sure whether I was bluffing or not.

"Thank you," said Joanna, her voice quite steady. "I was concerned there, for a moment. Who were they?"

"Demons."

"Is that the name of their gang?"

"No, they're demons, playing at being a street gang. Probably out on day release. We get all sorts here."

She thought about that. "They were frightened of you."

"Yes."

"What makes you so special, here?"

I had to smile. "Damned if I know. Let's just say I have something of a reputation in the Nightside. Or at least, I used to. Be interesting to see how much currency my name still has here, in some of the places we're going to have to visit."

Joanna looked around her. "Shouldn't we alert the police, or something? Those . . . demons might attack someone else."

"There are no police operating in the Nightside," I explained patiently.

"Not many laws, either. Anything goes here; that's part of the attraction. There are . . . Authorities. Those with power to punish serious transgressors. Pray we don't run into them."

Joanna took a deep breath, and let it out slowly. "All right; I can handle this. I came here to find my daughter, and I can cope with anything if it helps me retrieve her. You said you had a gift for finding people. Show me."

"It's not that simple."

"Why did I just know you were going to say that?"

I met her accusing gaze steadily, choosing my words with more than usual care. "I have a gift. Call it magic, or esp, or whatever current buzzword you feel most comfortable with. I can use that gift to track down missing people or objects, things that are hidden from normal view and normal investigative procedures. It only works here in the Nightside, where the laws of reality aren't as strictly nailed down as they might be.

But I have to be very careful how and where and when I use it. I have enemies here. Bad people. Using my gift is like shining a bright light in a dark place. It attracts attention. My enemies can follow the light to find me. And kill me."

"Who are these enemies?" said Joanna, and for the first time there was something like concern in her cool blue eyes. "Why are they so keen to kill you? What did you do? And why is a man who can scare off demons so frightened by these people?"

"They are many, and I am one. They've been after me for as long as I can remember. It started when I was still a child. They once burned down a whole city block, trying to get to me. Over the years they've killed a lot of people who were close to me. It's a wonder I have any friends left. They aren't always out there . . . sometimes I think they're afraid of me. Either way, I've never been able to find out who they are, or why they want me dead so badly. I'm safe in the mundane world. They can't track me there. But this is their territory as well as mine. I only agreed to take on this case because it seemed so simple and straightforward. With just a little bit of luck, we should be able to track down your daughter, put the two of you together for a little heart-to-heart, and then get the hell out of here. Without anyone who matters knowing I'm here. Now hush, and let me concentrate. The briefer I can keep this, the better."

I concentrated, reaching deep down inside myself, and my gift unfolded like a flower, blossoming up to fill my mind, then spilling out onto the night. My third eye opened wide, my private eye, and suddenly I could See. And there she was, right before me; Cathy Barrett's after-image, glowing and shimmering on the night. The ghost she left behind, stamped on Time by her presence; a semi-transparent wraith drawn in pastel shades. Passing pedestrians walked around and through her without seeing her. I concentrated on her image, rewinding the past, watching closely as Cathy emerged again from the Underground station entrance and looked around her, dazed and delighted at the new world she'd found. She was wearing Salvation Army cast-offs, but she looked happy and healthy enough. Cathy looked around suddenly, as though someone had called her name. She smiled then, a wide happy smile that transformed her face. She looked radiant, delighted, as though she'd found an old dear friend in an unexpected place. She started off down the street, hurrying towards . . . something. Something I couldn't See or sense, but it pulled her to it with a single-minded, implacable purpose, like a moth drawn to a blow-torch.

I replayed the image from the beginning, watching again as the ghost from the past came tripping out of the station entrance. Cathy's imprint was still too clear and uncorrupted to be more than a few weeks old at most. The impressions I was getting from the image puzzled me. Unlike most runaways Cathy hadn't come into the Nightside looking to hide from someone, or forget some past pain. She'd come here with a purpose, looking for some specific thing or person. Something or someone here had *called* her. I frowned, and opened up my mind just a crack further, but there was nothing unusual beating on the night air, no siren call strong enough to summon people from the safety of the mundane world.

Unless the caller was shielded from me. Which was a worrying thought. There's not much that can hide from me, when I put my mind to it. I'm John Taylor, damn it. I find things. Whether they want to be found or not.

Unless . . . I was dealing with one of the Major Powers.

I braced myself and pushed my mind all the way open. The hidden world snapped into focus all around me. Old paths of power criss-crossed each other, cutting unnoticed through the material world, burning so brightly I had to look away. Ghosts stamped and howled, going through their endless paces over and over, trapped in moments of Time like insects caught in amber. Wispy insubstantial giants strode slowly through the city, not deigning to look down on all the tiny mortals beneath them. The Faerie and the Transient Beings and the Awful Folk went about their various mysterious businesses, and none of them so much as looked at me. And still there was no trace anywhere of whatever had called so beguilingly to Cathy Barrett.

I shut my mind down again, layer by careful layer, re-establishing my shields. It had been so long since I'd had a chance to glory in the Sights of my gift that I'd forgotten all about being cautious. For a time there, I must have shone like the sun. Time to get this show on the road. I reached out and took Joanna firmly by the hand, linking her mind to mine, and she gasped as she saw the street through my private eye. She saw Cathy's translucent image, and called out to her, starting forward. Immediately I let go of her hand, and shut everything down, tamping down the edges of my gift with great thoroughness, so that not even a spark of light could get out to betray me. Joanna rounded on me angrily.

"What happened? Where is she? I saw her!"

"You saw an image from the past," I said carefully. "A footprint, left in Time. Cathy hasn't been here for at least two weeks, more than enough time for her to get into some serious trouble. But at least now we know for sure that she did get here, and that she was alive and well two weeks ago.

Did you see the look on her face? She came here for a reason. She was headed somewhere specific."

Joanna's face had quickly resumed its usual chilly mask, as though she was ashamed I'd caught her showing actual emotions. When she spoke, her voice was entirely calm again. "Specific. Is that good or bad?"

"Depends," I said honestly. "This is the Nightside. She could be anywhere by now. She might have found friends, protection, enlightenment, or damnation. They're all pretty cheap here. I think . . . I'm going to need a little help on this one. How would you like to visit the oldest established bar and nightclub in the world?"

One side of her dark red mouth twitched in something that might have been a smile. "Sounds good to me. I could use a stiff drink. Hell, I could use several stiff drinks and an adrenaline chaser. What's the name of this place?"

I grinned. "Strangefellows."

FOUR

Everyone Goes to Strangefellows.
If They Know What's Good for Them.

You get to Strangefellows, the oldest drinking hole, conversation pit and scumbag attractor in the history of Mankind, by walking down the kind of streets that raise the hairs on the back of your neck, and then slipping into a side alley that isn't always there. Mostly, I think it's ashamed to be associated with such a dive. The alley is dimly lit and the street had cobbles. The entrance to Strangefellows is a flat slab of steel set flush with the grimy wall. Above the door is a small but dignified neon sign that spells out the name of the bar in ancient Sanskrit. The owner doesn't believe in advertising. He doesn't need to. If you're meant to find your way to the oldest pub in England, you will. And if you're not, you could search all the days of your life and never find it. There's no waiting list to get in, but the dues can be murder. Sometimes literally. I translated the sign for Joanna, and she looked at it expressionlessly.

"Is this a gay bar?"

I had to smile. "No. Just a place where the stranger people in the world can come to drink in peace and quiet. No-one bothers you, no-one will expect you to talk sports, politics or religion, and no-one will ask for your autograph. Good and Bad can buy each other drinks, and neutrality is strictly enforced. Strangefellows has been around, in various identities, for centuries. No-one's really sure how old it is, but it's always been a bar of some kind. The last time I was here, the current incarnation was decidedly upmarket. Glamorous in a threatening kind of way, with excellent booze and an . . . interesting clientele. But identities can change fast in the Night-side, so once we get in there stick close to me, hang on to your bag and don't talk to any strange women."

"I have been to nightclubs before," Joanna said frostily.

"Not like this one, you haven't."

I walked up to the door, and it swung slowly open before me. Though I hated to admit it, I was more than a little relieved. The door only opens to people in good standing with the owner, and I hadn't been sure just what my standing was, after so long away. We hadn't exactly parted on good terms. Hell, I still had money owing on my bar bill. But the door had opened, so I made a point of walking in like I owned the place, with Joanna looking at her most alluring and intimidating at my side. Keep your chin up, and your gaze steady. Remember, they can smell fear here.

I stopped in the middle of the foyer, and looked about me, taking my time. The old place hadn't changed much after all. The same Tudor furni-ture, with people draped over them like bendy toys, trying to sleep some of it off before they had to go home. The same obscene murals on the walls and ceilings, some of them in bas-relief. The same stains on the Persian car-pet. I felt positively nostalgic. I glanced at Joanna, but she was carefully maintaining the straightest of straight faces. I led the way forward, step-ping over outstretched legs where necessary, until we could look down the metal stairs and into the wide stone-walled pit that held the bar proper.

The first word that came to mind on seeing the bar again was *seedy*. Though *sleazy* came a very close second. Clearly the upmarket experiment hadn't taken. I led the way down the stairs, which clanged noisily under our feet, by design. The bar's patrons preferred not to be taken by surprise. There was the usual sea of mismatched tables and chairs, with booths at the far end for those who felt in need of a little extra privacy. Or some-where to hide a body for a while. The lights were always kept low—partly for atmosphere, and partly so you couldn't get too good a look at your sur-roundings. Or your fellow company. Most of the tables were occupied, by the kind of mixed crowd that reminded me why I'd left the Nightside in the first place. I recognised a lot of the faces; though most of them were ostentatiously not looking at me. The usual babble of raised voices was half–drowned out by loud heavy metal rock being blasted through con-cealed speakers. The close unmoving air was heavy with smoke, some of it legal, some of it earthly. A sign on the wall at the bottom of the stairs said *Enter At Your Own Risk*. Joanna drew my attention to it.

"Are they serious?"

"Sure," I said calmly. "The bar food's terrible."

"So is the ambience," Joanna said dryly. "I can feel my credit rating dropping just from being here. Tell me we're here for a purpose."

"We're looking for information," I said patiently. It never hurts to spell it out for clients, especially when you know it irritates them. "We need to know who or what summoned Cathy into the Nightside, and where she went after my gift lost her. You can find the answer to practically any question at Strangefellows, if you know the right people to ask."

"And if you know the right palms to grease?"

"You see; you're learning. Money doesn't just talk in the Nightside; it shouts and screams and twists arms. It helps that most of the real movers and shakers have passed through here at one time or another, on their way up or on their way down. There are those who say this place has been around since civilisation began."

Joanna sniffed. "Doesn't look like it's been cleaned much since then, either."

"Merlin Satanspawn was buried here, under the wine cellar, after the fall of Logres. He still makes the occasional appearance, to keep everyone honest. Being dead doesn't stop you from being a major player, in the Nightside."

"Hold everything. *The* Merlin?"

"I'd hate to think there was more than one. I only saw him manifest once, but it scared the crap out of me."

Joanna shook her head. "I need a very large drink, right now."

"Lot of people feel that way in the Nightside."

I headed for the extended mahogany bar at the end of the room. It was good to be back. I could feel long-buried parts of me waking up and flexing their muscles. Sometimes I hated the Nightside, and sometimes I loved it, but running away to the real world had only served to show me how much I needed it. For all its threats and dangers, its casual brutality and deep-seated wickedness, it was only here that I felt truly alive. And I'd had some good times in this bar, back in my younger days. Admittedly mostly because back then I'd been strictly small change, and no-one gave a damn about who I was, or might be. I led Joanna through the packed tables, and the noise of conversation didn't even slip as we passed. The record on the speakers changed, and the Stranglers began shouting about there being "No More Heroes." The bar's owner's way of letting me know he'd noticed my arrival. Joanna winced at the noise, and put her mouth next to my ear.

"Is this racket all they play here?"

"Pretty much," I said loudly. "This is Alex Morrisey's place, and he plays what he wants. He likes heavy rock, he doesn't believe in being cheerful, and he doesn't take requests. Someone came in here once and asked for Country and Western, and Alex shot him. A lot of people applauded."

We came to the bar. Alex Morrisey was there, as always, a long streak of misery in basic black. He was the latest in a long line of bartender/owners, from a family that had been around longer than it was comfortable to contemplate. It's not clear whether they stick around to protect Merlin, or possibly vice versa, and no-one likes to ask because if you do Alex throws things. It's no secret he'd leave Strangefellows in a moment if he could, but he can't. His family is bound to the bar, by ancient and unpleasant pacts, and Alex can't leave until he can find someone else from his family line to take his place. And since Alex Morrisey is reputed to be the very last of his long line, it's just another reason for him to act up cranky and take it out on his customers.

The word is Alex was born in a bad mood, and has only got worse since. Permanently seething, viciously unfair just for the hell of it, and notoriously cavalier when it comes to giving you the right change. Though God protect your soul if you hold back one penny when he calls in your marker. He claims to be the true heir to the British Throne, being a (more or less) direct descendant of Uther Pendragon, on the wrong side of several blankets. He also claims he can see people's auras if he bangs his head against the wall just right. He was currently taking his own sweet time about serving another customer, but he knew I was there. Nothing happened in Alex's bar that he didn't know about, sometimes even before you knew you were going to do it. His party trick is to answer a phone just before it rings.

I leaned on the bar and studied him openly. He looked just as I remembered him, appalling and disturbing, in equal measures. Alex had to be in his late twenties by now, but looked ten years older; thin, pale and moody, and always thoroughly vexed about something. His scowl had etched a permanent notch above his nose, and on the few occasions when he smiled, you knew you were in trouble. He always wore black of some description, topped with designer shades and a snazzy black beret perched on the back of his head, to hide the bald spot that appeared when he was still a teenager. Proof if proof were needed, he always said, that God hated him personally. He shaved when he remembered, which wasn't often, and didn't wash the bar's glasses anywhere near often enough. His spiky black hair stuck out in tufts, because he tugged at it a lot, and his personal hygiene bordered on distressing.

He still had a large glamour calendar behind the bar, showing Elvira Mistress of the Dark, in a series of photographic poses that would probably upset her greatly if she ever found out about them, and the designs on the bar coasters were cheerfully pornographic. On the whole, Alex is very bad with women, most of whom don't live down to his expectations. He was married once, and still won't talk about it. And that . . . is Alex Morrisey for you. Pissed off at the entire world and proud of it, and mixer of the worst martinis in the Nightside.

I suppose we're friends. We both put up with a lot of things from each other that we wouldn't tolerate for a second from anyone else.

He finally gave up pretending I wasn't there and slouched along the bar to glare at me.

"I knew it was going to be a bad day when I woke up to find my rabbit's foot had grown itself a new rabbit," he said resentfully. "If I'd known it was a warning you were coming back into my life, I would have locked all the doors and windows and melted down the keys. What do you want?"

"Good to see you again, Alex. How's business?"

He sniffed, loudly. "Takings have dropped so low you'd need an excavator to find any profits, a poltergeist has moved into my cellar and is haunting my beer barrels, turning the taps on and off, and Pale Michael is claiming that since he is now a zombie and officially dead, with a coroner's certificate to prove it, he doesn't have to pay his not inconsiderable bar bill. And now you're here. It's nights like this that make me dream of bloody insurrection, and planting bombs in public places. What are you doing back here, John? You said you were never coming back, and it was the only sensible thing I ever heard you say."

"The lady at my side is Joanna Barrett. Her daughter's gone missing, in the Nightside. And I've drawn a blank."

Alex looked at me over his sunglasses. "I thought you could find anything?"

"So did I. But my gift could only show me so much before I got locked out. Someone's hiding this runaway. I won't be able to pick up her trail again till I can get a lot closer to her. Which means I need a lead. Is Eddie around?"

"Yes, and I do wish he wasn't. He's at his usual table in the corner, scaring off the reputable trade."

And that was when the three yuppies appeared out of nowhere to surround me. I turned around unhurriedly as I spotted their reflections in the long mirror behind the bar, and looked them over curiously. They seemed fairly generic; all young, all dressed in the very best-cut suits, with razor-trimmed hair, a single ear-ring, and perfectly manicured hands. Old school ties, of course. They all looked very unhappy with me, but the one glaring right into my face seemed vaguely familiar. Joanna, I noticed, was making a point of being distinctly unimpressed with them. Good for her. I leaned back against the bar, and raised a single eyebrow with just the right amount of insolence. The big bad businessman before me pushed his face even closer to mine and breathed spearmint into my face. I hate spearmint.

"John Taylor!" the yuppie said loudly, trying his very best to sound fierce and hard and menacing, in a high-pitched voice that really wasn't suited to it. "John *bloody* Taylor! Oh, God is good, isn't he? Sending you back to me. I always knew you'd come crawling back here someday, Taylor, so I could personally ensure you got what was coming to you!"

"I get the impression you know me," I said calmly. "Can't say the same, I'm afraid. Do I owe you money, by any chance?"

"Don't you dare pretend you don't remember! I told you never to come back here, Taylor. I told you never to show your face here again. You made me look bad."

"It wasn't difficult," observed Alex from behind the bar. He was watching interestedly and making absolutely no move to intervene.

The yuppie pretended he hadn't heard that. Mad as he was, he wasn't stupid enough to upset Alex. He turned the full force of his glare on me, his slightly bulging eyes all but protruding from their sockets, while his two friends did their best to lurk dangerously in the background, being supportive.

"I said I'd do for you, Taylor, if I ever saw you again. Interfering little turd, meddling in the affairs of your betters!"

"Ah," I said, the light finally dawning. "Sorry, but it has been five years. I remember you now. The limited vocabulary and repetitive threats finally rang a bell. Ffinch-Thomas, isn't it? You were in here one night slapping your girl about, because you were in a bad mood. And because you could. I wasn't going to interfere. Really, I wasn't. If she was stupid enough to go about with a hyphenated thug like you, just because you always had the money for the very best booze and blow and clubs, that was her affair. But then you knocked her down, and kicked her in the side till her ribs broke. Giggling while you did it. So I beat the crap out of you, stole all your credit cards, and finished up by throwing you through a window that happened to be closed at the time. As I recall, you made these famous threats of yours while hobbling away at speed, trying to pull bits of glass out of your arse. Anyone else would have derived a useful moral lesson from these events. Alex, I'm surprised you let this little swine back in here."

Alex shrugged, leaning his elbows on the bar. "What can I tell you? His father's something big in the city. Both of them."

The music in the bar broke off suddenly, and the general babble of voices quickly died away as people realised what was happening. There was interest from all sides now, and not a little money changing hands. Everyone wanted to see if John Taylor still had it. I was kind of curious myself.

"You can't talk to me like that," said Ffinch-Thomas, his voice so strained it was practically breaking.

"Of course I can. I just did. Weren't you paying attention?"

He drew a slender golden scythe from inside his jacket, a nasty little instrument expertly crafted to fit his hand. The blade gleamed brightly, and I just knew the edges would be razor-sharp. The other two yuppies drew similar weapons. Must be the latest thing. Druid chic.

"We're going to do it to you," said Ffinch-Thomas, grinning widely. His voice was light and breathy, and his eyes were bright with excitement. "We're going to do it and do it and do it. Make you scream, Taylor. Spread your blood and skin all over the bar, until you beg to be allowed to die. I never believed those stories about you. You just caught me by surprise last time. And after we've made you cry and squeal, we'll stop for a while, so you can watch us do it to your woman. And we'll . . . we'll . . . ."

His voice trailed away to nothing as I locked on to his eyes with mine. I'd heard enough. More than enough. Some insects just beg to be stepped on. He stood very still, trying to look away, but he couldn't. I had him. Beads of sweat popped out all over his suddenly grey face, as he tried to turn and run and found he couldn't. He whimpered, and wet himself, a large dark stain spreading across the front of his very expensive trousers. His hand opened, against his will, and the golden scythe tumbled from his nerveless fingers, clattering loudly on the floor in the hushed quiet. He was scared now, really scared. I smiled at him, and blood ran down his cheeks from his staring eyes. He was whining, a thin, trapped, animal sound, and then his eyes rolled up in his head, and he collapsed unconscious on the floor. His two yuppie friends stood gaping down at him, and then they looked at me. They held up their golden scythes with shaking hands, nerving themselves to attack, and Alex raised his voice.

"Lucy! Betty! *Trouble!*"

Lucy and Betty Coltrane were suddenly right there, behind the yuppies. The Coltranes have been Alex's bouncers for years. Tall and formidable body-builders, the girls never wore anything more than a T-shirt and shorts, the better to show off their impressive muscles. One is blonde and one is brunette, but otherwise there's not much to choose between them. They have a somewhat threatening glamour, and crack nuts by coughing loudly. They fell on the two yuppies, slapped the scythes out of their hands, slammed them back against the bar, kneed them briskly in the privates, and then frog-marched them out. The watching crowd cheered and applauded. A few wolf-whistled. I looked reproachfully at Alex.

"I could have handled them."

He sniffed loudly. "I've seen what happens when you handle things, and it takes ages to mop up the blood afterwards. Here; have one on the house, and for God's sake leave the rest of my customers alone."

I accepted the offered brandy with good grace. It was the nearest Alex could come to an apology. The Coltranes came back and carried off the still-twitching Ffinch-Thomas.

"He'll tell his daddy on you," observed Alex. "And Daddy will not be pleased. He might even be just a bit peeved with you."

"Tell him to take a number," I said, because you have to say things like that in public. God knows I've got enough enemies without making more, but the young Ffinch-Thomas and his type deserve a good slapping now and again. Just on general principles. Joanna had been watching the Coltranes.

"Who . . . *what* are they?"

"My pride and glory," Alex said fondly. "Betty and Lucy Coltrane. Best damned bouncers in the business. Though of course I'd never tell them that. Fiercer than pit bulls and cheaper to run. Married to each other. They had a dog once, but they ate it."

Joanna was looking just a little dazed. "I think we need to go talk with Eddie," I said kindly. "Talk to you later, Alex."

"If you must. I'd bar you, if I thought you'd listen. You're trouble, John, and you always will be."

Heavy rock started up again, loud and driving, and all the various conversations resumed, having decided regretfully that the show was over. Still, they had plenty to talk about now. John Taylor was definitely back, and as sharp as ever. I couldn't have planned it better. A good dramatic scene helps to keep the flies off. Though it can also attract the wrong kind of attention. I headed for the far corner of the pit, Joanna at my side. She was looking at me just a little oddly.

"Don't mind Alex," I said calmly. "He's the only man I know who suffers from permanent PMT."

"Did those women really eat their own dog?"

I shrugged. "Times were hard."

"And just what did you do to that poor bastard?"

"I stared him down."

Joanna gave me a hard look, and then clearly decided not to pursue that any further. Wise of her.

"Who's this Eddie we're going to see? And how can he help us find my daughter?"

"Razor Eddie," I said. "Punk God of the Straight Razor. Supposedly. Got his name quite a few years back, in a street war over territory between neighbouring gangs. Eddie was just fourteen at the time, and already a slick and vicious killer. Expert with a pearl-handled razor, and nasty with it. Already more than a little crazy. In the years that followed, he'd kill for anyone who had the price, or just for a little attention."

"You know the most charming people," murmured Joanna. "How is someone like that going to help us?"

"Wait. It gets better. Eddie went missing. Something happened to him on the Street of the Gods, something he still won't talk about, and when he came back it was as something both more and less than human. Now he sleeps in doorways, lives on handouts and eats leftovers, and wanders where he will, living a life of violent penance for his earlier sins. His chosen victims tend to be the bad guys no-one else can touch. The ones who think they're protected from the consequences of their actions by money or power. They tend to end up being found dead in mysterious, upsetting ways. And that's Razor Eddie; an extremely disturbing agent for the good. The good didn't get a say in the matter."

"You're lecturing me again." For the first time since I'd led her into the Nightside, Joanna looked a little unsettled. "All that matters . . . is whether he can help me find my Cathy. Will he want paying?"

"No. Eddie doesn't have any use for money, any more. But he does still owe me a favour."

"I'd hate to think what for."

"Best not to," I agreed.

We finally came to a halt before a table in a particularly dark and shadowy corner of the stone-walled pit. And behind that table, Razor Eddie, a painfully thin presence in an oversized grey coat apparently held together by accumulated filth and grease. Just looking at it was enough to make you itch, and the smell was appalling. Rats have been known to jump back into open sewers, just to get away from the smell of an approaching Razor Eddie. He hadn't changed at all in five years. The same hollowed face and fever-bright eyes, the same disturbing presence. Being around Eddie was as close as most people get to death before the real thing comes looking for them. He likes to drink at Strangefellows, somewhere at the back, away from bright lights. No-one judges him, and no-one bothers him. His drinks are on the house, and in return Eddie never kills anyone actually on the premises.

He had a bottle of designer water on the table in front of him, with flies crawling all over it. More flies buzzed around Eddie, except for the ones that got too close, and fell dead out of the air. I smiled at Eddie, and he nodded gravely back. I pulled up a chair opposite him. The smell was every bit as bad as I'd remembered it, but I like to think it didn't show in my face. Joanna pulled up a chair beside me, trying hard to breathe only through her mouth. When Eddie spoke, his voice was low, controlled, almost ghostly.

"Hello, John. Welcome home. You're looking well. Why is it you only ever come to see me when you want something?"

"You're not always the easiest man to find, Eddie. And, you're a spooky bastard. So, how are things? Killed anyone interesting recently?"

The ghost of a smile moved across his pale lips. "No-one you'd know. I hear you're looking for a runaway."

Joanna started. "How did you know that?"

"Word gets around, in the Nightside," said Eddie. He turned his disturbingly bright eyes on me. "Try the Fortress."

I nodded. I should have thought of that one myself. "Thanks, Eddie."

"You'll find Suzie there."

"Oh good," I said, trying to sound pleased. Suzie and I have a history. I was about to push back my chair when Eddie turned suddenly to look at Joanna, who started again under the impact of his gaze.

"You be careful around this man, miss. John isn't the safest of people to keep company with."

"Anything specific in mind, Eddie?" I said carefully.

"There are people looking for you, John."

"There are always people looking for me."

Eddie smiled gently. "These are *bad* people."

I waited, but he had nothing more to say. I nodded my thanks and rose to my feet. Joanna scrambled quickly to hers. I took her back to the bar. She breathed deeply all the way, and then shuddered suddenly.

"*Awful* little man. And what was that stench? I swear, he smelled like something that had died and then been dug up again."

"There are things about Razor Eddie it's best not to ask," I said wisely. "For our own peace of mind."

We were back at the bar again. Alex glowered at me in greeting. I looked at Joanna.

"You wait here, while I get word to the Fortress that we're coming. It's best not to surprise people with that many guns."

I moved off down the bar to use the courtesy phone. But even as I hit the numbers, listened to a recorded voice from the Fortress and left a brief message, I was still listening carefully to Joanna as she talked with Alex. Keep a close eye on your enemies, but a closer one on your friends. And clients. You tend to live longer that way, in my business. Alex gave Joanna what he thinks is his ingratiating smile. She didn't smile back.

"I'll have a large whiskey. Single malt. No ice."

"At last," said Alex. "A civilised drinker. You wouldn't believe what I get asked for some nights. Designer beers and flavoured spirits and bloody cocktails with soft porn names. One guy actually wanted a piledriver, vodka with prune juice. Animal."

He poured Joanna a generous measure in a reasonably clean glass. She looked at him thoughtfully. "You know John Taylor."

"For my sins, yes."

"How well do you know him?"

"As well as he'll let me," said Alex, unusually serious. He has a weakness for blondes, especially ones that don't take any shit from him. That's why I left them alone together. Alex leaned across the bar to Joanna. "John doesn't believe in letting people in. And it has been five years . . . Still, I knew he'd be back someday. This place has its claws in him. Born in the Nightside, he'll die in the Nightside, and it won't be of old age. Always has to be the white knight, riding in to rescue some poor bastard caught between a rock and a hard place. The ones with no-one else to turn to. John's always been a sucker for a hard luck story, and it would appear he's still arrogant enough to believe he knows what's best for everyone."

"Why did he become a private detective?"

"He has a gift for finding things. Only decent thing he got from his parents. You know the story? Everyone here does. How John's father killed himself by inches after finding out the woman he married wasn't . . . entirely human. I feel much the same about my ex-wife. May she rest in peace."

"I'm sorry," said Joanna. "When did she die?"

"She didn't," said Alex. "It's just wishful thinking on my part."

"Can I trust Taylor?" said Joanna forcefully.

"You can trust him to do what he feels is best. Which may or may not be what you want. So watch yourself."

"Razor Eddie said we should go to the Fortress."

Alex winced at the name, but nodded. "Sounds about right."

"What is it? Another bar?"

"Hardly. The Fortress is a heavily fortified refuge for people who've been abducted by aliens. A whole lot of them got together, bought a whole lot of guns, and made it clear to all and sundry that they weren't being taken again without one hell of a fight. There's a television camera in every room, so they can be watched over even while they sleep. Some of them even have explosive devices taped to their bodies, ready to be triggered at a moment's notice. Word is there's enough ammo and bombs in that place to fight a fairly major war."

"Does it work?" said Joanna.

Alex shrugged. "They're not the kind of people you ask personal questions of. They're always on the lookout for Men in Black. Anyway, over the years the Fortress has become something of a haven for anyone who needs help or protection, or just somewhere safe and secure to crash for a few days. A lot of runaways pass through the Fortress."

"Are they good people?"

"Oh sure. Paranoid, violent and crazy as a cat on crack, but . . ."

I decided I'd heard enough. I put the phone down and went back to join them. Alex might or might not have known I was listening. It didn't matter. I nodded to Joanna.

"All I can get is the answerphone. We'll have to go round there and ask in person."

"Can't wait," said Joanna. She downed the last of her drink in one. Alex blinked respectfully a few times. Joanna slammed the glass down on the bar. "Put it on Taylor's tab."

"You're learning," said Alex.

I headed for the metal stairs, Joanna at my side. No-one looked around as we passed. Joanna looked at me suddenly.

"John?"

"Yes?"

"Did they *really* eat their dog?"

FIVE

The Harrowing

We left Strangefellows, stepping out into the sullen gloom of the back alley, and the solid steel door shut itself firmly behind us. On the whole, things hadn't gone too badly. Eddie had come up with a solid lead, no-one serious had tried to kill me, and Alex hadn't even mentioned my long-standing bar bill. Presumably because he knew a rich client when he saw one. I'd hate to think he was getting soft. Joanna looked vaguely about her, frowned, and hugged herself tightly, shivering suddenly. Understandable. The alley was freezing cold, with thick whorls of hoarfrost on the walls and cobbled ground. The night had turned distinctly wintry in the short time we'd been inside. Joanna looked at me accusingly, her breath steaming thickly on the still air.

"All right, what happened to the weather? It was a nice balmy summer night when we went through that door."

"We don't really have weather, as such, in the Nightside," I explained patiently. "Or seasons, either. Here, the night never ends. Think of temperature changes here less as weather, and more as moods. Just the city, expressing itself. If you don't like the current conditions, wait a minute, and something new but equally distressing will come along. Sometimes, I think we get the weather we deserve here. Which is probably why it rains a lot."

I started off down the alley, and Joanna strode along beside me, her heels clacking loudly on the cobbles. She was working her way up to ask-ing me something intrusive. I could tell.

"Eddie said bad people were looking for you," she said finally.

"Don't worry. The Nightside is a big place to get lost in. We'll have found your daughter and be long gone before anyone can catch up to us."

"If people are always looking for you here . . . why don't you just stay out of the Nightside?"

I did her the courtesy of considering the matter for a few moments. It was a serious question, and deserved a serious answer. "I tried, for five long years. But the Nightside is seductive. There's nothing in everyday London to match it. It's like living in colour, instead of black and white. Everything's more in-tense here, more primal. Things matter more, here. Beliefs, actions, lives . . . can have more significance, in the great scheme of things. But in the end, it all comes down to the fact that I can make a much better living here, than I can in London. My gift only works in the Nightside. I'm somebody, here, even if I don't always like who that person is. Besides, you can't let anyone tell you where you can and can't go. It's bad for business."

"Alex said this was your home. Where you belong."

"Home is where the heart is," I said. "And most people don't dare re-veal their heart here. Someone would eat it."

"Eddie said they were *bad* people," Joanna said stubbornly. "And he looked like the kind who would know *bad*. Be honest with me. Are we in any immediate danger?"

"Always, in the Nightside. All kinds of people end up here, drawn and driven by passions and needs that can't properly be expressed or satisfied anywhere else. And a lot of them like to play rough. But most of them know better than to mess with me."

She looked at me, amused. "Hard man."

"Only when I have to be."

"Are you armed?"

"I don't carry a gun," I said. "I've never felt the need."

"I can look after myself too," she said suddenly.

"I don't doubt it," I assured her. "Or I would never have let you come with me."

"So, who's this Suzie, that Eddie said we'd meet at the Fortress?"

I looked straight ahead. "Ask a lot of questions, don't you?"

"I believe in getting my money's worth. Who is she? An old flame? An old enemy?"

"Yes."

"Is she going to be a problem?"

"Perhaps. We have a history."

Joanna was smiling. Women like to know things like that. "Does she owe you a favour too?"

I sighed, reluctantly realising that Joanna wasn't going to be put off by curt, monosyllabic answers. Some women just have to know everything, even when it's patently none of their business.

"Not so much a favour; more like a bullet in the back of the head. So . . . Suzie Shooter. Also known as Shotgun Suzie, also known as *Oh God, it's her, run!* The only woman ever thrown out of the SAS for unacceptable brutality. Works as a bounty hunter, in and around the Nightside. Probably got paper on someone hiding out in the Fortress."

Joanna was looking at me closely, but I kept on looking straight ahead, my face carefully calm. "All right," she said finally. "Would she be willing to help us?"

"She might. If you can afford her."

"Money is no object, where my daughter is concerned."

I looked at her. "If I'd known that, I'd have charged you more."

She started to laugh, and then it turned into a cough, as she hugged herself hard again. "*Damn*, it's cold! I can hardly feel my fingers. I'll be glad to get back into the light again. Maybe it'll be warmer, out on the street."

I stopped abruptly, and she stopped with me. She was right. It was cold. Unnaturally cold. And we'd been walking for far too long still to be in the alley. We should have reached the street long before this. I looked behind me, and Strangefellow's small neon sign was just a glowing coal in the dark, far away. I looked back at the alley exit, and it was no nearer now than when we'd started. The alley had grown while I was distracted by Joanna's questions. Someone had been playing with the structure of space, stretching the alley . . . the energy drain manifesting as the sudden cold . . . I could feel the trap closing in around me. Now I was looking for it, I could sense magic in the air, crackling like static, stirring the hair on my arms. Everything seemed far away, and what sounds there were came slow and dull, as though we were underwater. Someone had taken control of the space around us, like closing the lid on a box.

And as I looked, six dark silhouettes appeared, blocking the exit to the alley. Dark men in dark suits, waiting for me to come to them.

"Next time you want to pick a fight," Joanna said quietly, "do it on your own time. It would appear Ffinch-Thomas' daddy has sent reinforcements."

I nodded, trying hard not to let my relief show in my face. Of course; Ffinch-Thomas and his threats. Druid magic and city honour. No problem. I could handle half a dozen yuppie Druid wannabes, and send them home crying to their mothers. The alley spell would collapse soon enough, once I shattered their concentrated will with a little practiced brutality. And then a pale ruddy light filled the alley, leaking out of nowhere, illuminating the scene in shades of blood so Someone else could enjoy the show, and for the first time I saw clearly what was waiting for me at the end of the alley. And I was so scared I nearly vomited right there and then.

They stood together, six of them, things that looked like men but were not men. Human in shape, but not in nature, they wore plain black suits, with neat string ties and highly polished shoes, and slouch hats with the brims pulled low, but that was just part of the disguise. Something to help them blend in, so they could walk the streets without people screaming. It worked, until you looked under the brims of their hats, to where their faces should have been. They had no faces. Just utterly blank expanses of skin, from chin to brow. They had no eyes, but they could still see. No ears, but they could hear. No mouths or noses, but then, they didn't need to breathe. There was something uniquely horrid about the sight, an offence against nature and common sense, foul enough to sicken any sane man.

I knew them, from before. They were fast and they were strong, and they never got tired; and once they had been set on your trail they'd track you to Perdition itself and never once falter. I had seen them tear people literally limb from limb, and trample over screaming bodies. Oh yes, I knew them, of old. They moved forward suddenly, calm and unhurried, stepping out in perfect unison, advancing on me in complete silence, with not even the sound of their own footsteps to accompany them.

I made a sound in the back of my throat, the kind of sound a fox makes when it sees the hounds closing in. Or the sound of a man who can't wake up from a nightmare. I was so scared I was shaking, sweat running down my face. My own personal bogeymen, my pursuers since childhood, come for me at last. Joanna saw my fear, and it quickly infected her too. After seeing some of the things I'd taken in my stride, she knew these had to be really bad. She had no idea. Inside, I was screaming. After all the years of running and hiding, they'd finally found me. And I was going to die hard, and bloody, and people would vomit when they saw what was left of me. I'd seen their work.

I looked back over my shoulder, wondering if I had time to reach Strangefellows. Maybe run through the bar, and out the back, through the old cellars . . . but they were already there. Six more of them, standing together, cutting me off from hope and safety and all chance of escape. I hadn't even sensed them appearing. I'd spent too long in the everyday world. Got soft, and careless. I looked back at the six bearing down on me. I was breathing hard, my hands opening and closing helplessly.

"What . . . what are they?" said Joanna, clinging to my arm with both hands. She was as scared as I was.

"The Harrowing," I said, my voice little more than a whisper. It was an effort to talk. My mouth was painfully dry, my throat closed like there was a hand round it. "The ones who are always looking for me. Death given shape and form, the act of murder made manifest in flesh and blood and bone."

"The bad people Eddie warned you about?"

"No. These are their emissaries. The ones they always send to kill me. Someone has betrayed me. They couldn't have tracked me down this fast, set up so perfect a trap so quickly. Someone told them where and when to find me, the bastards. Someone sold me out. To the Harrowing."

All the time I was babbling, my mind was working furiously. There had to be a way out of this. Had to be. It couldn't all end so simply, so stupidly, with my guts torn out in a grimy back alley in the middle of a nothing case.

"Can you fight them?" said Joanna, her voice high, bordering on the hysterical.

"No. My bag of tricks is pretty much empty, after so long away."

"But you're the hard man, remember!"

"They're harder."

"Can't you just . . . stare them down? Like you did with Ffinch-Thomas?" Her voice broke off sharply. She could see them more clearly now. The Harrowing.

"They don't have any eyes!" I said, hysteria edging into my voice too. "You can't hurt them; they don't feel anything. You can't even kill them; they're not really alive."

I hit my gift for all it was worth. Most of it was still sleeping at the back of my head, unused for five years, but I forced it ruthlessly awake, knowing I'd pay in pain and damage later. If there was a later. I pushed against my limits, scrabbling with my mind at the spell surrounding me, probing it for weaknesses. Front and back were blocked, but maybe the alley walls . . . I can find things, so I tried as hard as I knew how to find a way out of that alley. The alley walls were solid brick, but walls can conceal a lot of things, in the Nightside. And sure enough my third eye, my private eye, found the outlines of an old door hidden underneath the bricks and mortar of the present wall. A door in the space currently occupied by the right-hand wall, hidden from all but those with a very special gift. From the look of it, the door hadn't been opened in a long time, but its temporal inertia was no match for my desperation. I hit it with all my mind, and space shuddered.

The Harrowing lifted their heads slightly, together, sensing something. I hit the door again and it groaned, springing open just a crack. Bright light flared around the edges of the door, spilling into the alley, pushing back the unnatural bloody light. It was sunlight, pure and uncorrupted, and the Harrowing flinched back from it, just a little. I could hear a wind blowing beyond the door, harsh and ragged, and it sounded like freedom.

"What is that?" said Joanna.

"Our way out." My voice was firmer. "Lots of weak spots and fracture lines in the Nightside, if you know where to look. Come on. We are out of here."

"I can't."

"What?"

"I can't move!" I looked at her. She wasn't kidding. Her face was white as a skull, her eyes as wide as an animal's in a slaughterhouse. Her hands gripped my arm with painful pressure. "I'm scared, John! They scare me. I can't . . . I can't move. I can't breathe. I can't think!"

She was panicking, lost to hysteria. The Nightside had finally pushed her too far. I'd seen it before. I had to act for us. I hauled her towards the door I'd opened, but her legs wouldn't cooperate, and she fell awkwardly, sprawling across the cobbles and almost dragging me down with her. I forced her hands off my arm, and she curled up on the ground, crying helplessly and shaking all over. I looked at the door, and then at the approaching Harrowing. It was so far, and they were so close. I couldn't drag her. But I could get away. I could still reach the door, force it open, fall through and slam it shut behind me, and be safe. But that would mean leaving Joanna behind. The Harrowing would kill her. Horribly. Partly because they never leave witnesses, and partly as a message to me, and others. They'd done it before.

She was nothing to me. Joanna bloody Barrett, all money and pride and snotty manners, dragging me back into the Nightside against my better judgement. Making me feel sorry for her, and her stupid bloody daughter. I owed her nothing. Nothing worth putting my life at risk, trying to save her. She couldn't run. She fell. She brought it on herself. All I had to do was leave her to the Harrowing, and I'd be safe.

I turned towards the door in the wall, and let go of my hold on it. The door slammed shut in a moment, the daylight snapped off, and the awful ruddy light took back its hold on the alley. I moved back to stand over Joanna, my hands balled into fists. She might not be a friend, or even an ally, but she was a client. I've failed myself more times than I care to remember, but I've always done my best never to fail a client. A man has to have some self-respect.

I threw aside the last of my pride and let out one last, desperate mental call for help. Not many would care, even if they heard, not in the Nightside, but Alex might hear . . . and do something. But even as I opened up my mind, the thoughts of the Harrowing crashed in on me; a deafening cacophony of alien, yammering voices, utterly inhuman, trying to fill my head and force out my own thoughts. I had to shut my mind down again, in self-defence. There wasn't going to be any help—no cavalry, no last-minute rescue. As always, I was all alone, in the night that never ends. Just me, and my enemies, at my throat at last.

The Harrowing closed in, six before and six behind, taking their time now they knew I had nowhere to go. They moved in silence, like ghosts or shadows, or deadly thoughts, and their blank faces were scarier than any murderous expressions could ever have been. Their purpose and intent were clear in their movements—sharp, economic, perfectly synchronised. Not graceful; that was too human an attribute for them. I raised my fists in one last gesture of defiance, and they held up their pale hands. For the first time I saw that their long slender fingers ended in hypodermic needles, protruding inches beyond their nail-less tips. Long slender needles, dripping a pale green liquid. That was new, something I'd never seen before. And I knew suddenly, on a level deeper than instinct, and more sure, that the game had changed while I was away. They weren't here to kill me. They were here to jab me with those needles, drug me till I couldn't fight any more, and then drag me away to . . . somewhere else. To their mysterious, unknown masters. The *bad* people.

I could have cried. I wasn't even going to be allowed the dignity of a quick, if nasty, death. My enemies had something slower, more lingering, planned for me. Torture, horror, madness; perhaps to make me one of them, to do their bidding. Saying their words, carrying out their commands, while some small part of me screamed helplessly, forever trapped and suffering behind my own eyes. I'd rather die. I was finally so scared I got angry. To hell with that, and to hell with them. If I couldn't escape, I could at least defy them. Make them kill me, and deny them their victory, or triumph.

And who knew; if I could hold them off long enough, maybe I'd find some way out of this mess, after all. Miracles do happen, sometimes, in the Nightside.

The first of the Harrowing came in reach, and I hit it right in its blank face, putting all my strength behind the blow. My fist sank deeply into its head, square in the middle where its nose should have been, the pale flesh *giving* unnaturally, stretching like dough. The skin clung stickily to my hand as I jerked it free, and the creature barely swayed under the impact. I spun round quickly, striking out at the others as they came crowding in around me. They were fast, but I was faster. They were strong, but I was desperate. I held them off for a while with sheer fury, but it was like hitting corpses. Their bodies were horribly yielding, as though there was really nothing inside them, and perhaps there wasn't. They were just vessels for my enemies' hatred. They absorbed punishment as a passing thing, of no importance at all, and came back for more. Their hands came at me from all directions, striking like snakes, trying over and over again to catch me with their needled fingers. They had the mindless tenacity of machines, and all I could do was keep moving, keep dodging, getting a little slower with every panting breath. Their needles ripped open my trench coat, and pale green liquid stained the material. I actually got mad enough to pick one of the things up, and throw it back against a wall; but though it hit hard enough to break the bones of a living man, the Harrowing just flattened slightly against the brickwork, like a horrid toy that wouldn't break, and came back at me again.

Faceless, remorseless, completely silent. It was like fighting nightmares. I yelled to Joanna to run, while they were still preoccupied with me, but she just lay huddled on the ground, mouth slack with shock, staring with wide, almost mindless eyes. The Harrowing were all over me by then, and I was so tired, so cold. The best I could do was fool them into working against each other, so that they stabbed each other rather than me. Even rage and terror can only keep you going for so long, and what strength I had left was fast fading away. I was working on how best to make them kill me, when the shadow came moving among them, and everything changed.

The Harrowing's heads all turned at once, as they suddenly realised they weren't alone. Something new had come into the alley, something scarier and even more dangerous than they were. They could feel it, the way predators can always sense a rival. They forgot all about me for the moment, and I collapsed gratefully onto the cobbles beside Joanna, my heart hammering painfully in my chest as I fought for breath. Joanna threw her arms about me, and clung to me, shuddering, hiding her face in my neck. I watched it all.

The Harrowing looked about them, all their blank faces moving as one. They were confused, disoriented. This wasn't in the plan. And then one of the faces was suddenly different from all the others. A long red line had appeared, crossing the empty face where the eyes should have been, immediately leaking blood. The creature hesitantly raised a needled hand to its bloody face, as though to examine the cut. A shadow swept across the Harrowing, fast as a fleeting thought, and the hand toppled from the wrist and fell away, neatly severed. Blood pumped out of the stump into the chill air, steaming thickly. And I smiled, a nasty gloating smile, as I re-

alised just who had come to my rescue. It was already over. The Harrowing were all finished. They just didn't know it yet.

Something moved among the blank-faced figures, too fast to be seen.
Blood flew on the air, spurting from a hundred wounds at once. The Harrowing tried to fight, but all they struck was each other. They tried to run,
but wherever they went the shadow was already there before them, cutting
and slicing at them, ripping them apart, tearing them to pieces. They
couldn't scream, but I like to think that in their last few moments of existence they knew something of the horror and suffering they had always
brought to others.

In a matter of seconds, it was all over. The dozen Harrowing, the
deadly hounds on my trail, were no more. They had been rendered into
hundreds, maybe thousands, of small scattered body parts, spread the
length of the alley. Some of them were still twitching. The grimy brick
walls ran red with blood, and the cobbled ground was slick with it, save
for a small empty circle around Joanna and myself. And a dozen featureless faces, expertly skinned from featureless heads, had been nailed to the
wall in neat rows beside the closed steel door leading to Strangefellows.

The bloody light snapped off, and the alley returned to its usual gloom.
The bitter chill slowly began to relax its hold. I murmured comfortingly to
Joanna, until her death grip on me began to relax, and then I nodded to
the still, quiet figure standing beneath the small neon sign.

"Thanks, Eddie."

Razor Eddie smiled faintly, his hands thrust into the pockets of his
oversized grey coat. There wasn't a speck of blood on him.

"That's your favour paid off, John."

Something about the way he said that made a lot of things fall into
place for me. "You knew this was going to happen!"

"Of course."

"Why didn't you wade in sooner?"

"Because I wanted to see if you still had it."

"You could at least have said something! Why couldn't you have
warned me?"

"Because you wouldn't have listened. Because I wanted to send the
Harrowing's bosses a warning. And because I do so hate to be indebted to
anyone."

And I knew, then. "You told them I was going to be here."

"Welcome back, John. The old place hasn't been the same without you."

Something moved like a fleeting shadow, or a passing breeze, and there
was no-one standing beneath the neon sign. The alley was empty, apart

from all the scattered body parts, and the blood sliding down the walls. I should have known. Everyone has their own agenda, in the Nightside. Joanna raised her pale face to look at me.

"Is it over?"

"Yes. It's over."

"I'm sorry. I know I should have run. But I was so *scared*. I've never been that scared before."

"It's all right," I said. "Not everyone can swim when they're thrown in the deep end. Nothing in your old life could ever have prepared you for the Harrowing."

"I always thought I could cope with anything," she said quietly. "I've always had to be hard—to be a fighter—to protect my interests, and those of my child. I knew the game, how it was played. How to use . . . what I have, to get my own way, do all the other people down. But this . . . this is beyond me. I feel like a child again. Lost. Helpless. Vulnerable."

"The rules aren't that different," I said, after a while. "It's still all about the powerful, getting away with murder because they can. And a few of us who won't be beaten down. Fighting our corner, helping those we can, because we must."

"My hero," said Joanna, smiling slightly for the first time.

"I'm no hero," I said, very definitely. "I just find things. I'm not here to clean up the Nightside. It's too big, and I'm too small. I'm just one man, using what gifts I have to help my clients, because everyone should have someone to turn to, in time of need."

"I never met a man I respected," said Joanna. "Before now. You could have run and left me. Saved yourself. But you didn't. My hero."

She raised her mouth to mine, and after a moment, we kissed. She was warm and comforting in my arms, pressing against my body, and for the first time in a long time, I felt alive again. For a time, I was happy. It was like waking up in a foreign country. Afterwards, we sat there on the bloody cobbles for a while, holding each other. And nothing else mattered at all.

SIX

Storming the Fortress

I hailed a horse and carriage to take us to the Fortress. It was too damned far to walk, especially after that business outside Strangefellows, and I felt in distinct need of a bit of a sit-down. And it was probably a good idea to get my face off the streets for a while. The horse came trotting over, glaring down any traffic that looked like getting in his way. He was a huge brute of a Clydesdale, white as the moon, with broad shoulders and massive silver-hoofed feet, hauling an ornate nineteenth-century hansom carriage, of dark ebony and sandalwood, with solid brass trimmings. The man sitting up top, wrapped in an old leather duster, was carrying a five-foot-long blunderbuss, its long stock etched with offensive charms and sigils. He looked carefully about him as the horse manoeuvred the carriage in beside Joanna and me, clearly ready to use his huge gun at a moment's notice. Joanna had recovered most of her composure by now, if not all her old arrogance, but she was immediately charmed by the horse. She went immediately over to him, to pat his shoulder and rub his nose. The horse whinnied appreciatively.

"What a wonderful animal," said Joanna, almost cooing. "Do you think he'd like some sugar, or a sweetie?"

"No thanks, lady," said the horse. "Gives me cavities. And I hate going to the dentist. Wouldn't say no to a carrot, mind, if you had such a thing about your person."

Joanna blinked a few times, and then looked at me accusingly. "You do this to me deliberately. Every time I think I'm finally getting my head round the Nightside, you spring something like this on me. I swear, my nerves are sitting in a corner, crying their eyes out." She looked back at the horse. "Sorry. No carrots."

"Then get in the carriage and stop wasting my time," said the horse. "Time is money, in this business, and I've got payments to make."

"Excuse me," said Joanna, diffidently, "but am I to understand that this . . . is your carriage? You're in charge here?"

"Damn right," said the horse. "Why not? I do all the hard work. Out in all weathers, wearing grooves in my shoulders from this bloody harness. And I know every road, route, and resurfaced bypass in the Nightside, plus a whole bunch of short cuts that aren't on anybody's maps. You name it, and I can get you there, and faster than any damned cab."

"And the . . . gentleman up top?" said Joanna.

"Old Henry? He's just there to take the fares, make change, and ride shotgun. No-one messes with us, unless they fancy going home with their lungs in a bucket. Handy things, hands. Once I've paid off the bank, I'm thinking about investing in some cybernetic arms. If only so I can scratch my own damned nose. Now are we going to stand around talking all night, for which I charge extra, or are we actually going somewhere?"

"You know the Fortress?" I said.

"Oh sure. No problem. Though I think I'll drop you off at the end of the block. Never know when those crazies are going to start shooting again."

Old Henry grunted loudly in agreement and hefted his blunderbuss. I held open the carriage door for Joanna, and she climbed in, somewhat dazed. I got in after her, slammed the door, and we were off. The seats were red leather, and very comfortable. Not a lot of room, but cosy. It was a smooth ride, which argued for some fairly sophisticated springs somewhere down below.

"I don't like cabs," I said, just to make conversation while Joanna got her mental breath back. "You never know who they're really working for, or who they're reporting back to. And the drivers always want to talk politics. The few horse and carriage outfits working the Nightside are strictly independent. Horses are stubborn that way. You might have noticed Old Henry doesn't even have any reins; the horse makes all the decisions. Besides, Old Henry probably needs both hands free to handle that massive shooting iron of his."

"Why does he need a gun?" said Joanna, her voice back to normal.

"Keeps the other traffic at bay. Not everything that looks like a car is a car. And you never know when the trolls are going to take up carjacking again."

"I feel a distinct need to change the subject," said Joanna. "Tell me more about this Suzie Shooter we might be running into at the Fortress. She sounds . . . fascinating."

"Oh, she's all that and more, is Suzie," I said, smiling. "She tracks down runaway villains like a hunter on the trail of big game. There's nowhere they can hide that she won't go after them, no protection so overwhelming that she won't go charging right in, guns blazing. Not the most subtle of people, Suzie, but definitely one of the most determined. No job ever turned down, no target ever too dangerous, if the price is right. Suzie's been known to use every kind of gun known to man, as well as a few she's had made up specially, but mostly she favours the pump-action shotgun. You can usually tell where she's been, because it's on fire. And you can track her down by following the kicked-in doors, scattered screaming and blood splashed up the walls. Her presence can start a fight, or stop one dead. Hell of a woman."

"Were you ever . . . close? You said you had a history . . ."

"We worked some cases together, but Suzie doesn't let anyone get close. I don't think she knows how. Men have been known to enter her life from time to time, but they usually exit running."

"Razor Eddie, Shotgun Suzie . . . you know the most *interesting* people, John. Don't you know any ordinary people?"

"Ordinary people don't tend to last long, in the Nightside."

"Is she likely to be a help, or a hindrance?"

"Hard to tell," I said honestly. "Suzie's not the easiest of people to work with, especially if you prefer to bring your quarry back alive. Suzie's a killer. She only became a bounty hunter because it provides her with a mostly legal excuse for shooting lots of people."

"But you like her, don't you? I can hear it in your voice."

"She's been through a lot. Endured things that would have broken a lesser person. I admire her."

"Do you trust her?"

I smiled briefly. "You can't trust anyone here. You should know that by now."

She nodded. "Razor Eddie."

"And he's my friend. Mostly."

We spent the rest of the ride in silence. We both had a lot to think about. Joanna spent a lot of the time looking out the window. I didn't. I'd seen it all before. The carriage finally lurched to a halt, and the horse yelled back that we'd reached our destination. I got out first, and paid Old Henry, while

Joanna got her first look at the Fortress. (I made sure Old Henry got a good tip, one he'd remember. Never know when you might need a ride in a hurry.) The horse waited till Old Henry nodded that everything was okay, and then he set off again. I went over to Joanna, who was still staring at the Fortress. It was worth looking at. Hadn't changed a bit in five years.

The Fortress started out life as a discount warehouse. Stack them high, sell them cheap, and absolutely no refunds. It dealt mostly in weapons, from all times and places, no questions asked, but it made the mistake of flooding the market. Even in the Nightside, there are only so many people who need killing at any given time. So the warehouse tried quietly instigating a few turf wars, to stimulate demand, and that was when the Authorities took an interest. Next day the property was up for sale. The alien abductees took it over, lock, stock and a whole lot of gun barrels.

The Fortress was a squarish building of several storeys, with all its windows and doors protected behind reinforced steel shutters. There were heavy-duty gun emplacements on the flat roof, looking up as well as down, and all kinds of electronic gear. No-one ever approached the Fortress without being carefully scrutinised well in advance. The word *FORTRESS* had been painted in big letters across the front wall, over and over, in every language under the sun, and a few spoken only in the Nightside. They weren't hiding. They're proud of what they are. The Fortress is still primarily a last refuge for alien abductees, but it was there for anyone in need, for short-term stays. They'd provide counseling, another address more suited to your needs, and whatever kind of weapons you needed to make you feel safe. The Fortress firmly believed in the *Kill them all and let God sort them out* school of therapy. Being abducted from the age of ten will do that to you. Those few people stupid enough to abuse the Fortress's hospitality never lived long enough to boast about it.

The Fortress stood between a Voodoo Business School and an Army Surplus Store. Joanna just had to stop and look in the windows. The Voodoo establishment's current display boasted St. John The Conqueror's Root in easy-to-swallow capsules, Mandrake Roots with screaming human faces, and a Pick & Mix section of assorted charms. They'd dressed up a window dummy as Baron Samedi, complete with mock graveyard, but it looked more tacky than anything.

The Army Surplus window had uniforms from throughout history, a display of medals from countries that didn't exist any more, and a single executive's suitcase, closed, marked *Backpack nuke; make us an offer.* Joanna looked at that for a long time, before turning to me.

"Are they *serious*? Could that actually be the real thing?"

"Must be something wrong with it," I said. "Otherwise, the Fortress would have bought it. Maybe you have to supply your own plutonium."

"Jesus wept," said Joanna.

"He did indeed," I agreed. "And over worse things than this."

We approached the Fortress's front door, and that was when I first got the feeling that something was seriously wrong. The security camera over the door had been smashed, and the reinforced steel door was standing slightly ajar. I frowned. That door was never left open. Never. I stopped Joanna with a gentle pressure on her arm, gestured for her to be quiet and stay well behind me, and then I carefully pushed the door open a way. From inside came the faint sounds of distant gun-fire and the occasional scream. I smiled briefly.

"Looks like Suzie's here. Stick close to me, Joanna, and try to look harmless."

I pushed the door all the way open and looked in. The lobby was deserted. I walked in, very quietly, and studied the situation carefully.

The lobby had probably been very comfortable originally, designed to put new visitors at their ease, but now it was just a mess. All the up-to-the-moment furniture had been overturned, the country-side scenes on the walls hung crookedly, punctured with bullet holes, and the tall rubber plant in the corner had been riddled with extremely unfriendly fire. Normally you had to pass through a bulky ex-airport metal detector to get into the lobby proper. Someone had thrown it half-way across the room. There was still some smoke drifting on the air, and the unmistakable smell of cordite. Someone had let off a whole lot of rounds in here, and pretty damned recently at that.

But there weren't any bodies, anywhere.

I slowly crossed the lobby, Joanna sticking as close to me as she could without actually climbing into my pockets. I checked out the security cameras in the ceiling corners. The little red lights showed they were still operating. Someone had to have seen what went down here, but there was no sign of any reinforcements. Which could only mean the real action was still going on, somewhere deeper inside the building. I was beginning to get a really bad feeling.

The door on the other side of the lobby, that gave access to the inner layers of the Fortress, was also standing ajar. All its locks and bolts had been smashed, and one of the door's hinges had been torn clean away from the door-jamb. I carefully pushed the door aside and peered out into the corridor beyond. There were fresh bullet scars on the walls, but still no bodies. From further ahead came the sound of multiple gun-shots and angry shouting.

"Maybe we should nip next door to the Army Surplus and pick up some guns of our own?" said Joanna.

"Would you know how to use one, if we did?"

"Yes."

I looked at her. "You're just full of surprises, aren't you? I don't like guns. They make it too easy to make the kind of mistakes you can't put right by saying 'Sorry' afterwards. Besides, I've never felt the need."

"What about the Harrowing?"

"Guns wouldn't have stopped them anyway."

Joanna gestured at the cameras up by the corridor ceiling. "Why all the security?"

"Abductee logic. They have cameras in every room, every corridor, every nook and cranny. And more hidden booby-traps than I feel comfortable thinking about. And, a whole team of people whose only job is to sit and watch the monitors, in shifts. These people are genuinely afraid that the aliens will come for them again. And since no-one knows how the little grey bastards come and go, the cameras are always running. The idea is, that while human eyes might be fooled, cameras would still catch them. I suppose once the security team spots them, they hit every alarm in sight, and everyone grabs the nearest weapon and shoots the shit out of anything that doesn't look entirely human. They even have cameras in the toilets and showers, just in case. No-one here is being taken again without one hell of a fight first."

Joanna pulled a face. "No privacy anywhere? *Seriously* paranoid."

"Not if They really are after you. And the more I look at what's happened here . . . the less I like it. All the signs are that someone, or something, crashed into the lobby, and the Fortress people opened fire. To no obvious effect. From the sound of it, they're still fighting, but they're clearly on the retreat. Something is pushing them further and further back, into the heart of their own territory. So far, so obvious. But, where are the bodies? Maybe, just maybe . . . the aliens have come at last, looking for their missing specimens . . ."

"Are you serious?" said Joanna. "*Aliens?*"

I looked down the empty corridor, considering the possibilities. "All sorts end up in the Nightside. Past, present and future. Aliens are no stranger than a lot of the things I've seen here."

"Maybe we should come back another time," said Joanna.

"No. These are good people. I can't walk away, when they might need help. I never could. And Suzie's probably in there somewhere . . . Damn. *Damn.* I really didn't need this right now. You can wait outside if you want, while I check this out."

"No. I feel safer with you, wherever you are. My hero."

We shared a quick smile, and then I led the way down the corridor. The sound of gun-fire slowly grew louder, along with incoherent shouting and cursing. Lots more structural damage along the way, but still no bodies. Not even any blood. Which, given the sheer amount of gun-fire, was disturbing . . . The corridor ended in a sharp right turn. We were right on top of the fire-fight now. I made sure Joanna was standing well back, and then peered quickly round the corner. Whereupon everything became extremely clear. I should have known. I sighed deeply, and stepped round the corner and into clear view. I raised my voice, cold and commanding and really annoyed.

"Everybody cut it out, right now!"

The shooting stopped immediately. Silence fell across the corridor before me. Smoke curled thickly on the still air. At the far end of the corridor, a whole crowd of people were sheltering behind furniture they'd dragged out of adjoining rooms to pile into a barricade. I counted at least twenty different kinds of guns protruding through the improvised barricade before I gave up. Most of them looked to be full automatic. And facing them, at my end of the corridor, was a tall blonde in black leathers, with a pump-action shotgun in her hands, kneeling behind her own improvised barricade. She looked back at me and nodded briskly.

"John. Heard you were back. Be with you in a minute, soon as I've dealt with this bunch of self-abuse experts."

"Put your gun down, Suzie," I said sternly. "I mean it. No more shooting from anyone. Or I am going to get seriously cranky with everyone. Suddenly and violently and all over the place."

"Oh hell," said a voice from behind the far barricade. "As if things weren't bad enough, now John Taylor's here. I could spit. All right, which of you idiots upset *him*?"

Suzie Shooter stood up and snarled at me. She had to be in her late twenties now, and still looked good enough to eat. If you didn't mind a meal that would very definitely bite back. As always, Suzie was dressed in black motorcycle leathers, adorned with steel chains and studs, and two bandoliers of bullets crossing her impressive chest. Knee-length leather boots with steel toe-caps completed the look. Suzie had seen *Girl on a Motorcycle* and *Easy Rider* more times than was healthy, and loved every Hells Angels movie Roger Corman ever made.

She had a striking face, with a strong bone structure, ending in a determined jaw, and she kept her shoulder-length straw-blonde hair back out of her face with a leather headband supposedly fashioned from the hide of the first man she'd killed. When she was twelve. Her eyes were a very dark blue, cold and unwavering, and her tightly pursed mouth rarely relaxed into a smile, except in the midst of mayhem and bloodshed, where she felt most at home. She'd never been known to suffer fools gladly, spent her money as fast as it came in, and in general kicked arse with vim and enthusiasm. She liked to say she had no friends and her enemies were dead, but a few people have been known to sneak their way into her life, almost despite her. I, for my sins, was one of them.

Standing there, set against the curling smoke and swaying lights of the corridor, she looked like a Valkyrie from Hell.

"Let me guess," I said, just a little tiredly. "You smashed your way in, demanded they turn your bounty over to you, and when they declined, you declared war. Right?"

"I have serious paper on this guy," said Suzie. "And they were very rude to me."

I considered the matter. "I'm sure they're very sorry. Well, try not to kill them all, Suzie. I need someone alive and mostly intact to answer a few questions."

"Hey! Hold everything!" said the voice from behind the far barricade. "It's possible . . . we may have been a bit hasty. Nobody here wants to take on Shotgun Suzie and John bloody Taylor unless it's absolutely necessary. Can't we talk about this?"

I looked at Suzie, who shrugged. "All they have to do is hand over my bounty, and I'm out of here."

"If we hand him over, you'll kill him," said the voice. "He came to us for sanctuary."

"The man has a point," I said. "You do tend towards bringing them in dead, rather than alive."

"Less paperwork," said Suzie.

I looked down the corridor at the twenty or so guns facing me. "If Suzie really wanted you dead, you'd be dead by now. She's given you every chance. I really think you should consider surrendering."

"We guarantee the safety of people who come here," the voice said stubbornly. "That's who we are. Why we are. We're willing to discuss a deal, but we won't betray our principles."

I looked at Suzie. "What poor soul are you after, this time?"

"No-one important. Just some scumbag lawyer who grabbed a client's settlement money and did a runner with it. Five million pounds, and change. I'm down for ten per cent of whatever I recover."

"A *lawyer*?" said the voice. "Oh hell, why didn't you say? If we'd known he was one of them, we'd have given him to you."

I smiled at Suzie. "Another triumph for common sense and diplomacy in action. You see how easy it is, if you just try a little reason first?"

Suzie growled, lowering her shotgun for the first time. "I hate being reasonable. It's bad for my reputation."

I turned back to the far barricade, so she wouldn't see me smile. "I'm here looking for a teenage runaway, name of Cathy Barrett. Who may have got herself into more trouble than she realises. Name ring any bells?"

"I'm not coming out while Suzie's still there," said the voice from behind the barricade.

"You don't have to come out," I said patiently. "Just answer the question. Unless you want me to get a bit peeved with you too."

"Cathy was here," the voice said quickly, "but she took off, a week or so back. Said something was calling to her. Something wonderful. We all tried to talk her out of it, but she wouldn't listen. And this isn't a prison, so . . . She said something about Blaiston Street. And that's all I know."

"Thank you," I said. "You've been very helpful."

"Not like we had much of a choice," said the voice. "Word's already going around about what you did to those poor bastards outside Strangefellows. They're still mopping up the mess."

I just nodded. It wasn't the first time things had been attributed to me that were none of my doing. Eddie probably started this particular rumour, as a way of saying sorry. It helps to have a reputation for being a bit of a bastard. People will believe anything of you.

"I'll leave you and Suzie to sort this out between you," I said. "Just give her everything she asks for, and you shouldn't have any more problems with her."

"Thanks a whole bunch," said the voice bitterly. "I think I'd rather face the aliens again."

I gestured for Suzie to step around the corner for a moment, so we could talk privately. I introduced her to Joanna, and the two women smiled at each other. I just knew they weren't going to get on.

"So," said Suzie, "found another lost lamb to look after, have you, John?"

"It's a living," I said. "Been a while, Suzie."

"Five years, three months. I always knew you'd come crawling back to me someday."

"Sorry, Suzie. I'm only here because I'm working a case. Soon as I find my runaway, I'm out of here. Back to the safe, sane, everyday world."

She stepped forward, fixing me with her wild, serious gaze. "You'll never fit in there, John. You belong here. With the rest of us monsters."

I didn't have an answer for that, so Joanna stepped into the silence. "What, precisely, is your connection with John, Miss Shooter?"

Suzie snorted, loudly. "I shot him once, but he got over it. Paper I had on him turned out to be fake. We've worked together, on and off. Good man in a tight corner. And he always leads me where the action is. The real action. Never a dull moment, when John's around."

"Is that all there is to your life?" said Joanna. "Violence, and killing?"

"It's enough," said Suzie.

I decided the conversation had gone about as far as it was safe for it to go, and turned to Joanna. "I know Blaiston Street. Not far from here. Bad neighbourhood, even for the Nightside. If Cathy has gone to ground there, the sooner we find her, the better."

"Need any help?" said Suzie.

I looked at her thoughtfully. "Wouldn't say no, if you're offering. You busy?"

She shrugged. "Things have been quiet recently. I hate quiet. Just let me finish up here and collect what I'm owed, and I'll catch up with you. Usual fee?"

"Sure," I said. "My client's good for it."

Suzie looked at Joanna. "She'd better be."

Joanna started to say something, noticed that Suzie's shotgun was pointing right at her, and very sensibly decided not to take offence. She ostentatiously turned her back on Suzie, and fixed her attention on me.

"At least now we've got an address. What are the odds Cathy could have got into serious trouble there?"

"Hard to say, without knowing what drew her there. I wouldn't have thought there was anything on Blaiston Street to attract anyone. There isn't anywhere lower, except maybe the sewers. It's where you end up when you can't fall any further. Unless things have changed dramatically, since I was away. Suzie?"

She shook her head. "Still a snake pit. If you burned the street down, the whole city would smell better."

"Don't worry," I said quickly to Joanna. "She's your daughter. You said yourself she can look after herself. And we're right on her heels now."

"Don't put money on it," said Joanna, the corners of her mouth turning down. "Cathy's always been good at giving people the slip."

"Not people like us," I said confidently.

"There are no people like us," said Suzie Shooter.

"Thank God," said the voice from behind the far barricade.

SEVEN

Where the Really Wild Things Are

Joanna and I left Suzie Shooter intimidating the entire Fortress through the sheer force of her appalling personality, and headed for Blaiston Street. Where the wild things are. Every city has at least one area where all the rules have broken down, where humanity comes and goes, and civilisation is a sometime thing. Blaiston Street is the kind of area where no-one has ever paid any rent, where even the little comforts of life go only to the strongest, and plague rats go around in pairs because they're frightened. It's mob rule, on the few occasions when the brutal inhabitants can get their act together long enough to form a mob. They live in the dark because they like it that way. Because that way they can't see how far they've fallen. Drink, drugs and despair are the order of the day on Blaiston Street, and no-one ends up there by accident. Which made Cathy's choice of destination all the more disturbing. What on earth, or under it, could have called a vital, mostly sensible young girl like her to such a place?

What did she think was waiting for her there?

It was raining, soft pitterpatters of blood temperature that made the streets glisten with the illusion of freshness. The air was heavy with the smell of restaurants, of cuisines from a hundred times and places, not all of them especially appealing. The ever-present neon seemed subtly out of focus behind the rain, and the people passing by had hungry, angry faces. The Nightside was getting into its stride.

"This is a hell of a place," Joanna said abruptly.

"Sometimes literally," I said. "But it has its attractions. Just as it's ways the bad boy that makes the good girl's heart beat that little bit fast so it's the darker pleasures that seduce us out of the everyday world, an into the Nightside."

Joanna snorted. "I always thought you could find every kind of pleasure in London. I've seen the postcards in public phone kiosks, advertising perversion at reasonable rates. Every kind of sex, with and without bodily contact, performed by people of every kind of sex. And a few proudly in between. Pre-op, post-op, during the op . . . I mean, what's left?"

"Trust me," I said seriously. "You really don't want to know. Now change the subject."

"All right. What was it like, growing up here, in the Nightside?" Joanna looked at me earnestly. "This must have been . . . an unusual place, for a child."

I shrugged. "It was all I knew. When miracles and wonders happen every day, they lose their powers to amaze. This is a magical place, in every sense of the word, and if nothing else, growing up here was never boring. Always some new trouble to get into, and what more could a curious child ask for? And it's a great place to learn self-discipline. When they tell you to behave or the bogeyman will get you, they aren't necessarily kidding here. You either learn to be a survivor early on, or you don't get to grow up. You can't trust anyone to watch your back for you . . . not friends or family. But there's an honesty to that, at least.

"This all seems normal to me, Joanna. Your world, the calm and reasonable, mostly logical, everyday London was a revelation to me. Safe, sane, reassuringly predictable . . . There's a deal of comfort in being blessedly anonymous, of knowing that sometimes things can just *happen*, with no great significance, for you or anyone else. The Nightside is lousy with omens and prophecies, and intrusions and interventions from Above and Below. But though your world is mostly secure and protected, it's also . . . grey, boring, and bloody hard to earn a living in. I'll go back there, when I'm through with this case, but I couldn't honestly say whether that's because I prefer it, or because I've lost my touch in how to survive in a place of gods and monsters."

"This Blaiston Street," said Joanna. "It sounds a dangerous location, even for the Nightside. Are you sure Cathy was heading there?"

I stopped, and she stopped with me. It was a question I'd been asking myself. The voice at the Fortress might have said anything, just to get rid

o and get Suzie off his back. I would have. But . . . it was my only lead.
wled, frustrated, and the people passing by gave us a little more room.
always been able to find anything with my gift. That was how I'd
e my reputation. To be back in the Nightside, and blind in my private
was almost too much to bear. I ought to be able to pick up at least a
npse of her, if she really was so close, on Blaiston Street.

I lashed out with my mind, hitting the night like a hammer-blow, forc-
g my gift out across the secret terrains of the hidden world. It beat on the
, wild and angry, pushing open locked doors with grim abandon, and
eople around me clutched their heads, cried out and shrank away. My
ands closed into fists at my sides, and I could feel myself smiling that old
icious smile, that wolf on a trail smile, from a time when nothing mat-
ered but getting to the truth. There was a sick, vicious pain throbbing in
my left temple. I could do myself some serious damage by forcing my gift
beyond its natural limits, after so long asleep, but right then I was so angry
and frustrated I didn't care.

I could feel her out there, Cathy, not long gone, her traces still vibrat-
ing on the membrane of the hidden world, but it was like reaching out for
something you can sense in the dark, but not see. Someone, some thing,
didn't want me to see her. My smile widened nastily. Hell with that. I
pushed harder, and it was like slamming my mind against a barbed-wire
fence. Blood was dripping steadily from my left nostril now, and I couldn't
feel my hands. Serious damage. And then some tension, some defence,
broke under my determination, and Cathy's ghost sprang into being before
me. It was a recent image, a manifestation only days old, shimmering right
there on the street before me. I grabbed Joanna's hand so she could see it
too. Cathy hurried down the street, really striding out, and we hurried
after her. Her face sparkled and shimmered, but there was no mistaking the
broad smile on her face. She was listening to something only she could
hear, something *wonderful*, that called to the very heart of her, and it was
drawing her in like an angler plays a fish, leading her straight to Blaiston
Street. The smile was the most terrible thing. I couldn't think of anything
in my life I'd ever wanted as much as Cathy clearly wanted what the un-
heard voice was promising her.

"Something's calling her," said Joanna, gripping my hand so hard it
hurt.

"Summoning her," I said. "Like the Sirens called the Greek sailors of
old. It could be a lie, but it might not. This is the Nightside, after all. What
disturbs the hell out of me is that I can't even sense the shape of whatever
it is that's out there. As far as my gift's concerned, there's nothing there,

never has been. Nothing at all. Which implies major shields, and really heavy-duty magic. But something that powerful should have showed up on everyone's radar the moment it appeared in the Nightside. The whole place should be buzzing with the news. A new major player could upset everyone's apple carts. But no one knows it's here . . . except me. And I'm damned if I can even guess what anything that powerful would want with a teenage runaway."

Cathy's ghost snapped out, despite everything I could do to hang on to it. My gift retreated back into my head and slammed the door shut after it. The headache was really bad now, and for a moment all I could do was stand there in the middle of the pavement, eyes clenched shut, fighting to hold my thoughts together. When this case was finally over, I was going to need some serious healing time. I opened my eyes and Joanna offered me a handkerchief, gesturing at my nose. I dabbed at my left nostril until the bleeding finally gave up. I hadn't even felt her let go of my hand. I was pushing myself way too hard, for my first time back. Joanna stood close to me, trying to comfort me with her presence. The headache quickly faded away. I gave Joanna her bloodied handkerchief back, she received it with a certain dignity, and we set off towards Blaiston Street again. I didn't mention my lapse, and neither did she.

"Is Suzie really as dangerous as everyone seems to think she is?" said Joanna, after a while, just to be saying something.

"More, if anything," I said honestly. "She built her reputation on the bodies of her enemies, and a complete willingness to take risks even Norse berserkers would have balked at. Suzie doesn't know the meaning of the word *fear*. Other concepts she has trouble grasping are *restraint, mercy* and *self-preservation*."

Joanna had to laugh. "Damn it, John; don't you know any normal people here?"

I laughed a little myself. "There are no normal people here. Normal people would have more sense than to stick around in a place like this."

We walked on, and though people were giving me plenty of room, no-one even glanced at me. Privacy is greatly valued in the Nightside, if only because so many of us have so much to hide. The traffic roared past, never stopping, rarely slowing, always in such a hurry to be somewhere else, to be doing something somebody else would be sure to disapprove of. There are no traffic lights in the Nightside. No-one would pay them any attention anyway. There are no official street crossings, either. You get to the other side of the street through courage and resolve and intimidating the traffic to get out of your way. Though I'm told bribery is also pretty effective. I looked at Joanna, and asked her a question I'd been putting off for too long. Now we were finally getting close to Cathy, I felt I needed to know the answer.

"You said this wasn't the first time Cathy ran away. Why does she keep running away, Joanna?"

"I try to spend time with her," said Joanna, looking straight ahead. "Quality time, when I can. But it isn't always possible. I lead a very busy life. I work all the hours God sends, just to stay in one place. It's ten times harder for a woman than a man, to get ahead and stay ahead in the business world. The people I have to deal with every day would eat sharks for breakfast, as an appetizer, and have turned betrayal and back-stabbing into a fine art. I work bloody hard, for the security Cathy takes for granted, to get the money to pay for all the things she just has to have. Though Heaven forfend she should show the slightest interest in the business that makes her comfortable world possible."

"Do you enjoy your work?"

"Sometimes."

"Ever thought about trying something else?"

"It's what I'm good at," she said, and I had to nod. I knew all about that.

"No stepfathers?" I said casually. "Or father figures? Someone else she could turn to, talk to?"

"Hell, no. I swore I'd never make the mistake of being tied to a man again," Joanna said fiercely. "Not after what Cathy's father put me through, just because he thought he could. I'm my own woman now, and whoever comes into my life does so on my terms. Not a lot of men can cope with that. And I have trouble hanging on to the few that can. The work, again. Still, Cathy never wanted for anything she really needed. I raised her to be bright, and sharp, and independent."

"Even from you?" I said quietly. Joanna wouldn't even look at me.

And that was when the world suddenly changed. The living city disappeared, and abruptly we were somewhere else. Somewhere much worse. Joanna and I stumbled on for a few steps, caught off guard, and then we stopped and looked quickly about us. The street was empty of people and the road was empty of traffic. Most of the buildings surrounding us were nothing more than ruins and rubble. The taller buildings had apparently collapsed, long ago, and everywhere I looked nothing was more than a storey or two high. I could see for miles now, all the way to the horizon, and it was all destruction and devastation. I turned in a slow circle, and everywhere was the same. We had come to a dead place. London, the

Nightside, the old city, was now a thing of the past. Something bad had come, and stamped it all flat.

It was very dark now, with all the street-lights and the glaring neon gone. What light there was had a dull, purple cast, as though the night itself was bruised. It was hard to make out anything clearly. There were shadows everywhere, very deep and very dark. Not a normal light to be seen anywhere, in any of the wrecked and tumbledown buildings; not even the flicker of a camp-fire. We were all alone, in the night. Joanna fumbled in her bag and finally produced her cigarette lighter. Her hands shook so much it took her half a dozen goes to get it to light. The warm yellow flame seemed out of place in such a night, and the glow didn't travel far. She held the lighter up high as we looked around, trying to get some sense of where we were, although I already had a sinking feeling I knew what had happened.

It was quiet. Very quiet. No sounds at all, save for the shuffling of our feet and our own unsteady breathing. Such utter quiet was eerie, unsettling. The roar of the city was gone, along with its inhabitants. London had been silenced, the hard way. I only had to look around in the awful purple light to know that we had come to an empty place. The heavy silence was almost overpowering, until I felt like shouting out . . . something, just to emphasize my presence. But I didn't. There might have been something listening. Even worse, there might not.

I'd never felt so alone in my life.

All around us the buildings were squat, deformed, their shapes altered and the edges softened by exposure to wind and rain. Long exposure. All the windows were empty, every trace of glass gone, and I couldn't see a single doorway with a door; just dark openings, like eyes or mouths, or maybe wounds. There was something almost unbearably sad in seeing such a mighty city brought so low. All those centuries of building and expanding, all those many lives supporting and giving it purpose, all for nothing, in the end. I moved slowly forward, and puffs of dust sprang up around my feet. Joanna made a noise at the back of her throat and moved slowly after me.

It was cold. Stark and bitter cold, as though all the heat had gone out of the world. The air was still, with not even a breath of wind blowing. Our footsteps seemed very loud in the quiet, loud and carrying as we walked down the middle of what had once been a street, through what had once been a vital, thriving place. We were both shivering now, and it had nothing to do with the cold. This was a bad place, and we didn't belong here. Off in the distance, broken buildings stood blackly against the horizon in jagged silhouettes, shadows of what they had once been. The city, inside and out, was over.

"Where are we?" Joanna said finally. The hand holding up the lighter was steadier now, but her voice trembled. I didn't blame her.

"Not . . . where," I said. "When. This is the future. The far future, by the look of it. London has fallen, and civilisation has come and gone. This isn't even an epilogue. Someone closed the book on London and the Nightside, and closed it hard. We've stumbled into a Timeslip. An enclosed area where Time can jump back and forth, into the past and the future and everything in between. Needless to say, there wasn't a Timeslip here the last time I came this way. Anyone with two brain cells to rub together knows enough to avoid Timeslips, and they're always well sign-posted. If only because they're such arbitrary things. No-one understands how they work, or even what causes them. They come and they go, and so do whatever poor bastards get sucked up in them."

"You mean we're trapped here?"

"Not necessarily. I've been using my gift to try and find us a way out. The physical area of a Timeslip isn't very large. If I can just locate the boundaries, crack open a weak spot . . ."

"Not very large!" Joanna's voice rose, harsh with emotion. "I can see for miles, all the way to the horizon! It'll take us weeks to walk out of here!"

"Things aren't always as they appear. You should know that by now." I kept my voice calm and light, trying to sound knowledgeable and reassuring, and not at all as though I was just guessing. "While we're in the Timeslip, we see all of it; but the actual affected area is comparatively small. Once I can crack a hole in the boundary, and we walk through, we'll snap back to our own time. And I'd say we're only half an hour away. Easy walk. Assuming, of course, that nothing goes wrong."

"Wrong?" said Joanna, seizing on the word. "What could possibly go wrong? We're all alone here. This is the far future, and everyone's dead. Can't you feel it? The lights of London have finally gone out . . ."

"Nothing lasts forever," I said. "Everything comes to an end, in Time. Even the Nightside, I suppose. Let enough centuries pass, and even the greatest of monuments will fall."

"Maybe they dropped the Bomb, after all."

"No. The Nightside would survive the Bomb, I think. Whatever did happen here . . . was much more final."

"I hate to see London like this," Joanna said quietly. "It was always so *alive*. I always thought it would go on forever. That we built it so well, ran it so tightly, loved it so much, that London would outlast us all. I guess I was wrong. We all were."

"Maybe we just went away and built another London somewhere else," I said. "And as long as people are around, we'll always need a Nightside, or something like it."

"And what if people aren't around, any longer? Who knows how far into the future we are now? Centuries? Millennia? Look at this place! It's dead. It's all dead. Everything ends. Even us." She shuddered abruptly, and then glared at me, as though it was all my fault. "Nothing's ever easy around you, is it? A Timeslip . . . Is this sort of thing usual, in the Nightside?"

"Well," I said carefully, "it's not unusual."

"Typical," said Joanna. "You can't even trust *Time* in the Nightside."

I couldn't argue with that, so I looked around me some more. Millennia? The ruins looked old, but surely not that old. "I wonder where everyone is. Did they just up and leave, when they saw the city was doomed? And if so, where did they go?"

"Maybe everyone's gone to the moon. Like in the song."

That was when I finally looked up, and the chill sank past my bones and into my soul. It was suddenly, horribly, clear why it was so dark. There was no moon. It was gone. The great swollen orb that had dominated the Nightside sky for as long as anyone could remember was missing from the dark sky. Most of the stars were gone too. Only a handful still remained, scattered in ones and twos across the great black expanse, shining only dimly, a few last sentinels of light against the fall of night. And since the stars are so very far away, perhaps they were gone too, and this was just the last of their light to reach us . . .

How could the stars be gone? What the hell had happened . . .

"I always thought the moon seemed so much bigger in the Nightside because it was so much closer here," I said finally. "Perhaps . . . it finally fell. Dear Jesus, how far forward have we come?"

"If the stars are gone," Joanna said softly, "do you suppose our sun has gone out too?"

"I don't know what to think . . ."

"But . . ."

"We're wasting time," I said roughly. "Asking questions we have no way of answering. It doesn't matter. We're not staying. I've got the far boundary fixed in my head. I'm taking you there, and we are getting the hell out of here, and back to where we belong."

"Wait a minute," said Joanna. "The *far* boundary? Why can't we just turn around and go back the way we came, through the door that brought us here?"

"It's not that simple," I said. "Once a Timeslip has established itself, nothing less than an edict from the Courts of the Holy is going to shift it. It's here for the duration. If we go back, we'll just re-emerge by the Fortress again, and the Timeslip will still be between us and Blaiston Street. We'd have to go around the Timeslip to reach Blaiston Street, and for that we'll need a fairly major player to map the Timeslip's extent and affected area. Or we'll just keep ending up here again."

"How long could such a mapping take?"

"Good question. Even if we could find someone powerful enough who wouldn't charge us an arm and a leg, and could fit it into his schedule straightaway . . . we're talking days, maybe even weeks."

"How big could a Timeslip be?"

"Another good question. Maybe miles."

"That's ridiculous," said Joanna. "There must be another way of reaching Blaiston Street!"

I shook my head reluctantly. "The Timeslip's connected to Blaiston Street, on some level. I can feel it. Which makes me think this can't be co-incidental. Someone, or something, is protecting its territory. It doesn't want us interfering. No. Our best bet is to cross this space to the far boundary, where I can force an opening, and we should emerge right next to Blaiston Street. Shouldn't be too difficult. This is all pretty unpleasant, but I don't see any obvious dangers. Just stick with me. My gift will guide us right there."

Joanna looked at me, and I looked back, trying hard to seem confident. Truth be told, I was just winging it, going by my guts and my instincts. In the end, she looked away first, staring unhappily about her.

"I hate this place," she said flatly. "We don't belong here. No-one does, any more. But Cathy's been gone too long already, so . . . Which way?"

I pointed straight ahead, and we set off together. Joanna held her lighter out before her, but the yellow glow didn't travel far at all. The small flame stood still and upright, untroubled by even the slightest murmur of breeze. I tried not to think about how much longer it would last. The purple light around us seemed even darker in comparison. I was feeling colder all the time, as though the empty night was leeching all the human warmth out of me. I would have improvised a rough torch of some kind, but I hadn't seen any wood anywhere. Just bricks and rubble, and the endless dust.

The quiet was getting on my nerves. It just wasn't natural, to be so completely quiet. This was the quiet of the tomb. Of the grave. It had an almost anticipatory quality, as though somewhere off in the darkest and deepest of the shadows, *something* was watching, and waiting, and biding its time to attack. The city might be empty, but that didn't mean the night was. I was reminded suddenly of how I'd felt as a small child, when my father would put me to bed at night and turn out the light. Back when he still cared enough, and was sober enough, to do such things. Children know the secret of the dark. They know it has monsters in it, which might or might not choose to reveal themselves. Now here we were, in the darkest night of all; and more and more I was convinced something was watching us. There are always monsters. That's the first thing you learn, in the Nightside.

Some of them look just like you and me.

Perhaps the monster here was London itself. The dead city, resenting the return of the living. Or maybe the monster was just loneliness. A man and a woman, in a place that life had left behind. Man isn't meant to be alone.

Our footsteps seemed to grow louder and more carrying as we made our way down what had once been a main street. The dust should have absorbed the sound. There was enough of it. It was everywhere, thick layers of it, undisturbed for God alone knew how long. It was at its worst in the street, but we'd learned the hard way that we had no choice but to stick to the very middle of the street. Buildings had a tendency to collapse, if we got too close. Just the vibrations of our tread were enough to disturb their precarious rest, and whole sections of wall would crumble and fall away, crashing to the ground in great angry clouds of the grey dust. I picked up one brick, and it fell apart in my hand. I tried to work out how ancient it must be, to have become so delicate, but the answers I came up with made no sense. The human mind isn't comfortable with numbers that big.

Just when I thought I was finally coming to terms with where and when I was, things got worse. I started hearing things. Sounds, noises, so faint at first I thought I'd imagined them. But soon they were coming from all around us, from before and behind, subtle, disturbing sounds that seemed to be gradually creeping closer. I don't have that good an imagination. The sounds were almost familiar, but not quite, giving them a strange, sinister feel. And all the time, drawing gradually, remorselessly, closer. I didn't turn my head, but my eyes probed every shadow as I approached it. Nothing. I increased our pace, and the sounds kept right up with me. Following us, tracking us, keeping their distance for the moment, but never too far away. My hands were sweating now. Clattering, chattering noises, that I could almost put a name to. Joanna had picked up on them too, and was glaring openly about her. The flame in the lighter flickered so wildly I was afraid it would go out, and I put a hand on her arm, ostensibly to slow our pace again.

"What the hell is *that*?" she said fiercely. "Could there be something here with us, after all? Something alive?"

"I don't know. But the sound's coming from a lot of directions at once, which suggests that there's a lot of them, and they're all around us." I glared at the shadows from which the ruins grew, but I couldn't make out a damned thing. Anything could have been hiding in there. Anything at all. I was getting less happy by the minute. "Whatever they are, they seem to be content for the moment to keep their distance. Could be they're more afraid of us than we are of them."

"Don't take bets on it," said Joanna. "How much further to the boundary?"

I checked with my gift. "Half an hour's walk. Maybe half that, if we run. But running might send the wrong message."

She looked at me abruptly. "Could it be the Harrowing, after you again?"

I shook my head firmly. "Not so soon after Razor Eddie's little message. Whoever's behind the Harrowing will want to consider the ramifications of that for a while. I would. Even the major players can get really twitchy whenever Razor Eddie's name comes up. Besides, the Harrowing have never been able to track me that accurately. Or I wouldn't have survived this long. Maybe . . . it's insects. I always thought that if anything would outlast Humanity, it would be the bloody insects. Scientists were always saying the damn things would be the only creatures to survive a nuclear war. It could well be insects. *Damn.* I hate creepy-crawlies."

"You're sure it couldn't be anything human? Maybe some other poor soul who got sucked into the Timeslip, maybe hurt and trapped and trying to get our attention?"

I scowled. I should have thought of that. Unlikely, but . . . I sent my gift out into the night, trying to find the source of the sounds, and to my astonishment I locked on to a human trace straightaway. We had to be right on top of him.

"There is someone here! A man . . . one man, on his own. Not moving. Could be hurt . . . this way."

I ran down the street, clouds of dust billowing up around my pounding feet, Joanna right there at my side. I was starting to get used to that. I kind of liked it. We lost track of the sounds around us, caught up in the excitement of finding another human being alive in this awful, dead place. Could be a visitor, could be a survivor . . . could be the answer to a whole lot of questions. And it could be just some poor soul who needed help. First things first. My gift tracked his location as accurately as any radar, leading us off the main street and down a side alley. We slowed to a walk immediately, for fear our footsteps would bring down the brick walls on either side of the alley. But the walls stood firm, not even trembling as we passed.

Finally, we came to a halt beside a large ragged hole in the left-hand wall. The jagged edges of the hole made it seem . . . organic, more like a wound than an entrance. I prodded a protruding brick with a careful fingertip, but it didn't crumble at my touch. Odd. It was very dark beyond the hole, and the air had a faint but distinct mouldy smell. I gestured for Joanna to hold her lighter closer, but the light didn't penetrate more than an inch or two.

"He's in *there*?" said Joanna. "Are you sure? It's pitch-black . . . and I can't hear anything."

"He's in there," I said firmly. "My gift is never wrong about such things. But it does feel . . . odd." I put my head cautiously into the hole. "Hello? Can you hear me? Hello!"

We waited, but there was no reply. The brickwork didn't even shudder at the vibrations of my raised voice. As I listened, I realised the faint sounds that had been following us had stopped. I told myself we'd left them behind, but I wasn't convinced. I pulled my head back and studied the hole in the wall. The more I looked at the situation, the less I liked it. The whole thing smelled of a trap, with the (possibly) injured man as bait. There could be anything waiting in the darkness beyond the hole. But there was definitely a man in there, even if he wasn't answering, and if he was hurt . . . we could be his only chance. And I was damned if I'd abandon anyone here in this Godforsaken place. So . . . I took a deep breath, the smell of mould tickling my nostrils and the back of my throat, and then I eased myself cautiously through the hole in the wall. It was a tight fit. I found the floor with my foot and stepped into the utter darkness of the room beyond. I stood very still for a long moment, listening, but there was no reaction anywhere. I stepped aside, and Joanna followed me in, bringing the feeble yellow light with her.

It looked like two rooms had been knocked through into one, and pretty messily at that. There were dark objects all over the floor. They didn't look like bricks, but I didn't feel like touching them to find out what they were, so I stepped carefully round them as I moved further into the room. The air was close and foul, dry and acrid, but with an underlying scent of decay, as though something had died here, not that long ago. There was no dust on the floor, but the bare brick walls were thick with ugly mounds of grey furry mould. I kept moving, following my gift, Joanna holding her lighter out before us. Shadows danced menacingly around us. It soon became clear we were heading for the far corner, occupied by what seemed to be a huge, dirty grey cocoon. It filled the corner from floor to ceiling; nine feet tall and three feet wide. I thought about what kind of insect might emerge from a cocoon of such size, and then decided very firmly that I wasn't going to think about that any more. *Hate* creepy-crawlies. I kept looking around for the subject of our search, but he was nowhere to be seen, despite my gift urging me forward.

Until finally we were standing right in front of the cocoon, glistening palely in the glow from the lighter, and there was nowhere else to go.

"Tell me you're not thinking what I'm thinking," said Joanna.

"He's in there," I said reluctantly. "He's still alive. Alive, and in there . . . because there's nowhere else he can be."

I swallowed hard, and reached out one hand to the cocoon. The material was hot and sweaty to the touch, something like silk, something like spiderweb, and my flesh crawled instinctively just at the feel of it. I grabbed a handful at about head height, and tore it away by brute strength. The horrid stuff clung stickily to my fingers, stretching unnaturally rather than breaking, and it took all my strength to open up a hole in the outer layer of the cocoon. There was a face underneath. A human face. The skin was grey, the eyes were closed. I hesitated, sure he must be dead, even though my gift was never wrong, and then the eyelids quivered, as though the eyes were trying to open.

I thrust both hands into the hole I'd made and tore the material away from his face. It fought me, clinging to my fingers and the face, trying to repair the broken threads even as I tore them apart. I yelled for Joanna to help, and between us we broke open a larger gap, freeing the head and shoulders. I pulled the last of the stuff away from the face, the eyes finally opened, and I was forced to admit that I knew the face. It was older than I remembered, and much more lined, and the eyes held more horror than I ever want to think about, but it was still, clearly, Razor Eddie.

His eyes slowly came into focus as they looked at me. I scrubbed the last sticky traces from his face with Joanna's handkerchief. The eyes were aware, but that was all. There was no recognition in them, no sense of self, of humanity. Joanna and I talked loudly and comfortingly as we forced open the cocoon, splitting it apart inch by inch, until finally we had an opening large enough to drag him out of. His whole body was limp, unresponsive. He was wearing his old grey coat, even more of a mess than I remembered, much holed and tattered, soaked with slime and darkened with what looked like a whole lot of bloodstains.

We hauled him away from the cocoon, but his legs wouldn't work, so we had to lower him to the floor and set him down with his back against the wall to support him. He was breathing heavily now, great gasping breaths, as though he wasn't used to it. I didn't even want to guess how long he'd been in the cocoon, or what it had done to him. I had a hundred questions, but I kept talking calmly, trying to reach Eddie, bring him up out of the place he'd had to hide in, deep inside himself, for the sake of his own sanity. His eyes fixed on me, ignoring Joanna.

"It's all right, Eddie," I said. "It's me. John Taylor. You're out of that . . . thing. You get your strength back, and your legs working, and we'll get you out of here and back to the Nightside. Eddie? Can you hear me, Eddie?"

A slow knowledge came into his unblinking eyes, though the horror never quite left them. His mouth worked slowly. I leaned closer, to hear his quiet voice. It was rough and harsh, and painful, as though he hadn't used it in a long, long time.

"John . . . Taylor. After all this time. You . . . bastard. God damn you to Hell."

"What?" I jerked back, shocked, sure he must have misunderstood. "I'm going to get you out of here, Eddie. It's going to be all right."

"It'll never be all right . . . Never again. This is all your fault. All of this."

"Eddie . . ."

"I should have killed you . . . when I had the chance. Before you . . . destroyed us all."

"What are you talking about?" Joanna said angrily. "We only just got here! He hasn't done anything! This is a Timeslip!"

"Then damn you, John . . . for what you will do."

"You're blaming me for this?" I said slowly. "You're blaming me . . . for something I haven't even done yet? Eddie, you must know I'd never do anything to bring the world to this. The end of everything. Not by choice, anyway. You have to tell me. Tell me what to do, to prevent this happening."

Razor Eddie's mouth moved in a slow, utterly mirthless smile. "Kill yourself."

"You betrayed John to the Harrowing," said Joanna. "Why should we believe anything you say? Maybe we should forget about rescuing you. Just stick you back in the cocoon again."

"That's not going to happen, Eddie," I said quickly, as the horror filled his eyes again. "Come with us. Help us prevent this. We're not far from the Timeslip's boundary. I can crack it open, get us home again. Back where we belong."

"Back . . . into the past?"

That stopped me for a moment. If this Eddie had got here the hard way, the long way, could I risk taking him back? Would the Nightside accept two Razor Eddies? I pushed the thought aside. It didn't matter. There was no way I was going to leave Eddie here. In the dark. In the cocoon. Some things you just can't do and still call yourself a man.

We got him on his feet, and this time his legs supported him. Even after all he'd been through, he was still Razor Eddie, and tough as nails. Joanna and I helped him across the room, pushed and pulled him through the hole in the wall, and out into the alley. As soon as we were all out into the night, the sounds started up again. Eddie actually cringed for a moment as he heard them, but only for a moment. His gaze was steady now, and his mouth was firm. By the time we reached the main street again, he was walking on his own. Something had broken him, something awful, but he was still Razor Eddie.

"How did you end up the only living person here?" I said finally. "*When* is this, anyway? How far in my future? I've just come back into the Nightside, after five years away. Does that help you date it? Dammit, Eddie, how many centuries have passed, since the city fell?"

"Centuries?" said Eddie. "It seems like centuries. But I've always had a good grasp of time. Not centuries, John. It's only been eighty-two years since you betrayed us all, and the Nightside fell."

Joanna and I looked at each other, and then out over the deserted city. The crumbling buildings, the starless, moonless night.

"How could all this have happened in just eighty-two years?" I said.

"You were very thorough, John. All of this is down to you. Because of what you did." Eddie tried to sound more accusing, but he was just too tired. "All Humanity is dead . . . thanks to you. The world is dead. Cold and corrupt, the only remaining life . . . like maggots writhing in a rotten fruit. And only I am left . . . to tell the tale. Because I can't die. Part of the deal I made . . . all those years ago. On the Street of the Gods. Fool. Damned fool. I have lived long enough . . . to see the end of everything and everyone I ever cared for. To see all my dreams dashed, and made into nightmares. And now I want so badly to die . . . and I can't."

"What did John do?" Joanna said urgently. "What could he have done . . . to bring about this?"

"You should never have gone looking for your mother," said Eddie. "You couldn't cope, with what you found. You couldn't cope with the truth."

"Hang in there, Eddie," I said lamely. "You're going home. Back in Time, to the Nightside as it was. And I swear to you . . . we'll find a way to prevent this. I'll die, rather than let this happen."

Razor Eddie turned his head away and wouldn't look at me. He breathed deeply of the relatively fresh air, as though it had been a long time since he'd breathed anything like it. He was walking more or less normally now, and we were making a good pace as I headed us towards the boundary. But we were still in the same street when it all went to hell.

They came up out of holes in the ground, before and behind and all around us. Dark and glistening, squeezing and forcing their flexible bodies through the ragged openings in the dusty ground. We stopped dead in our tracks, looking quickly around us. And everywhere there were long spindly legs, hard-shelled bodies, compound eyes, grinding teeth and clattering mandibles, and long, quivering antennae. Insects, of all shapes and breeds, species I'd never seen before, all horribly, unnaturally large. More of them came scuttling and scurrying out of the ruined buildings, or skittering down the crumbling walls, light as a breath of air for all their size, joining the hundreds and hundreds already circling us, hopping and seething in a living carpet, covering the ground. The smallest were six inches long, the largest two and even three feet in length, with great serrated mandibles that looked sharp enough and strong enough to take off a man's arm or leg in a single vicious bite. Sometimes the insects crawled right over each other to get a better look at us, but for the moment at least they maintained a safe distance.

I could feel my gorge rising. I really can't stand creepy-crawlies.

"Well," I made myself say lightly, "I always thought insects would end up inheriting the world. Just never thought they'd be so bloody *big*."

"Cockroaches," said Joanna, her voice thick with loathing and disgust. "Revolting things. I should have stomped on more when I had the chance." She waved her cigarette lighter at the nearest insects, and they actually seemed to shrink back a little. It had to be the light. It wasn't any real threat now, but their instincts remembered. Maybe we could use it to open up a path, make a run for it . . . I glanced at Eddie, to see how he was doing, and was horrified to discover he was quietly crying. What had they *done* to him? The great and terrible Razor Eddie, Punk God of the Straight

Razor, reduced to tears by a bunch of bloody bugs? I was suddenly so angry I couldn't speak. Somehow, before I left this place, there was going to be some serious payback.

"This . . . is disgusting," said Joanna. "We've come to where the really wild things are. Nature at its most basic and appalling."

"Got that right," said a familiar, cheerful and self-satisfied voice. I looked round sharply, and there he was, in a little circle entirely clear of insects—the Collector. An old acquaintance of mine, from before I left the Nightside. Not a friend. I don't think the Collector has friends. Got a hell of a lot of enemies, though. He was currently dressed as a gangster from the Roaring Twenties; every detail correct, from the white spats on his shoes to the overbearing colour scheme of the waistcoat, to the snap-brimmed hat. But he was at least thirty pounds too heavy for the suit, and his stomach strained against the half-buttoned waistcoat. As always there was an impression of the utterly false about him. Of someone hiding behind a whole series of masks. His face was almost painfully florid, his eyes gleamed fiercely, and his smile was totally insincere. No change there, then. Warm yellow sunlight surrounded him, from no obvious source, and the insects gave it plenty of room.

"What the hell are you doing here, Collector?" I said. "And who did you steal that incredibly vulgar suit from?"

"It is rather good, isn't it?" said the Collector smugly. "It's an original Al Capone, acquired from his very own wardrobe when he wasn't looking. He won't miss it. He had twenty others just like it. I even have a letter of authentification, from Capone's tailor." He beamed about him, not in the least disturbed by his surroundings. "We do meet in the strangest places, don't we, John?"

"Do I take it you know this person?" said Joanna, looking at me almost accusingly.

"This is the Collector," I explained resignedly. "You name it and he collects it; even if it's nailed down and surrounded by barbed wire. Nothing too rare or too obscure but he hasn't got a line on it. He has an endless appetite for the unique item, and the thrill of the chase. Word is he gets off just indexing his hoard. The Collector, thief, con man, cheat, and quite possibly the most conscienceless individual in the Nightside. There's nothing he won't go after, no matter how precious it might be to other people. I know other collectors, not in his league, who'd give everything they owned, and everything you owned, just for a tour of the Collector's famous and very well hidden warehouse. How's it going, Collector? Found the Phoenix's Egg yet?"

He shrugged. "Hard to tell, until it hatches." He turned his entirely unconvincing smile on Joanna. "You don't want to believe everything you hear about me, my dear. I am a very misunderstood man."

"No you're not," I said. "You're a grave robber, a miser and a meddler in history. Archaeologists use your name to frighten their children. You don't care who gets hurt, as long as you get what you want."

"I save things that would otherwise disappear into the mists of history," said the Collector, unperturbed. "One day I'll open a museum in the Nightside, so everyone can appreciate my treasures . . . But for the moment there are just too many competitors, jealous people, who would cheerfully rob me blind."

"What are you doing here, Collector?" I said. "I wouldn't have thought there was anything valuable left here for you to appropriate."

"You have such limited vision, John," said the Collector, shaking his head sadly. "Surrounded by treasures, and so blind to them. Look around you. There are species of insect here unknown to the world we came from. Unique variations, unavailable anywhere else. I know collectors who speculate in insects who will piss blood when they hear what I've got. I'll take back a few duplicates, of course, to auction off for utterly extortionate prices. Travelling in Time can be so expensive these days."

"Time travel?" Joanna said quickly. "You have a time machine?"

"Nothing so crude," said the Collector. "Though I do have rather a nice display of some of the more rococo mechanisms . . . No, I have a gift. Many do, in the Nightside. Dear John here finds things, Eddie kills with a razor that no-one ever sees . . . and I flit back and forth in Time. It's how I've been able to acquire so many lovely pieces. But to answer your next question; no, I don't carry passengers. How did you get here, John?"

"Timeslip," I said. "I was heading for the boundary when these insects appeared. When exactly are you from, Collector?"

"You've just left the Nightside," said the Collector. "In something of a hurry, swearing never to return. Do I take it you're back?"

"Five years up the line, after you left," I said. "I'm back, and my mood has not improved."

"Can't say I'm surprised," said the Collector. He grinned happily about him. "Ah, so many beauties, I don't know where to start. I can't wait to get them back to my warehouse and start pinning them to display boards!"

Joanna snorted. "Hope you brought a really big killing bottle."

The insects were stirring restlessly all around us, antennae twitching with dangerous agitation. I decided to get to the point. "Collector, Eddie says we're only eighty-two years in my future, but everything here is destroyed. Do you know what brought this about?"

The Collector spread his fat, nail-bitten hands in an innocent gesture. "There are so many futures, so many possible timelines. This is just one possibility. If it's any comfort, there's nothing inevitable about this."

"You knew this future well enough for your gift to bring you here," I said. "You knew about the insects. Talk to me, Collector. Before I get upset with you."

The Collector just kept on smiling his insufferable self-satisfied smile. "You're in no position to make threats, John. In fact, you don't even recognise just how much danger you're in. You're right; I have studied these insects, from a safe distance. I know why they're so interested in us. In humans. I even know why they haven't just killed you. I'm afraid it's rather an unpleasant reason, but then, that's insects for you. Such wonderfully uncluttered minds. No room for fear, or other emotions. They don't even bother with sentience, as we understand it. They're concerned only with survival. I've always admired their ruthlessness. Their single-minded, implacable nature."

"You always were strange," I said. "Get to the point." It seemed to me that the insects around us were edging closer.

"You never studied," said the Collector. "Insects lay their eggs in host bodies. Non-insect host bodies. The eggs grow and hatch inside the host, and the larvae then eat their way out. A bit hard on the host, of course, but . . . Nasty, totally without conscience and compassion, and utterly insect. However, the only living species left in this future world are insects. So all they've got left to use for a host is . . . that unfortunate fellow with you. For eighty-two years now, the undying form of Razor Eddie has been host to generation after generation of insects. Eggs go in, larvae with teeth come out, and the insect race survives. Rather unpleasant for poor Eddie, of course, eaten alive over and over again, but then . . . I never liked him."

I didn't look at Eddie. He didn't need to see my shock and horror at what had been done to him. Especially if it really was my fault. I knew now why the insects had kept him imprisoned in a cocoon. They couldn't risk his finding a way to kill himself. I was so angry then . . . if I'd been big enough, I'd have stamped on every damned insect in the world.

"And now here you are, John," said the Collector. "You and your lady friend. New hosts, for more insect young. I shouldn't think you'll last anywhere near as long as Eddie, but I'm sure they'll make good use of you, while you do last. I suppose I could help you escape . . . but then, I never liked you much either, John."

Razor Eddie cried out suddenly, his back arching, his whole body shaking and shuddering. I grabbed him by the shoulders, but his spasms were so violent I couldn't hold on to him. He fell to the ground, gritting his teeth to keep from crying out again, but his eyes were leaking tears in spite of him. I knelt beside him. I think I already knew what was happening. I didn't back away as hundreds of insect young the size of thumbs burst out of his flesh, eating their way out of his convulsing body. Black soft squishy things, with teeth like tiny razors. They even came out through his eyes. His coat soaked up most of the blood. Joanna fell to one knee and vomited, but still managed to hang on to her lighter. I grabbed handfuls of the emerging larve and crushed them viciously. Their innards ran down my wrists, but there were just too many of them.

"What can I do, Eddie?" I said desperately, but he couldn't hear me.

"Only one thing you can do," the Collector said reasonably. "Kill him. Put him out of his long misery. Except, of course, you can't. This is after all the remarkable Razor Eddie, who cannot die. Take a good look at him, John. Once that cigarette lighter runs out of fuel, they'll come for you . . . and this will be your future, and hers, for as long as they can make you last . . ."

I pushed his hateful words aside, concentrating on my gift. If there was anything that could still kill Razor Eddie, and give him peace at last, my gift would find it. It didn't take long. Pretty obvious, once I had the answer. The only thing that could kill Eddie was his own straight razor. The weapon that no-one ever saw. I already knew it wouldn't be anywhere about his person, or he'd have used it on himself before now. The insects couldn't separate him from it, either. Eddie and his Razor were bound together by a pact only a god could break. I focused my gift further, and there it was, in the one place the insects could put it that Eddie couldn't reach it. They'd buried it deep inside his own body, in his guts.

I made myself act without thinking, without feeling. I thrust my hand into one of the insects' exit wounds, forcing it open, and then drove my hand deep into Eddie's guts, not listening as he screamed, holding him down with all my weight as he kicked. Joanna was dry-heaving by now, but she couldn't bring herself to look away. My arm was bloody up to the elbow by the time my fingers closed around the pearl handle of the old-fashioned straight razor, and Eddie howled like a damned thing as I pulled my hand back out again. Blood dripped thickly from my fingers and my prize. Eddie lay shuddering, moaning quietly. I opened the razor and set the edge against his throat, and I like to think there was gratitude in his eyes.

"Good-bye, Eddie," I said softly. "I'm so sorry. Trust me. I won't let this happen."

"How very sentimental," said the Collector, "but you haven't really thought this through, have you?" I didn't need to look round to know that he was enjoying every moment of this. "You see, if you destroy the insects' only host, and then remove yourself and the woman from this Time, you will be condemning every species here to extinction. Are you really ready to commit genocide, to wipe out the only living things left on the earth?"

"Hell yes," I said, and Razor Eddie didn't even twitch as I cut his throat, pressing down so hard with the blade that I could feel the steel edge grate against his neckbones. I needed to be sure. Blood pumped out under pressure, soaking his clothes and mine, and the dusty ground around us. Eddie lay there peacefully as he died, and afterwards I held him in my arms and cried the tears he couldn't. Because for all our differences, and there had been many, he had always been my friend. When the very last of his life went out of him with a sigh, his razor disappeared from my hand. I lowered his body to the ground and clambered unsteadily to my feet. The Collector was looking at me, utterly stupefied.

"*Hate* creepy-crawlies," I explained.

The insects screamed suddenly; a shrill inhuman sound that filled the purple night. It had taken them a while, but they'd finally understood the significance of what I'd done. The scream rose and rose as more and more of them took it up, until it seemed to be coming from everywhere in the desolate city. I smiled my old smile, my devilish smile, and the Collector flinched at the sight of it. The insects were boiling all around us, pressing right up to the limits of the yellow light. I had just murdered all their future generations . . . unless they could find a way to make use of me, and Joanna. I checked the distance to the far boundary again. Fifteen minutes' running time, maybe ten, depending on how motivated we were. As long as the lighter fuel held out.

The Collector cried out suddenly as holes opened up in the ground around his feet. The insects down below weren't intimidated by his light, and they had finally come for him. One of the Collector's legs plunged down into a gaping hole, and he cried out in pain and shock as unseen jaws sank deep into the meat of his leg. More holes opened up in the ground around me and Joanna, but I had already hauled her to her feet by main force, and we were off and running. We left Eddie's body behind. He was past caring, at last. And already decaying, as the long years finally caught up with him.

We ran past the Collector, who was screaming shrilly as he scrabbled in his suit pockets for something. He finally pulled out a shiny canister, and sprayed the contents down the hole. More of the insects screamed underground, and the Collector was able to pull his leg free. Huge chunks of flesh were missing, the cracked bone clear among red strings of meat. The Collector whimpered, and then sprayed his canister wildly about him as more holes opened up. The light he stood in was flickering unsteadily now as his concentration wavered. He swore briefly, like a disappointed child, and vanished, back into Time. The light snapped off, and the insects charged forward, coming after Joanna and me as we ran for the boundary.

Joanna was back in control again, her face grim and focused as she held the lighter out before her, almost like a cross to ward off the undead. It seemed to me the flame was smaller than it had been, but I didn't say anything. Either it would last, or it wouldn't. Insects crowded in all around us, scrambling over each other in their eagerness to get at us, but still they couldn't bring themselves to enter the gradually shrinking pool of yellow light. There were some the size of dogs, and some the size of pigs, and I hated them all. Joanna and I ran straight at them, and they fell aside at the very last moment, huge dark mandibles snapping shut like bear traps. I glanced again at Joanna's lighter, and didn't like what I saw. The flame wasn't going to last until we reached the boundary, and if it didn't, neither would we. So I called on my gift one more time, to find a path of power.

There are lots of them, in the Nightside, with lots of names; from the uber science of the ley lines to the shimmering magic of the Rainbow Run, there have always been roads of glory, hidden from all but the keenest of gazes, holding the substance of the world together with their immaterial energies. If you had the courage to run them, you could gain your heart's desire. Supposedly. And even now, in this desolate and deserted place, the paths of power remained. My gift locked on to one that led right to the Timeslip boundary, and called it up into existence. A bright, vivid, scintillating path appeared before us, and the insects fell back from the new light as though they'd been burned. Joanna and I ran on, hand in hand, pushing ourselves hard, and sparks flew up from our pounding feet.

But I was already slowing. Using the gift had taken a lot out of me, at the end of a long, hard day. I'd used my gift too often, pushed it too hard, and I was paying the price now. My head was throbbing so hard I could barely see anything outside of the path, and blood ran steadily from both my nostrils and dripped from my chin. My legs felt very far away. Joanna was having to drag me along now, keeping me moving through sheer determination. I could feel the boundary drawing closer, but it still seemed a hell of a way off. Like in those dreams where you run as hard as you can, and still never get anywhere. Joanna was yelling at me now, but I could hardly hear her. And the insects were all around us, a scuttling carpet of dark intent.

I was tired and hurting, but even so I was surprised when my legs just suddenly gave out, and I fell. I hit the glory path hard, and small shocks ran through me, none of them enough to get me back on my feet again. So close, the magic was almost painful. The insects surged right up to the edge of the light, staring at me with expressionless compound eyes. Joanna leaned over me, and tried to raise me up, but I was too heavy. I rolled over onto my side and looked up at her.

"Get the hell out of here," I said. "I've taken you as far as I can. There's nothing more I can do for you. Boundary's straight ahead. I've already cracked an opening that will take you back to the Nightside. Go find your daughter, Joanna. And be kind to her. In memory of me."

She let go of my arm, and it dropped limply to the bright track. I couldn't even feel it.

"I won't leave you," said Joanna. "I can't just leave you."

"Of course you can. If we both die here, who'll help your daughter? Don't worry; I'll be dead before the insects get to me. I'll see to that. Maybe . . . by dying here, now, I can prevent this ever happening. Time's funny that way, sometimes. Now go. Please."

She stood looking down at me, and suddenly her face was utterly blank. All the emotion had gone out of it. Shell-shocked, again, perhaps. Or just considering the matter. She turned away from me, staring down the glowing path towards a boundary whose existence she could only take on faith. She was going to leave me behind, to die. I could feel it. Part of me cursed her, and part of me urged her on. I'd always known something in the Nightside would kill me, and I hated the thought that I might drag someone else down with me. And then she turned back, all the blankness gone from her face, and she grabbed me by the arm again with both hands.

"Get up!" she said fiercely. "Damn you, get up on your feet, you bastard! We haven't come this far together for you to give up now! I'm not leaving without you, so if you don't get up, you're killing me along with you. So move, damn you!"

"Well," I said, or thought I said. "If you put it that way . . ."

Between the two of us, we got me back on my feet again, and we staggered down the shimmering path. I kept thinking that the next step would be my last, that there just wasn't anything left in me, but Joanna kept me going. Half-supporting, half-carrying me, urging me on with comforting words and shouted obscenities. She dragged me down the path, all the way to the boundary, the insects screaming shrilly all the way, until suddenly we crashed through the crack I'd opened and back into our own Time.

We collapsed together on a rain-slick street, fighting for breath, and the wonderful roar of the living city was all around us. Bright neon and thundering traffic, and people, people everywhere. The night sky was full of the blaze of stars, and the great and glorious moon. It was good to be home. We lay side by side on the pavement, and people walked around us, ignoring the blood that soaked my clothes. The Nightside is a great place for minding your own business. I looked at the moon in its bright unblinking eye, and said sorry. Not everyone gets to see the possible results of their own future actions. The world that could be, if they really screw up. I wondered whether I should tell the present-day Razor Eddie of what I'd seen in the possible future. I thought not. There are some horrors no man should have to contemplate, not even the Punk God of the Straight Razor.

Not every future is etched in stone. I should know. I'd seen enough, before now. But I still felt guilty, even if I didn't know what for.

You should never have gone looking for your mother. That's what the future Eddie had said. I'd always been curious about the mother who abandoned me. The woman who wasn't actually human after all. In the early hours of the morning, when a man just can't sleep, I'd often wondered if I help other people find things that matter to them because I can't find the one thing that really matters to me. Well, now I'd have something else to think about at three o'clock in the morning.

I looked at Joanna. "You know, I really thought you were going to leave me there, for a moment."

"For a moment," she said slowly, "I was. I surprised myself. I didn't know I had that kind of determination in me." She frowned. "But it was . . . strange. Something in me didn't want to help you. Don't ask me to explain, because I can't. It's like there's something on the tip of my tongue, a word or a memory I can't quite grasp . . . Oh hell, it doesn't matter. We both got out. Now let's get up off this freezing-wet pavement and go find Blaiston Street. After all we've been through to get there, I'm curious to see what it looks like. It had better be worth it."

"Cathy will be there," I said.

"And we will find her, and save her from whatever damn fool mess she's got herself into this time. Anything else can wait. Right?"

"Right," I said, not entirely sure just what it was I was agreeing to.

When I did find out it was, of course, far too late.

EIGHT

Time Out at the Hawk's Wind Bar & Grill

I'd just seen the end of the world, murdered one of my oldest friends, and discovered that the one quest I'd always intended to give my life to was now forever barred to me; so I decided I was owed a break. Luckily there was a really good café close by, so I took Joanna firmly by the hand and led her there, so that we could both get our mental breath back. The Nightside will grind down the toughest of spirits, if you don't learn to take the occasional pit stop, when you can. Joanna didn't want to go, with Blaiston Street and the answer to her daughter's fate now so close at hand, hopefully, but I insisted. And she must have been tired and shaky too, because she'd actually stopped arguing before we reached our destination.

The Hawk's Wind Bar & Grill is a sight to see, something special even among the Nightside's many dark wonders, and I stopped outside a moment, so Joanna could appreciate it. Unfortunately, she wasn't in the mood. Which was a pity. It's not every day you get to see such a perfect monument to the psychedelic glories of the sixties, complete with rococo Day-Glo neon and Pop Art posters with colours so bright they practically seared themselves onto your retinas. The Hindu latticed doors swung politely open before us as I urged Joanna in, and I breathed deeply of the familiar air of the sixties as we entered the café; joss sticks and patchouli oils, a dozen kinds of smoke, all kinds of freshly brewing coffee, and a few brands of hair oil best forgotten.

The place was packed and jumping, as always, all the hits of the sixties throbbing loudly on the thick air, and I smiled about me at familiar
faces as I led Joanna through the maze of tables to find a reasonably private spot at the rear of the café. Strangefellows is where I go to do business, or a little private brooding; Hawk's Wind is where I go for the peace
of my soul. Joanna looked disparagingly at the stylised plastic table and
chairs, but sat down with a minimum of fuss. I liked to think she was beginning to trust my instincts. Her nostrils twitched suspiciously at the mul-
ticultural atmosphere, and I pretended to study the oversized hand-written
menu while she looked about her. There was always a lot worth looking at
in the Hawk's Wind Bar & Grill.

The decor was mostly flashing lights and psychedelia, with great swirls
of primary colours on the walls, the ceiling and even the floor. A jukebox
the size of a Tardis was pumping out an endless stream of hits and classics
from the sixties pop scene, blithely ignoring the choices of those stupid
enough to put money in it. The Kinks had just finished "Sunny Afternoon,"
and the Lovin' Spoonful launched into "Daydream." My foot tapped along
as I unobtrusively studied Joanna while she studied the faces around her.
The tables around us were crowded with travellers from distant lands and
times, heroes and villains and everything in between. Plus a special sprin-
kling of the kind of people who could only ever have felt at home in a place
like this. Names and faces, movers and shakers, and all the unusual
suspects.

The Sonic Assassin was showing off his new vibragun to the Notting
Hill Sorcerer. The timelost Victorian Adventurer was treating his new sixties stripper girlfriend to the very best champagne. The Amber Prince was
sitting alone, as usual, trying to remember how he got there. Any number
of spies, ostentatiously not noticing each other. And for a wonder, all five
Tracy brothers at the same table. While off in a far corner, what looked
like the whole damned Cornelius clan were being their usual raucous
selves, running up a tab they had no intention of paying. I had to smile.
Nothing much ever changed here. Which was, of course, part of the attraction. The Hawk's Wind Bar & Grill was happily and proudly free of
the tyranny of passing Time.

In the centre of the great open floor, two go-go dancers dressed in little more than bunches of white feathers were dancing energetically in ornate golden cages, frugging and bobbing their heads for all they were
worth. The one in the silver wig winked at me, and I smiled politely back.
A waitress came tripping over to our table in eight-inch pink stiletto heels,
plastic mini skirt, starched white man's shirt and a positively precarious

beehive hairdo. I stood up and peeled off my trench coat, indicating the blood-soaked material, and the waitress nodded brightly.

"Oh sure, JT; anything for you, baby! Welcome back, daddy-o; looking good! You wanna order yet?"

She was chewing gum, and her voice was an irritatingly high-pitched squeal, but there was no denying she was authentic as hell. I sat back down and handed her the menu.

"Two Cokes, please, Veronica. Nothing else. And fast as you can with the coat. I'm in the middle of a case."

"Never knew you when you weren't, dearie. Any messages from the future?"

"Invest in computers."

"Groovy!"

And off she went, swaying on her heels like a ship at sea. Friendly hands reached out to her from all sides, but she avoided them with practised ease and vicious put-downs. A beatnik stood up to recite some poetry, and we all threw things at him. The Animals were singing an uncensored version of "House of the Rising Sun." Try and find that one on a CD compilation. Joanna leaned forward across the plastic table to glare at me.

"Tell me you haven't dragged me into some hideous sixties theme café. I lived through the sixties, and once was more than enough. And we definitely don't have the time to hang around here while they launder your coat! Cathy is close now. I can feel it."

"We could spend a month in here, and not one second would have passed in the street outside," I said calmly. "It's that kind of place. And the laundry here really is something special. They ship your clothes all the way to China and back, and guarantee it'll come back spotless. They could get all the markings out of the Turin Shroud, and add double starch for no extra charge."

"I need a drink," Joanna said heavily. "And not some damned Coke, either."

"Trust me; you're going to love the Cokes they serve here. Because this café isn't a re-creation of the sixties. This is the genuine article."

"Oh bloody hell. Not another Timeslip."

"Not as such . . . The original Hawk's Wind Bar & Grill was a hangout for all the great sixties adventurers and cosmic spirits, and much loved in its day, but unfortunately the café burned down in 1970; possibly in self-immolation, as a protest over the Beatles splitting up. It was due to be replaced by some soulless, boring business school, but luckily the café was so fondly remembered by its famous and gifted patrons that it came back, as a ghost. This whole establishment is one big haunting, a deceased building still stubbornly manifesting long after the original was destroyed.

"A ghost café.

"The people, on the other hand, are mostly real. Either Time-tripping in from the sixties, or just getting into the spirit of the thing. The Hawk's Wind is a genius loci for all that was good and great about the Swingingest era of them all. And because the café isn't real, you can order all kinds of things here that haven't existed since the sixties. Ghost food and drink, which as it isn't real, can't affect a real body. The ultimate in slimming diets; and your last chance to wallow in some serious nostalgia. How long has it been since you've tasted a real Coke, Joanna?"

Our waitress was back, bearing two old-fashioned chunky glass bottles with crimped-on caps, balanced expertly on a tin tray decorated with photos of the Monkees. She slammed the crimped tops expertly against the edge of the table. The caps flew through the air, but not one frothy bubble rose above the mouth of the neck. She placed a bottle before each of us, and dipped in curly-wurly plastic straws. She flashed a grin, cracked her gum, and wiggled off while Joanna looked dubiously at the bottle before her.

"I do not need a straw. I am not a child."

"Go with it. It's all part of the experience. This . . . is *real* Coke. The old, sugar-rich, caffeine-heavy, thick syrup and taste-intensive kind you can't get any more; except in certain parts of Mexico, apparently, which just goes to show. Try it, Joanna. Your taste-buds are about to convulse in ecstasy."

She took a sip, and so did I. She took several more, and so did I. And then we both sat back in our plastic chairs, *ooh*ing and *aah*ing appreciatively, while the dark liquid ran through our bodies, jump-starting all our tired systems. *You don't know what you've got till it's gone,* was crooning from the jukebox, and I could only nod in agreement.

"Damn," said Joanna, after a respectful pause. "*Damn.* This *is* the real thing, isn't it? I'd forgotten how good Coke used to be. Is it expensive?"

"Not here," I said. "This is the sixties, remember? They accept coins from all periods here, and IOUs. No-one wants to risk being barred."

Joanna had relaxed a little, but her mouth was still set in a firm line. "This is all very pleasant, John, but I didn't come into the Nightside to be entertained. My daughter is only a few streets away now, according to you. What are we doing here, when we should be rescuing her?"

"We're here because we need to get our breath back. If we're going to venture into Blaiston Street, we're going to have to be fresh, sharp, and have every last one of our wits about us. Or they'll chop us off at the ankles before we even see them coming. Blaiston Street is only a few blocks away, but it's a whole other world. Vicious, violent, and possibly even more dangerous than the place we just left. And yes, I know that makes you even more desperate to go rushing off to save Cathy, but we're going to need to be at the top of our form for this. And remember, Time doesn't pass out there, while we're in here.

"You're holding up really well after all you've been through, Joanna. I'm impressed. Really. But even the sharpest edge will go blunt if you beat it against a brick wall often enough. So I want you to sit here, enjoy your Coke and the surroundings, until we're both ready to take on the Nightside again. You only think you've seen the bad places. You mess up in Blaiston Street and they'll eat you alive. Possibly literally. And I think . . . there are things we need to talk about, you and I, before we go anywhere else."

"Things?" said Joanna, raising a perfect eyebrow.

"There are things about Cathy, and her situation, that need . . . clarifying," I said carefully. "There's more to this than meets the eye. More to this whole situation. I can feel it."

"There are a lot of unanswered questions," said Joanna. "I know that. Who called Cathy here, and why? Why choose her? She's no-one important, except to me. I'm a successful businesswoman, but I don't earn the kind of money that would make kidnap or blackmail attractive. And this is the Nightside. People like me don't matter here. So why pick on Cathy? Just another teenage runaway? If I knew the answers to questions like those, I wouldn't have needed to hire someone like you, would I?"

I nodded slowly, acknowledging the point. Joanna pressed on.

"I don't think we're in here because I need a rest, John. I think this is your rest stop. You've been through a lot too. You killed Razor Eddie. He was your friend, and you killed him."

"I killed him because he was my friend. Because he'd suffered so much. Because it was the only thing left I could do for him. And because I've always been able to do the hard, necessary things."

"Then why are your hands shaking?"

I looked down, and they were. I honestly hadn't noticed. Joanna put one of her hands on top of mine, and the shaking slowly stopped.

"Tell me about Eddie," she said. "Not the Street of the Gods stuff. Tell me about you, and Eddie."

"We worked a lot of cases together," I said, after a while. "Eddie's . . . powerful, but he's not the most subtle of people. There are some problems you can't solve with power, without destroying what you're trying to save. That's when Eddie would turn up at Strangefellows, asking for my help.

Not openly, of course. But we'd talk, and eventually the conversation would come around to what was troubling him, and then he and I would go out into the night, and find a way to put things right that didn't involve hitting the problem with a sledgehammer. Or a straight razor.

"And sometimes . . . he'd just appear out of nowhere, to back me up. When I got in over my head."

"This sounds more like partners than friends," said Joanna.

"He's a killer," I said. "Razor Eddie. Punk God of the Straight Razor. These days he kills with good rather than bad intentions, but in the end all he is, is killing. And he wouldn't have it any other way. Hard to get close to a man like that. Someone who's gone much further into the dark than I ever have. But . . . he turned his life around, Joanna. Whatever epiphany he found on the Street of the Gods, he threw aside everything that had ever had power over him, in order to earn redemption. How can you not admire courage like that? If someone like him can change, there's hope for all of us.

"I've tried to be a good friend to him. Tried to steer him towards a different kind of life, where he doesn't have to define who he is by killing. And he . . . listens, when I have bad times, and need someone I can talk to who won't repeat it. He warns people away from me, if he thinks they're a threat. He hurts people, if he thinks they're planning to hurt me. He thinks I don't know that.

"I killed him in the Timeslip to put an end to his suffering. I've always been able to bite the bullet, and do what has to be done. I never said it was easy."

"John . . ."

"No. Don't try and bond me with me, Joanna. There's no room in my life for people who can't protect themselves."

"Is that why your only friends are damaged souls like Razor Eddie and Suzie Shooter? Or do you deliberately only befriend people already so preoccupied with their own inner demons that they won't put pressure on you to confront your own? You're afraid, John. Afraid to really open up to anyone, because that would make you vulnerable. This is no way to live, John. Living vicariously through the problems of your clients."

"You don't know me," I said. "Don't you dare think that you know me. I am . . . who I have to be. To survive. I live alone, because I won't risk endangering someone I might care for. And if it's sometimes very cold and very dark where I am; at least when I do go down, I won't drag anyone else with me."

"That's no way to live," said Joanna.

"And you, of course, are the expert on how to run your life successfully. A mother whose child runs away at every opportunity. Let's talk about some of the questions you have to consider, before we go any further. What if, we finally go to Blaiston Street, find the right house, kick in the door and find that Cathy's actually very happy where she is, thank you? That she's happy and safe and doesn't need rescuing? What if she's found someone or something worth running to, and doesn't want to leave? Stranger things have happened, in the Nightside. Could you turn and walk away, leave her there, after all we've been through to track her down? Or would you insist she come back with you, back to a life you could understand and approve of, where you could keep a watchful eye on her, to ensure she won't grow up to make your mistakes?"

Joanna took her hand away from mine. "If she was genuinely happy . . . I could live with that. You don't last long in the business world if you can't distinguish between the world as it is and the world as you want it to be. What matters is that she's safe. I need to know that. I could always come back and visit."

"All right," I said. "Try this one. What if she is in a bad place, and we haul her out of there, and you take her back home with you? What are you going to do to ensure she won't just run away again, first chance she gets?"

"I don't know," said Joanna, and I had to give her points for honesty. "Hopefully, the fact that I've come this far for her, gone through so much for her . . . will make an impression. Make her see that I do care about her, even if I'm not always very good at showing it. And if nothing else, this whole experience should give us something in common to talk about, for once. We've always found it difficult to talk."

"Or listen. Make time for your daughter, Joanna. I really don't want to have to do this again."

"I had managed to work that out for myself," said Joanna, just a little coldly. "I always thought Cathy had everything she needed. Clearly, I was wrong. My business can survive without me for a while. And if it can't, the hell with it. There are more important things."

I nodded and smiled, and after a moment she smiled back. It wasn't going to be as simple or as easy as that, and both of us knew it, but recognising a problem is at least half-way to solving it. I was pleased at how far she had come. I just hoped she could go the distance. We sipped our Cokes for a while. The Fifth Dimension finished "Aquarius" and went straight into "Let the Sun Shine."

"That future we ended up in," Joanna said, after a while. "It may not be *the* future, or even the most likely, but it was still a bloody frightening one. How could *you* possibly be responsible for destroying the whole damned world? Are you really that powerful?"

"No," I said. "At least, not at present. It's got to be tied in to what I inherited, or perhaps stand to inherit, from my missing mother. I never knew her. I have no idea who or what she really was. No-one does. My father found out, and the knowledge made him drink himself to death. And this was a man well used and inured to all the worst excesses of the Nightside."

"What did he do here?" said Joanna.

"He worked for the Authorities. The ones who watch over us, whether we like it or not. After my father died, I went through his papers. Hoping to find some kind of legacy, or message, or just an explanation, something to help me understand. I was ten years old, and I still believed in neat answers like that then. But it was all just junk. No diary, no letters, no photos of him and my mother together. Not even a wedding photo. He must have destroyed them all. And the few people who'd known both my parents had vanished long ago. Driven away by . . . many things. None of them turned up for his funeral.

"Over the years, all kinds of people have come up with all kinds of theories as to who and what my mother might have been. Why she appeared out of nowhere, married my father, produced me, and then disappeared again. And why she didn't take me with her. But no-one's ever been able to prove anything out of the ordinary about me, apart from my gift. And gifts are as common as freckles among the sons and daughters of the Nightside."

Joanna frowned suddenly. "On the tube train, coming here, the Brittle Sisters of the Hive recognised your name. They backed off, rather than upset you. And they asked to be remembered, when you finally came into your kingdom."

I had to smile. "That doesn't necessarily mean anything. In the Nightside, you can never be sure which ugly duckling might grow up to be a beautiful swan, or even a phoenix. So if you're sensible you hedge your bets and back as many horses as possible. And never make an enemy you don't have to."

Joanna leaned forward across the plastic table, pushing her Coke bottle aside so she could stare at me the more fiercely. "And do you still intend to go on looking for your mother, now you know what might happen to the world if you find her?"

"It's a hell of a wake-up call, isn't it? It's certainly given me a lot of food for thought."

"That isn't answering the question."

"I know. Look, I hadn't even intended to stay here, in the Nightside, once this case was over and done with. I left this madhouse five years ago for good reasons, and none of them have changed. But . . . more and more, this dangerous and appalling place feels like home to me. Like I belong here. Your safe and sane everyday world didn't seem to have any place for me. At least here I get the feeling I could do some real good for my clients. That I could . . . make a difference."

"Oh yes," said Joanna. "You could make a hell of a difference here."

I met Joanna's gaze as calmly as I could. "All I can honestly say is this—I really don't care enough about my mother to risk bringing about the future we both saw."

"But that could change."

"Yes. It could. Anything can happen, in the Nightside. Drink your nice Coke, Joanna, and try not to worry about it."

The Crazy World of Arthur Brown was belting out "Fire," by the time Joanna had calmed down enough to ask another question.

"I need you to be straight with me, John. Do you think Cathy is still alive?"

"I have no reason to believe she's not," I said honestly. "We know she was alive very recently. The last image my gift picked up was only a few days old. We know Someone or Something called her into the Nightside, but there's no direct evidence that individual means Cathy any harm. There's no evidence that he doesn't, either, but when you're groping in the dark it's best to be optimistic. As yet, no clear threat or danger has manifested. We have to proceed on the assumption that she's still alive. We have . . . to have hope."

"Hope? Even here?" said Joanna. "In the Nightside?"

"Especially here," I said. This time I put my hand on hers. Our hands felt good together, natural. "I'll do everything I can for you, Joanna. I won't give up, as long as there's a shred of hope left."

"I know," said Joanna. "You're a good man at heart, John Taylor."

We looked into each other's eyes for a long time, and both of us were smiling. We believed in each other, even if we weren't too sure about ourselves. I knew this wasn't a good idea. *Never get personally involved with a client.* It's written in large capital letters on page one of *How to Be a Private Detective.* Right next to *Get as much cash as you can up front, just in case the cheque bounces,* and *Don't go looking for the Maltese Falcon because it'll all end in tears.* I'm not stupid. I've read Raymond Chandler. But right then, I just didn't care. I did make one last effort, for the good of my soul.

"It's not too late for you to back out," I said. "You've been through enough. Stay here, and let me handle Blaiston Street. You'll be safe here."

"No," Joanna said immediately, pulling her hands away from mine. "I have to do this. I have to be there, when you find . . . what's happened to my daughter. I have to know the truth, and she has to know . . . that I cared enough to come myself. Dammit, John, I've earned the right to be there."

"Yes," I said, quietly proud of her. "You have."

"John Taylor, as I live and breathe," said a cold, cheerful voice. "I really couldn't believe it when they told me you'd showed up again. I thought you had more sense, Taylor."

I knew the voice, and took my time turning around. There aren't many people who can sneak up on me. Sure enough, standing behind me was Walker, large as life and twice as official. Every inch the City Gent, sharp and stylish and sophisticated. Handsome, if a little on the heavy side, with cold eyes and smile and an even colder heart. Had to be in his late forties by now, but you still wouldn't bet on the other guy. People like Walker don't slow down; they just get sneakier. His perfect city suit was expertly cut, and he tipped his bowler hat to Joanna with something very like charm. I glared at him.

"How did you know where to find me, Walker? I didn't know I was coming here till a few minutes ago."

"I know where everyone is, Taylor. You'd do well to remember that."

"John, who is this . . . person?" asked Joanna, and I could have blessed her for the sheer unimpressed indifference in her voice.

"Perhaps you should introduce me to your client," said Walker. "I would so hate for us to start off on the wrong foot."

"Your tie's crooked," said Joanna, and I could have kissed her.

"This is Walker," I said. "If he has a first name, no-one knows it. Probably not even his wife. Ex-Eton and ex-Guards, because his sort always is. Mentioned in dispatches for being underhanded, treacherous and more dangerous than a shark in a swimming pool. Walker represents the Authorities, here in the Nightside. Don't ask what Authorities, because he doesn't answer questions like that. All that matters is he could have you or me or anyone else dragged off without warning, with no guarantee we'd ever be seen again. Unless he had a use for us. He plays games with people's lives, all in the name of preserving his precious status quo."

"I preserve the balance," Walker said easily, flicking an invisible speck of dust from his impeccable sleeve. "Because someone has to."

"No-one knows who or what Walker reports to, or where his orders come from," I continued, "Government or Church or Army. But in an emergency he has been known to call for backup from any damned force he wants; and they come running every time. His word is law, and he enforces it with whatever measures it takes. Always immaculately turned out, charming in a ruthless kind of way, and never, ever, to be trusted. No-one ever sees him coming. You can never tell when he's going to come strolling out of the shadows with a smile and a quip, to pour oil on troubled waters, or occasionally vice versa.

"He has a gift for getting answers. There aren't many who can say no to him. They say he once made a corpse sit up on an autopsy table and talk with him."

"You flatter me," said Walker.

"You'll notice he's not denying it. Walker can call on powers and dominations, and make them answer to him. He has power, but no accountability. And damn all conscience, either. In a place where the Light and the Dark are more than just aphorisms, Walker remains determinedly grey. Like any good civil servant."

"It's all about duty and responsibility, Taylor," said Walker. "You wouldn't understand."

"Walker disapproves of people like me," I said, smiling coldly. "Rogue agents, individuals who insist on being in charge of their own destinies, and their own souls. He thinks we muddy the waters. It's not often you'll see him out in the open, like this. He much prefers to stay in the shadows, so people can't see him pulling strings. Anyone at all could be working for him, knowingly or unknowingly, doing his bidding, so Walker doesn't have to get his own hands dirty. And of course, if one of his unofficial agents should get killed in the process, well, there are always more where they came from. For Walker the end always justifies the means, because the end is keeping the Nightside and its occupants strictly separate from the everyday world that surrounds it."

Walker bowed his head slightly, as though anticipating applause. "I do so love it when you introduce me, Taylor. You do it so much better than I ever could."

"He's been known to fit up people," I said. The words were coming faster now, as my anger rose. "When he finds it necessary, to throw someone to the wolves. He is much feared, occasionally admired, and practically everyone in the Nightside has tried to kill him, at one time or another. At the end of the day, he goes home to his wife and his family, in the everyday world, and forgets all about the Nightside. We're just a job to him. Personally, I think he sees this whole damned place as nothing more than a hideously dangerous freak show, full of things that bite. He'd nuke the Nightside and wipe us all out, if he thought he could get away with it. Except he can't, because his mysterious masters won't let him. Because they, and those like them, need somewhere to come and play the games they can't play anywhere else, to wallow in the awful pleasures they can't even admit to in the everyday world.

"This is Walker, Joanna. Don't trust him."

"How very unkind," Walker murmured. He pulled up another chair and sat down at our table, exactly half-way between Joanna and me. He crossed his legs elegantly and laced his fingers together on the table before him. All around us conversations were starting up again, as it became clear Walker hadn't come for any of them. He leaned forward across the table, and despite myself I leaned forward a little too, to hear what he had to say. If Walker had taken an interest in me and my case, the situation had to be even more serious than I thought.

"People have been disappearing on Blaiston Street for some time now," Walker said briskly. "It took us a while to realise this, because they were the kind of people no-one misses. The homeless, the beggars, the drunks and drug-users. All the usual street trash. And even after the situation became clear, I saw no reason to become involved. Because, after all, no-one cared. Or at least, no-one who mattered. If anything, the area actually seemed to improve, for a while. By definition, anyone who ends up on Blaiston Street by choice has already opted out of the human race. But just recently . . . a number of rather important people have walked into Blaiston Street, and never come out again. So the word has come down from Above for me to investigate."

"Hold everything." I gave Walker my best hard look. "Just what would these *rather important people* have been doing in a cesspit like Blaiston Street?"

"Quite," said Walker. If my hard look was bothering him, he hid it very well. "None of them had any business being there. Blaiston Street has none of the usual attractions or temptations that might lead a normally sensible person to go slumming. It seems much more likely they were called, or possibly even summoned, there, by forces or individuals unknown. Except . . . if something that powerful had come into the Nightside, we should have detected its presence long before now. Unless it's hiding from us. Which, strictly speaking, is supposed to be impossible. So, a mystery. And you know how much I hate mysteries, Taylor. I was considering what to do for the best when I learned you'd reappeared in the Nightside; and then everything just fell into place. I understand you're tracking a runaway."

"This lady's daughter," I said. Walker inclined his head to Joanna again.

"And your gift leads you to believe she's in Blaiston Street?"

"Yes."

"And you have reason to believe she was called there?"

"Not necessarily against her will."

Walker made a vague dismissive gesture with one elegant hand. "Then you have twelve hours, Taylor, to discover the secrets of Blaiston Street and do whatever is necessary to re-establish the status quo. Should you fail, I will have no choice but to fall back on my original plan, and destroy the whole damned street, and everything in it, now and forever."

"You can't do that!" said Joanna. "Not while my Cathy's still in there!"

"Oh yes he can," I said. "He's done it before. Walker's always been a great admirer of the scorched earth option. And it wouldn't bother him in the least if he had to sacrifice a few innocents along the way. Walker doesn't believe anyone's innocent. Plus, by involving me he doesn't have to put one of his own people at risk."

"Exactly," said Walker. He rose gracefully to his feet, checking the time on an old-fashioned gold fob watch from his waistcoat pocket. "Twelve hours, Taylor, and not a minute more." He put the watch away and looked at me thoughtfully. "A final warning. Remember . . . that nothing is ever what it seems, in the Nightside. I'd hate to think you've been away so long that you've forgotten such a basic fact of life here."

He hesitated, and for a moment I thought he might be about to say something more, but then our waitress came trotting back with my freshly laundered trench coat, and the moment passed. Walker smiled tolerantly as the waitress displayed the spotless coat for my approval.

"Very nice, Taylor. Very retro. I must be off now, about my business. So much to do, and so many to be doing it to. Welcome back, Taylor. Don't screw up."

He was already turning away to leave when I stopped him with my voice. "Walker, you were my father's friend."

He looked back at me. "Yes, John, I was."

"Did you ever find out what my mother was?"

"No," he said. "I never did. But if I ever do find her, I'll make her tell me. Before I kill her."

He smiled briefly, touched his fingertips to the brim of his bowler hat, and left the café. No-one actually watched him go, but the general murmur of voices rose significantly once the door was safely shut behind him.

"Just what is it with you and him?" Joanna said finally. "Why did you let him talk to you like that?"

"Walker? Hell, I'd let him shit on my shoes if he wanted to."

"I haven't seen you back down to anyone since we got here," said Joanna. "What makes him so special?"

"Walker's different," I said. "Everyone gives Walker plenty of space. Not for who he is, but for what he represents."

"The Authorities?"

"Got it in one. Some questions are all the scarier for having no answer."

"But who watches the watchmen?" said Joanna. "Who keeps the Authorities honest?"

"We are drifting into decidedly murky philosophical waters," I said. "And we really don't have the time. Finish your nice Coke, and we'll go pay Blaiston Street a visit."

"About time!" said Joanna. And she gulped down the last of her icy Coke so fast it must have given her a headache.

NINE

A House on Blaiston Street

Blaiston Street butts onto the back end of nowhere. Shabby houses on a shabby street, where all the street-lights have been smashed, because the inhabitants feel more at home in the dark. Perhaps so they won't have to see how far they've fallen. I could practically feel the rats running for cover as I led Joanna down the street, but otherwise it was almost unnaturally still and quiet. Litter was piled everywhere in great festering heaps, and every inch of the dirty stone walls was covered in obscene graffiti. The whole place stank of decay—material, emotional and spiritual. All down the street, windows were missing, patched up with cardboard or paper or nothing at all. Filth everywhere, from animals marking their territory, or from people who just didn't care any more. The houses were two rows of ancient tenements, neglected and despised, that would probably have fallen down if they hadn't been propping each other up.

Maybe Walker was right. A good bomb here could do millions of pounds of civic improvements.

And yet . . . something was wrong here. More than usually wrong. The street was strangely empty, deserted, abandoned. There were no homeless huddled in doorways, or under sagging fire-escapes. No beggars or muggers, no desperate souls looking to buy or sell; not even a single pale face peering from a window. Blaiston Street usually seethed with life like maggots in an open wound. I could hear the sounds of traffic and people from adjoining streets, but the sound was muted, strangely far away, as though from another world.

"Where the hell is everybody?" said Joanna quietly.

"Good question," I said. "And I don't think we're going to like the answer, when we find it. I'd like to think everyone just ran away, but . . . I'm beginning to suspect they weren't that lucky. I don't think anyone here got out alive. Something bad happened here. And it's still happening."

Joanna looked around her, and shuddered. "What in sweet Jesus' name could have summoned Cathy to a place like this?"

"Let's find out," I said, and calling up my gift I opened my private eye again. My gift was getting weaker, and so was I, but I was so close now it was just strong enough to show me Cathy's ghost prancing down the street, lit up from within by her own blazing emotions. I'd never seen anyone look so happy. She came to one particular house, that looked no different from any of the others, and stopped before it, studying it with solemn, child-wide eyes. The door opened slowly before her, and she ran up the stone steps and disappeared into the darkness beyond the door, smiling widely all the time, as though she was going to the best party in all the world. The door closed behind her, and that was that. I'd come to the end of the trail. For whatever reason, she'd never left that house again. I took Joanna by the hand and replayed the ghost so she could see it too.

"We've found her!" said Joanna, her hand clamping down on mine so hard it hurt. "She's here!"

"She was here," I said, pulling my hand free. "Let me check the house out before we go any further, see what my gift can tell us about the house's past and present occupants."

We walked right up to the house, and stopped at the foot of the dirty stone steps that led up to the paint-peeling door. Old bricks and mortar, smeared windows, and no signs of life anywhere. The door looked flimsy enough. I didn't think it could keep me out if I decided I wanted in, but this was the Nightside, so you never knew . . . I raised my gift and concentrated on the house, and despite myself I made a sudden, startled sound. There was no house before me. No history, no emotions, no memories, not even a simple sense of presence. As far as my gift was concerned, I was standing before a vacant lot. There was no house here, and never had been.

I grabbed Joanna's hand again, so she could see what I wasn't seeing, and she jumped too.

"I don't understand. Where did the house go?"

"It didn't go anywhere," I said. "As far as I can tell, there's never been any kind of house here."

I let go her hand and dropped my gift, and there was the house again, right in front of me. Large as life and twice as ugly.

"Is it another ghost?" said Joanna. "Like the café?"

"No. I'd recognise that. This is solid. It has a physical presence. We saw Cathy go into it. Something here . . . is playing games with us. Disguising its true nature."

"Something inside the house?"

"Presumably. Which means the only way we're going to get any answers is to force our way in, and see for ourselves. A house . . . that isn't just a house. I wonder what it is?"

"I don't give a damn what it is," Joanna said hotly. "All that matters is finding my Cathy, and getting her the hell out of here."

I grabbed her by the arm to stop her from charging up the steps. Her face was flushed with emotion at coming so close to the end of the chase, and her arm trembled under my hand. She looked at me angrily as I stopped her, and I made myself speak calmly and soothingly.

"We can't help Cathy by plunging headlong into traps. I don't believe in charging blindly into strange situations."

"Just as well I'm here then, isn't it?" said Suzie Shooter.

I looked round sharply, and there she was in the street behind me; Shotgun Suzie, smiling just a little smugly, the stock of her holstered pump-action shotgun peering at me over her leather-clad shoulder. I gave her my best glare.

"First Walker, and now you. I can remember when people weren't able to sneak up on me all the time."

"Getting old, Taylor," said Suzie. "Getting soft. Found anything for me to shoot yet?"

"Maybe," I said. I gestured at the house before us. "Our runaway is in there. Only my gift says there's something decidedly unnatural about this place."

Suzie sniffed. "Doesn't look like much. Let's do it. I'll lead the way, if you're worried."

"Not this time, Suzie," I said. "I have a really bad feeling about this house."

"You're always having bad feelings."

"And I'm usually right."

"True."

I made my way slowly up the stone steps. There still wasn't anyone around, but I could feel the pressure of watching eyes. Suzie moved in beside me like I'd never been away, like she belonged there, her shotgun already in her hands. Joanna brought up the rear, looking a little upset at being pushed into the background by Suzie's presence. The sound of our feet on the stone steps seemed unusually loud and carrying, but it didn't matter. Whatever was waiting for us inside the house that wasn't just a house, it knew we were there. I stopped before the door. There was no bell. No knocker or letter-box, either. I rapped on the door with my fist, and the wood seemed to give slightly under each blow, as though it was rotten. The sound of my knocking was eerily soft, muffled. There was no response from within.

"Want me to blow the lock out?" said Suzie.

I tried the door-handle, and it turned easily in my grasp. The discoloured metal of the door-knob was unpleasantly warm and moist to the touch. I rubbed my hand roughly on the side of my coat, and pushed the door open with the tip of my shoe. It fell back easily. Inside, there was only an impenetrable darkness, and not a sound anywhere. Joanna pushed in beside me, staring eagerly into the dark. She opened her mouth as though to call out to Cathy, but I stopped her. She glared at me again. There was an urgency in her now. I could feel it. Suzie produced a flashlight from some hidden pocket, turned it on and handed it to me. I nodded my thanks, and played the bright beam back and forth across the hallway before me. Hardly anything showed outside the beam, but the hall seemed long and wide and empty. I moved slowly forward, and Joanna and Suzie came with me.

Once we were safely inside, the door closed behind us if its own volition, and none of us were a bit surprised.

TEN

In the Belly of the Beast

The house was dark and empty, utterly quiet and almost unnaturally still. It was like walking into a hole in the world. It felt like something was holding its breath, while it waited to see what we would do next. My back and stomach muscles tensed as I walked slowly down the wide hallway, anticipating an attack that somehow never came. There was danger all around me, but I couldn't put a name to it, couldn't even tell what direction it might come from. I hadn't felt this nervous in the future Timeslip. But some traps you just have to walk into to get to where you're going.

Shadows danced jerkily around me as I played the beam of my flashlight back and forth. For all its brightness, the beam didn't make much of an impression on the dark. I could make out the hall before me, two doors leading off to the right, and a stairway to my left that led up to the next floor. Ordinary, everyday sights made somehow sinister by the atmosphere they were generating. This was not a healthy place. Not for three small humans, wandering blindly in the dark. The air was thick and oppressive, hot and moist, like the artificial heat of a greenhouse, where great fleshy things are forced into life that could not normally survive. Suzie moved silently along beside me, glaring about her. She hefted her shotgun and sniffed heavily.

"Damp in here. Like the tropics. And the smell . . . I think it's decay . . ."

"It's an old place," I said. "No-one's looked after it in years."

"Not that kind of decay. Smells more like . . . rotting meat."

We exchanged a look, and then carried on down the hallway. Our slow footsteps echoed hollowly back from the bare plaster walls. No furniture, no fittings; no carpets or comforts of any kind. No decorations, no posters or paintings or even calendars on the walls. Nothing to show that anyone had ever lived here. That thought seemed significant, though I couldn't for the moment see how. We were, after all, in Blaiston Street. This wasn't a place where people came to live like people . . .

"Have you noticed the floor?" Suzie said quietly.

"What in particular?" I said.

"It's sticky."

"Oh, thanks a bunch," said Joanna. "I really didn't need to know that, thank you. The moment I get out of here I'm going to have to burn my shoes. This whole place is *diseased*."

She was right back at my side again, staring almost twitchily about her. But she seemed more . . . impatient, than anything else. She didn't like the house, but it was clear the setting wasn't disturbing her anywhere near as much as it was getting to Suzie and me. Which was . . . curious. I assumed being this close to finding Cathy at last had driven all other thoughts aside. We stopped in the middle of the hall and looked around us. Suzie lowered her shotgun a little, having no-one to point it at.

"Looks like the last occupants of this dump did a moonlight flit, and took everything with them that wasn't actually nailed down."

I just nodded. I didn't trust myself to say anything sane and sensible, for the moment. I was feeling increasingly jumpy. There was an over-whelming sense of being watched, by unseen, unfriendly eyes. I kept wanting to look back over my shoulder, convinced I'd find something awful crouching there, waiting to spring; but I didn't. There was no-one there. Suzie would have known. And you don't last long in the Nightside if you can't learn to control your own instincts.

A mirror on the wall beside me caught my attention. It took me a moment to figure out what was wrong with it. The mirror wasn't showing any reflection. It was just a piece of clear glass in a wooden frame. It wasn't a mirror at all.

There were two doors to my right, leading to rooms beyond. Ordinary, unremarkable doors. I moved slowly over to the nearest, and immediately Suzie was right there with me, shotgun at the ready. Joanna hung back a little. I listened carefully at the first door, but all I could hear was my own breathing. I turned the handle slowly. It was wet in my hand, dripping moisture, like it was sweating from the heat. I wiped my palm on the side of my coat, and then pushed the door open. *Come into my parlour, said the spider to the fly.*

The door swung easily open. The hinges didn't make a sound. The room beyond was completely dark. I stayed just inside the doorway and flashed my light around the room. The darkness seemed to suck up the light. Still no furnishings or fittings, no personal signs or touches. It looked more like a film set than anything someone might call home. I stepped back into the hall and moved down to the next door. The second room was just like the first.

"Whatever was going on here, I think we missed it," said Suzie. "Someone must have told them I was coming."

"No," I said. "That's not it. Something's still here. It's just hiding from us."

I walked over to the foot of the staircase. Bare wooden boards, simple banisters. No frills or fancies. No scuff marks or traces of wear, either. It could have been old or new or anything in between. Almost as though untouched by humans hands . . . I raised my voice in a carrying call.

"Hello! Anybody home?"

The close air flattened my voice, making it sound small and weak. And then from somewhere up on the next floor came the sound of a single door, slamming shut. Suzie and Joanna moved quickly over to join me at the foot of the stairs. And the door banged shut again, and again, and again. There was a horrid deliberateness to the sound, almost taunting, an open violence that was both a threat and an invitation. *Come up and see, if you dare.* I put my foot on the first step, and the banging door stopped immediately. Somehow, it knew. I looked at Suzie, and then at Joanna.

"Someone's home."

Joanna surged forward, and would have gone running blindly up the stairs, if I hadn't grabbed her by the arm and made her stop. She pulled fiercely away, fighting to be free, not even looking back at me, and I had to use all my strength to hang on to her. I said her name over and over, increasingly loudly, until finally she spun on me, breathing hard. Her face was hot and red and angry, almost furious.

"Let go of me, you bastard! Cathy's up there! I can feel it!"

"Joanna, we don't know *what's* up there . . ."

"I know! I have to go to her, she needs me! Let go of my arm, you . . ."

When she found she couldn't pull or twist her arm out of my grasp, Joanna went for my face with her other hand. Her fingers were like claws. Suzie interrupted the blow easily, catching Joanna's wrist in a grip so hard it had to hurt her. Joanna snarled, and fought against her. Suzie applied pressure, forcing the wrist back against itself, and Joanna gasped, and stopped struggling. She glared at Suzie, who looked coldly back at her.

"No-one gets to hit John but me, Mrs. Barrett. Now behave yourself; or you can listen to the bones in your wrist breaking, one by one."

"Easy, Suzie," I said. "She's new to the Nightside. She doesn't understand the kind of dangers we could be facing."

Except she should have known, by now.

"Then she'd better learn fast," said Suzie. "I won't have her putting us at risk. I'll kill her myself first."

"Dead clients don't pay their bills," I reminded her.

Suzie sniffed and let go of Joanna's wrist, though she pointedly stayed where she was, ready to intervene again, if necessary. I released Joanna's arm. She scowled at both of us, rubbing sulkily at her throbbing wrist. I tried really hard to sound calm and reasonable.

"You mustn't lose it now, Joanna. Not when we're this close. You've trusted me this far; trust me now to know what I'm doing. There could be anything at all up there, apart from Cathy, just waiting for us to walk into some cleverly set trap. We do this slowly and carefully, or we don't do it at all. Understood?"

Her mouth was a sulky pout, her eyes bright and almost viciously angry. "You don't understand what I'm feeling. You know nothing about a mother's love. She's up there. She needs me. I have to go to her!"

"Either you control yourself, or I'll have Suzie drag you back to the front door and kick your arse out onto the street," I said steadily. "For your own protection. I mean it, Joanna. The way you're acting now, you're not just a liability, you're a danger to us all. I know this place is . . . upsetting, but you can't let it get to you like this. This isn't like you, Joanna. You know it isn't."

"You don't know me at all, John," said Joanna, but her voice was markedly calmer. "I'm sorry. I'll behave. It's just . . . being this close is driving me crazy. Cathy's in trouble. I can feel it. I have to go to her. Let me stay, John. I'll be good, I promise."

That wasn't like Joanna either, but I nodded reluctantly, putting it all down to the influence the house was having on her. I was born in the Nightside, and this damned house was already playing games with my head. I made Joanna take several deep breaths, and it seemed to help her. I didn't like the effect the house was having on her. This frantic, almost out of control Joanna, wasn't at all the woman I'd come to know, and care for. She hadn't been this freaked out before, even in the Timeslip. It had to be the house.

"You shouldn't have brought her here, John," said Suzie. "She doesn't belong here."

Her voice wasn't especially harsh, or unforgiving. She was speaking the truth as she saw it, just as she always did.

Joanna glared at her, her voice rising angrily again. "You don't give a damn about what might have happened to my daughter! You're only here because I'm paying you to be here!"

"Damn right," said Suzie, entirely unmoved. "And you'd better be good for the money."

They went on snarling at each other for a while, in their own hot and cold way, but I wasn't really paying attention. The house, what there was of it, baffled me. I kept thinking I was missing something. Something had called, or even summoned, Cathy to this place, and all those missing *important people* Walker had mentioned, but now I was here, at the heart of the mystery, *there was nothing here*. Except for whatever was playing games up on the next floor. Nothing in the house, nothing at all . . . I started up the stairs, and Joanna and Suzie immediately stopped arguing and hurried after me, Suzie pushing forward to take her place at my side again, shotgun to the fore.

No more slamming doors. No reaction at all. When we got to the next floor, all we found were more bare walls and more doors leading off. All the doors were safely, securely, closed. Suzie looked slowly about her, checking for targets, the shotgun tracking along with her gaze. Joanna was all but trembling with eagerness, and I took a few seconds to impress on her that Suzie and I were going to take the point. I looked at the closed doors, and they looked smugly back at me. Suzie raised her voice suddenly.

"Is it me, or is it lighter up here?"

I frowned, as I realised I could make out much more on this floor, even outside of the flashlight's beam. "It's not you, Suzie. The gloom seems to be lifting; though I'm damned if I can see where the light's coming from . . ." I broke off, as I looked up at the ceiling and realised for the first time that there were no light bulbs, or even any sign of the original light fittings. Which was . . . unusual, even for Blaiston Street.

"I just had another thought," said Suzie. "And a rather unsettling one, at that. If this house isn't really here, what are we standing on, right now? Are we actually floating in mid air, over some vacant lot?"

"You're right," I said. "That is an unsettling thought. Just what I needed right now. Hang about while I check it out."

But when I went to raise my gift, nothing happened. Something from outside had wrapped itself around my head, unfelt but immovable, forcibly preventing me from opening my private eye, from seeing the world as it really was. I struggled against it, with what strength I had left, but there was nothing there that I could get a grip on. I swore briefly. What was going on here, that Something didn't want me to see, to understand? Suzie scowled about her, desperate for something solid she could attack.

"What do you want to do, John? Kick in all the doors and take it room by room? Shoot anything that moves and isn't the runaway?"

I gestured abruptly for her to be quiet, straining my ears for the sound I thought I'd caught. It was there, faint but definite. Not too far away, behind one of the closed doors; someone was giggling. Like a child with a secret. I padded quickly down the corridor, Joanna and Suzie right on my heels, stopping to listen at each door until I'd found the right one. I tried the handle, and it turned easily in my grasp, like an invitation. I pushed the door in an inch, and then stepped back. I gestured for Joanna to stick close to me, and then nodded to Suzie. She grinned briefly, kicked the door in, and we all surged forward into the room beyond.

It was bare and empty like the rest of the house, except for Cathy Barrett, found at last, lying flat on her back on a bare wooden floor on the other side of the room, covered from neck to toe by a long grubby raincoat, tucked under her chin like a blanket. She made no move to rise as her would-be rescuers charged in, just smiled happily at us as though she didn't have a care in the world.

"Hello," she said. "Come in. We've been expecting you."

I looked carefully about me, but there was no-one else in the room with her. I didn't discount the *we*, though. The continuing sense of an unseen watching presence was stronger than ever here. The light was brighter too, though there was still no obvious source for it. The more I studied the room, the more disturbing it felt. The room had no window, no contents, no details. Just walls and a floor and a ceiling. A sketch of a room. It was as though the house felt it didn't have to pretend any more, now that we'd come this far. I put away the flashlight and took a firm hold on Joanna's arm, to make sure she stayed with me. She didn't even seem to notice, all her attention fixed on her daughter, who hadn't even tried to raise up on one elbow to look at us more easily. I began to wonder if she could move.

Her gaunt face smiled equally at all of us, peering over the collar of the raincoat. I almost didn't recognise her. She'd lost a hell of a lot of weight since the photo Joanna had shown me, back in my office, in another world. The bones of her face pressed out against taut, grey skin, and her once golden hair hung down across her hollowed features in dark greasy strings. She looked half-starved, her great eyes sunk right back into the sockets. In fact, she looked like she hadn't eaten properly in months, not just the few weeks she was supposed to have been missing. I glanced at Joanna, wondering if I should have been quite so ready to believe everything she'd told me. But no; that wasn't it. My gift had shown me Cathy entering this house only a few days ago, and she'd looked nothing like this then.

Suzie glared about her, the pump-action shotgun steady in her hands. "This stinks, John. Something's very wrong here."

"I know," I said. "I can feel it. It's the house."

"It's her!" said Joanna. "My Cathy. She's here!"

"She's not the only one here," I said. "Suzie, keep an eye on Joanna. Don't let her do anything silly."

I moved slowly forwards and knelt beside Cathy. The wooden floor seemed to give slightly under my weight. Cathy smiled happily at me, as though there was nowhere else in the world she'd rather be. Up close, she smelled *bad*, as though she'd been sick for weeks.

"Hello, Cathy," I said. "Your mother asked me to come and find you."

She considered this for a moment, still smiling her awful smile. "Why?"

"She was worried about you."

"She never was before." Her voice was calm but empty, as though she was remembering something that had happened a long time ago. "She had her business and her money and her boyfriends . . . She never needed me. I just got in the way. I'm free now. I'm happy here. I've got everything I ever wanted."

I didn't look around the empty room. "Cathy, we've come to take you out of here. Take you home."

"I am home," said Cathy, smiling her interminable smile. "And you're not taking me anywhere. The house won't let you."

And I fell screaming to the floor as something huge and dark and ravenously hungry smashed its way into my mind, revealing itself at last.

It hit me from all sides at once, tearing through my defences like they weren't even there. It was the house, and it was alive. Once it had looked like something else, and might again, but for now it was a house. And it was feeding.

Inch by inch I forced it out of my mind, my shields re-forming one by one until my thoughts were my own again, the house was gone, and the only one in my head was me. The effort alone would probably have killed anyone else. I came to myself again lying curled up on the bare floor beside Cathy, shaking and shuddering. A vicious headache beat in my temples, and blood was dripping steadily from my nose. Suzie was kneeling beside me, one hand on my shoulder, shouting something, but I couldn't hear her. Joanna was watching from the doorway, her face completely blank. With my cheek pressed against the bare wood of the floor, I slowly realised how warm it was. Warm and sweaty and curiously smooth. Deep within the pale wood, I could feel a faint pulsing.

I struggled up onto my hands and knees, Suzie helping me as best she could. Blood dripped onto the floor from my nose. I watched almost emotionlessly as the pale wood soaked up the blood, until there was no trace of it left. I knew what was happening now. I knew just what kind of trap I'd walked into. I reached out and pulled Cathy's coat away from her, revealing the truth. Naked and horribly emaciated, Cathy's body was slowly melting into the wooden floor. Already I could no longer tell where her flesh ended, and the floor's began.

ELEVEN

All Masks Thrown Aside

"It's the house," I said. "It's alive. And it's hungry."

I could feel the house all around me now, pulsing with alien life, roaring triumphantly at the edges of my mind. Laughing at me, now it didn't have to hide any more. I looked up and there was Suzie, breathing harshly, her knuckles showing white as she clung to her gun, the only thing that had always made sense to her. Her eyes darted wildly round the room, as she searched desperately for something she could hit or shoot. Joanna was standing very still by the doorway, not looking at Cathy. Her pale face was completely without expression, and when her gaze briefly crossed mine, I might as well have been a stranger. I looked back at Cathy.

"Tell me," I said. "Tell me why, Cathy. Why did you come here, to this place, of your own free will?"

"The house called me," she said happily. "It opened up a door, and I stepped through, and found myself in a whole new world. So bright and vivid; so *alive*. Like a movie going from black and white to colour. The house . . . needed me. I'd never felt needed before. It felt so good. And so I came here, and gave myself to the house, and now . . . I don't have to care about anything any more. The house made me happy, for the first time in my life. It loves me. It'll love you too."

I wiped the blood from my nose on the back of my hand, leaving a long crimson smear. "It's eating you, Cathy. The house is swallowing you up."

"I know," she said blissfully. "Isn't it wonderful? It's going to make me a part of it. Make me part of something greater, something more important than I could ever have been on my own. And I'll never have to feel bad again, never feel lost or alone or unhappy. Never have to worry about anything, ever again."

"That's because you'll be dead! It's lying to you, Cathy. Telling you what you want to hear. When the house attacked my mind, I was able to see it clearly at last, see it for what it really is. It's hungry. That's all it ever is. And you're just food, like all the other victims it's absorbed."

Cathy smiled at me, dying by inches and not caring, because the house wouldn't let her care. Suzie moved in beside me and hauled me bodily to my feet. She held me upright by brute strength until my legs stabilised again, and stuck her face right into mine.

"Talk to me, John! What's happening here? What is this house, really?"

I took a deep breath. It didn't steady me nearly as much as I'd hoped, but at least the shakes were starting to wear off now. Like so many times before in the Nightside, I had found the truth at last, and it didn't please or comfort me one bit.

"The house is a predator," I said. "An alien thing, from some alien place, far outside our own space, where life has taken very different forms. It makes itself into what it needs to be, taking on the colour of its surroundings, hiding in plain sight, calling its prey to it with a voice that cannot be resisted. Its prey is the lost and the lonely, the unloved and the uncared for, the discarded flotsam and jetsam of the city that no-one ever misses when it washes up here, on Blaiston Street. The house calls, in a voice that no-one ever disbelieves, because it tells them just what they want to hear. It even sucked in a few supposedly important people, people perhaps a little too susceptible for their own good. Being important doesn't necessarily protect you from the secret despairs of the hidden heart."

"Stick to the point, John," said Suzie, shaking me by the shoulder. "The house lures people into it, and then?"

"And then it feeds on them," I said. "It sucks them dry, absorbing all they are into itself. It grows strong by feeding on their strength, keeping them happy while they last, so they won't try to escape. So they won't even want to."

"Jesus," said Suzie, looking down at Cathy's emaciated body. "From the look of the kid, the house has already taken most of her. Shame. We have to get out of here, John."

"What?" I said, not understanding, or perhaps not wanting to.

"There's nothing we can do," Suzie said flatly. "We got here too late. Even if we could maybe cut the kid free from the floor, odds are she'd bleed to death before we even got her to the street. She's already as good as dead. So we leave her, and get the hell out of here while we still can. Before the house turns on us."

I shook my head slowly. "I can't do that, Suzie. I can't just walk away and leave her here."

"Listen to me, John! I don't do lost causes. This case is *over*. All that's left to us is to give the kid a quick death, maybe cheat the house out of some of its victory. Then we get out of here, and come back with something heavy in the explosive line. You get Joanna moving. I'll take care of the kid."

"I didn't come all this way, just to abandon her! She's coming back with us!"

"No-one's leaving," said Cathy. "No-one's going anywhere."

Behind us, the door groaned loudly in its frame. Suzie and I looked round sharply, just in time to see the door slam shut and then vanish, its edges absorbed into the surrounding wall. The door's colours faded out, and within moments there was only an unmarked, unbroken expanse of wall, with no sign to show there'd ever been a door there. And all around us, the four walls of the enclosed room *rippled* suddenly, expanding and contracting in slow sluggish movements; becoming steadily more organic in appearance, soft and puffy and malleable. Thick purple traceries of veins spread across the walls, pulsing rhythmically. And a great inhuman eye opened in the ceiling above us, cold and alien, staring unblinkingly down at its new victims like some ancient and unsympathetic god. A sickly phosphorescent glow blazed from the walls, and I finally knew where the light had been coming from all along. There was a new smell on the air, thick and heavy, of blood and iron and caustic chemicals.

"No-one's going anywhere," said Cathy. "There's nowhere to go." There was another voice under hers now, harsh and deliberate and utterly inhuman.

Suzie stalked over to where the door had been, reversed her gun and slammed the butt of the shotgun against the wall. The awful pulsing surface gave a little under the blow, but it didn't break or even crack. Suzie hit it again and again, grunting with the effort she put into it, to no avail. She glared at the wall, breathing hard, and then kicked it in frustration. The leather toe of her boot clung stickily to the wall, and she had to use all her strength to pull it free. Part of the leather toe was missing, already absorbed. Drops of dark liquid fell from the ceiling, and more slid slowly down the walls and oozed up out of the floor. Suzie hissed suddenly, in surprise as much as pain, as a drop fell on her bare hand, and steam rose up from the scorched flesh.

"John, what the hell is this? What's going on?"

"Digestive juices," I said. "We're in a stomach. The house has decided we're too dangerous to absorb slowly, like Cathy. It doesn't want to savour us. We're going to be soup. Suzie, make us an exit. Blast a hole right through that wall."

Suzie grinned fiercely. "I thought you'd never ask. Stand back. This could splatter."

She trained her shotgun on the wall where the door had been, and let fly. The wall absorbed the blast, the point-blank impact producing only ripples spreading slowly outwards, like when you throw a stone into a pond. Suzie swore briefly and tried again, reloading and firing repeatedly till the close air stank of cordite, and the sound was overwhelming. But even as the roar of the gun died away, the ripples were already disappearing from the unmarked wall. Suzie looked back at me.

"We are in serious trouble, John. And don't look now, but your shoes are steaming."

"Of course," I said. "The house isn't fussy about what it eats."

Suzie looked at me steadily, waiting. Without an enemy she could hit or shoot, she was pretty much lost for another option; but she trusted me to find a way out of this mess. She'd always been too ready to trust me. That was one of the reasons why I'd left the Nightside in the first place. I got tired of letting my friends down. I thought hard. There had to be a way out of this. I hadn't come back after all these years, fought my way through all the madness, just to die in an oversized stomach. I hadn't come back to fail again. I looked at Cathy, and then I looked at Joanna, still standing very still by the living wall. She hadn't said a word or moved an inch since the house revealed itself. Her face was eerily calm, her eyes unfocused. She hadn't even flinched when Suzie opened fire right next to her. Shock, I supposed, then.

"Joanna!" I said loudly. "Come over here and talk to your daughter. See if you can focus her mind on you, separate her from the house. I think I've got an idea on how to break her and us free, but I don't know what effect it might have on her . . . Joanna! Listen to me!"

She turned her head slowly to look at me, and there was a slow horror forming in her eyes that made me want to look away.

"Why are you talking to her about me?" said Cathy.

"Because I need your mother's help in this," I said.

"But that's not my mother," said Cathy.

The words seemed to resonate endlessly in the quiet room, their sudden awful significance driving all other thoughts out of my head. It never even occurred to me to doubt Cathy's word. I could hear the truth in her voice, even if I didn't want to. So many little things that hadn't made sense suddenly came together, in one terrible moment of insight. Joanna looked at me, and there was nothing in her eyes but a calm, resigned sadness. All the vitality had gone out of her. As though she didn't have to pretend any more.

"I'm sorry, John," she said slowly. "But I think it's all over now. My purpose is over, now you're here. I think I did care for you . . . but I don't think I'm who I thought I was . . ." Her voice changed, and under it I heard the harsh alien voice that had briefly spoken through Cathy. "I'm just a Judas Goat, the perfect bait, designed and programmed specifically to lure you back into the Nightside, so that you could be . . . dealt with."

"Why?" I said, and my voice was little more than a whisper.

"The house was provided with all the necessary details—the exact kind of client, the exact kind of case, the exact kind of woman who would most appeal to you. Someone who would slip past all your defences, make you disregard all your instincts, and lead you unresisting to your doom. There never was a Joanna Barrett—only a role to play, a function to perform. But they made me too well, John; and for a time I actually forgot what I was. I thought I was a real woman, with real feelings. There's enough left of me to be sorry about what's going to happen to you . . . but not enough for me to stop it."

"Was none of what we had real?" I said.

"Only you were real, John. Only you."

"And all . . . this?" I said. "Was all this set up just for me? Was the house invited into the Nightside, allowed to hunt and feed and kill, just to get *me*? Why? I'd left the Nightside! I was no threat to anyone any more! Why bring me back now?"

"Ask your mother," said the thing with Joanna's voice. "It seems she's coming back. And you . . . are a loose thread that could unravel everything."

"Who did this?" I said. "Who's behind this?"

"Can't you guess?" said Joanna. And her face slowly melted away, leaving behind only the perfect blank mask of the Harrowing.

I think I cried out then; the sound of some small animal as the steel trap finally closes on it. Joanna leaned back into the living wall, and sank into it, the soft pulsing surface closing over her as the house reabsorbed the thing it had created, or birthed. In a moment she was gone, leaving only slow ripples behind, and soon they were gone too. I should have known. I should have remembered. You can't trust anyone, or anything, in the Nightside, to be what it appears to be. Walker had tried to warn me, but I didn't listen. I'd forgotten that here, love is just another weapon they can use to hurt you, and that the past never goes away. I felt the tears running down my cheek long before I knew I was crying.

"Damn," said Suzie, glowering at the wall Joanna had disappeared into. "Guess I'm not going to get paid for this one after all."

She looked at me, and sighed when I didn't react. The digestive juices were falling from the ceiling in a steady rain now, stinging and burning my bare face and hands, and I didn't care at all. Someone, or something, had just punched my heart out, and I didn't care about anything. Suzie came over and put a hand on my shoulder, staring right into my face. She wasn't very good with emotions, but she did her best.

"John, you have to listen to me. You can mourn her later. Whatever she was, or might have been. You can't fall apart now. We have to get out of here."

"Why?" I said. "Everyone wants me dead; and maybe I do too."

She slapped me across the face, more professionally than angrily. "What about me, John?"

"What about you?"

"All right, maybe I deserved that. I never should have let you go running off to hide in London. And I wasn't always the best of friends to you; I don't seem to have the knack. But what about the kid, John? Cathy? Remember her? The one you came back into the Nightside to save? Are you going to let her down now? Are you going to let her die, just because you're feeling sorry for yourself?"

I turned my head slowly, and looked at Cathy. What was left of her. "No," I said finally. "None of this is her fault. And I never let a client down. Take my hand, Suzie."

"What? This is no time to be getting sentimental, John."

I looked back at her. "You have to trust me on this, Suzie. Trust me to know what I'm doing. We can't fight our way out, so that just leaves me, and my gift."

Suzie looked at me for a long moment, reassuring herself that I was back in control again, and then nodded briskly. She slid her shotgun into the holster behind her shoulder and took my hand in hers. I could feel the calluses on her palm, but her grip was firm and steady. She had faith in me. Which made one of us. I sighed, tiredly, getting ready to fight the good fight one more time, because that was all I had left.

"We need to find the heart of the house," I said. "Kill the heart, and kill the house. But the heart won't be anywhere here. The house will have hidden it somewhere else, for protection. Somewhere . . . no-one would be able to reach it, normally. But then, I'm not normal. I can find it. I can find anything."

Except what matters most. I reached inside myself and summoned up my gift, opening my mind again. And the house pounced.

• • •

For a long time I was nowhere, and it felt good. Good not to have to worry about bills that needed paying, cases that couldn't be solved, clients who couldn't be helped. Good not to have to worry about all the mysteries of my life, and the endless pain they brought to me and those I cared for. When I started out I had a dream, a dream of helping people who had nowhere else to turn; but dreams don't last. They can't compete with reality. The reality of struggling to find money for food and rent, and the way your feet hurt from pounding the streets looking for people who don't want to be found.

The harsh, unyielding reality of having to compromise your ideals bit by bit, day by day, just to achieve a few little victories in the face of the world's malice, or indifference. Until sometimes you wonder if there's nothing left of you but the shell of the man you intended to be, just going through the motions because you've nothing better to do.

But somehow the dream doesn't quite die. Because in the Nightside, sometimes dreams are all that can keep you going. Give them up, and you're dead.

Growing up in the Nightside, I saw a lot of dead men walking about. They could walk and talk and go through the motions, drifting from bar to bar and from drink to drink, but there was nothing left behind their eyes. Nothing that mattered. My father was a dead man for years, long before his heart finally, mercifully, gave out, and they nailed the coffin lid down. I couldn't help him. I was only a kid.

My gift didn't kick in until much later. A gift I could use, to make a difference. For other people, if not myself.

In the safe nowhere nothing that surrounded and comforted me, gentle waves of love and affection lapped against my mind, wanting me to forget all that. To forget everything but an eternal now of love and happiness, an end to all wanting and needing, and a rest that would never end. A quiet murmuring voice promised me I could have everything I ever wanted; all I had to do was lie back and accept, and give up the fight. But I didn't believe the voice. Because the only thing I really wanted had already been taken from me, when the house took Joanna back into itself. The voice spoke more urgently, and I sneered at it. Because underneath the voice I could still hear the endless, insatiable hunger.

My dreams. My reality. I clung to them like a drowning man, and would not give them up. They made me what I am. Not the father who ignored me, or the mother who abandoned me. Not the mysterious inheritance I never wanted, and not even the faceless hordes who'd hounded me all my life. So many influences trying to shape me, and I disowned them all. I chose to help people, because there'd been no-one there to help me when I needed it. I knew even then that I couldn't trust the Authorities to save me. My father had been one of them, and they still hadn't been able to protect him, or comfort him. I shaped my own life, determined my own destiny; and to hell with everyone and everything else.

My anger was rising now, hot and fierce and strong, and it pushed back the false promises of love and happiness, perhaps because deep down I'd never believed in such things. Not for me, anyway. The empty nothingness was fragmenting, falling apart. I could sense other people around me. Suzie Shooter, a ghost hand in mine, quietly confident in me. Cathy Barrett, understanding for the first time just how much she'd been lied to, manipulated and abused, almost as angry as I was. And somewhere close at hand . . . a faint presence, a quiet voice, like the last echoes of someone who had briefly believed themselves to be a woman called Joanna. And I swear I felt another ghostly hand in mine.

I reached out and embraced them, binding them to me with my gift; and together we were stronger than any damned house.

I don't just find things with my gift. It can do other things too. Like identify an enemy's weak spot and attack it. I lashed out with my gift, and the house screamed, in shock and rage, pain and horror. I think it had been a very long time since anyone had been able to hurt it.

The nothing was replaced by something. An in-between place. I was standing on a bare plain that stretched out to infinity in all directions. It was a grey place, soft and hazy and indistinct. Not a real place, but real enough. A place to make a stand. Suzie and Cathy were there with me. Suzie was wearing silver armour, studded with vicious spikes. Cathy looked like she had in her old photo, only mad as hell now. I didn't look down to see how I appeared. It didn't matter. Not too far away there was another presence, too faint to be clearly seen, but I knew who it was. Who it had to be. We were all shining brightly now, luminous beings in a grey world. Together we formed a wide circle around a column of swirling darkness, shot with vivid blood-red traces, that towered endlessly up into the featureless sky. From it came the voice of the house, beating against us like hammer-blows, harsh and inhuman.

"Mine! Mine! Mine!"

But the gift was strong in me, and I just laughed at the voice. All it really had on its side was stealth and lies, and neither could serve the house here. I stepped forward, and Suzie and Cathy moved with me. The dark column actually shrank back from our light, shrinking and contracting away from us. We closed in, and the column became narrower. And all around us, on that wide and endless plain; hundreds and hundreds of insubstantial figures, standing silently, watching and hoping. All the house's victims. It hadn't just eaten their bodies; the damned thing had consumed their souls too, holding them within itself to power its unnatural existence. What was left of a woman called Joanna came forward, holding herself together despite everything the house could do to tear her apart and assimilate her, and again I felt her hand in mine. Through her I reached out to the other captive shades, silently offering them a chance for revenge, and the only freedom they could ever know now . . . and they reached out to me.

Power surged through me, igniting my gift, and I blazed so very brightly as I advanced on the dark column before me. Suzie and Cathy and all the other victims advanced with me, and the house screamed and screamed. The column shrank and compacted, growing thinner and thinner, until finally I was able to join my shining hands with the trusting Suzie, the furious and betrayed Cathy, and the ghost of a woman I could have loved. We were all shining like suns now. I gathered together all our rage and hate and need, channeling all the many victims through my gift, and struck out at the dark heart of the thing that pretended to be a house. It howled once, with impotent horror, and then the dark swirling column was suddenly gone, and the voice of the house was stilled forever.

The other side of my gift. To find another's death.

I've never carried a gun. I don't need one.

I looked around the endless plain, that grey and empty place, and all the hundreds of victims were gone, their souls released at last to find the only peace left to them. And gone with them, a designed and programmed piece of bait that had briefly learned what it was to be human, and would not give it up.

You have to believe in dreams, because sometimes they believe in you.

● ● ●

I fell back into my body and glared wildly about me. All my strength was back, restored by the departed souls of the house's victims. I was still trapped in an enclosed room, with no way out, but the house was dead now. Already the air was thick with the sweet cloying stench of decay. The eye in the ceiling was closed and gone, and the phosphorescent glow from the walls was slowly fading. Ragged cracks spread slowly across the walls, tearing them apart like rotting flesh. And there, on the floor, what was left of Cathy Barrett. Gaunt, desiccated and half-dead, but finally separate from the consuming floor, ejected by the house's dying spasms, as I'd hoped. She was struggling to sit up, her face mad as hell. I helped her sit up, and wrapped the long coat around her. She held it closed with hands that were little more than bone and skin, and managed a brief, but real, smile for me.

"It lied to me," she said. "It told me everything I secretly wanted to hear, so I believed it. And when it finally had me, it made me happy; but inside I was screaming all the time. You saved me."

"It's what I do," I said. "It's my job."

She studied me for a while. "If my mother had known I was here, and in trouble, I like to think she would have sent someone like you. Someone . . . reliable."

"Look, this is all touching as hell," Suzie said briskly, "but I'd really like to get out of here."

"Good point," I said. "I've only just had this trench coat cleaned."

Together, we got Cathy onto her feet and helped support her. It wasn't difficult. She couldn't have weighed more than seventy pounds.

"Where were we?" she said abruptly. "The grey place. What was that?"

"The house was only vulnerable through its heart," I said, urging her towards the place in the wall where the door had been. "So, the house hid its heart in another place. Another dimension of reality, if you like. It's an old magical trick. But I can find anything."

"Are you sure it's dead?" said Suzie. "All the way, not coming back in the last reel, dead? I mean, it's still here, and we're still trapped inside it."

"It's dead," I said. "And from the smell and general state of things, I'd say its body is already starting to decay. It never really belonged in our world. Only its augmented will allowed it to survive here. Suzie, make us a door."

She looked at me. "You might remember, my gun didn't work too well, last time."

"I think you'll find it will now."

Suzie grinned like a child who's just been presented with an unexpected present, and drew her shotgun while I supported Cathy. Suzie opened fire on the wall at point-blank range again, and this time the blast punched a hole right through the wall, blowing it apart like rotten meat. Suzie loaded and fired again and again, laughing aloud as she widened the hole, and finally stepped forward to tear at the edges of the hole with her bare hands, widening it still further. She looked at the filth dripping from her hands, and grimaced.

"Damn stuff is falling apart."

"The whole house will fall apart soon," I said. "And lose what's left of its precarious hold on our reality. I really don't think we should be here when that happens; do you? Give me a hand here, Suzie."

We took a firm hold on Cathy's frail body and forced our way through the ragged gap in the wall, half-falling out onto the trembling corridor beyond. We'd barely got our feet under us before the edges of the hole in the wall behind us ran together like melting wax. Strange lights glowed everywhere, like the dim unhealthy glows of corpsefires, and the sickly-sweet stench of corruption was fast becoming overwhelming. I hurried us along the corridor towards the stairs, and the walls we passed were already developing black, diseased patches. The ceiling was bowing down towards our heads, as though it could no longer support itself. The whole floor was shuddering now, and the jagged cracks in the walls were lengthening in sudden spurts. By the time we got to the top of the stairs, the floor was sagging dangerously under our feet.

"Let's move like we have a purpose, people," I said. "I don't think this house is long for this world. And I really don't think we'd like being trapped in the kind of world that could produce a creature such as this."

"Right," said Suzie. "I'd have to kill everything in it, just on general principles. And I didn't bring enough ammunition with me."

We hurried down the swaying stairs, Cathy helping as best she could, which wasn't much. The house had eaten most of her muscles. She was still game as hell, though. The wall beside the stairs was melting slowly, like wax running down a candle. The steps clung to our feet like sticky toffee, until we had to drag them free by brute force. I grabbed at the banister for support, and a whole chunk of it came away in my hand, rotting and purulent. I pulled a face, and threw the stuff away.

We hit the wide hallway running, mostly carrying Cathy now, while the swaying walls bulged forwards on all sides, and the ceiling fell on us in thick muddy drops. Where the front door had been there was only a slumping, rotting hole, dark and purple, its edges dripping like a diseased wound. It was slowly irising shut, collapsing in on itself. Already it was far too small for any of us to get through.

"Oh God," said Cathy. "We're never going to get out of here. It's never going to let us go."

"It's dead," said Suzie. "It doesn't have a say in the matter. And we are leaving, whatever it takes. Right, Taylor?"

"Right," I said.

Beyond the collapsing hole that had once pretended to be a door, I could see a glimpse of the outside world, clear and calm and relatively sane. I glared at the closing hole, bludgeoning it with my gift, and it winced open, reluctantly widening again. Suzie and I took firm hold of Cathy and charged the hole, hitting it at a dead run. The decaying tissues grabbed at us, but we crashed through and out in a moment. We burst onto Blaiston Street, back into the world of men, and the newly falling rain washed us clean.

We staggered to a halt in the middle of the street, whooping like crazy in celebration, and lowered Cathy to the ground. She ran her hands over the solid street, that might have been filthy dirty but never pretended to be anything other than what it was, and started to cry. I looked back at the dead house. It was slowly sagging and falling in on itself, the windows drooping shut like so many tired eyes. What was left of the hole we'd crashed through looked like nothing more than a bruised, pouting mouth.

"Rot in hell," I said.

I hit the dead thing with my gift one last time, pushing it over the edge, and what was left of the creature that had pretended to be a house dropped out of the Nightside and was gone, back to whatever awful place it had come from, leaving behind only a few decaying chunks and a stench of corruption already slowly dissipating in the rain. By the time Walker arrived with his people, there wasn't even anything left to bury.

EPILOGUE

The rain had mostly died away. I was shaking just a little, probably not from the cold. At least the night sky was still packed with stars and a huge white moon, and I tried to take some comfort from that. I sat on the pavement, hunched inside my filthy trench coat, watching Walker's people on the other side of the road as they swarmed all over the vacant lot where the house had been. They didn't seem to be having much luck, but every now and again they'd get all excited over some mess of decaying tissue, and make a big deal about sealing it into a snap-lock plastic bag. For evidence, or later analysis, perhaps. Or maybe Walker just fancied his chances of growing himself a new house. Walker was always on the look-out for some new dirty trick he could spring on whoever happened to be his enemy that week. He was currently ordering his people about from a very safe distance, careful as always not to get his own hands dirty.

He turned up with a small army of his people not long after I'd brought Suzie and Cathy out of the dead house. He and they had been standing by, observing, just in case I screwed up after all. Apparently Walker had heard the house scream as it died. I had no trouble believing that. I'd always thought Walker would make a really good vulture.

Cathy sat beside me, still wrapped in the long grubby coat she refused to give up, leaning companionably against me. Walker had conjured up a large mug of beef tea for her from somewhere, and she sipped at it now and again, when she remembered. Her body had been so reduced by the house it had even forgotten how to be hungry. Suzie stood guard over us with her shotgun in her hands, giving Walker the hard look if he even looked like drifting too close to us. Even Walker knew better than to cross Suzie Shooter unnecessarily.

The memory of Joanna still haunted me, though her ghost had disappeared along with the house. I couldn't believe she'd fooled me for so long . . . but she'd seemed so real. I had to wonder whether I'd believed in her for the same reasons that Cathy had believed the house's promises, because we were told just what we wanted to hear. That I'd loved Joanna because she'd been created specifically by my enemies to be my perfect love. Hard, but vulnerable. Strong, but desperate. A lot like me, in fact. Someone had done their homework very well, the bastards. But I still think that in the end Joanna believed in herself because I believed in her, that she became, if only briefly, a real person through an effort of will. Her own will. Dreams can come true, in the Nightside. Everyone knows that.

But they still vanish when you wake up.

Suzie looked down at me, frowning, correctly divining my thoughts. "You always were too soft for your own good, Taylor. You'll get over her. Hey, you still got me."

"Lucky me," I said. She meant well, in her own way.

"And we kicked that house's arse, didn't we?"

"Yes," I said. "We did that."

Suzie looked across at the vacant lot, unimpressed by Walker's people and their efforts. "How many people did that thing eat, do you think, before we shut it down?"

I shrugged. "How many lost souls and losers are there, in the Nightside? And how many of them would have to go missing, before anyone noticed? Or cared? Walker only got involved after a few movers and shakers accidentally got sucked in."

Walker picked up on his name, and strolled casually over to join us, keeping a wary eye on Suzie. She turned her gun on him, smiling unpleasantly, but I gestured for her to let him approach. There were things I needed to know, now I was feeling a little stronger. He tipped his bowler hat to us politely.

"You knew," I said.

"I suspected," said Walker.

"If you'd been sure," I said slowly, "would you still have let me go in there, not knowing?"

"Probably. You're not one of my people, Taylor. I don't owe you anything."

"Not even the truth?"

"Oh, especially not that."

Suzie frowned. "Are you two talking about the house, or Joanna?"

"It doesn't matter," I said. "Walker has always been very jealous of the secrets he guards. Tell me this, Walker. Is my mother really coming back?"

"I don't know," he said, holding my gaze calmly. His manner was open and sincere, but then, it always was. "There are rumours . . . but there are always rumours, aren't there? Perhaps . . . you should stick around, just in case." He looked across at the vacant lot, so he wouldn't have to look at me. "I could always put a little work your way, now and again. Unofficially, of course. Since it seems you haven't lost your touch, after all."

"You've got some nerve," said Suzie.

He smiled at her, every inch the polite and demure civil servant. "Comes with the job, my dear."

"I am not your dear, Walker."

"And don't think I'm not grateful."

I intervened, before things started getting out of hand. "Walker, can you look after Cathy for me? See that she gets back to the real world, and her mother? Her real mother?"

"Of course," said Walker.

"You can forget that shit," Cathy said sharply. "I'm not going back. I'm not ever going back. I'm staying here, in the Nightside."

I gave her my best harsh glare. "Are you crazy? After everything you've been through?"

She smiled at me over her mug of beef tea, and there wasn't a trace of humour in that smile. "There's more than one kind of nightmare. Trust me; bad as this place can be, it's still nothing compared to what I ran away from. I thought I'd stay with you, John. Could you use a secretary? Every private eye has to have a smart-mouthed secretary who knows a thing or two. I think it's in the rule book."

Suzie started to laugh, and then turned it into an unconvincing coughing fit when I glared at her. Walker became very interested in the vacant lot again. I glowered at Cathy.

"I just saved your life; I haven't adopted you!"

"We'll sort something out," Cathy said confidently. She looked across the road too. "What was it, do you think, really?"

"Just another predator," I said. "A little less obvious than most. Just . . . something from the Nightside."

AGENTS OF LIGHT AND DARKNESS

ONE

Everyone Believes in Something

There is only the one church in the Nightside. It's called St. Jude's. I only ever go there on business. It's nowhere near the Street of the Gods, with its many and varied places of worship. It's tucked away in a quiet corner, shadowed and obscured, no part of the Nightside's usual bright and gaudy neon noir. It doesn't advertise, and it doesn't care if you habitually pass by on the other side. It's just there, for when you need it. Dedicated to the patron saint of lost causes, St. Jude's is an old, old place; a cold stone structure possibly older even than Christianity itself. The bare stone walls are grey and featureless, unmarked by time or design, with only a series of narrow slits for windows. One great slab of stone, covered with a cloth of white samite, serves as an altar, facing two rows of blocky wooden pews. A single silver cross hangs on the wall beyond the altar; and that's it. St. Jude's isn't a place for comfort, for frills and fancies and the trappings of religion. There is no priest or attendant, and there are no services. St. Jude's is, quite simply, your last chance in the Nightside for salvation, sanctuary, or one final desperate word with your God. Come to this church looking for a spiritual Band-Aid, and you could end up with a hell of a lot more than you bargained for.

Prayers are heard in St. Jude's; and sometimes answered.

I use the church occasionally as a meeting place. Neutral ground is so hard to come by in the Nightside. Only occasionally, though. All are welcome to enter St. Jude's, but not everyone comes out again. The church protects and preserves itself, and no-one wants to know how. But this time, I had a specific reason for being here. I was counting on the nature of the place to protect me from the terrible thing that was coming. From the awful creature I had very reluctantly agreed to meet.

I sat stiffly on the hard wooden seat of the front pew, huddled inside my white trench coat against the bitter chill that always permeated the place. I glared about me and tried not to fidget. Nothing to look at and nothing to do, and I wasn't about to waste my time in prayer. Ever since my enemies first tried to kill me as a child, I've learned the hard way that I can't depend on anyone but myself. I stirred restlessly, resisting the urge to get up and pace back and forth. Somewhere out there in the night, a force of destruction was heading straight for me, and all I could do was sit tight and wait for it to come. I let one hand drift down to the shoe box on the seat beside me, just to reassure myself it hadn't gone anywhere since the last time I checked. What was in the box might protect me from what was coming, or it might not. Life's like that; particularly in the Nightside. And especially when you're the famous—or infamous—John Taylor, who has been known to boast he can find anything. Even when it gets him into situations like this.

The dozen candles I'd brought and lit and placed around the church didn't do much to dispel the general gloom of the place. The air was still and cold and dank, and there were far too many shadows. Sitting there, in the quiet, listening to the dust fall, I could feel the age of the place, feel all the endless centuries pressing down on me. St. Jude's was supposed to be one of the oldest surviving buildings in the Nightside. Older than the Street of the Gods, or the Time Tower, older even than Strangefellows, the longest-running bar in the world. So old, in fact, and so long established as a place of worship that there are those who hint it might not even have been a church, originally. Just a place where you could talk to your God, and sometimes get an answer. Whether you liked the answer you got was, of course, your problem.

It's only a short step from a burning bush to a burning heretic, after all. I try not to bother God, and hope He'll do me the same courtesy.

I don't know why there aren't any other churches in the Nightside. It's not that the people who come here aren't religious; it's more that the Nightside is where you go to do the things you know your God wouldn't approve of. Souls aren't lost here; they're sold or bartered or just plain thrown away in utter abandon. There are presences and avatars, and even Powers and Dominations, to be found on the Street of the Gods; and you can bargain with them for all the things you know your God wouldn't want you to have.

There are those who've tried to destroy St. Jude's, down the centuries. They aren't around any more, and St. Jude's still is. Though that could change this night, if I was wrong about what I had in the shoe box.

It was three o'clock in the morning, but then it always is in the Night-side. The night that never ends, and the hour that stretches. Three o'clock in the morning, the hour of the wolf, when a man's defences are at their weakest. The time when most babies are born and most people die. That lowest of points, when a man can lie awake in his bed and wonder how his life could have turned out so very differently from what he'd intended. And, of course, the very best time to make deals with the devil.

All the hairs on the back of my neck stood up suddenly, and my heart missed a beat, as though a cold hand had closed fleetingly around it. I lurched to my feet, an almost violent shudder running through me. She was close now. I could feel her presence, feel her gaze and cold intent turned upon me as she drew nearer. I grabbed up my shoe box and clutched it to my chest like a life preserver. I moved reluctantly out into the aisle, and turned to stand facing the only door. A single great slab of solid oak, five feet tall and five inches thick, locked and bolted. It wouldn't stop her. Nothing could. She was Jessica Sorrow the Unbeliever, and nothing in the world could stand against her. She was close now, very close. The monster, the abomination, the Unbeliever. There was a stillness to the air, like the tension that precedes the coming storm. The kind of storm that rips off roofs and drops dead birds out of the sky. Jessica Sorrow was coming to St. Jude's, because she'd been told I was there, and I had what she was looking for. And if they and I were wrong about that, she would make us all pay.

I don't carry a gun, or any other kind of weapon. I've never felt the need. And weapons wouldn't do any good against Jessica Sorrow anyway. Nothing could touch her any more. Something happened to her, long ago, and she gave up her humanity to become the Unbeliever. Now she doesn't believe in anything. And because she doesn't believe with such utter cer-tainty, all the world and everything in it are nothing to her. None of it can affect her in the least. She can go anywhere, and do anything, and she does. She can do terrible, distressing things, and she does, and nothing touches her. She has no conscience and no morality, no pity and no restraint. The material world is like paper to her, and she rips it apart as she walks through it. Luckily for the world, she doesn't leave the Nightside much. And luckily for the rest of us here, there are long periods when she just sleeps or drops out of sight. But when she's up and walking, everyone gets the hell out of her way. Because when she concentrates her unbelief on anything or anyone, they disappear. Gone forever. Even the Street of the Gods closes up shop and goes home early when Jessica Sorrow is abroad in the night.

Her most recent rampage had been one of her worst, as she stormed through all the most sensitive parts of the Nightside, leaving a trail of chaos and destruction behind her as she searched obsessively for . . . something. No one seemed too sure of exactly what that might be, and absolutely no one had any intention of getting close enough to her to ask. It had to be something special, something really powerful . . . but this was Jessica Sorrow, who was famous for not believing anything was special or powerful. What use could the Unbeliever have for material possessions any more? There was no shortage of objects of power in the Nightside, anything from wishing rings to description theory bombs, and every damn one of them was up for sale. But Jessica Sorrow would have none of them, and people and places vanished under her angry glare as she continued her rampage. The word was, she was looking for something so real she would *have* to believe in it . . . perhaps something real enough and powerful enough finally to kill her, and put her out of everyone's misery.

So Walker came to me, and told me to find it. Walker represents the Authorities. No-one really runs the Nightside, though many have tried, but the Authorities are the ones who step in and bang heads together whenever any of the movers and shakers look like they're getting out of hand. Walker is a calm and quiet sort, in a neat city suit, and he never raises his voice because he doesn't have to. He doesn't approve of lone operatives like me, but he throws me the odd job occasionally, because no-one else can do the things I can. And because as far as he's concerned, I am entirely expendable.

Which is why I make him pay through the nose for those jobs.

I can find anything. It's a gift. From my dear departed mother, who turned out not to be human. She's really not dead; that's just wishful thinking on my part.

Anyway, I found what Jessica Sorrow was looking for, and now it lay in the shoe box I was crushing to my chest. She knew it was here, and she was coming to get it. My job was to present it to her in exactly the right way, so that it would defuse her anger and send her back to wherever she went when she wasn't scaring the crap out of the rest of us. Assuming, of course, that I had found the right thing. And that she didn't just storm right in and unbelieve me out of existence.

She was outside the church now. The solid flagstones under my feet vibrated strongly, echoing to the tread of her approaching feet, crashing down heavily on the world she refused to believe in. All the candle flames were dancing wildly, and the shadows leapt around me, as though they were frightened too. My mouth was very dry, and my hands were crushing the shoe box out of shape. I made myself put it down on the pew, then straightened up and thrust my hands deep into my coat pockets. Looking casual was out of the question, but I couldn't afford to seem weak or indecisive in the presence of Jessica Sorrow the Unbeliever. I had hoped that St. Jude's accumulated centuries of faith and sanctity would offer me some protection against the force of Jessica's unbelief, but I wasn't so sure about that any more. She was coming, like a storm, like a tidal wave, like some implacable force of nature that would sweep me effortlessly aside in a moment. She was coming, like cancer or depression, and all the other things that cannot be denied or negotiated with. She was the Unbeliever, and compared to that St. Jude's was nothing and I was nothing . . . I took a deep breath, and held my head up. To hell with that. I was John Taylor, dammit, and I'd talked my way out of worse scrapes than this. I'd *make* her believe in me.

The heavy oaken door was reinforced with heavy bands of black iron. It must have weighed five hundred pounds, easy. It didn't even slow Jessica down. Her thunderous feet marched right up to the door, then her fingers plunged through the thick wood and tore it like cloth. The whole door came apart in her hands, and she walked through it like a hanging curtain. She came striding down the aisle towards me, naked and emaciated and corpse pale, the heavy flagstones exploding under the tread of her bare feet. Her eyes were wide and staring, as focussed as a feral cat's, and as impersonal. Her thin lips were stretched wide in something that was as much a snarl as a smile. She had no hair, her face was as drawn and gaunt as the rest of her, and her eyes were yellow as urine. But there was a force to her, a terrible energy that drove her on even as it ate her up. I held my ground, giving her back glare for glare, until finally she crashed to a halt right in front of me. She smelled . . . bad, like something that had spoiled. Her eyes didn't blink, and her breathing was unsteady, as though it was something she had to keep reminding herself to do. She was hardly five feet tall, but she seemed to tower over me. I could feel my thoughts and plans disintegrating in my head, blown away by the sheer force of her presence. I made myself smile at her.

"Hello, Jessica. You're looking . . . very yourself. I have what you need."

"How can you know what I need?" she said, in a voice that was frightening because it was so nearly normal. "How can you, when I don't know myself?"

"Because I'm John Taylor, and I find things. I found what you need. But you have to believe in me, or you'll never get what I have for you. If I just disappear, you'll never know . . ."

"Show me," she said, and I knew I'd pushed it as far as I could. I reached carefully down into the pew, picked up the shoe box, and presented it to her. She snatched it from me, and the cardboard box disintegrated under her gaze, revealing the contents. A battered old teddy bear with one glass eye missing. Jessica Sorrow held the bear in her dead white hands, looking and looking at it with her wild unblinking eyes, and then, finally, she held it to her shrunken chest and cuddled it to her, like a sleeping child. And I began to breathe once more.

"This is mine," she said, still looking at the bear rather than at me, for which I was grateful. "It . . . was mine, when I was a small child. Long ago, when I was still human. I haven't thought of him in . . . so long, so very long . . ."

"It's what you need," I said carefully. "Something that matters to you. Something that's as real to you as you are. Something to believe in."

Her head rose sharply, and she turned her unwavering regard on me. I did my best not to wince. She cocked her head to one side, like a bird. "Where did you find this?"

"In the teddy bears' graveyard."

She laughed briefly, but it surprised me anyway. "Never ask the magician how he does his tricks. I know. I'm crazy, but I know that. And I know I'm crazy. I knew what I was buying with the price I paid. I'm always alone now, divorced from the world and everyone in it; because of what I did to myself, what I made of myself. La la la . . . just me, talking to myself . . . It wasn't an easy or a pleasant thing, to cut away my humanity and become the Unbeliever. I walk through the world, and I'm the only one in it. Until now. Now there's me and teddy. Yes. Something to believe in. What do you believe in, John Taylor?"

"My gift. My job. And perhaps my honour. What happened to you, Jessica?"

"I don't know, any more. That was the point. My past was so appalling, I had to make myself forget it, had to make it unreal, had to make it never have happened. But in doing that I lost my faith in reality, or it lost faith in me, and now I only exist through a constant effort of will. If I ever stop concentrating, I'll be the one to disappear. I've been alone for so long, surrounded by shadows and whispers that mean nothing, nothing at all.

Sometimes I pretend, just to have someone to talk to, but I know it's not real . . . But now I have my bear. A comfort, and a reminder. Of who and what I was." She smiled down at the battered old bear in her stick-thin arms. "I've enjoyed our little chat, John Taylor. Made possible by this place, and this moment. Don't ever try this again. I wouldn't know you. Wouldn't remember you. Wouldn't be safe."

"Remember the bear," I said. "Just maybe, it can lead you home."

But she was already gone, striding out of the church and back into the night. I let out my breath slowly and sat down on the front pew before I fell down. Jessica Sorrow was too damned spooky, even for the Nightside. It's not easy having a conversation with someone you know thinks she's only listening to voices in her head. And who can drop you out of existence on the merest whim. I got to my feet and went over to the altar to collect up my candles. And that was when I heard running footsteps approaching the church from outside. Not Jessica. Human footsteps, this time. I retreated to the very back of the church and hid myself in the deepest of the shadows. Apart from Jessica, and, of course, Walker, no-one was supposed to know I was there. But I have enemies. Their dread agents, the Harrowing, have been trying to kill me since I was born. And besides, I'd had enough excitement for one night. Whoever was coming, I didn't want to know.

A man in black came running through the gap where the door used to be. His dark suit was tattered and torn, and his face was slack with exhaustion. He looked like he'd been running for a really long time. He looked like he'd been scared for a really long time. He was wearing sunglasses, black and blank as a beetle's eyes, even though he'd come out of the night. He staggered down the aisle towards the altar, clutching at the pews with one hand as he passed, to hold himself up. His other hand pressed an object wrapped in black cloth to his chest. He kept glancing back over his shoulder, clearly afraid that whoever or whatever pursued him was close behind. He finally collapsed onto his knees before the altar, shaking and shuddering. He pulled off his sunglasses and threw them aside. His eyelids had been stitched together. He held out his parcel to the altar with unsteady hands.

"Sanctuary!" he cried, his voice rough and hoarse, as though it hadn't been used in a long time. "In God's name, sanctuary!"

For a long moment there was only silence, then I heard slow, steady footsteps approaching the church from outside. Measured, unhurried footsteps. The man in black heard them too, flinching at the sound, but he wouldn't look back; his mutilated face was fixed desperately on the altar.

The footsteps stopped, just at the doorway to the church. A slow wind blew in from the night, gusting heavily down the aisle like someone breathing. The candles nearest the door guttered and went out. The wind reached me, even in my shadows, and slapped against my face, hot and sweaty like fever in the night. It smelled of attar, the perfume crushed out of roses, but sick and heavy, almost overpowering. The man in black whimpered before the altar. He tried to say *sanctuary* again, but he couldn't get his voice to work.

Another voice answered him, from the darkness beyond the church's doorway. Harsh and menacing, and yet soft and slow as bitter treacle, it sounded like several voices whispering together, in subtle harmonies that grated on the soul like fingernails drawn down a blackboard. It wasn't a human voice. It was both more and less than human.

"There is no sanctuary, here or anywhere, for such as you," it said, and the man in black trembled to hear it. "There is nowhere you can run where we cannot follow. Nowhere you can hide where we cannot find you. Give back what you have taken."

The man in black still couldn't find the courage to look back at what had finally caught up to him, but he clutched his black cloth parcel to his breast and did his best to sound defiant.

"You can't have it! It chose me! It's mine!"

There was something standing in the doorway now, something darker and deeper than the shadows. I could feel its presence, its pressure, like a great weight in the night, as though something huge and dense and utterly abhuman had found its way into the human world. It didn't belong here, but it had come anyway, because it could. The odd, whispering voice spoke again.

"Give it to us. Give it to us now. Or we will tear the soul out of your body and throw it down into the Pit, there to burn in the flames of the Inferno forever."

The face of the man in black contorted, caught in an agony of indecision. Tears forced themselves past the heavy black stitches that closed his eyes and ran jerkily down his shuddering cheeks. And, finally, he nodded, his whole body slumping forward in defeat. He seemed too tired to run any more, and too scared even to think of fighting. I didn't blame him. Even as I hid deep in my concealing shadows, that sick and pitiless voice scared the crap out of me. The man in black unwrapped his cloth parcel, slowly and reverently, to reveal a great silver chalice, studded with precious stones. It shone brilliantly in the dim light, like a piece of heaven fallen to earth.

"Take it!" the man in black said bitterly, through his tears. "Take the Grail! Just . . . don't hurt me any more. Please."

There was a long pause, as though the whole world was listening and waiting. The man in black's hands began to shake so hard he was in danger of dropping the chalice. The harmonied voice spoke again, heavy and immutable as fate.

"That is not the Grail."

A great shadow leapt forward out of the doorway, rushed down the aisle, and enveloped the man in black before he even had time to cry out. I pressed my back against the cold stone wall, praying for my shadows to hide me. There was a great roaring in the church, like all the lions in the world giving voice at once. And then the shadow retreated, seeping slowly back up the aisle, as though . . . satiated. It swept through the open doorway and was gone. I couldn't feel its presence in the night any more. I stepped cautiously forward, and studied the figure still crouching before the altar. It was now a gleaming white statue, wearing a tattered black suit. The white hands still held the rejected chalice. The frozen white face was caught in a never-ending scream of horror.

I collected all my candles, checked to make sure I'd left no traces of my presence anywhere, and left St. Jude's. I walked home slowly, taking the pretty route. I had a lot to think about. The Grail . . . if the Holy Grail had come to the Nightside, or if the usual interested parties even thought it had, we were all in a for a world of trouble. The kind of beings who would fight for possession of the Grail would give even the Nightside's toughest movers and shakers a real run for their money. A wise man would consider the implications of this, take a long holiday, and not come back till the rubble had finished settling. But if the Grail really was here, somewhere . . . I'm John Taylor. I find things.

There just had to be a way for me to make a hell of a lot of money out of this.

Possibly literally.

TWO

The Gathering Storm

Strangefellows is the kind of bar where no-one gives a damn what your name is, and the regulars go armed. It's a good place to meet people, and an even better place to get conned, robbed, and killed. Not necessarily in that order. Pretty much everybody who is anybody, or thinks they are or should be, has paid Strangefellows a visit at one time or another. Tourists are not encouraged, and are occasionally shot at on sight. I spend a lot of time there, which says more about me than I'm comfortable admitting. I do pick up a lot of work there. I could probably justify my bar bill as a business expense. If I paid taxes.

It was still three o'clock in the morning as I descended the echoing metal staircase into the bar proper. The place seemed unusually quiet, with most of the usual suspects conspicuous by their absence. There were people, here and there, at the bar and sitting at tables, plus a whole bunch of customers who couldn't have passed for people even if I'd put a bag over my head as well as theirs . . . but no-one important. No-one who mattered. I stopped at the foot of the stairs and looked around thoughtfully. Must be something big happening somewhere. But then, this is the Nightside. There's always something big happening somewhere in the Nightside, and someone small getting shafted.

The bar's hidden speakers were pumping out King Crimson's "Red," which meant the bar's owner was feeling nostalgic again. Alex Morrisey, owner and bartender, was behind the long wooden bar as usual, pretending to polish a glass while a sour-faced customer bent his ear. Alex is a good person to talk to when you're feeling down, because he has absolutely no sympathy, or the slightest tolerance for self-pity, on the grounds that he's a full-time gloomy bugger himself. Alex could gloom for the Olympics. No matter how bad your troubles are, his are always worse. He was in his late twenties, but looked at least ten years older. He sulked a lot, brooded loudly over the general unfairness of life, and had a tendency to throw things when he got stroppy. He always wore black of some description, (because as yet no-one had invented a darker colour) including designer shades and a snazzy black beret he wore pushed well back on his head to hide a growing bald patch.

He's bound to the bar by a family geas, and hates every minute of it. As a result, wise people avoid the bar snacks.

Above and behind the bar, inside a sturdy glass case fixed firmly to the wall, was a large leather-bound Bible with a raised silver cross on the cover. A sign below the glass case read *In case of Apocalypse, break glass.* Alex believed in being prepared.

The handful of patrons bellying up to the bar were the usual mixed bunch. A smoke ghost in shades of blue and grey was inhaling the memory of a cigarette and blowing little puffs of himself into the already murky atmosphere. Two lesbian undines were drinking each other with straws, and getting giggly as the water levels rose and fell on their liquid bodies. The smoke ghost moved a little further down the bar, just in case they got too drunk and their surface tensions collapsed. One of Baron Frankenstein's more successful patchwork creations lurched up to the bar, seated itself on a barstool, then checked carefully to see whether anything had dropped off recently. The Baron was an undoubted scientific genius, but his sewing skills left a lot to be desired. Alex nodded hello and pushed across an opened can of motor oil with a curly-wurly straw sticking out of it. At the end of the bar, a werewolf was curled up on the floor on a threadbare blanket, searching his fur for fleas and occasionally licking his balls. Because he could, presumably.

Alex looked up and down the bar and sniffed disgustedly. "It was never like this on *Cheers*. I have got to get a better class of customers." He broke off as the magician's top hat on the bar beside him juddered briefly, then a hand emerged holding an empty martini glass. Alex refilled the glass from a cocktail shaker, and the hand withdrew into the hat again. Alex sighed. "One of these days we're going to have to get him out of there. Man, that rabbit was mad at him." He turned back to the musician he'd been listening to and glared at him pointedly. "You ready for another one, Leo?"

"Always." Leo Morn finished off the last of his beer and pushed the glass forward. He was a tall slender figure, who looked so insubstantial it was probably only the weight of his heavy leather jacket that kept him from drifting away. He had a long pale face under a permanent bad hair day, enlivened by bright eyes and a distinctly wolfish smile. A battered guitar case leaned against the bar beside him. He gave Alex his best ingratiating smile. "Come on, Alex, you know this place could use a good live set. The band's back together again, and we're setting up a comeback tour."

"How can you have a comeback when you've never been anywhere? *No,* Leo. I remember the last time I let you talk me into playing here. My customers have made it very clear that they would rather projectile vomit their own intestines rather than have to listen to you again, and I don't necessarily disagree. What's the band called . . . this week? I take it you are still changing the name on a regular basis, so you can still get bookings?"

"For the moment, we're Druid Chic," Leo admitted. "It does help to have the element of surprise on our side."

"Leo, I wouldn't book you to play at a convention for the deaf." Alex glared across at the werewolf on his blanket. "And take your drummer with you. He is lowering the tone, which in this place is a real accomplishment."

Leo ostentatiously looked around, then gestured for Alex to lean closer. "You know," he said conspiratorially, "if you're looking for something new, something just that little bit special to pull in some new customers, I might be able to help you out. Would you be interested in . . . a pinch of Elvis?"

Alex looked at him suspiciously. "Tell me this has nothing at all to do with fried banana sandwiches."

"Only indirectly. Listen. A few years back, a certain group of depraved drug fiends of my acquaintance hatched a diabolical plan in search of the greatest possible high. They had tried absolutely everything, singly and in combination, and were desperate for something new. Something more potent, to scramble what few working brain cells they had left. So they went to Graceland. Elvis, as we all know, was so full of pills when he died they had to bury him in a coffin with a childproof lid. By the time he died, the man's system was saturated with every weird drug under the sun, including several he had made up specially. So my appalling friends sneaked into Graceland under cover of a heavy-duty camouflage spell, dug up Elvis's body, and replaced it with a simulacrum. Then they scampered back home with their prize. You can see where this is going, can't you? They cremated

Elvis's body, collected the ashes, and smoked them. The word is, there's no high like . . . a pinch of Elvis."

Alex considered the matter for a moment. "Congratulations," he said finally. "That is the most disgusting thing I've ever heard, Leo. And there's been a lot of competition. *Get out of here. Leo. Now.*"

Leo Morn shrugged and grinned, finished his drink, and went to grab his drummer by the collar. His place at the bar was immediately taken by a new arrival, a fat middle-aged man in a crumpled suit. Slobby, sweaty, and furtive, he looked like he should have been standing in a police identification parade somewhere. He smiled widely at Alex, who didn't smile back.

"A splendid night, Alex! Indeed, a most fortunate night! You're looking well, sir, very well. A glass of your very finest, if you please!"

Alex folded his arms across his chest. "Tate. Just when I think my day can't get any worse, you turn up. I don't suppose there's any chance of you paying your bar bill, is there?"

"You wound me, sir! You positively wound me!" Tate tried to look aggrieved. It didn't suit him. He switched to an ingratiating smile. "My impecunious days are over, Alex! As of today, I am astonishingly solvent. I . . ."

At which point he was suddenly pushed aside by a tall, cadaverous individual, in a smart tuxedo and a billowing black opera cape. His face was deathly pale, his eyes were a savage crimson, and his mouth was full of sharp teeth. He smelled of grave dirt. He pounded a corpse-pale fist on the bar and glared at Alex.

"You! Giff me blut! Fresh blut!"

Alex calmly picked up a nearby soda syphon and let the newcomer have it full in the face. He shrieked loudly as his face dissolved under the jet of water, then he suddenly disappeared, his clothes and cloak slumping to the floor. A large black bat flapped around the bar. Everyone present took the opportunity to throw things at it, until finally it flapped away up the stairs. Alex put down the syphon.

"Holy soda water," he explained, to the somewhat startled Tate. "I keep it handy for certain cocktails. Bloody vampires . . . that's the third we've had this week. Must be a convention on again."

"Put it from your thoughts, dear fellow," Tate said grandly. "Tonight is your lucky night. All your troubles are over. I will indeed be paying my bar bill, and more than that. Tonight, the drinks are on me!"

Everyone in the bar perked up their ears at that. They never had any trouble hearing the offer of a free drink, even with King Crimson going full blast. It wasn't something that happened very often. A crowd began to form around the grinning Tate, pleased but somewhat surprised. Frankenstein's creature pushed forward his can for a refill. Alex still hadn't uncrossed his arms.

"Absolutely no more credit for you, Tate. Let's see the colour of your money first."

Tate looked around him, taking his time, making sure he had everyone's full attention, and produced from inside his jacket a substantial wad of cash. The crowd murmured, impressed. Tate turned back to Alex.

"I have inherited a fortune, my dear boy. Taylor finally found the missing will, and I have been legally proclaimed the one and only true heir; and I am now so rich I could spit on a Rockefeller."

"Good," said Alex. He neatly plucked the wad of cash out of Tate's hand, peeled off half of it and gave the rest back. "That should just about cover your tab. Hopefully once you've paid Taylor, he'll be able to settle up his bill too."

"Taylor?" Tate said disdainfully. He gestured grandly with what remained of his wad of cash. "I have creditors of long-standing and exhausted patience waiting to be paid. They come first. Taylor is just hired help. He can take a number, and wait."

He laughed loudly, inviting everyone else to join him. Instead, everyone went very quiet. Some actually began to back away from him. Alex leaned forward over the bar and gave Tate a hard look.

"You're planning on stiffing Taylor? Are you tired of living, Tate?"

The fat man pulled himself up to his full height, but unfortunately he didn't have far to go. He glared at Alex, his mouth pulled into a vicious pout. "Taylor doesn't scare me!"

Alex smiled coldly. "He would, if you had the sense God gave a boll weevil."

He looked past Tate, and nodded a hello. After a moment, everyone else looked round too. And that was when Tate finally turned around, and saw me standing at the foot of the stairs, from where I'd been watching and listening. I started towards the bar, and people who weren't even in my way hurried to get out of it. The crowd around Tate quickly melted away, falling back to what they hoped was a safe distance. Tate stood his ground, chin held high, trying to look unconcerned and failing miserably. I finally came to a halt right in front of him. He was sweating hard. I smiled at him, and he swallowed audibly.

"Hello, Tate," I said calmly. "Good to see you. You're looking your usual appalling self. I'm pleased to hear the inheritance is everything you thought it would be. I do so love it when a case has a happy ending. Now, you owe me money, Tate. And I really don't feel like waiting."

"You can't bully me," Tate said hoarsely. "I'm rich now. I can afford protection."

His podgy left hand went to a golden charm bracelet around his right wrist. He grabbed two of the bulky, ugly-looking charms, pulled them free, and threw them onto the floor between us. There was a brief lurch in the bar as a dimensional gateway opened between the worlds and the two charms were replaced by the two creatures they'd summoned. They stood glowering between me and Tate, two huge reptiloid figures with muscles on their muscles and great wedge-shaped heads absolutely bristling with serrated teeth. The reptiloids looked at me, and I looked at them, and then they both turned to look at Tate.

"*He's* why you called us?" said the one on the left. "You summoned us here to take on *John bloody Taylor?* Are you *crazy?*"

"Right," said the one on the right. "We don't do lost causes."

And with that, they disappeared back to where they'd come from. Tate tried all the other charms on his bracelet, in increasing desperation, but none of them would budge. I just stood there, looking calm and relaxed and not at all bothered, while my heart slowly returned to its usual rate. Those reptiloids really had been worryingly large . . . Sometimes it helps to have a reputation as a dangerous and extremely ruthless bastard. Tate finally gave up on the bracelet and looked, very reluctantly, back at me. I smiled at him, and he seemed very, very upset.

In the end, he gave me every piece of cash, all his credit cards, all his jewellery, including the charm bracelet, and basically everything else he had on his person. And I let him walk out of the bar alive. He was lucky I let him keep his clothes. I settled down to chat with Alex, and everyone else went back to what they were doing before, vaguely disappointed because there hadn't been any blood.

Alex poured me a large brandy. "So, John, where are you living these days?"

"In the real world," I said, deliberately vague. "I commute into the Nightside to work. It's safer."

"You're not still sleeping in your office, are you?"

"No, now I'm getting regular work here, I can afford a decent place again." I checked the money I'd taken off Tate. "In fact, it may be time for an upgrade."

"Stick to the real world," said Alex. "Now you're back on the scene again, there are a lot of people out there looking for you with bad intent in their hearts. Some of them have looked in here. You'd be surprised how much certain people are willing to pay for hard information on where you rest your head. I take their money and give them all different lies."

"I sleep more soundly in the real world," I admitted. The Harrowing are always out there, somewhere. It was why I'd stayed away from the Nightside for so long.

"Glad to be back?" said Alex.

"I don't know yet. It's good to be working again. I do my best work here. It might even be where I belong. But . . ."

"Yeah," said Alex. "But. This is the Nightside, the dark side of everyone's dreams." It was hard to tell past the sunglasses, but there was an expression on his face that in anyone else I would have said was concern. "Word is, a lot of people want you dead, John. *Lot* of people. You know . . . you're always welcome to crash here, for a while. If you need a place. Somewhere you could feel safe."

"Thanks," I said. I was touched, but knew better than to show it. It would only embarrass him. "I'll bear it in mind. So, what's new?"

Alex considered. "Surprisingly, not a lot. Jessica Sorrow, of course, but you know about that. Don't know if it's connected, but a lot of the usual players have dropped out of sight just recently. Keeping their heads down and hoping not to be noticed. Or it could be connected with the latest hot rumour, which is that angels have come to the Nightside."

I had to raise an eyebrow at that. "Angels? Really?"

"From Above and Below, apparently. No-one's reported any actual sightings as yet. Probably because no-one's too sure what to look for. It's been a long time since any angel manifested in the material worlds. Demons, yes, but they're not in the same league as the Fallen . . ."

"I encountered . . . something, at St. Jude's," I said thoughtfully. "Something very nearly as upsetting as the Unbeliever herself . . . Angels in the Nightside . . . That's got to be a Sign. Of something.

"They'd better watch their step around here," Alex said briskly. "Some of the scumbags in this locale will steal anything that isn't actually nailed down, electrified, or cursed. Wouldn't surprise me if I looked out of here one morning and found St. Michael himself propped up on bricks with his wings missing."

I looked at him thoughtfully. "You don't know much about angels, do you, Alex?"

"I do my best to steer clear of moral absolutes," said Alex. "They tend not to approve of establishments like this. And they leave lousy tips."

He didn't mention his own ancestry. He didn't have to. Alex is famously descended from Arthur Pendragon on one side, and Merlin Satanspawn on the other. Merlin himself was buried somewhere under the wine cellar. He still manifested on occasion, to lay down the law and scare the crap out of everyone. Being dead doesn't necessarily stop you being a major player in the Nightside.

"Forget all your usual notions about angels," I said patiently. "All the usual images of angels as nice guys with wings, long nighties, and a harp fixation. Angels are God's enforcers, his Will made manifest in the world of men. The spiritual equivalent of the SAS. When God wants a city destroyed, or the firstborn of a whole generation slaughtered, he sends an angel. When the Day of Judgement finally comes, and the world is brought to an end, it will be the angels who do all the dirty work. They are powerful, implacable beings. I don't even want to talk about the Fallen kind."

And then there was a voice behind me. Polite, well-spoken, and tinged with an accent I couldn't place.

"Excuse me, please. Would you be John Taylor?"

I took my time turning around, careful not to look startled, even though my heart had just missed a beat. There aren't many people capable of catching me by surprise. I pride myself on being very hard to sneak up on. In the Nightside, that's a survival skill.

Standing before me was a short, stocky type with a dark complexion, kind eyes, and jet-black hair and beard, both carefully shaped. He was wearing a long, flowing coat of a very expensive cut.

"I might be," I said. "Depends. Who might you be?"

"I am Jude."

"Hey, Jude."

He frowned slightly. It was clear he didn't get the reference. I smiled patiently.

"I'm Taylor. What can I do for you, Jude?"

He glanced at Alex, then took in the other beings lining the bar, all pretending not to listen with varying amounts of skill. Jude turned back and met my gaze steadily. "If we could talk in a private place, Mr Taylor. I have a commission for you. It pays very well."

"You just said the magic words, Jude. Step into my office."

I led him to one of the private booths at the back of the bar, and we sat down facing each other across the table. Jude gazed around the bar. It was clear this was all unknown territory to him. He didn't look like the kind of person you'd find in a bar, though on the other hand I wasn't sure where I would place him. There was something about the man . . . He didn't fit any of the usual patterns. He looked like someone with secrets. He fixed me again with those warm brown eyes, as though willing me to like him, and leaned forward across the table to address me, his voice low and confidential.

"I represent the Vatican, Mr Taylor. The Holy Father wishes you to find something for him."

"The Pope wants to hire me? What happened? Somebody steal his ring?"

"Nothing so trivial, Mr Taylor."

"Why didn't he send a priest?"

"He did. I'm . . . undercover." He glanced around the bar again, and didn't seem at all pleased or comfortable with what he saw. It wasn't so much that he looked judgemental, more . . . mystified, and perhaps even uneasy. He looked back at me and smiled almost shyly. "I don't get out much, these days. It's been a long time since I was out in the world. I was chosen to approach you because I have . . . some special knowledge of the missing item. You see, normally I'm in charge of the Forbidden Library at the Vatican. The secret, hidden chambers underground, where the Church stores texts too dangerous or too disturbing for most people."

"Like the Gospel According to Pilate?" I couldn't help showing off a little. "The translation of the Voynich Manuscript? The Testimony of Grendel Rex?"

Jude nodded slightly, giving nothing away. "Things like that, yes. I am here because an object of great power has suddenly resurfaced in the world, after being missing for centuries. And, of course, it has turned up here in the Nightside."

It was my turn to nod and look thoughtful. "This object of power must be something really important, if the Vatican's getting personally involved. Or . . . something really dangerous. What exactly are we talking about here?"

"The Unholy Grail. The cup that Judas drank from at the Last Supper."

That stopped me in my tracks. I had to sit back in my chair and consider that for a few moments. "I never heard . . . of an Unholy Grail."

"Not many have," said Jude. "Luckily for us all. The Unholy Grail magnifies all evil by its presence, encourages and accelerates evil trends and events, and utterly corrupts all who come into contact with it. It is also a source of great power . . . It's passed from hand to hand down the centuries. Previous owners are said to include Torquemada, Rasputin, and Adolf Hitler. Though if Hitler had possessed all the mystical items rumour has gifted him with, he wouldn't have lost the war. Anyway, the Unholy

Grail is currently on the loose and up for grabs, somewhere in the Nightside."

I felt like whistling loudly, impressed, but I didn't. I had a reputation to maintain. "No wonder there are angels in the Nightside."

"Already?" Jude leaned forward sharply. His eyes didn't look kind any more. "Are you sure?"

"No," I said calmly. "So far it's only talk. But the word is, we have visitors from Above and Below."

"Shit," said Jude, startling me just a bit. You don't expect language like that from a priest and librarian. "Mr Taylor, it's imperative you locate the Unholy Grail for us, before agents of the Lord or the Enemy become directly involved. Make no mistake, if agents of the Principalities go to war here, they could level the Nightside."

"If the Unholy Grail is here, I can find it," I said, giving Jude my best confident smile. He didn't seem impressed or reassured.

"It won't be easy, Mr Taylor. Even with your famous talent. A lot of people are going to be searching for the Unholy Grail, for all manner of good and bad reasons. And in the wrong hands, its power could conceivably upset the balance between Above and Below. The Last Days could come early, and we're not nearly ready yet."

"So if the angels don't destroy the Nightside, whoever gets to the Unholy Grail first could do the job too? Wonderful. I just love working under pressure."

"But you'll take the commission?"

"I can find anything. It's what I do. That is why you came to me, isn't it?"

"You came highly recommended," said Jude. "Though for the sake of your ego, I don't think I'll say by whom. Now, the Unholy Grail was being kept in the House of Blue Lights, one of the hidden complexes deep under the Pentagon. But a guard somehow got past all the defences and protections, and smuggled it out. He couldn't hang on to it, of course, the poor fool. It had just used him to escape."

I remembered the man in black at St. Jude's, and what had happened to him. The awful voice(s) had mentioned a Grail. But I didn't say anything. I had no reason to keep things from Jude, but I still wasn't ready to trust him entirely either. I was pretty sure he was keeping things from me.

"If it's here, I can find it," I said flatly. "But I'm not so sure I should turn it over to the Vatican. Your reputation's taken a series of knocks recently. Everything from banking to the Ratlines."

"The Unholy Grail would go straight from me to the Holy Father," Jude said earnestly. "And he would ensure it would be locked away and properly contained. Until the End of Time, if necessary. If you can't trust the Pope to do the right thing, Mr. Taylor, whom can you trust?"

"Good question," I said. I wasn't convinced, and he could tell. He thought for a moment.

"We only want to preserve the status quo, Mr Taylor. Because Humanity isn't ready yet for any of the alternatives. I have been authorised to offer you a quarter of a million pounds. In cash. Fifty thousand in advance."

He placed a stuffed envelope on the table between us. I didn't touch it, though my fingers were itching to. A quarter of a bloody million?

"Danger money?"

"Quite," said Jude. "You'll get the rest when you place the Unholy Grail in my hands."

"Sounds good to me," I said. I picked up the envelope and tucked it away, giving Jude my best confident smile. "You've got yourself a deal, Jude."

And then we both looked up as three large gentlemen loomed over us. They took up positions standing as close as they could get without actually joining us in the booth. I'd heard them coming, but hadn't said anything because I didn't want Jude distracted while he was talking about money. The three gentlemen glared at us both impartially. They were the best-dressed thugs I'd seen in some time, but the attitude gave them away. They might as well have been wearing *I am a mafiosa hit man* T-shirts. They looked slick and heavy and dangerous, and each of them had a gun. All three were professionally calm, forming a semicircle to cover both me and Jude, while efficiently blocking us off from the rest of the bar. No-one could see what was happening, and we wouldn't be allowed to shout for help. Not that I had any intention of doing so. The largest of the three gunmen flashed me a humourless smile.

"Forget the pew-polisher, Taylor. From now on, you're working for us."

I considered the matter. "And if I prefer not to?"

The gunman shrugged. "You can find the Unholy Grail for us, or you can die. Right here, right now. Your choice."

I smiled nastily at him, and to his credit he didn't flinch. "Your guns aren't loaded," I said.

The three gunmen looked at each other, confused. I held up my closed hands, opened them, and let a stream of bullets fall out to clatter loudly on the tabletop. They pulled the triggers on their guns, and looked very upset when nothing happened.

"I think you should leave now," I said. "Before I decide to do something similar with your internal organs."

They put away their guns and left, not quite running. I smiled apologetically at Jude. "Boys will be boys. You leave the matter with me, and I'll see what I can turn up."

"Soon, please, Mr Taylor," said Jude. He fixed me with his deep brown eyes, positively radiating sincerity and earnestness. On anyone else, it would probably have worked. "We're all running out of time."

He rose to his feet, and I got up too. "How will I find you, when I have something to report?"

"You won't," he said calmly. "I'll find you."

He walked off through the bar, not looking back. Interestingly enough, people moved to get out of his way without even seeming to notice they were doing it. There was more to Jude than met the eye. Mind you, there would have to be. The Vatican wouldn't send just anybody into the Nightside. I went back to Alex, who was refilling the hand in the top hat's glass. Frankenstein's creature was moodily tightening the stitches in his left wrist. Alex nodded to me.

"Got yourself a new client?"

"Looks like it."

"Interesting case?"

"Well, different, anyway. I think I'm going to need Suzie's help for this one."

"Ah," said Alex. "One of *those* cases."

There was a crack of thunder, a flash of lightning, a billowing of dark sulphurous smoke, and a sorcerer appeared at the bar right next to me. He wore dark purple robes and the traditional pointy hat. He was tall, dark, and imposing, with long black fingernails, a neat goatee, and piercing eyes. He gestured dramatically at me, while fixing me with a ferocious glare.

"Taylor! Find the Unholy Grail for me, or suffer an eternity of my wrath!"

While the sorcerer's attention was fixed on me, Alex calmly produced a heavy bung-starter from behind the bar. He plucked off the sorcerer's tall pointy hat and hit him over the head with the bung-starter. The sorcerer yelped once, and collapsed. Alex raised his voice.

"Lucy! Betty! Time to take out the trash!"

Lucy and Betty Coltrane, Alex's body-building bouncers, arrived and cheerfully hauled away the unconscious sorcerer. Alex glared at me.

"Unholy Grail?"

"Trust me, Alex. You really don't want to know."

He sighed. "Taylor, get out of here. You're bad for business."

THREE

Meetings in Dark Places

The long and narrow alleyway outside Strangefellows was as dark, gloomy, and filthy dirty as always. The heavy blue light from the huge moon hanging overhead gave the cobbled alley a bleak, sinister air, like the uneasy streets we walk in our dreams, and never to anywhere good. Business as usual, in the Nightside. I headed for the bright city lights at the end of the alley, picking my way carefully through the rubbish littering the way. There were severed hands everywhere, and not a few feet, all hard as ice and dusted with hoarfrost. The Little Sisters of the Immaculate Chain Saw had been busy tonight. The Christmas season must be starting early this year.

A figure appeared suddenly at the far end of the alley, standing silhouetted against the glaring neon, and I stopped dead in my tracks. For a moment my heart slammed painfully against my chest, and I forgot how to breathe. The last time I'd walked down this alley, I'd been ambushed by my enemies. The faceless horrors of the Harrowing had come for me, and I'd only escaped with the help of my old friend Razor Eddie. Of course, he'd been the one who set me up for the ambush; but that's friends for you, in the Nightside.

But this time there was only the one figure, with a distinctly female silhouette, and as she started down the dark alleyway towards me, a soft golden glow appeared around her, lighting her way. She was exceedingly blonde and pretty, and almost overpoweringly voluptuous, moving with easy grace in her own pool of light. Marilyn Monroe, in her glorious prime, in her iconic white halter dress. Not a look-alike or a double, but indisputably the real thing, wrapped in glamour, bursting with life and laughter, just like in her films. Sweet and sexy Marilyn, walking in her own spotlight.

She came to a halt before me, and smiled dazzlingly. She smelled of sex and sweat and sandalwood, of roses and rot, and though her smile was as inviting as ever, there was no matching warmth in her eyes.

"Hello, sugar," she said, in a voice like a caress. "I'm so glad I found you. I've got a message for you."

"That's nice," I said, carefully non-commital.

She laughed her famous laugh, wrinkled her nose at me, and handed me a long white envelope with the tips of her fingers. "This is for you, sweetie. Inside the envelope, there's a blank cheque! Signed by Mr. Hughes himself. He wants the Unholy Grail for his collection. All you have to do is find it for him, and you can fill in the cheque for whatever amount you like. Isn't that generous of him?"

"Pardon me for asking?" I said. "But aren't you dead?"

She laughed huskily and tossed her head. Her wavy hair moved in slow sensuous waves. Being bathed in the glow of her open sexuality was like staring into a blast furnace.

"Oh, that wasn't me. Howard looks after his friends."

"I rather thought he was dead too."

"Men that rich don't die, sugar. Not if they don't want to. They just move to another plane, for tax reasons. He's mixing with some really powerful people these days."

"People?"

"Loosely speaking."

I weighed the envelope in my hands thoughtfully. I'd never been offered a blank cheque before. I was tempted. But . . . I smiled regretfully at Marilyn.

"Sorry, dear. I already have a client. I'm spoken for."

"I'm sure Mr. Hughes can match any offer . . ."

"It isn't the money. I gave my word."

"Oh. Are you sure . . . I couldn't do anything to persuade you?"

She took a deep breath, and her breasts seemed to surge towards me. I was finding it hard to breathe again.

"I'm probably going to hate myself in the morning," I said finally, "but I have to say no. My services are for sale, but I'm not."

She pouted at me with her luscious mouth. "Everyone has their price, darling. We just haven't found yours yet."

"I'm always loyal to my client," I said. "It's all the honour I have left."

"Honour," said Marilyn, wrinkling her nose again. "See how far that gets you, in the Nightside. See you again, sugar. Boop boop de boop."

She blew me a kiss, turned elegantly on her left high heel, and strode off down the alley. Her shoes made no sound on the cobbles. She walked in glamour, still in her own spotlight, like the star she was. I watched her disappear back into the neon noir of the city streets, and only then looked down at the envelope in my hand. My first impulse was to tear it up, but wiser thoughts prevailed, and I put it carefully in my inside coat pocket. You never knew when a cheque with Howard Hughes's signature on it might come in handy.

I looked around for a dark doorway. They tended to come and go, but you could always rely on a few, this close to Strangefellows. I walked over to the nearest, kicked a few hands aside, and sat down cross-legged. No-one would disturb me here, and I had work to do. If one major player already knew I was on the trail of the Unholy Grail, then it was a safe bet everyone knew. Or at least, everyone that mattered. They'd all be looking for me, and the people they'd send wouldn't all be as pleasant and polite as Marilyn. This was the kind of treasure hunt that started serious turf wars. And the last thing I needed was the Authorities getting involved. No, I needed to get my hands on the Unholy Grail as quickly as possible, and that meant using my gift. I'm always reluctant to do that, because when I use my special talent, my mind blazes like a beacon in the darkness of the Nightside, signalling to all my enemies exactly where I am. But it's my gift that makes me what I am, that enables me to be so very good at what I do.

My gift. I can find anything, or anyone. No matter how well hidden they are.

So I sat there in the deep dark shadows, my back pressed against the wall, breathed deeply, and closed my eyes, concentrating. And opened the eye deep in my mind; my third eye, my private eye. Energies swirled within me, rough and roaring, then flowed out of me, rushing off in all directions, lighting up the night so I could See everything. The thunder of a million voices descended upon me, not all of them in any way human, and I had to struggle to focus, to narrow my vision to the one thing I was searching for. The bedlam died away, and already I could begin to sense a direction, and the beginnings of distance. And then Something reached down out of the overworld, snatched my mind right out of my body, and bore it away. There was a sensation that might have been flying or falling, as the alley and the material world disappeared. And I was somewhere else.

This time, it was my turn to stand in the spotlight. A light stabbed down from somewhere above me, brilliant and blinding, holding me in place like a bug transfixed on a pin. I felt horribly naked and exposed, as though the light showed up everything inside me, the good and the bad. All around me there was only darkness, a deep concealing darkness, and somehow I could tell it was there to protect me, because I was not worthy or strong enough to see what lay beyond my small pool of light. But I could sense that I was not alone, that to either side of me there were vast and powerful presences, two great armies assembled on an endless unseen plain. There was a feeling of restless movement, and what might have been the fluttering and flapping of wings. My mind, or more likely my soul, had been hijacked. Brought into the overworld, the boundaries of the immaterial. The overworld wasn't Heaven or Hell, but it was said you could see them both from there.

A voice spoke to me from one side, and it was a harmony of many voices, like a crowd chanting in syncopation, a choir that sang only in descants. My skin crawled at the sound of it. I'd heard such a voice before, in St. Jude's. It was a powerful, imperious voice, steeped in ancient, unanswerable authority.

"The dark chalice is loose once more, travelling in the world of mortal men. This cannot be permitted. It is too powerful a thing to be abandoned to merely human hands, and so it has been decided that we shall descend from the glory plains and walk in the material world again."

A second harmonied voice spoke from the other side, rich and complex and full of discords. "Too long has the Unholy Grail wandered at random in the world of mortal men. The sombre chalice, the great corrupter. It must be placed in the right hands and allowed to fulfill its purpose. Its time has come round at last. And so it has been decided that we shall ascend from the infernal plains and walk in the material world again."

All I could think was *Oh shit . . .*

"Tell us what you know of the Unholy Grail," said the first voice, and the second echoed, "Tell us, tell us . . ."

"I don't really know anything yet," I said. It didn't even occur to me to lie. "I've only just started looking."

"Find it for us," said the first voice, implacable as fate, as an iceberg seeking out a ship.

"Find it for us," said the second voice, relentless as cancer, as torture.

Both their voices were very loud now, beating about me in the darkness, but I refused to allow myself to flinch or quail. Show weakness before overbearing bastards like these, and they'd walk all over me. I was scared, but I couldn't afford to show it. Both sides could destroy me in a moment, for any reason or none. But they wouldn't, as long as they thought I could be of use to them. I glared out into the dark, showing impartial contempt. Angels or devils, they both spoke with the arrogance of anyone who speaks from a position of strength. But I felt pretty sure I had a question that would reveal their true position.

"If you're so powerful," I said, "why can't you find the Unholy Grail for yourselves? I thought nothing was hidden from you, or your bosses?"

"We cannot see it," said the first voice. "Its nature hides it."

"We cannot see it," said the second voice. "Its power hides it."

"But you can See what is hidden."

"So See for us."

"I don't work for free," I said flatly. "And if either of you could compel me, you'd have done it by now. So stop trying to bully me, and make me a proper offer."

There was a long pause, and the voices said together, "What would you want?"

"Information," I said. "Tell me about my mother. My missing, mysterious mother. Tell me who and what and where she is."

"We cannot tell you that," said the first voice. "We only know what it is given to us to know, and some things are forbidden, even to us."

"We cannot tell you that," said the second voice. "We know only what is said in darkness, and some things are too awful, even for us."

"So essentially," I said, "you're really nothing more than glorified messenger boys, working on a need-to-know basis. Send me back. I've got work to do."

"You do not speak to us that way," said the first voice, its harmonies rising and falling. "Defy us, and there will be punishment."

I looked across at the other presences. "Are you going to let them get away with that? If I'm hurt or damaged, you risk losing the one person who can definitely find the Unholy Grail for you."

"Do not touch the mortal," the second voice said immediately.

"You do not speak to us that way!"

"We speak how we will! We always have!"

There was a stirring and a disturbance in the darkness, as of two great armies readying themselves for war. There were angry voices, with vicious threats and vows, and ominous intent. And it was the easiest thing in the world for me to quietly slip away from them, and drop back into my body, which waited in the doorway in the alley outside Strangefellows. It had grown cold and stiff in my brief absence, and I groaned aloud as I made myself stretch reluctant muscles and pounded my hands together to get the circulation moving again. I closed my mind down tightly, pulling all my strongest mental shields into place. You don't last long in the Nightside if you don't learn a few useful tricks to guard your mind and soul from outside attack or influence. Walk around here with an open mind, and your head will end up more crowded than the underground during rush hour.

But it did mean I wouldn't be able to use my gift again. Anytime I let down my defences long enough to See, you could bet agents from Above and Below would be waiting for a chance to grab me again. And make me an offer I wouldn't be allowed to refuse. So it looked like I was going to have to solve this case the hard way: lots of legwork, asking impertinent questions, and the occasional twisting of arms.

Which meant I was going to need Suzie Shooter even more than I'd thought.

• • •

Shotgun Suzie lived in one of the sleazier areas of the Nightside, up one of those narrow side streets that lurk furtively in the shadows of the more travelled ways. Lit starkly by glaring neon signs advertising nasty little shops and studios, offering access to all the viler and more suspect pleasures and goods, at extortionate prices, of course, it was the kind of place where even the air tastes foul. The neon flickered with almost stroboscopic intensity, and painted men and women and others who were both and neither smiled coldly from backlit windows. Somewhere music was playing, harsh and tempting, and somewhere else someone was screaming, and begging for the pain to never stop.

I walked down the centre of the street, avoiding the greasy rain-slick garbage-strewn pavements. I didn't want anyone tugging at my arm or whispering coaxingly in my ear. I was careful not to catch anyone's eye, or even glance at the shop windows. It was safer that way. I didn't want to have to hurt anyone this early in the case. Suzie's place was set right in the middle of it all, between a flaying parlour and a long pig franchise. From the outside, her section of the old tenement building looked broken-down, decayed, almost abandoned. The brickwork had been blackened by countless years of pollution and neglect, covered over with layers of peeling posters, and the occasional obscene graffiti. All the windows had been boarded up. But I knew that the single paint-peeling door had a thick core of solid steel, protected by state-of-the-art locks and defences, both high-tech and magical. Suzie took her security very seriously.

I was one of the very few people she'd ever trusted with the correct

entry codes. I looked around to make sure no-one was too close, or showing too much interest, then I bent over the hidden keypad and grille. (No
point in knocking or shouting; she wouldn't respond. She never did.) I
punched in the right numbers, and spoke my name into the grille. I waited,
and a face rose slowly up out of the door, forming its details from the splin-
tered wood. It wasn't a human face. The eyes opened, one after another
after another, and studied my face, then the ugly shape sank back into the
wood again and was gone. It looked disappointed that it wasn't going to
get to do something nasty to me after all. The door swung open, and I
walked in. I was barely out of its way before it slammed shut very firmly
behind me.

The empty hallway was lit by a single naked light bulb, hanging for-
lornly from the low ceiling. Someone had nailed a dead wolf to the wall
with a rivet gun. The blood on the floor still looked sticky. A mouse was
struggling feebly in a spider's web. Suzie never was much of a one for
housekeeping. I strode down the hall and started up the rickety stairs to
the next floor. The air was damp and fusty. The light was so dim it was like
walking underwater. My feet sounded loudly on the bare wooden steps,
which was, of course, the point.

The next floor held the only two furnished rooms in the house. Suzie
had a room to sleep in, and a room to crash, and that was all that mattered to her. The bedroom door was open, and I looked in. There was a
rumpled pile of blankets in the middle of the bare wooden floor, churned
up like a nest. A filthy toilet stood in one corner, next to a battered mini-
bar she'd looted from some hotel. A wardrobe and a dressing table and a
shotgun rack holding a dozen different weapons. No Suzie. The room
smelled ripe, heavy, female, feverish.

At least she was up. That was something.

I walked down the landing. The plastered walls were cracked, and
pocked here and there with old bullet holes. Telephone numbers, hexes,
and obscure mnemonic reminders had been scrawled everywhere in lip-
stick and eyebrow pencil, in Suzie's thick blocky handwriting. The door to
the next room was closed. I pushed it open and looked in.

The blinds were drawn, as always, blocking out the lights and sounds
of the street outside, and for that matter, the rest of the world as well. Suzie
valued her privacy. Another naked light bulb provided the main illumination. Its pull chain was held together by a knot in the middle. Takeaway
food cartons littered the bare floor, along with discarded gun magazines,
empty gin bottles, and crumpled cigarette packets. Video and DVD cases
were stacked in tottering piles all along one wall. Another wall held a

huge, life-size poster of Diana Rigg as Mrs. Emma Peel, from the old *Avengers* TV show. Underneath the poster, Suzie had scrawled *My Idol* in what looked like dried blood.

Suzie Shooter was lying sprawled across a scuffed and faded green leather couch, a bottle of gin in one hand, a cigarette in one corner of her downturned mouth. She was watching a film on a great big fuck-off wide-screen television set. I strolled into the room, and into Suzie's line of view, giving her plenty of time to get used to my presence. There was a shotgun propped up against the couch, ready to hand, and a small pile of grenades on the floor by her feet. Suzie liked to be prepared for anyone who might just feel like dropping in unannounced. She didn't look round as I came to a halt beside the couch and looked at the film she was watching. It was a Jackie Chan fight fest; that scene towards the end of *Armour Of God* where four big busty black women in leather gang up on Jackie and kick the crap out of him. Good scene. The sound track seemed to consist entirely of screams and exaggerated blows. I glanced around me, but nothing had changed since my last visit. There was still no other furniture, just a bog standard computer set up on the floor. Suzie didn't even have a phone any more. She wasn't sociable. If anyone needed to contact her, there was e-mail, and that was it. Which she might not get round to reading for several days, if she didn't feel like it.

As always when she wasn't working, Suzie had let herself go. She was wearing a grubby Cleopatra Jones T-shirt, and a pair of jeans that had been laundered almost to the point of no return. No shoes, no make-up. From the look of her, it had been some time since her last gig. She was overweight, her belly bulging out over her jeans, her long blonde hair was a mess, and she smelled bad. Without taking her eyes off the mayhem on the screen, she took a long pull from her gin bottle, not bothering to take the cigarette out of her mouth first, then offered me the bottle. I took it away from her and put it on the floor, carefully out of her reach.

"Almost six years since I was last here, Suze," I said, just loud enough to be heard over the television. "Six years, and the old place hasn't changed a bit. Still utterly appalling, with a side order of downright disgusting. Garbage from all across the country probably comes here to die. I'll bet the only reason this building isn't overrun with rats is that you probably eat them."

"They're good with fries, and a few onions," said Suzie, not looking round.

"How can you live like this, Suze?"

"Practice. And don't call me Suze. Now sit down and shut up. You're interrupting a good bit."

"God, you're a slob, Suzie." I didn't sit down on the couch. I'd just had my coat cleaned. "Don't you ever clean up in here?"

"No. That way I know where everything is. What do you want, Taylor?"

"Well, apart from world peace, and Gillian Anderson dipped in melted chocolate, I'd like to see some evidence that you've been eating sensibly. You can't live on junk food. When was the last time you had some fresh fruit? What do you do for vitamin C?"

"Pills, mostly. Isn't science wonderful? I hate fruit."

"I seem to recall you're not too keen on vegetables either. It's a wonder to me you haven't come down with scurvy."

Suzie sniggered. "My system would self-destruct if it encountered anything that healthy. I eat soup with vegetables in. Occasionally. That sneaks them past my defences."

I kicked an empty ice cream tub out of the way and sighed heavily. "I hate to see you like this, Suzie."

"Then don't look."

"Fat and lazy and smug with it. Don't you have any ambitions?"

"To die gloriously." She took a deep drag on her cigarette and sighed luxuriously.

I sat on the arm of the couch. "I don't know why I keep coming back here, Suze."

"Because we monsters have to stick together." She finally turned her head to look at me, unsmiling. "Who else would have us?"

I met her gaze squarely. "You deserve better than this."

"Shows how much you know. What do you want, Taylor?"

"How long have you been lounging around here? Days? Weeks?"

She shrugged. "I am currently between cases. Bottom's dropped out of the bounty-hunting business lately."

"Most people have a life apart from their work."

"I'm not most people. Just as well, really, considering most people depress me unutterably. My work is my life."

"Killing people is a life?"

"Stick to what you're good at, that's what I always say. Hell! When I do it, it's an art form. I wonder if I could get a grant . . . Shut up and watch the film, Taylor. I hate it when people talk during the good bits."

I sat with her and watched quietly for a while. As far as I knew, I was the closest thing Shotgun Suzie had to a friend. She wasn't much of a one for getting out and meeting people, unless it involved killing them later. She only really came alive when she was working. In between cases, she shut down and vegetated, waiting for her next chance to go out and do the only thing she did well, the thing she was born to do.

"I worry about you, Suzie."

"Don't."

"You need to get out of this dump and get to know people. There *are* some out there worth knowing."

"Men have been known to walk into my life, from time to time."

It was my turn to sniff loudly. "They usually leave running."

"Not my fault if they can't keep up." She shifted her weight on the couch and farted unself-consciously.

I glared at her. "They usually leave because you made them watch *Girl On A Motorcycle* one time too many."

"That film is a classic!" Suzie said automatically. "Marianne Faithful never looked better. That film is right up there with *Easy Rider* and Roger Corman's Hells Angels movies."

"Why did you shoot me, six years ago?" I didn't know I was going to ask that until I said it.

"I had paper on you," said Suzie. "Serious paper, backed by serious money."

"You knew that paper was false. The whole thing was a setup. You had to know that . . . but you shot me anyway. Why?"

"You were leaving," she said quietly. "How else could I stop you?"

"Oh, Suze . . ."

"Why do you think you were only wounded? You know I never miss. If I'd wanted you dead, you'd be dead."

"Why was it so important for you to stop me leaving?"

She finally turned to look at me. "Because you belong here. Because . . . even monsters need to feel they're not alone. Look, what do you want here, Taylor? You're interrupting a classic."

"Bruce Lee again?" I said, just to tease her. And because I knew I'd got as much honesty out of her as both of us could stand.

"Don't show your ignorance. This is Jackie Chan."

"There's a difference?"

"Blasphemer. Jackie's got some great moves, but Bruce Lee is God."

"Speaking of whom," I said casually, "I have a case I could use some help on."

Suzie sat up and gave me her full attention for the first time. "You have a case involving Bruce Lee?"

"No. God. There are angels in the Nightside."

Suzie shrugged and gave her attention back to the television screen. "About time. Maybe they'll clean the place up."

"Maybe. But there's a distinct possibility there might not be much left of the place by the time they'd finished with it. They're looking for the Unholy Grail. I've got a client who wants me to find it first. Thought you might like to help. The money really is extremely good."

Suzie produced a remote control from somewhere underneath her and put the film on hold. Jackie froze in mid kick. Suzie looked at me. "How good?"

"I'm offering fifty thousand, out of my fee. You get twenty-five up front, and the rest when the job's done."

Suzie considered, her face impassive. "Is the job very dangerous? Will I have to kill lots of people?"

"Odds are . . . yes and yes."

She smiled. "Then I'm in."

And that was it. Suzie didn't really care about the money; she never did. She just went through the motions, so people wouldn't think they could take advantage of her. With her, it was always the job that mattered, the challenge. The only feelings of self-worth she had came from testing herself against forces that could destroy her. I took the money out of the envelope Jude had given me, peeled off half, and dropped it onto the couch beside her. She nodded, but made no move to pick it up. She didn't have a safe, or even a strongbox, on the unanswerable grounds that no-one was going to be stupid enough to steal from her. There were less painful ways to commit suicide. She turned off the television, stubbed out the last half inch of her cigarette on the leather couch, flicked it away, then fixed me with a steady stare.

"You have my full attention. Angels . . . and an Unholy Grail. Kinky. Bit out of our usual territory. Would silver work against angels?"

"Not even if you loaded it into a bazooka. You could probably strap an angel to a backpack nuke and set it off, and he wouldn't even blink. Angels are major hard-core."

Suzie looked at me for a long moment. It was always hard to tell what she was thinking, behind the cold mask she used for a face. "You religious, Taylor?"

I shrugged. "Hard not to be, in the Nightside. If only because there are no atheists in foxholes. I'm pretty sure there is a God, a Creator. I just don't think he cares about us. I don't think we matter to him. You?"

"I used to tell people I was a lapsed agnostic," she said easily. "Now I tell them I'm a born-again heretic. I hung out with this bunch of Kali worshippers for a while, but they said I was too hard-core, the wimps. Mostly . . . I believe in guns, knives, and things that go bang. All of which we're probably going to need if we're going after the Unholy Grail. I take it there will be competition?"

"Lots and lots. So you don't have any problems, about going up against angels or devils?"

She smiled coldly. "Just give me something to aim at and leave the rest to me." She frowned thoughtfully. "There was a weapon I heard of once . . . The Speaking Gun. Created specifically to kill angels. The Collector tried to bribe me with it one time, to get into my pants . . ."

"I think we'll save that for a last resort," I said, diplomatically.

She shrugged. "So, where do we start?"

"Well, I thought we'd go and have a word with the Demon Lordz."

"Those gangsta wannabes? I have seen puppies in toilet paper commercials that were more threatening than that bunch of poseurs."

"There's more to them than meets the eye."

She sniffed. "There would have to be."

I stood up. Time to get the show on the road. "Grab what you need, and let's get moving, Suzie. Above and Below have already tried to lean on me. I'm pretty sure we're working against the clock on this one."

Suzie lurched ungracefully to her feet and stomped out of the room, heading for her bedroom. I waited patiently while she threw things about, looking for what she wanted. When she came back, she looked like Shotgun Suzie again. The grubby T-shirt and faded jeans were gone, replaced by gleaming black leather jacket, trousers and knee-high boots, generously adorned with steel chains and studs. She wore two bandoliers of bullets across her impressive chest, and the hilt of her favourite pump-action shotgun peered over her right shoulder from its holster on her back. A dozen assorted grenades hung from her belt. She'd even brushed her hair and slapped on some make-up. She looked sharp and deadly and very alive. Suzie Shooter was on the job, heading into deadly peril, and she couldn't have been any happier.

"Damn," I said. "Clark Kent becomes Superman."

"Big Boy Scout," she sneered. "Who's our client on this one, Taylor?"

"The Vatican. So watch your language. You ready?"

"Does the Pope shit in the woods? I was born ready."

I made a mental note to keep her well away from Jude, and led the way out. It was a good day for someone else to die.

FOUR

Demons, Nazis, and Other Undesirables

We went uptown. The nastiest, scariest, sleaziest joints are always uptown. Where the beautiful people go, to act out their inner ugliness in private places. Uptown, where the neon becomes more stylised and the come-ons are more subtle. Where the best food and the best wine and the best drugs, and all the very best music can be yours, for a price. Which is sometimes money and sometimes self-respect, and nearly always your soul, in the end. Uptown, you can see everybody on the way up, and everyone on the way down. Birds of a feather groom together.

Walking the rain-slick streets under hot neon, with Suzie at my side like a barely restrained attack dog, it quickly became clear that there really were a lot fewer people about than usual. Just the thought of visiting angels, from Above or Below, had been enough to scare a lot of familiar faces into lying low for a while. But there were still crowds of people out and about, hurrying along temptation's rows, avoiding eye contact, lips wet with anticipation. On their way to business or pleasures they couldn't or wouldn't put off, even for the threat of Judgement Day.

Now and again, certain individuals would spot Suzie Shooter coming down the street towards them, and they would quickly and quietly disappear, slipping into convenient side streets and alleyways. Others would hide in doorways or deep shadows, shoulders hunched, heads down, hoping not to be noticed. A few actually stepped off the pavement and out into the road, to be sure of giving her plenty of room. A dangerous act in itself. It was never wise to get too close to any of the endless traffic that roared through the Nightside. Not everything that looked like a car was a car. And some of them were hungry.

When you go uptown, into neatly laid-out squares with tree-lined streets and ornate old-fashioned lamp-posts, passing increasingly expensive establishments with pretence to class and sophistication, you move among a much higher class of scumbag. There are restaurants where you have to book months in advance just to be sneered at by a waiter. Huge department stores, selling every bright and gaudy useless luxury the covetous heart could desire. Wine cellars, dispensing beverages older than civilisation that madden and inflame and bestow terrible insights. Weapon shops and influence peddlers, and quiet parlours where destinies can be adjusted and reputations restored. And, of course, all the hottest brand names and the very latest fads. Love for sale, or at least for rent, and vengeance guaranteed.

And nightclubs like you wouldn't believe.

The Nightside has the best nightclubs, hot spots, and watering holes in the world. The doors never close, the music keeps on playing, and the excitement never ends. Nowhere is the scene more now, the girls more glamorous, the setting more decadent, or the shadows more dangerous. These are places where they eat the unwary alive, but that's always been part of the attraction. The Blue Parrot, The Hanging Man, Caliban's Cavern, and Pagan Place. Once past the ominous doormen and the reinforced doors, there's every kind of music on the menu, including some live acts you would have sworn were dead. Robert Johnson, still playing the blues with weary fingers, to pay off the lien on his soul. Glenn Miller and his big band sound, still calling Pennsylvania 6-500. (The Collector had Miller on ice for a long time, but was leasing him out now, in return for a consideration best not discussed in public.) Buddy Holly, hitting his guitar like it might fight back, headlining the Rock & Roll Sky-Diving All-Stars. And the Lizard King himself, on tour from Shadows Fall, that small town in the back of beyond where legends go to die when the world stops believing in them. Plus a whole bunch of Elvises, John Lennons, and Jimi Hendrixes, of varying authenticity. You paid your money and you took your choices.

Suzie and I were on our way to The Pit. A relatively new concern, recommended for the seriously discerning pleasure-seeker. An extremely private place, for those in whom pleasure and pain combine to form a whole far greater than the sum of its parts. Where caressing hands had sharpened fingernails, and every kiss left a little blood in the mouth. The Pit, not sur-

prisingly, was underground. From the street up, the place was just another
restaurant, specialising in meals made from extinct animals. To get to The
Pit, you had to go down a long set of dirty stone steps, to an alley well
below street level. No flashing neon here, no dazzling come-ons. You either knew what you were looking for, and where to find it, or you weren't
the kind of patron The Pit wanted to attract. It was the kind of place where
if you had to ask the price of something, you couldn't afford it. I'd been
there once before, to rescue a succubus who wanted out of her contract. It
all got rather messy and unpleasant, but that's life for you. In the
Nightside.

Suzie and I walked down the alley, ignoring the long queue. A few of
those we passed scowled and muttered, but no-one said anything. Suzie
and I are well-known faces, and our reputations went before us. A few
people produced camcorders, just in case there was trouble. The solid steel
door that was the only entry into The Pit was guarded by two of the
Demon Lordz, scowling menacingly at one and all, their muscular arms
folded across their heavy chests.

At first glance, the Lordz looked like just another street gang. Both
wore dark, polished leathers, fashionably scruffy, and heavy with metal
studs and hanging chains. They wore bright tribal colours on their faces,
gaudy daubs on skin so black it glistened blue. They wore strap-on devil's
horns on their foreheads, and when they smiled or scowled they showed
teeth filed to sharp points. But there was something more about them, in
their unnatural stillness, in the boiling air of menace they projected, that
showed they were so much more than just another set of gangsta
wannabes. Certainly none of the punters waiting patiently to get in even
thought about trying to jump the queue. They were mostly rich kids, in all
the latest fetish gear, whose parents could probably buy and sell The Pit
out of petty cash, but none of that mattered here. It wasn't who you were,
but who you knew, that got you in.

Suzie studied the two Lordz standing guard before the firmly closed
door and scowled ominously as they refused even to notice our presence.
She tended to take such slights personally. She looked around the alley,
then sneered impartially at the Lordz and the queue.

"You know all the best places to bring a girl, Taylor. I just know I'm
going to have to disinfect my boots later. Do we have anything resembling
a plan?"

"Oh, I thought we'd just barge our way in, insult all the right people,
and kick the crap out of anyone who annoys us."

Suzie smiled briefly. "My kind of party."

I walked right up to the Lordz, radiating confidence. Suzie stuck close beside me, still scowling. Some of the queue decided that they'd try another club. The doormen finally deigned to acknowledge our existence. They were trying hard to look cool and aloof, and not quite bringing it off. The clenched fists gave it away. The one on the left looked down on me from his full six feet four.

"Back of the queue," he growled out of one corner of his mouth. "No jumping. No bribes. No exceptions. Members only. And you two would be wasting your time anyway. We have a very strict dress code."

"So piss off," said the one on the right, from his full six foot six. "Before we have to do something to you that might upset the nice ladies and gentlemen in the queue."

"Let me kill them, Taylor," said Suzie. "It's been a slow night so far."

"Keep your bitch under control, Taylor," said the one on the left. "Or we'll take her inside and teach her some manners. We might let you have her back, in a week or two, when we've broken her in properly."

Suzie's shotgun all but whistled as it flew out of the holster on her back, and the Demon Lord shut up suddenly as she rammed both barrels up his nostrils.

"I'd really like to see you try," she said, smiling her awful smile.

"This," I explained to the Demon Lordz, "Is Suzie Shooter. Also known as Shotgun Suzie, also known as Oh Christ, it's her, run."

"Oh *shit*," said both doormen, pretty much in unison. Most of the waiting queue decided at that point that it was time they were somewhere else, their hurrying feet clattered loudly down the alley. But a few actually pressed forward a little, murmuring with excitement, their eyes hot and hungry for a little real blood and death to start the evening off with a bang. The Demon Lord with the gun up his nose tried to stand even stiller than usual, while the other doorman spoke urgently into a concealed speaker grille beside the door. There was a pause, just long enough for all parties concerned to get uneasy, then the heavy steel door swung backwards, and bright light and hot and heavy music spilled out into the night air. I sauntered into The Pit, doing my best to look like I was slumming, while Suzie gave the doormen a really nasty grin before following me in, still covering both Demonz with her shotgun, until the door had closed completely between them. She started to holster her gun, then took a good look around her, and decided to hold on to it.

It was hellishly noisy inside The Pit, with death metal guitars blasting from concealed speakers. The lighting was stark and harsh and almost painfully bright. No comforting gloom here, no shadows to hide in; everything was right out in the open, so every act and reaction could be enjoyed and savoured by the milling crowd. Most of the club's patrons eddied back and forth across the open floor of the great ballroom, looking tastefully chic in gothic leathers, cut-away rubber, and spray-on latex. But the real action was taking place in spotlit nooks and crannies around the perimeter.

The bare stone walls had been decorated to look as much like a medieval dungeon as possible, and everywhere you looked there were happy victims being stretched on racks, or suspended in hanging cages, or enjoying the embrace of an iron maiden, filled with hypodermic needles instead of metal spikes. There were always new shrieks of pain and joy, and howls of approval from the rapt onlookers. The victims writhed languorously as they suffered, playing to the crowd. Here and there a tall dominatrix, beautiful as a sharpened knife, all dark leathers and straps and buckles, would stride proudly through the throng in search of prey, her painted face haughty with indifference. Men and women bowed low to these mistresses of pain and tried to lick their polished boots as they passed. There were whippings and scourgings and brandings, to the delight of all concerned. Blood flowed and fell, and trickled away down hidden runnels in the floor. The close air stank of fresh sweat, cheap perfume, and industrial-strength disinfectant.

Not unlike a dentist's, really.

Suzie looked about her, entirely unimpressed, her face heavy with disinterest. "I thought the Demon Lordz were supposed to be a street gang? What are they doing running a joint like this for high-class pervs with more money than sense?"

"They're only playing at being gangstas," I said. "This . . . is their true nature coming out."

One of the dominatrixes stalked towards us, a heavy bullwhip coiled in her hands. Her black lips widened in a cruel smile. Suzie looked round and caught the dominatrix's eye. Without missing a beat, the mistress of pain changed direction and kept going, losing herself in the crowd. She knew the real thing when she saw it. I looked around me, taking my time. None of it moved me. Here, they only played at sin and damnation. I had far too much experience of the real thing to be impressed.

Over in a corner, a man was having his nipple pierced and being a real wimp about it.

I finally caught the eye of one of the female Demon Lordz, and she came through the crowd towards me. People hurried to get out of her way. She was tall and blonde, all legs and high tits, every inch the Aryan ideal. She wore the same scruffy outfit and bright tribal colours as the two at the door, right down to the fake horns on her head. She came to a halt before me, smiling coldly with blue lips to show off her pointed teeth. Her eyes were black on black. She had to know Suzie was covering her with the shotgun, but she showed no signs of caring.

"What are you doing back here, Taylor? I thought we made it very clear after your last visit that you were never to darken our doors again."

"Just visiting," I said calmly. "Seeing how the other five per cent lives. I love what you've done with this place. Very atmospheric. Just the ticket, if you want to play at being damned for a while. But then, you'd know all about that, wouldn't you?"

"You don't belong here," said the female Demon. "Either of you. Not your kind of scene, is it?"

Suzie sniffed loudly, entirely unmoved by the sweaty suffering going on around her. She didn't care much about other people's lives at the best of times. And I knew better than to show any signs of condemnation or compassion. The Demon would only have seen it as a sign of weakness. I've never had any time for emotional excesses. I can't afford to be vulnerable, or give up any part of my self-control. Only rigid self-discipline has kept me alive in the Nightside. It keeps me one step ahead of the forces that have been trying to kill me ever since I was a small child.

I felt almost wistful, watching the happy S&M freaks at their play. Must be nice to be able to *pretend* that you're in danger, while still being absolutely safe. Their various practices didn't upset or disturb me. You learn tolerance early in the Nightside. You can't keep on being outraged all the time. It wears you out.

"What do you *want*, Taylor?"

I smiled pleasantly at the female Demon. "I want to see Mr. Bones and Mr. Blood. I'm here on business. And the sooner they agree to see me, the sooner I can get my business over with, and Suzie and I can be on our way. Keep us waiting around, and we're bound to find some trouble to get into. We're already freaking out some of your customers. They came here for the illusion of danger, not the real thing."

The female Demon looked around quickly. A few of the bright young things were already drifting towards the door, shooting uneasy glances at Suzie. The blonde Demon snarled and headed for the winding metal steps that led up to the next floor. Suzie and I followed after her, sticking close as we passed through the merry throng. Someone pinched my arse. They wouldn't have dared pinch Suzie's. Out of the corners of my eyes, I could see other Demon Lordz working their way through the crowd to join us. There seemed to be quite a few of them.

The steps led up to a private office that took up the whole of the next floor. Another steel door sealed the office off from the partying below. The female Demon hammered on the door with her fist, while glaring into the lens of an overhead security camera. More Demon Lordz were climbing the steps, cutting off our retreat. Not that I had any intention of retreating until I'd got what I wanted. Suzie was looking out over the company below. Her upper lip curled briefly.

"You don't approve?" I said quietly.

"Amateur night," Suzie said dismissively. "I take pain seriously."

There were any number of ways I could have pursued that remark, but I chose not to follow any of them. Sometimes, that's what friends are for. I looked down the steps, and a dozen Demonz glared back at me. I gave them my best *I know something you don't* smile. They didn't seem particularly impressed. The door finally opened, and the female Demon led us into the private office.

The noise shut off abruptly as the door closed behind the last of the Demon Lordz. We could have been on another planet. Excellent sound-proofing, though whether magical or high-tech wasn't immediately apparent. The whole floor had been converted into one very comfortable meeting place, stuffed with every kind of luxury and indulgence imaginable. Chairs so comfortable that Rip Van Winkle would never have woken up if he'd dozed off in one of them. A massive drinks cabinet, with every potable in the world, plus a few from stranger places. Winter wine, worm-wood brandy, crème de Tartarus. Bowls on low tables, full of multi-coloured pills and assorted powders. A dozen large television screens covered one wall, all showing different video games. A fifteenth-century hanging tapestry, depicting the fall of Lucifer, not quite long enough to conceal the old and recent blood-stains on the carpet below it, shut off one corner. Most of the floor was glass, presumably reinforced, so that we could all look down on the mortals below, going about their various painful pleasures in eerie silence. All they saw was a mirror, showing what they loved most: themselves. Somebody cleared his throat pointedly, and I looked down the length of the office at Mr. Blood and Mr. Bones, standing on either side of their heavy mahogany desk. They ran the Demon Lordz, as well as The Pit. Neither of them looked at all happy to see me.

Unlike their fellow gang members, Mr. Blood and Mr. Bones had no time for the traditional street cred look. They both wore power suits, expertly cut and tailored. Their thick black hair was slicked back from their foreheads, and there were bright flashes of gold when they smiled to show off their pointed teeth. They looked sharp and keen and very businesslike. Yuppies from Hell. Mr. Bones was tall and slender, with wasted aesthetic features. His eyes were a pale, pale blue, and the only thing colder was his smile. Mr. Blood was large and ponderous, with red beefy features. His eyes were bright pink, like an albino's. Both Lordz held themselves with the easy arrogance of accustomed power. Behind us, the rest of the gang had filed into the office. I counted thirty-two, half and half men and women. They lounged around in various cocky postures, trying to look hard. I ignored them, knowing that would upset them the most. Suzie still had her pump-action shotgun in her hands, pointed exactly half-way between Mr. Blood and Mr. Bones. It didn't seem to worry them too much.

"Good of you to join us," said Mr. Bones. His voice was soft and effortlessly vicious, a mere breath of air. "You were beginning to disturb the dear patrons, and we can't have that, can we?"

"Indeed not," said Mr. Blood. His voice was hearty with false cheer. "Can I interest either of you in a chilled glass of Moët & Chandon? We've just opened a bottle. A little caviar, perhaps? Or maybe something a little tastier to chew on?"

He gestured amiably with a fat hand, and the hanging tapestry drew back of its own accord, to reveal a young woman hanging in chains, slumped in the corner. She was barely out of her teens, entirely naked, and quite dead. There was a big hole in her side, from where something had been feeding on her. Stubs of broken-off ribs showed in the pale red meat, and from the dark depths of the hole, it was clear that some of her internal organs had been removed. There were tooth marks on the broken ribs. Her hair was black as night, her skin was white as snow, with not even the faintest tinge of colour in her lips or nipples. And then my heart missed a beat as the dead woman slowly raised her head and looked at me. Her body was dead, but her soul remained, trapped inside. Her eyes were focussed on me, and full of suffering. She knew what was happening to her. Her mouth moved silently.

Help me . . . help me . . .

"The suffering on offer below wasn't enough for this one," said Mr. Blood. "She insisted on the real thing. And we were only too happy to oblige her. A tasty young morsel, eh, Mr. Bones?"

"What fools these mortals be," breathed Mr. Bones. "But they do make such wonderful snacks."

Suzie stepped forward and shot the dead woman in the head. At point-blank range, both barrels together blew her whole head apart, leaving nothing behind but a great crimson-and-grey splatter of blood and brains and bone fragments on the wall behind her. The headless body kicked a few times, then was still. Suzie pumped fresh bullets into position and looked calmly at Mr. Bones and Mr. Blood.

"Some things I don't put up with."

"Quite right," I said, while the two gang leaders were still numb with shock and outrage. "You forget your place, Demon Lordz. You're not at home now. Time for us to talk seriously, I think. So drop the illusions. We're not tourists. Show us your real faces."

And in the blink of an eye, the gangsta street gang and their two yuppie leaders were gone, replaced by a whole crowd of crimson-skinned medieval demons. Eight feet tall and overpoweringly brutal, they crowded together before and around us, scarlet as sin, stinking of brimstone, with goats' horns curling up from their foreheads and cloven hooves for feet. Their male and female attributes were sarcastically exaggerated. So were their fangs and claws. Long, twitching tails hung down between their bent legs. Suzie sniffed loudly, unimpressed, and glared at me.

"You know I hate surprises. So this is why you had me carve a cross in each of my bullets and dip them in holy water."

"I believe in being prepared," I said calmly. "Allow me to introduce the real Demon Lordz. A batch of very minor demons, on the run from Hell, living among us as humans for the pleasures it affords them."

"Coffee!" said the Demonz, their snarling voices overlapping. "Ice cream! Cold showers!"

"And all the mortals we can torture," said Mr. Bones. "We can't keep them away. And they pay us to do it to them!"

"Not that we do much of the tormenting ourselves, these days," said Mr. Blood. "We find it better to delegate. All our dominatrixes are fully human. No-one understands how to inflict pain better than a trained professional human. You mortals are subtler than we could ever be . . ."

"And besides, some of us had trouble with the concept of safe words," said Mr. Bones, glaring about him.

"If you're all real demons," said Suzie, "how did you escape from Hell?"

The Demonz sniggered and elbowed each other in the ribs. Mr. Blood giggled. "Why, this is Hell, Faustus, nor are we out of it. Ah, the old jokes are still the best."

"Answer the lady," I said.

Mr. Bones shrugged. "Let's just say we're political refugees, and leave it at that. We're hiding out from those who would seek to drag us back."

"If you're trying to hide," said Suzie, "why call your place The Pit? Isn't that kinda drawing attention to yourselves?"

"No-one ever said demons were smart," I observed. "And they really are only very minor demons."

The Demon Lordz moved in a little closer, flexing their claws. The stench of brimstone was almost overpowering. I could feel my eyes smarting. I smiled kindly upon them, utterly casual.

"What do you want here, Taylor?" said Mr. Bones.

"The Unholy Grail has come to the Nightside," I said.

"We know. We don't have it," Mr. Blood said immediately.

"Never thought for a moment that you did," I said easily. "It's way out of your league. But you know people. You have contacts. You hear things, from others of your kind. So if anyone knows who's got the Unholy Grail, or is closest to getting it, it's you."

Mr. Blood shook his horned head firmly. He sat on one corner of his desk, and it groaned loudly under his weight. "We don't know, and we don't want to know. We've put a lot of effort into finding our niche and not being returned. If the dark chalice, Iscariot's Bane, really has come here, then you can bet good money that all the real movers and shakers will be out after it, like sharks tasting blood in the water."

"There are angels in the Nightside," said Mr. Bones, grimacing as though he'd tasted something bitter. "Ranks and degrees far greater than us. They are death and destruction; the will of the Highest and the Lowest made manifest in the mortal world. Nothing material can hope to stand against them."

"So we are keeping our heads down and staying very quiet on the sidelines," said Mr. Blood. "Until the Elect and the Damned have finished their business here and departed. We have no intention of being found out, and dragged back Below. Not when there are still so many subtle pleasures to be enjoyed here."

"Life is sweet," said Mr. Bones. "In this tastiest of worlds."

"The Unholy Grail is a major prize," I suggested. "You could use it to bargain for power and wealth and protection."

"You don't use the Judas Cup," said Mr. Blood. "It uses you. It is temptation and corruption, and the seduction of fools. It gives nothing that it does not take away, and damnation follows in its wake. Even such as we are frightened of the Unholy Grail."

The Demonz stirred uneasily, as though even the mention of the dark chalice was enough to call it.

"However," said Mr. Bones, "there is a prize that we could present to the movers and shakers of the Nightside that might well win us power and wealth and protection."

"Oh yes?" I said politely. "And what might that be?"

"The heads of John Taylor and Suzie Shooter," said Mr. Bones, smiling unpleasantly. "Separated from your annoying and intrusive bodies, of course. And thus we avenge ourselves on your many slights, while winning respect from all. A plan with no drawbacks."

"Hold everything," said Mr. Blood urgently. "Can I have a word with you? Have you lost your mind? This is *John Taylor* and *Shotgun Suzie* we're talking about!"

"So?"

"So I like having my internal organs where they are, and not splattered all over the surroundings! It's rather difficult to enjoy the subtler pleasures when your passionate parts have been ripped off and stuffed where the sun don't shine! These are dangerous people!"

"*We outnumber them!*"

"So?"

"Sweet Lucifer, you're a wimp!" said Mr. Bones. "Don't know how you got to be a demon in the first place. Kill the mortals! Rend their bodies and eat their flesh, but make sure the heads are intact!"

"Oh shut the hell up," said Suzie Shooter.

She lifted her shotgun and shot Mr. Bones point-blank. The blessed and sanctified bullets tore his crimson face right off, revealing a dirty yellow skull. He fell backwards, screaming piteously. Mr. Blood got up off his desk in a hurry and glared at his partner, writhing in agony on the floor.

"*See!*"

"He'll repair himself in a minute or two," I said quietly to Suzie, as she pumped fresh ammunition into place. The Demonz were circling us slowly now, nerving themselves up to attack. "No earthly weapon can defeat a demon."

"In which case," said Suzie, tracking the nearest Demonz with her gun, "this would be a really good time for the cavalry to make an appearance. Or failing that, for you to produce one of your last-minute miracle saves."

I considered the matter thoughtfully. The Demonz were closing in. Mr. Bones sat up, holding his tattered face together with his hands, as the crimson features slowly knit themselves back together. Even Mr. Blood came out from behind his desk.

"Taylor!" said Suzie. "Anytime now would be good!"

I held up a hand and smiled. Everyone stopped moving.

"In the Beginning," I said, "God said *Let there be light,* and there was. If a man could summon up that light, from the very first moments of creation, and look into it without burning out his eyes or his reason, then that man would have at his command a light that could burn away all the darkness in the world."

For a long moment, nobody said anything. Mr. Bones stood up, glaring out of his ravaged face.

"You don't have that kind of power!"

"Don't I?" I said.

The Demonz looked at each other, remembering things I'd done and other things I was supposed to have done. I smiled at them easily.

"Just . . . get out of here," said Mr. Bones. "Get out, and leave us alone. We don't have your bloody Grail."

"Then point me at someone who might."

"Try the Fourth Reich," Mr. Blood said quietly. "They've been throwing around some serious money for information on the dark chalice. If nothing else, they'll have better information than we do."

"See how easy it can be, when everyone acts reasonable?" I said. "There's a lesson for us all in that, I feel. Time we were leaving. Don't bother to show us out."

• • •

We left The Pit behind us and strolled off into the night. If anything, the streets were even emptier. I knew where the Fourth Reich had their quarters. Everyone did. They publicized it hard enough, with everything from leaflets handed out in the street to prime-time advertising. The New Nazi Crusade, or the panzerpoofters, as everyone else called them, weren't short of money. Just followers. They met regularly in an old assembly room right on the edge of uptown. Monied or not, no-one wanted them any closer than that. Last I heard, they were down to a hundred members or so, and they'd given up holding uniformed parades after a dozen golems turned up at the last one to kick their nasty arses up one side of the street and down the other. But they did still have serious financial backers. They might not have the Unholy Grail themselves, but they might well have been able to buy information on who did.

Suzie looked at me suddenly. "Could you really have summoned up the light of Creation?"

I smiled. "What do you think?"

"I never know when you're bluffing."

"Neither does anyone else. That's the point."

"I notice you're not answering the question."

"Ah, Suzie, don't you want a little mystery in your life?"

She sniffed. "The only mystery in my life is why I continue to put up with you."

And that was when a figure stepped imperiously out of the shadows ahead, blocking our way. A city gent in a smart suit, complete with bowler hat and rolled umbrella, stood smiling before us. Late forties, cold eyes and colder smile, charming and sophisticated and every bit as dangerous as a coiled cobra. Suzie drew her shotgun and aimed it at him in one smooth motion.

"Relax, Suzie," said Walker. "It's only me."

"I know it's you," said Suzie.

She kept her shotgun trained on him as he approached unhurriedly. Walker, to do him credit, didn't seem in the least perturbed. It was part of his style that nothing ever touched him, despite the many fateful decisions he had to make every day. Walker represented the Authorities, the people in the background who really run things in the Nightside. Inasmuch as anybody does. Don't ask me who these shadowy people might be. I've no idea. No-one has. Sometimes I wonder if even Walker knows for sure. Still, he spoke on their behalf, and his word was law, with any amount of force available to back him up. People lived and died at Walker's word, and he'd never been known to give a damn. He came to a halt before us, leaned casually upon his umbrella and raised his bowler politely to Suzie.

"I hear you're looking for the Unholy Grail," he said. "Along with practically everyone else in the Nightside who considers himself or herself a power or a player. I, on the other hand, have been instructed by my superiors to withdraw all my people from the Nightside. The word is that I am to let the angels from Above and Below fight it out among themselves. And if anyone here gets hurt, well, if they're in the Nightside, they deserve everything that comes to them. I have the feeling the Authorities see the coming of the angels as an opportunity for a little spring cleaning. Take out the trash, so to speak. The Authorities don't care about individuals, you see. They only care about the long view, and the big picture."

"And preserving the status quo," I said.

"Exactly. Their feeling seems to be that the sooner one side or the other acquires the appalling object, the sooner they'll all leave and things around here can get back to what passes for normal. They don't like upsets like this; it's bad for business. It doesn't really matter which side ends up with the Unholy Grail; the Authorities will work out some way to turn a profit. They always do."

"This is insane," I said, keeping my voice level as my temper rose. "Don't they realise how powerful the Unholy Grail is?"

"Possibly not. Perhaps they are being overconfident. But I have my orders. Officially, none of my people can get involved. But of course, you're not one of my people, Taylor. Officially. So such restrictions don't apply to you, do they?"

I nodded slowly. "So, once again I'm doing your dirty work, am I? Cleaning up the messes you're not allowed to touch."

"It is what you do best," said Walker. "I have every confidence in you. Of course, if you screw up, you're nothing to do with me." He looked at Suzie's shotgun, still trained rock steady on him, and raised an elegant eyebrow. "My dear Suzie, as bloodthirsty as ever. You don't really think guns are going to help you against angels, do you?"

"There's always the Speaking Gun," I said, and Walker looked at me sharply.

"The depths and range of your knowledge never cease to amaze me, Taylor. But a word of warning: some cures are worse than the disease."

Suzie gave him a hard look. "You know about the Speaking Gun?"

Walker smiled coldly. "Of course, my dear. It's my job to know about things like that. I know all the weapons powerful enough to bring down or destroy the Nightside. As for the Speaking Gun, only the truly irresponsible or the seriously deluded would even consider using such a weapon."

"Any idea where such a thing might be found?" I said. "The Collector's supposed to have had it for a while."

"And couldn't hold on to it," said Walker. "Which should tell you something. Even if I did know, I wouldn't tell you. For your and everyone else's good. Trust me on this, Taylor. You're in deep enough waters as it is."

"What is the Authorities' position on the angels themselves?" I asked, acting like I'd given up on the Speaking Gun. It didn't fool Walker in the least, but he went along with it.

"Their position is that they don't have a position. We are on the sidelines in this, and intend to stay there until all the violence and mass destruction are safely over, one way or another. Then we will return, to supervise the picking up of pieces."

"People are going to get hurt," I said. "Good people."

"This is the Nightside," said Walker. "Good people don't come here." He smiled at Suzie. "Good to see you out and working again, my dear. You know I worry about you so."

"I like to think of you being worried," said Suzie. The gun she had on him hadn't wavered once.

"Don't you care at all about the carnage that's coming?" I said, and the anger rising in my voice brought his gaze snapping back to me. "If angels go to war in the Nightside, the whole place could end up as rubble, or one big cemetery. What happens to your precious status quo then?"

Walker looked at me almost sadly. "The Nightside will survive, no matter how many people die. The major players will survive, and all the more important businesses. They're protected. No-one else matters, in the great scheme of things. And no, Taylor, I don't care how many die. Because the Nightside has never been more than a job to me. If I had my way, I'd wipe out the whole sick freak show and start over. But I have my orders."

"And the Unholy Grail?"

Walker pursed his lips, and shrugged. "I wouldn't worry too much about that. The odds are it's just another religious con job, another fake relic for fools to fight over. There have been more versions of the true Grail passing through here than there were copies of the Maltese Falcon. And even if this Unholy Grail does turn out to be the real thing, from what I've seen of its history, it's never brought anyone any real happiness or lasting power. Let the angels take it away, to Above or Below. We're better off without it. The Unholy Grail is nothing more than tinsel and glamour and shoddy dreams, just like everything else in the Nightside."

"And if it is . . . what everyone's afraid it is?" said Suzie.

"Then it's just as well you and Taylor are on the job, isn't it? So, off you go. Have fun. Try not to break anything too important. But if you do get your hands on the Unholy Grail, don't be foolish enough to hang on to the dreadful thing yourselves. I have to go to enough funerals in the line of duty as it is. The best you'll be able to achieve in this appalling business is to decide which side to hand it over to. Which may not be as straight-forward as you think. You see, I know who your client really is. And you only think you do."

I started to say something, but Walker had already turned his back on us and was walking unhurriedly away. Head held high and back ramrod straight, as always. He'd said everything he'd come to say, sowed all the right doubts, and now wild horses couldn't drag another word out of him. I shook my head slowly. No-one can mess with your mind like Walker.

Suzie continued to cover him with her shotgun until he rounded a corner and was safely out of sight, then she holstered the gun with one swift motion, and turned to me. "What was that all about, Taylor? Who is our client?"

"The Vatican, supposedly." I scowled thoughtfully. "Represented by an undercover priest called Jude."

"Like in St. Jude's?"

"Presumably. It occurs to me now that I never did check out his credentials properly. I don't usually slip up like that. There's just something about the man . . . that makes you want to trust him. Which in the Nightside should be automatic grounds for suspicion. If we do get our hands on the Unholy

Grail, I think I'll make a point of asking some really awkward and pointed questions before I hand it over to anyone. Come on, Suzie. Let's get over to the Fourth Reich's headquarters. Before someone else does."

• • •

The old assembly room currently hosting the last great hope of the Fourth Reich was situated at the end of a quiet side street, in a largely residential area. The kind of place where people kept to themselves, minded their own business, and watched the world from behind drawn curtains. The street was empty, the night unusually quiet. Suzie and I strolled down the deserted street, our footsteps sounding unusually loud and carrying. No-one appeared to challenge us as we approached the assembly room. Which was also not usual. Suzie and I stopped outside the front door. It was standing slightly ajar. Suzie unholstered her shotgun, and scowled at the door. I looked at her enquiringly.

"What is it, Suze?"

"Don't call me that. It's too quiet. Those Nazi freaks always have their martial music running full blast, so they can puff out their chests and march up and down to it and shout *Heil!* at each other. This is their usual meeting time, but I can't hear a damned thing." She stepped cautiously forward and put her face to the crack of the door. She sniffed a few times. "Cordite. Smoke. Someone's been firing guns in there."

She looked at me, and I nodded. Suzie kicked the door in and charged on in, gun at the ready. I followed after her, at a more sedate pace. I don't carry a gun. I've never felt the need. I soon caught up with Suzie. She'd stopped not far inside. We stood together and looked around the old assembly room, taking our time. There was no need to hurry any more.

The long hall the Fourth Reich used as their headquarters and meeting place was a fair size. Far too big for the small-scale rallies that were all they could manage these days. And every inch of the great open floor was covered with dead bodies. Dozens of dead Nazis, all in full uniform, all of them soaked in blood and riddled with bullet holes. They lay where they had fallen, outstretched hands reaching out for help that never came, like so many discarded toy soldiers. The walls had taken a lot of hits too. The swastikaed flags and Nazi memorabilia and old curling photos covering the walls had been torn apart by sustained gun-fire. Most hung in tatters, pitiful remnants of a dead empire. And there was blood everywhere, splashed and splattered across the walls, running down to form thick pools between the bodies on the floor.

Suzie was on full alert, raking every inch of the hall with savage eyes, swivelling her shotgun back and forth, searching for an enemy or a target. Suzie only ever really came alive when there was a chance of killing someone.

But there was nothing moving in the assembly room but us. The Fourth Reich was over before it even got started. This was a place of the dead now.

"Whatever happened here, we missed it," said Suzie.

"Someone else looking for the Unholy Grail got here first," I said, stepping carefully forward, over and around the piled-together bodies. "And whatever questions they asked, they sure as hell didn't like the answers they got."

"Whoever that someone was, they had a hell of a lot of firepower," said Suzie, moving cautiously forward after me. "You couldn't do this much damage with handguns. We're talking heavy-duty weaponry. Given the fire patterns, at least a dozen automatic weapons, maybe more. If the Nazis had any weapons, it doesn't look like they got the chance to use them. I don't see anyone dead not wearing a uniform." She knelt beside one corpse and checked for a pulse in the neck. She shook her head briefly and stood up. "Still warm, though. This all happened fairly recently."

I looked around me, estimating the numbers. "We're looking at . . . at least a hundred dead people here. Most of their organisation. Maybe all of it."

Suzie sniggered suddenly. "Hey, Taylor, what do you call a hundred dead Nazis? A good start."

"Cheap, Suzie, even for you. You'll be doing knock-knock jokes next." I stopped and looked at a huge poster of Adolf Hitler on the wall beside me. Blood had splashed across half his face. Some symbols are just too obvious, even for me. "They say he owned the Holy Grail."

"Didn't do the silly bugger a lot of good in the long run, did it?"

"Good point." I looked back at the dead Nazis, trying to summon up some sympathy, and failing. Given a chance, they would have done this to the whole world, and laughed while they did it. To hell with them. A thought struck me. "Men with guns did this, Suzie. Not angels."

Suzie nodded. "Hard to visualise an angel with an Uzi. What do we do now?"

"We search the place thoroughly. Just in case whoever did this missed something. Something that might tell us where to go next. I'm a private detective, remember? Find me some nice juicy clues, so I can smile enigmatically over them."

It took us the best part of an hour, but eventually we found our clue. He was kneeling behind a piano at the far end of the hall, next to a half-open fire exit door. A white statue of a man, dressed in a smart black suit. He was crouched down right next to the piano, as though trying to hide from something. And given the horrified scream still fixed on his gleaming white face, a pretty damned awful something at that. Suzie and I studied him carefully.

"Just when you think you've seen everything," Suzie said finally. "Marble?"

"I don't think so." I touched a fingertip to the contorted white face, brought the fingertip to my mouth, and tasted it.

"Well?" said Suzie.

"Salt," I said. "It's salt."

"A statue made of salt?"

"This isn't a statue. I've seen this work before, at St. Jude's. Someone, or more properly something, turned a living human being into salt, just like this."

Suzie curled her upper lip. "Kinky. Why salt?"

"Lot's wife looked back to see the Lord's angels at work. And was turned to salt."

"Creepy," said Suzie. "Big-time creepy. But why just this man, and not any of the others?"

I considered the matter. "This isn't one of the Nazis. He isn't wearing a uniform. More likely, this was one of the people who wiped out the Nazis. Because they couldn't, or wouldn't, deliver the Unholy Grail to their attackers. Then . . . the angels turned up. The ambushers disappeared out this fire exit at speed, but this poor bastard either didn't move fast enough, or thought he could hide here. Search his pockets, Suzie."

She looked at me. "Why do I have to do it?"

"Hey, I tasted his face."

Suzie sniffed, put away her gun, and frisked the statue's clothing with practiced thoroughness. A small pile of all the usual junk formed on the floor before him, while I studied the silently screaming face.

"You know, Suzie, there's something familiar about this guy."

"Nothing in the coat pockets."

"I've seen him before somewhere . . ."

"Nothing in the trouser pockets . . . except a piece of old gum in his handkerchief. Now that is really disgusting."

"Got it!" I said triumphantly. "This guy braced me in Strangefellows, earlier tonight. He wanted me to work for his boss and didn't take it at all well when I declined."

"Who was he working for?" said Suzie, straightening up and rubbing her hands briskly against her jacket.

"He didn't say. But he knew my client was a priest, even though Jude was travelling incognito. Called him a 'pew-polisher.' Which means this guy has to be working for one of the major players. Someone with real information as to what's going on in the Nightside."

Suzie frowned. "Walker?"

"No. This isn't his style. Too crude. Besides, he said he'd taken all his people out, and I believe him. No, this has to be the work of some of the real movers and shakers. The Collector, Nasty Jack Starlight, the Smoke Ghosts, the Lord of Tears . . ."

And then my eye fell on something on the floor, tucked under the statue's ankle. A small black case, almost hidden in the shadows. I gestured to Suzie, and she helped me manhandle the salt statue to one side. It felt eerily light and strangely delicate, as though it might shatter and fall apart under rough handling. I pushed the black case out into the light with the tip of my shoe. It was about a foot long, eight inches wide, and its surface was a strangely dull matte black. Suzie prodded it with the barrel of her gun. Nothing happened. We both knelt down to study the case more closely. Neither of us felt like rushing things. We both had extensive experience of booby-traps. It took me a while to make it out, but I finally recognised a familiar symbol, set out in bas-relief on the case's lid. A large initial C, containing a stylised crown.

"The Collector," said Suzie. "I'd know his mark anywhere."

"Whatever's in the case must be important," I said slowly. "This guy stopped here to try and open the case, and the angel got him."

"A weapon?" said Suzie.

"Seems likely. But he never got a chance to use it."

"Do we open it?" said Suzie.

"Give me a minute," I said.

I couldn't afford to open my gift for finding things all the way, not with angels hovering in the overworld, waiting for the chance to grab me again. But I could ease my third eye, my private eye, open just a crack, just enough to find out what defences the Collector had built into the case. I braced myself, ready to shut down all of the way if I even sensed anyone watching me, but it only took me a few seconds to sense there were no defences, and no booby-traps. Faced with an angel, this guy must have revoked all the case's protections to try and get at the contents faster. I shut down my third eye, and re-established all my mental shields.

And then I opened the case.

The smell hit me first. The smell of hardworking horses, the scent of dogs maddened on heat, the stench of freshly spilled guts. I pushed the lid all the way back. And there, nestled in a bed of black velvet, was the ugliest handgun I have ever seen. It was made of meat. Of flesh and bone, dark-veined gristle, and shards of cartilage, held together with strips of pale skin. Living tissues, shaped into a killing tool. Thin slabs of bone made up the handle, surrounded by freckled skin. The flushed skin had a hot and sweaty look. The trigger was a long canine tooth, and the red meat of the barrel glistened wetly.

"Is that . . . what I think it is?" said Suzie.

I swallowed hard. "It fits the description." We were both speaking very quietly.

"The Speaking Gun. The Collector had it after all."

"Yes."

"Is it . . . alive, do you think?"

"Good question. No, don't touch it. You might wake it."

Suzie leaned in close, wrinkling her nose at the smell, then frowned and turned her head to one side. Strands of her long blonde hair fell down, almost touching the thing as she listened. She straightened up again and looked at me. "I think it's breathing."

"The Speaking Gun," I said. "A gun created specifically to kill angels, from Above and Below. Damn . . . We are in deep spiritual waters here, Suzie."

"Who made it?" she said suddenly. "Who'd want to be able to kill angels?"

"No-one knows for sure. Merlin's name has been bandied about, but he gets blamed for a lot of stuff . . . There's always The Lamentation or The Engineer, but they usually deal in more abstract threats . . ." Something on the bone handle caught my eye, and I leaned forward. Etched deep into the bone were lines of tiny writing. I struggled with it for a while, then admitted defeat. "Suzie, you take a look at this. You've got better eyes than me."

She leaned in close again, holding her long hair back, and slowly read out the words on the bone handle. "Abraxus Artificers. The old firm. Solving problems since the Beginning." She straightened up again, frowned, and looked at me. "Any of that mean anything to you?"

"Not much."

"So, are we going to take it with us?"

I snorted. "I'm certainly not leaving something this powerful lying around here. It'll be safer with us."

"Great!" said Suzie. "A whole new kind of gun for me to use!"

"Hold everything, Suzie. I'm not sure we can afford to use a weapon like this. We kill an angel, even a Fallen one, and you can bet *Someone* is going to get really mad at us."

Suzie shrugged. "It's got to beat getting turned into salt."

"There is that, yes." I carefully closed the lid on the Speaking Gun, picked the case up, and slipped it carefully into my coat pocket, next to my heart. "Still, I think we should consider using this only as a very last resort."

Suzie pouted, but didn't object. "Any idea how it's supposed to work?"

"Only roughly. According to the Voynich Manuscript, the Speaking Gun re-creates God's Word. You know, in the Beginning was the Word? The great Sound at the start of Creation, that lives on in the real, secret, names of everything. The Speaking Gun recognises the secret name of whatever you point it at, and then Says it backwards, uncreating it. Theoretically, this Gun could destroy anything. Or everything."

"*Cool . . .*" said Suzie.

"The Gun is also supposed to exert a very heavy price on whoever uses it," I said sternly. "No-one today knows what. But given the fact that no-one's dared use the awful thing in centuries, I think we should be extremely cautious."

"All right," said Suzie. "No need to look at me like that. I can take a hint. I can be cautious, when I have to be. So, where do we go now?"

"Well, given that the lid of this case bears the Collector's mark, I think it's fair to assume this guy and his friends worked for the Collector. Which makes sense. He'd sell what's left of his scavenging soul to get his hands on a unique item like the Unholy Grail. He'd certainly sell any number of other people's souls for it. And you can bet good money he'll have the very latest information on where it might be. If he doesn't already have it . . . So I think we should pay him a little visit."

"Good idea," said Suzie. "Except nobody knows where to find him."

"There is that problem, yes. The location of his secret hideout is one of the great mysteries of the Nightside. Not too surprising, really. If people knew where he kept his legendary collection, they'd be lining up a dozen deep to burgle and loot it. But someone must know. This guy would have had some way of reporting back to the Collector, but his associates are long gone. So, who else do we know that works for him?"

"The Bedlam Boys!" said Suzie.

"Of course . . . They wouldn't normally betray the Collector's confidence, not even to hard cases like us, but now we have something to bargain with. He's bound to want the Speaking Gun back."

"And we'll only agree to hand it over in person."

"Got it in one. Let's go."

The Bedlam Boys, nasty little bastards that they were, often did work for the Collector. They specialised in running protection rackets, using their appalling abilities to extract regular payments from small businesses and the like. They were also very good at recovering debts. The Collector used them to persuade reluctant owners to hand over some special item that he had his eye on. Few people had the strength of will to stand against the Bedlam Boys. It shouldn't be too difficult to track them down; they made enough noise and commotion when they were working.

The black case lay snugly in my coat pocket as Suzie and I left the assembly room. It pressed heavily against my side, almost painfully hot. Suzie was right. It was breathing.

• • •

Outside the hall of the dead, in the deserted street, we stopped and looked up. The great moon hung heavily in the sky, full and bright and a dozen times larger than it seemed outside the Nightside. Things were flying across the night sky, silhouetted against the pallid face of the moon. Dark shapes, vaguely human, with huge wingspans. As Suzie and I watched, more of the things flew past, crowding together in ever greater numbers until there were hundreds of them, darkening the night, blocking out the light of the moon and the stars.

Angels had come to the Nightside. Armies of angels.

FIVE

Angels, Bedlam Boys, and Nasty Jack Starlight

There were angels all over the Nightside, crossing the night sky in such numbers that they blocked out the stars in places. At first, people came crowding out onto the streets, laughing and pointing, marvelling and loudly blaspheming, and more often than not discussing ways to profit from the new situation. And then the angels started dropping down into the Nightside like birds of prey, winged Furies in search of information and retribution, and God and the devil help anyone who dared refuse them. People were snatched up into the boiling skies, and after a time dropped screaming back into the city streets. Sometimes, only blood or body parts fell back. And sometimes, worse and stranger things were returned that were no longer in any way human. Angels are creatures of purpose and intent only, and know nothing of mercy. Soon anyone with a grain of common sense had disappeared from the streets. Suzie and I walked alone down deserted ways, and from all around came the sound of doors being locked and bolted, and even barricaded.

Like that was going to help.

"So," Suzie said, after a while, "when are you going to use your gift, to find out where the Bedlam Boys are practicing their appalling trade these days?"

"I'm not," I said shortly. "The last time I tried to use my gift, the angels ripped me right out of my head and hauled me up into the shimmering realms to interrogate me. I was lucky to get away with my thoughts intact, and I daren't risk it again. We're going to have to solve this case the old-fashioned way."

Suzie brightened up a little. "You mean kicking in doors, asking loud and pointed questions, threatening life and property, and maybe just a touch of senseless violence?"

"I was thinking more of gathering clues, piecing together information, and developing useful theories. Though there's a lot to be said for your way too."

I took my mobile out of my coat pocket and called my secretary. Actually, she's my secretary, receptionist, junior partner, and general dogsbody of all trades. I acquired Cathy Barrett on an earlier case, when I rescued her from a house that tried to eat her. I took her in, gave her a bowl of milk, and now I can't get rid of her. To be fair, she runs my office in the Nightside far more efficiently than I ever could. She understands things like filing, and keeping an appointment diary, and paying bills on time. I've never had the knack for being organised. I think it's a genetic thing. In the few months she's been working for me, Cathy's made herself indispensable, though God forbid she should ever find that out. She's insufferable enough as it is, and besides, I'd have to pay her more.

"Cathy! This is John. Your boss, John. I need some information on the current whereabouts of the Bedlam Boys. What have you got?"

"Give me a minute to check, oh mighty lord and master, and I'll see what I can dig out of the computer. Seems to me I heard something about them the other day. Do I take it it's their turn for a good kicking? Oh happy day." Cathy sounded bright and cheerful, but then she always did. I think she just did it to annoy me. "Okay, boss, got them. Seems they're running the old protection racket again, down on Brewer Street. In fact, the computer's getting updates from the crystal ball that they're shaking down the Hot N Spicy franchise on Brewer Street right now. If you hurry, you should get there before they leave. If the blonde one's there, feel free to give him a good slap on my account."

Part of Cathy's duties, when she's not working tirelessly to keep my business solvent in spite of me, is to keep track of all the major players in the Nightside, where they are, and who they're doing this week. Information is currency, and forewarned is definitely forearmed. Cathy makes a lot of contacts through her incessant clubbing, and her cheerful willingness to chat, drink, and dance with anyone still warm and breathing. It helps that she can chat, dance, and drink under the table pretty much anyone who isn't actually already dead and pickled. Cathy seems to regard alcohol as a food group, and has the endless energy of every teenager. It also helps that she's sweet and pretty and charming, and people like to talk to her. They tell her things they'd never tell anyone else, and Cathy feeds it all into the computer.

There was a time I'd have been doing the rounds myself, but I just don't have the energy any more to drink and debauch till dawn. Especially since dawn doesn't ever happen. It's always night in the Nightside. Luckily, Cathy seems to positively thrive on a regular diet of booze, caffeine, and adrenaline, and is on a first-name basis with practically every doorman and bouncer in the Nightside. You'd be surprised what people will say in front of them, not even noticing they're there because, after all, they're only servants.

I do keep up my own circle of contacts, of course. Old friends and enemies. You'd be surprised how often they turn out to be the same person, as the years go by. Some movers, some shakers, and a few that most people don't even suspect are major players. There aren't many doors that are closed to me. People tell me things. Mostly because they're afraid not to. And it all goes into the computer, too.

Between us, Cathy and I keep tabs on most things and people that matter. Cathy updates every day, and is always busy trying to spot upcoming trends and significant connections. Though we nearly lost everything last month, when the mainframe got possessed by Sumerian demons, and we had to call in a technodruid to exorcise it. I'd never heard language like that before, and even after it was all over, the office still smelled of burning mistletoe for weeks.

And I might add that the computer Helpline people were no bloody use at all.

"I'm getting mass reports of angel sightings," said Cathy. "Wings and blood everywhere, and several manifestation of statues weeping, bleeding, and soiling themselves. Either the Pholio Brothers are pushing a really potent brand of weed this week, or the Nightside's being invaded. This got anything to do with you, John?"

"Only indirectly."

"Angels in the Nightside . . . that is so cool! Hey, do you think you could get me a feather from one of their wings? I've got this new hat that could look absolutely killer with just the right feather . . ."

"You want me to sneak up on an angel and rip out its pinfeathers, so you can make a fashion statement? Oh right, like that's going to happen. *No*, Cathy. Stay away from the angels, as a personal favour to me. Concentrate on the Bedlam Boys. Is there any particular reason why I should be annoyed with the blonde one?"

"He tried to chat me up last week at the Dancin' Fool," said Cathy. "Thought he could impress me because he and his brothers used to be this big boy band. As if! That is so nineties . . . Anyway, he wouldn't take *No, Get lost* or *Fuck off and die!* for an answer, so I ended up smacking him right in the eye. I swear, he was so surprised he hit top C above A. Then he started crying, so I got all guilty and danced with him anyway. And I have to say his moves were complete rubbish without his old choreographer on hand to help him out. Then he pulled me in close for a slow dance, and stuck his tongue in my ear, so I rammed the heel of my stiletto through his foot and left him to it. Wanker." She paused.

"Ooh, ooh! I just remembered! I have messages for you . . . Yes. The Pit's management called to say you and Suzie are banned. Forever. And, they may sue for emotional distress and/or post-traumatic stress disorder. And Big Nina called to say Not to worry, it wasn't crabs after all. It was lobsters."

I hung up. Some conversations, you know they're not going to go anywhere you want.

• • •

It didn't take us long to get to the Hot N Spicy franchise on Brewer Street. We could hear the trouble half-way up the street. Screams and shouts and the sounds of things breaking; all the usual signs of the Bedlam Boys at their work. People were expressing a polite interest, but from a very safe distance. The Boys' powers tend to leak out in all directions once they get started. Suzie and I threaded our way through the crowd and cautiously approached the franchise's open door. We looked in. Nobody noticed us. Everyone had problems of their own.

It was a cheap place, all ugly wallpaper and over-bright lighting and plastic tablecloths. Plastic so that they could be wiped down between customers. You can wipe pretty much anything off plastic. The Hot N Spicy franchise specialises in fire alarm chillies, all variations, one mouthful of which could melt all your fillings and set fire to your hair. Chillies from hell. Three toilets, no waiting, and they keep the loo rolls in the fridge. We are talking *atomic* chillies, and I don't want to even think about the fallout. For *real* chilli fans only. A sign on the wall just inside the door proudly proclaimed Today's Special, wasabe chilli. Wasabe is a really fierce Japanese green mustard, which ought by right to be banned under the Geneva Convention for being more dangerous than napalm.

There was another sign below that, saying *Free sushi; you supply the fish.* Enterprise is a wonderful thing.

Suzie and I eased ourselves through the open door and watched the

Bedlam Boys practicing their particularly unpleasant version of the protection racket. Though consumer terrorism would probably be a better description. Once upon a time, the Boys really had been a successful boy band, but it had been a long time since any of their saccharine cover versions had even come close to troubling the charts. On the scrap heap while barely into their twenties, the Boys had drifted into the Nightside in search of a new direction, and the Collector had supplied them with a useful psychic gift in return for their talent, which he apparently keeps in a jar. A very small jar. These days, the Bedlam Boys mostly worked as muscle for hire or frighteners. And when business is slow they pick up pin money by freelancing. Either you agreed to pay them regular insurance payments, or they guaranteed bad things would happen to your business. To be exact, they turned up on your doorstep and demonstrated their awful ability on whoever happened to be present. The Boys could psionically inflict all kinds of different phobias and manias on anyone in their immediate proximity. They were currently hitting the Hot N Spicy's staff and customers with every kind of fear and anxiety they could think of, grinning widely all the while.

The place was full of screaming and crying people, staggering helplessly between overturned tables, blind to everything but the horrors that had been thrust into their minds. Staff and customers alike clutched at their heads, lashed about them with trembling arms, and pleaded pitifully for help. Some lay on the floor, crying hopelessly, thrashing like epileptics. And in the middle of all this horror and chaos, the Bedlam Boys, standing tall, looking proudly about them, and sniggering and giggling and elbowing each other in the ribs as they thrust people into Hell.

There were four of them, so alike they might have been mass-produced, with perfect bubble gum pink skin, perfect flashing white teeth, and immaculately styled hair. Hair colour seemed to be the only way to tell them apart. They all wore spangled white jumpsuits, cut away in the front to show plenty of hairy chest. They looked almost glamorous, until you looked closely at their faces. Each had the look of a dissipated Adonis, their once handsome features now marked with lines of cruelty and indulgence, like the fallen idols they were.

The franchise had become Panic Attack Central. People howled and screeched and sobbed bitterly as they were suddenly and irrationally afraid of spiders, of falling, of the walls closing in, of open spaces or enclosed places. If they could only have gathered their thoughts for a moment, they would have known these fears weren't real, but the hysteria that filled their heads left no room for rational thought. There was only the fear, and the horror, and no escape anywhere. Some of the franchise's staff and customers were made terrified of really obscure things. The Boys liked to show off. And so there was the fear of genitals shrinking and disappearing, the fear of people suddenly speaking in French accents, the fear of people showing you their holiday photos, and the fear of not being able to find your jacket.

Some of that was almost funny, until I saw one customer digging long bloody furrows in his bare arms with his fingernails, as he tried to scrape away all the bugs he felt were crawling all over him. Another man tore out his eyes with clawed fingers, and threw them on the floor and stamped on them, rather than see what he was being made to see. On the floor, people writhed and cried out in the grip of strokes and heart attacks and convulsions. The Bedlam Boys looked upon their work, and laughed and laughed.

"This is too much, even for me," Suzie said flatly. "Give me the Speaking Gun, Taylor."

"Hell no," I said immediately. "Save that for the angels. It's too big, too dangerous to risk using on anything else. Don't be impatient, Suzie. I know you're eager to try the thing out, but it didn't come with a user's manual. We have no idea of the side effects or drawbacks."

"What's there to know? It's a gun. Point and shoot."

"*No*, Suzie. We don't need the Speaking Gun to deal with cheap punks like these."

"Then what do you suggest?" said Suzie, with heavy patience. "I can't open fire with my shotgun from here. Too many innocent parties in the way. And we can't risk getting any closer, or the Boys' power will affect us too."

"What do you have a fear of, apart from tidying up? They can't affect us, as long as we shield our minds against them."

She looked at me dubiously. "Are you sure about that?"

"Actually, no. But that's what I was told. And we can't just stand here and do nothing."

But even as we stood there debating the point, one of the Bedlam Boys looked round and spotted us. He cried out, and all four Boys turned their power on us, reaching out to the very edge of their range. Their spell fell upon us, and fear stabbed into my brain like so many shards of broken glass. Concentration and willpower did me no good at all.

• • •

I was alone, standing in the ruins of London, in the Nightside of the future. I'd been here before, seen this before, courtesy of a Timeslip. A future that might be, of death and destruction, and all of it supposedly my fault.

For as far as I could see in the dim purple twilight, I was surrounded by tumbled buildings and seas of rubble. There was no moon in the almost starless sky, and the still air was bitterly cold. And somewhere, hidden in the deepest, darkest shadows, something was watching me. I could feel its presence, huge and awful, potent and powerful, drawing steadily closer. It was coming for me, with blood and worse on its breath. I wanted to run, but there was nowhere left to go, nowhere left to hide. It was close now. So close I could hear its eager breathing. It was coming for me, to take me away from everything I knew and cared for, and make me its own at last. The terrible shadow that loomed over everything I did, that had dominated my life ever since I was born. Close now, vast and powerful. A great dark shape, threatening to unmake everything I'd so painstakingly made of myself.

I knew what it was. I knew its name. And that knowledge frightened me more than anything else. That finally she was coming for me, after pursuing me my whole damned life. It was almost a relief to say her name.

Mother . . . I whispered.

And in naming my fear, that unknown creature who had birthed and then abandoned me, I was suddenly so full of rage it was the easiest thing in the world to push back the fear, and deny it. My mental shields slammed back into place, one by one, and the dead world around me shuddered, becoming flat and **grey** and unconvincing. I pushed the Bedlam Boys out of my mind with almost contemptuous ease, and in the blink of an eye I was back in the Hot N Spicy franchise again.

I'd fallen to my knees on the grimy floor, my whole body shaking with the strain of what I'd been put through. Suzie was kneeling beside me, tears running jerkily down her face from wide, unseeing eyes, lost inside herself. I put a hand on her shoulder, and in that moment I saw what she saw.

• • •

Suzie was lying in bed in a hospital ward, held in place by heavy restraining straps. Her throat was raw from screaming. She lunged against the leather straps, but they were far stronger than her. So all she could do was lie there and watch helplessly as her fear crawled slowly, laboriously, across the ward floor towards her. It was small and weak, but determination kept it moving. It was soft and scarlet and barely formed, and it left a scuffed bloody trail behind it as it crawled slowly towards her. It was almost at the side of her bed when it painfully raised its oversized head and looked at her.

And called her *Mommy . . .*

It took all my strength to wrap my mental shields around Suzie too, and drag her out of there and back into the waking world. She pulled away from me immediately, kneeling alone, hugging herself tightly as though afraid she might fly apart. Her face was a snarling mask of outrage and horror, tears still dripping off her chin. It was actually shocking to see her so vulnerable, so hurt. I hadn't thought there was anything that could hurt Shotgun Suzie. I started to reach out to her; then her puffed-up eyes fell upon the Bedlam Boys, and she reached for the shotgun holstered on her back. The Boys gaped at us, amazed that we'd been able to break free from their power. I fired up the dark side of my gift. For a moment, anything could have happened.

And that was when the angel arrived.

A vivid, overwhelming presence suddenly filled the restaurant, slapping up against the walls and suppressing everything else. The Bedlam Boys' power snapped off in an instant, blown out like four tiny candles in a hurricane. They just stood there and blinked stupidly at the angel. At first, it looked like a grey man in a grey suit, so average-looking in every way as to seem almost generic. You couldn't quite look at him, only glimpse him out of the corner of your eyes. And then he grew more and more real, more and more solid, more *there,* until you couldn't look at anything else. The angel lifted his grey head and looked at the Boys, and suddenly erupted into a pillar of fire in human form. His light was blinding, dazzling, too bright to look at directly. Vast glowing wings spread out behind him, sparking and spitting. There was a stench of ozone and burning feathers. The Bedlam Boys stared into the heart of that terrible light, mesmerised.

And turned to salt.

One moment they were living and breathing people, and the next there were four salt statues, paler than death, still wearing their stupid spangled jumpsuits. And all four fixed white faces were screaming horribly, silently, forever. The franchise's staff and customers, freed from their imposed fears, now had something real to be afraid of. They screamed and howled and ran for the open door. I hauled Suzie back out of the way as they stampeded past us, fighting and clawing each other in their need to get away. I felt very much like joining them. The sheer presence of the angel was viscerally disturbing, like every authority figure you ever knew was out to get you, all rolled into one.

I've never got on well with authority figures.

The angel gestured with a brightly glowing hand, and one of the salt statues toppled over and shattered. Suzie slapped me hard on the arm to get my attention.

"The Gun, Taylor. Give me the Gun, dammit. Give me the Speaking Gun!"

Her voice was back under control, but her eyes were fey and wild. "No," I said. "I get to try it first."

I yanked the case out of my inner coat pocket. It felt unpleasantly warm to the touch. I snapped open the lid and took out the Speaking Gun. The case fell unnoticed to the floor as I stood paralysed, unable to move even the smallest part of me. My skin crawled, revulsed at contact with the Gun made of meat. It was like holding the hand of someone long dead, but still horribly, eagerly active. It felt hot and sweaty and feverish. It felt sick and powerful. The Speaking Gun had woken up. It breathed wetly in my hand, and its slow heavy thoughts crawled sluggishly across the front of my mind. The Gun was awake, and it wanted to be used. On everything. It ached to say the backward Words that would uncreate all the material world. It had been made to destroy angels, but its appetite had grown down the many, many years. And yet the Gun was dependent on others to use it, to pull its trigger formed from a tooth, and it *hated* that. Hated me. Hated everything that lived. The Speaking Gun forced its filthy thoughts upon me, determined to control and compel me, to make me its weapon. Its thoughts and feelings were in no way human. It was as though death and decay and destruction had found a voice, and hideous ambition. It knew my Name, and ached to say it.

It took all my self-control, all my rigid self-discipline, and all the outrage raised in me by the Bedlam Boys, to force my fingers open one at a time, until the Speaking Gun fell stickily from my hand and hit the floor, still howling defiantly in my mind. I shut it out, behind my strongest shields, and leaned back against the wall behind me, shaking and shuddering.

The angel was gone. It had seen the Speaking Gun, and that was enough.

The restaurant was quiet now. The staff and customers were gone, the angel had escaped, and the Bedlam Boys were salt. There was just me and Suzie. My whole body was shaking, my hands beating a noisy tattoo against the wall. My mind felt like it had been violated. I could feel tears running down my cheeks. Walker had been right. Some cures are far worse than the diseases. I looked down at the Gun on the floor, lying beside its case, but I couldn't bring myself to reach down and touched the damned thing. So Suzie knelt and did it for me, closing the case around the Gun without actually touching it herself. She slipped the case into her jacket pocket, then stood patiently beside me while I got myself under control again. It was the closest she could come to comforting me.

Soon enough the shuddering stopped, and I was myself again. I felt tired, bone tired and soul tired, as though I hadn't slept for a week. I wiped the drying tears off my face with my hands, sniffed a few times, and gave Suzie my best reassuring smile. It felt fairly convincing. Suzie took it in the spirit with which it was intended and nodded briskly, all business again. Suzie's always been uncomfortable around naked emotions.

"I'll carry the case," she said. "I'm more used to guns than you are."

"It isn't just a gun, Suzie."

She shrugged. "That angel. Do you think it was from Above or Below?"

It was my turn to shrug. "Does it matter, Suzie? When the Bedlam Boys had us, trapped in our fears, for a moment I saw what you saw . . ."

"We won't talk about that," Suzie said flatly. "Not now. Not ever. If you are my friend."

Sometimes being a friend means knowing when to let things go and shut the hell up. So I pushed myself away from the wall and headed for the nearest of the three remaining salt statues. Suzie followed after me. The scattered remains of the shattered statue crunched loudly under our feet. I looked at the three white faces, trapped in a moment of horror, forever. Sometimes I think the whole universe runs on irony.

"Well, there goes our chances of finding the Collector's location," said Suzie, her voice and face utterly calm and easy.

"Not necessarily," I said. "Remember the first rule of the private detective, when in doubt, check their pockets for clues."

"I thought the first rule was wait until the client's cheque has cleared?"

"Picky picky."

It took a while, but eventually we turned up a single embossed business card, proclaiming a performance by Nasty Jack Starlight at the old Styx Theatre, dated that very day. Or, more properly, night.

"So Starlight's back in town," I said. "Wouldn't have thought he was the Boys' cup of tea."

"Has to be a connection," said Suzie. "I know for a fact that Starlight's supposed to have supplied certain items to the Collector in the past."

"Let's go talk to the man," I said. "See what he knows."

"Let's," said Suzie. "I'm in the mood to talk forcibly to someone. Possibly even violently."

"Never knew a time when you weren't," I said generously.

• • •

We walked through the streets of the Nightside, through a city under siege. There were angels everywhere now, soaring across the night sky, plunging down to snatch victims right out of the street, spreading terror and destruction. There were screams and cries, fires and explosions. Dark plumes of smoke rose from burning buildings on all sides. People had been driven out into the streets, as homes and businesses and hiding places collapsed into rubble behind them. Everywhere I looked there were salt statues, and bodies impaled on lamp-posts. Burned and blackened corpses lay piled up in the gutters, and once I saw someone turned inside out, still horribly alive and suffering. Suzie put him out of his misery. Judgement Day had come to the Nightside, and it wasn't pretty. There was gun-fire all over the place, and fiery explosions, and now and again I felt the fabric of the world shake as some poor desperate fool levelled heavy-duty magics against the invading angels. Nothing stopped them, or even slowed them down. Grey men in grey suits stood unnaturally still in doorways, or looked out of alleyways, or walked untouched out of fire-gutted buildings. They were everywhere, and people ran howling before them, driven like cattle to the slaughter.

Suzie and I hadn't been out in the street five minutes before an angel came swooping down out of the night sky, brilliant as a falling star, fierce and irrevocable, blazing wings spread wide, heading straight for me. I gave it my best significant glare, but it kept coming. Suzie pulled the Speaking Gun's case out of her jacket, and the angel changed course immediately, sweeping over our heads and flashing down the street behind us like a snow-white comet. Suzie and I stopped and looked at each other. Suzie weighed the case in her hand.

"Guess word about the Speaking Gun has got around."

"So much for the element of surprise," I said.

She sniffed. "I'd rather have the element of naked threat any day."

We started off down the street again, walking unhurriedly while everyone else ran, and blood and chaos flowed around us. Suzie put the Gun's case away again, then unconsciously rubbed that hand against her jacket, over and over, as though trying to clean it.

• • •

The Styx was an old, abandoned theatre, set well back from the main drag, in one of the quieter backwaters of the Nightside. There are enough dramas in the Nightside's everyday life that most people don't feel any need for the theatre, but we have to have somewhere for vain and bitchy people to show off in public. Suzie and I stopped outside the large, slumping building and studied it cautiously from a safe distance. It didn't look like much. The whole of the boarded-up front was plastered with peeling, overlapping posters for local rock groups, political meetings, and religious revivals. The once proud sign above the double doors was choked with grime and dirt.

Property doesn't normally stay untenanted long in the Nightside; someone's always got a use for it. But this place was different. Some thirty years ago, some poor fool tried to open a Gate to Hell during a performance of the Caledonian Tragedy, and that kind of thing plays havoc with property values. The three witches killed and ate the guy responsible, but didn't have the skills to close what he'd partway opened. The Authorities had to bring in an outside troubleshooter, one Augusta Moon, and while she sewed the thing up tighter than a frog's arse, the incident still left a nasty taste in everyone's spiritual mouth.

Even unsuccessful Hellgates can affect the tone of a whole neighbourhood.

Unsurprisingly enough, the theatre's double doors were locked, so Suzie kicked them in, and we strolled nonchalantly into the lobby. It was dirty and dusty, with thick shrouds of cobwebs everywhere. The shadows were very dark, and the still air smelled stale and sour. Dust motes swirled slowly in the shafts of light that had followed us in through the open door, as though they were disturbed by the light's intrusion. The once plush carpet was dry and crunchy under our feet. The whole place reeked of faded nostalgia, of better times long gone. It was like walking back into the shadows of the past. Old posters advertising old productions still clung stubbornly to the walls, faded and fly-specked. The Patchwork Players Present: Marlowe's *King Lier*, Webster's *Revenger's Triumph*, Ibsen's *Salad Days*. There was no sign anyone had been here for thirty years.

"Odd name for a theatre," Suzie said finally, her voice echoing loudly in the quiet. "What's a Styx, when it's at home?"

"The Styx is a river that runs through Hell," I said. "Made up from the tears shed by suicides. Sometimes it bothers me that I know things like that. Maybe the theatre specialised in tragedies. We may be in the wrong place, Suzie. Look around you. No-one's disturbed this dust in years."

"In which case," said Suzie, "where's that music coming from?"

I listened carefully, and sure enough, faint strains of music were coming from somewhere up ahead. Suzie drew her shotgun, and we crossed the lobby and made our way up to the stage doors. The music was definitely louder. We pushed the doors open and stepped through into the theatre proper. It was very dark, and we stood there for a while till our eyes adjusted. Up on the stage, in two brilliant following spotlights was Nasty Jack Starlight with his life-sized living rag doll partner, singing and dancing.

The music was an old sixties classic, the Seekers' "The Carnival Is Over." Nasty Jack Starlight sang along cheerfully, stepping it out across the dusty stage with more style than precision. He was dressed as Pierrot, in a Harlequin suit of black and white squares, and his face was made up to resemble a grinning skull, with dark, hollowed eyes and white teeth painted on his smiling lips, all of it topped with a jaunty sailor's cap. He was tall and gangling, and he danced with more deliberation than grace as his voice soared along with the melancholy song.

He danced a fiercely merry two-step with his partner, a living rag doll costumed as Columbine. She was almost as tall as he was, her arms and legs amazingly flexible as she danced, without joints to get in the way. She had a sadly erotic look, in her patched dress of many colours, and her face of tightly stretched white satin had garishly painted-on features. Her movements were disturbingly sexual, her dance provocative in every lascivious movement.

Pierrot and Columbine capered across the whole stage, making the most of the space, dancing and leaping and pirouetting in the two spotlights that followed them faithfully wherever they went. I looked back and above me, but there was no sign anywhere of a source for the spotlights. They just were. The music also seemed to come from nowhere. It changed abruptly to "Sweet Little Jazz Baby, That's Me," a staple from the Roaring Twenties, and Pierrot and Columbine came together and Charlestoned for all they were worth. Their feet on the stage made no sound at all. The music had a distorted, eerily echoing quality, as though it had had to travel a long way to get there and lost something of itself along the way. And for all the effort Nasty Jack Starlight and his partner put into their performance, it all had a dull, flat feeling. There was no appeal to it, no charisma or emotion. But the packed audience was in ecstatics, sheer raptures of emotion.

The audience.

Nasty Jack Starlight and his living rag doll were singing and dancing for the dead. Now that my eyes had adjusted to the gloom, I could see the stalls were full of zombies, vampires, mummies, werewolves, and ghosts of varying density. Every form of undead or half-life the Nightside had to offer, all come together in one place under a strict pact of non-aggression that wouldn't have lasted five minutes anywhere else. But no-one would destroy the truce here; no-one would dare. This was the one place they could come to recapture just a little of their lost or discarded humanity. To remember what it felt like to be alive.

The vampires looked right at home in their formal tuxedos and ball gowns, daintily sipping blood from discreet thermoses, passed back and forth. In comparison, the mummies looked distinctly drab and dirty in their yellowing bandages, and dust puffed out when they clapped their hands together. The werewolves huddled together in a clump, howling along to the tune, their alpha male distinguished by an impressive leather jacket made from human hide, the tattooed words on its back proclaiming him Leader of the Pack. The ghouls mostly kept to themselves, snacking on fingers from a takeaway tub. The zombies tended to sit very still, and applauded very carefully, in case anything dropped off. They sat as far away from the ghouls as possible. The ghosts varied from full manifestations to pale misty shapes, some so thinly spread their hands passed through each other when they tried to clap along. Others had to concentrate all their sense of personality just to keep from falling through their chairs. But dead, undead, partly human, or mostly inhuman, they all seemed to be having a good time. They laughed and cheered, sighed and wept, and applauded in unison, as though reacting to what was happening on the stage, though their responses seemed to have little to do with the performance.

Nasty Jack Starlight performed exclusively for the dead, or those feeling distanced from their original humanity. He remembered old emotions for them, evoked them through his singing and dancing, and *made* his audience feel them. He made them feel alive again, if only fleetingly. His patrons paid very well for the illusion of life he gave them, for a while . . . and while they wallowed in second-hand emotions, Starlight fed off their unnatural vitality, sucking it out of them as he danced, gorging on their inhuman energies like a happy little parasite. He had lived many lifetimes in this fashion, and intended to live many more. Long ago, he'd made a really bad deal with Something he was still afraid to name aloud, and now he couldn't afford to die. Ever.

I had to explain all this to Suzie. She'd never had any interest in the theatre. At the end, she sniffed, unimpressed.

"So what's the deal with the rag doll?" she said.

"The word is she was human once, and Jack Starlight's lover. He needed a dancing partner, but he didn't feel at all inclined to share what he'd be taking from his audience. So he had her made over into what she is now. A living rag doll, endlessly compliant, a partner who'll follow his every move and whim, and never complain. Of course, that was a long time ago . . . She's probably quite insane by now. If she's lucky. Now you know why they call him *Nasty* Jack Starlight."

"Who was she, originally?" said Suzie, glaring at the stage.

"No-one knows who she was any more. Except Jack, of course, and he'll never tell. Nasty little man that he is. Come on, let's go on up and ruin his day."

"Let's. I might even ruin his posture while I'm at it."

We strode off down the central aisle, side by side. The dead in the seats nearest us didn't even glance round as we passed, utterly transfixed by the performance onstage, and the old emotions flooding through what was left of their hearts. There was magic in the air, and it had nothing to do with sorcery. On and on they danced, Pierrot and Columbine, Harlequin and his rag doll, never stopping or resting as the music changed inexorably from one sentimental ditty to another . . . as though they had no need to pause, to refresh their strength or regain their breath. And perhaps they didn't. He was feeding, and she . . . she was just a rag doll, after all, her wide eyes and smiling lips only painted on. Neither of them suffered from human limitations any more. They mimed love and tenderness for their audience, and meant none of it.

It was all just an act.

Suzie and I vaulted up onto the stage, and everything stopped. The music cut off, and Starlight and his rag doll immediately ended their dance. They each stood very still in their separate spotlights, as Suzie and I approached them. Nasty Jack Starlight struck an elegant pose, calm and relaxed, smiling his skullface smile while his eyes gleamed brightly from darkened hollows. The rag doll had frozen in mid move, her head turned away, her arms and legs interrupted at impossible angles, inhumanly flexible. The audience was still only for a moment as the performance was interrupted, then they burst out into a roar of boos and yells and insults, quickly descending into open threats and menaces. Suzie glared out at them, to little effect. I turned and gave them my best thoughtful stare, and everyone shut up.

"I'm impressed," Suzie said quietly.

"To tell the truth, so am I," I said. "But don't tell them that. Jack Starlight! It's been a while, hasn't it, Jack? You still on your world tour of the Nightside?"

"Still playing to packed houses," Starlight said easily. "And they say the theatre's dead . . ." His voice was soft and precise, completely without accent or background. He could have been from anywhere, anywhen. His unwavering smile was very wide, and his eyes never blinked. "You know, most hecklers have the decency to do it from their seats. What do you want, Taylor? You are interrupting genius at work."

"We found your card in the possession of one of the Bedlam Boys," I said. "They worked for the Collector."

"I notice you're using the past tense. Am I to presume the little shits are all dead? My my, Taylor, you have become hard-core since your return."

"Tell me about the card, Jack," I said, deliberately not correcting his presumption. "What's your connection with the Collector?"

He shrugged easily enough. "There's not much to tell. The Collector sent the Boys round to lean on me, because he'd heard I once very nearly got my hands on the Unholy Grail, some years ago in France. I was excavating at Rennes-le-Château, in search of the Maltese Falcon . . ."

I winced. "I thought you had more sense, Jack. Never go after the Maltese Falcon. That's the first rule of private investigators."

Suzie frowned. "I thought the first rule was . . ."

"Not now, Suzie. Continue, Jack."

"Well, imagine my surprise when my companions unwrapped the contents of the hidden grave, and we found ourselves face to face with the Unholy Grail. It all got rather unpleasant after that. It's always sad when friends fall out over money. . . . Anyway, after the dust had settled and the blood had dried, I ended up having to leave the chateau empty-handed, and at speed. But I still remain one of the few men who has actually seen the Unholy Grail with his own eyes, and lived to tell of it."

"What did it look like?" said Suzie.

Nasty Jack Starlight considered for a moment. "Cold. Ugly. Seductive. I wasn't stupid enough to touch it, even then. I know evil when I see it."

"You should," I said. "You've had enough practice. So, what did you tell the Bedlam Boys, when they came calling?"

He laughed softly. It was a dark, unpleasant sound. "I didn't tell them a damned thing. I kicked their over-padded arses and sent them home crying to their master. Teach the Collector to set his dogs on me. Their fears were no match for my emotions. I am a master of my craft, and don't you forget it. And that is it. There's nothing more I can tell you about the Unholy Grail or the Collector. Just ships that passed in the Nightside, that's all. Now, do either of you happen to be in show business? Then perhaps you'll both be good enough to get the hell off my stage. I am making art here. Why is there never a guy with a long hook around when you need him?"

"There are angels all over the Nightside," I said. "They're looking for anyone with any knowledge of, or connection to, the Unholy Grail. And they're not playing nicely. They don't have to. They're angels. Now, impressive though your audience is, the whole lot of them put together wouldn't be enough to even slow down an angel. Even if they did feel disposed to try and protect you, which I personally doubt. The dead can be so fickle. On the other hand, you help us track down the Unholy Grail, and/or the Collector, and Suzie and I will protect you."

Nasty Jack Starlight shook his head slowly. "Just when you think it can't get any worse . . . Angels in the Nightside. Right! That is it. I am out of here." He turned to face the audience. "Ladies and gentlemen, tonight's show is cancelled on account of Biblical intervention. Good night, God bless, hope it was good for you too. Form an orderly queue for the exits. Sorry, no refunds."

He stalked over to his rag doll partner, snapped his fingers sharply, and she collapsed limply over his waiting shoulder, as though there was nothing inside her but straw and stuffing. And perhaps there wasn't. Certainly she seemed no weight at all to Starlight as he headed determinedly for the wings. I didn't see any point in trying to stop him. He didn't have anything I needed, and an unwilling partner would only slow us down. But then Nasty Jack Starlight stopped abruptly, turned round and looked back, moving slowly, almost reluctantly. And that was when we all realised there was someone else onstage with us. We looked slowly at the back of the stage, even the rag doll raising her satin face. There, standing behind us, still and silent like a living shadow, was a grey man in a grey suit.

He waited till we were all looking, then he blazed like the sun, a light so bright it was painful to merely human eyes. Suzie and I stumbled back, shielding our faces with upraised arms. Starlight turned and ran for the edge of the stage. The rag doll hanging down over his shoulder was the only one to stare adoringly at the angel, with her dark-painted eyes. The audience was in a panic, shrieking and crying out in alarm, while the word *angel* moved swiftly among them like a curse. Ghosts disappeared, snapping out of existence like popping soap bubbles. Vampires became bats and flapped away. Those still burdened with material bodies fought their way out into the aisles and sprinted for the lobby doors.

The angel became a pillar of fire in human form, spreading wide his glowing wings, brilliant and terrible and incandescent with glory. There was a stench of burning flesh and melting metals. The rag doll hanging limply over Starlight's shoulder burst into flames. They leapt up impossibly fast, consuming the doll from head to toe. And still she stared adoringly through the flames at the angel. Starlight cried out in pain and rage, and threw her from him. She flopped about on the stage, burning fiercely. She tried to crawl towards Starlight, but the flames were too hot, too eager, and she was only rags and stuffing. She burned up, and she was gone, and in moments there was nothing left of her but a scorch mark on the stage, and dark smoke drifting slowly though the air. It smelled of violets.

Starlight didn't spare the burning doll a glance once he'd thrown her aside. He ran for the edge of the stage, and had almost made it when his clothes burst into flames. The sailor's cap went up first, burning fiercely with a pale blue flame, setting his hair on fire. Then the Harlequin's costume caught alight, flames leaping everywhere at once. He beat at the flames with his bare hands, but soon they were burning too. In a matter of seconds, his whole body was burning hotter than a furnace. He screamed once, and a long jet of yellow flame shot out of his mouth from his burning lungs. He fell forward onto the stage, and lay there kicking and jerking, while the flames leapt even higher. They quickly consumed Nasty Jack Starlight, until there was nothing left but a few charred and blackened bones, and sizzling melted fat dripping slowly off the edge of the stage.

By that time, Suzie Shooter had the Speaking Gun out of its case, and was holding it rock steady in her hand, aimed right at the angel. But I could see from her twisted features that she was feeling the same sick horror at the Gun's touch that I had. Her iron self-control fought off its attempt to seize control of her mind, but her whole body was shaking from the effort of the struggle, even while the hand holding the Gun remained perfectly steady. All she had to do was pull the trigger. But she couldn't spare enough willpower to do it.

The angel turned its gaze away from Starlight's remains and looked at Suzie. It saw the Speaking Gun in her hand, and in a moment it was gone, flying upwards on wings of dazzling brightness, crashing through the roof of the theatre and up and out into the safety of the night skies.

Suzie didn't move, still aiming the Speaking Gun at where the angel had been. Her face was pale, and slick with sweat. Her eyes were fixed and wild. Her whole body was shaking now, as she and the Gun fought for control of her mind, and her soul. And in the end she won, and threw the Gun from her. Perhaps because in the end she was Shotgun Suzie, who owned guns, and not the other way round. She won, and I never knew how much it cost her. I never asked. Because what she did tell me was so much worse.

She sat down suddenly on the stage, as though her legs had just given out. Her hands twitched meaninglessly in her lap, and she rocked back and forth like a troubled child. She wasn't crying; she was beyond that. Her eyes were wild, desperate, feral. She was making a low, moaning sound, like an animal in pain. I sat down beside her, and put an arm round her shoulders to comfort her. She shrieked dismally, and scuttled away from me like a child afraid of a beating. I moved cautiously after her, careful not to get too close.

"It's all right, Suzie," I said. "I'm here. It's over. Let me help you."

"You can't," she said, not looking at me.

"I'm here . . . it's me, John."

"But you can't touch me," she said, her voice so harsh now it was almost inhuman. "No-one can. I can't bear to be touched, by anyone. Not ever again. Can't be vulnerable, to anyone."

I knelt before her, trying to hold her darting gaze with mine. I was desperate to help her, to haul her back from the edge, but it felt like the wrong choice of words might shatter her into so many pieces, she'd never recover. I'd never seen her like this before. So . . . defenceless.

"When the Bedlam Boys brought out our fears," I said slowly, "I saw what you saw. I was there with you, in the hospital. I saw . . . the baby."

"There was no baby," she said tiredly. "It has to be born to be a baby. What you saw was how the foetus looked, after I had it aborted. I left it so late because I was ashamed. Too ashamed to tell my parents that my brother had been abusing me since I was thirteen, and the baby would be his. It wasn't rape, not really. Sometimes he'd buy me things, little presents. And sometimes he'd say he'd kill me if I ever told anyone. He used me. And when the truth came out, my parents blamed me. Said I must have led him on.

"I had an abortion, just after my fifteenth birthday. No cake and candles for me that year. They made me look at the foetus, afterwards. So I wouldn't forget the lesson. Like I could ever forget. I killed my brother. Shot him dead with a gun I stole. My first gun. Pissed on his body, and then ran away to the Nightside. Been here ever since. Swore I'd never be weak and vulnerable, not ever again. I'm Shotgun Suzie now, death on two legs. But I can't be touched. Not by anyone. Not even by a friend, or a lover. I'm safe now. Safe from everyone. Even myself."

"You mean . . . there's never been anyone in your life?" I said. "No-one you could ever trust enough to . . ."

"No. Never."

"I had no idea how alone you really were, Suze."

"Don't call me that," she said in a dead voice. "That's what he used to call me."

"Oh Jesus, I'm so sorry, Suzie. I am so sorry."

Some life came back into her eyes as she looked at me, and her mouth turned down in a bitter smile. "I would trust you with my life, John. But I can't bear to have you touch me. My brother won after all. Because even though I killed him, he's always with me."

I didn't know what to say, so I just said "I'm here, Suzie."

"I know," she said. "And sometimes, that's enough."

She got up, retrieved the Speaking Gun by wrapping the case around it, and put the case back in her jacket. She stood on the edge of the stage, looking out into the darkness. She seemed entirely composed again. I came and stood beside her.

"It's just a gun," she said, not looking at me. "I know how to handle guns. Next time, I'll use it."

I nodded. And after a while we walked out of the Styx Theatre together, side by side and miles and miles between us.

● ● ●

We'd only just got out into the street when my mobile rang again. This time it was Razor Eddie, Punk God of the Straight Razor. Or so he claims, and since he tends to kill people who disagree, not many people contest the point any more. Certainly he's one of the strangest and most dangerous people in the Nightside, and that takes some doing. I suppose we're friends. It's hard to tell sometimes, in the Nightside. This time he had information for me.

"I hear you're looking for the Unholy Grail," he said, without preamble. "I know where it is. The Collector's got it."

"I'd pretty much worked that out for myself," I said. "What makes you think the Collector's got it?"

"Because I got it for him," said Eddie. His voice was a ghostly whisper, as always. "To be exact, he hired me to take it away from the bastards who had it. The Collector got a bit jumpy after his people lost the Speaking Gun, so he came to me. Normally he'd know better, but this time he had something I wanted, so we struck a deal. The Unholy Grail was in the hands of the Warriors of the Cross, a bunch of hard-core Christian evangelists who planned to use the Unholy Grail's power to launch a Crusade against the Nightside and slaughter everyone and everything that even smacked of magic. Anything that wasn't pure, untainted human was to be exterminated as ungodly and unChristian. Since that definitely included me, I was only too happy to get my own pre-emptive strike in first."

"The Collector hired you?" I said. "I didn't think you had any use for money any more?"

"I don't," said Razor Eddie. "His payment was the current location of the Warriors of the Cross. I'd been looking for those bastards for some time. They'd been hauling teenage runaways off to their hidden base and brainwashing them, then sending them out to act as spies, and honey to trap more kids. They were going to be the cannon fodder of the Crusade."

"So the Collector definitely has the Unholy Grail now?" I said.

"Put it into his hands myself. Ugly thing. But more and more it seemed to me that he is not a fit person to have such a thing. I can't touch him. I gave my word. But I never said anything about you. So you come to me, and I'll tell you where the Collector is hiding out these days. Then you can take the damned thing away from him and put it somewhere safe. Sound good to you?"

"Best thing I've heard all day. Where are you, Eddie?"

"Back at the Warriors of the Cross's hideout, having a bit of a look round for anything else of interest."

"You mean looting," I said.

He chuckled dryly. "Old habits die hard. You know Big Sergei's Warehouse, on Kaynek Avenue?"

"I know it. Be with you in twenty minutes. You do know that there are angels in the Nightside, from Above and Below, kicking the crap out of anyone they even suspect has any connection with the Unholy Grail?"

"I don't bother them, they don't bother me," said Razor Eddie. He hung up.

I put my mobile away, and turned to Suzie. She looked as calm and composed as usual, ice-cold and perfectly poised. I filled her in on the parts of the conversation she'd missed, and she frowned.

"Why couldn't he just tell you where the Collector is over the phone?"

"Because you never know who might be listening," I said. "There's no such thing as a secure line in the Nightside. You know Big Sergei's place?"

"Can't say I do."

"He's Russian mafiosi. You want it, he can get it for you. Guns and armour a speciality, which is presumably why the Warriors of the Cross went to him. You'll like him, Suzie, if Razor Eddie's left anything of him."

"You know all the best people, Taylor. Let's go. I want to get this case over with."

"Suzie . . ."

"Let's go."

So we went, together, once more side by side.

SIX

Death Comes Suddenly

Suzie and I hurried through largely deserted streets, while fires burned all across the Nightside, like warning balefires set against the dark. The air was thick with smoke and drifting ashes, and the smell of bodies burning. Buildings exploded, blown apart by angelic light, like party favours in Hell. There were so many angels flying overhead now that they blocked out most of the light from the moon and the stars. Most of the street-lights were smashed. The Nightside was at its lowest ebb, illuminated mostly by the leaping flames of its own destruction. Suzie and I stuck to the shadows and sprinted through the shifting pools of light. The streets seemed eerily still and quiet without the usual massed traffic rushing endlessly past, but everyone who could leave the Nightside was long gone by now, and no-one outside was stupid enough to come in.

Angels had come to the Nightside, from Above and Below, and the night had never seemed so dark.

Down in Time Tower Square, some of the area's major players had come out into the streets, out into the open, to make a last stand against the invading forces. Suzie and I watched from the shadows of a recessed doorway and hoped not to be noticed. The Lord of Thorns stood proudly with his staff of power, cut from the Tree of Life itself. Lightning crackled around him, and he laughed like a crow on a battlefield as angels wheeled away rather than meet his baleful gaze. Count Video leaned casually against a lamp-post, wrapped in static and shifting plasma lights, his pale skin studded with silicon nodes and sorcerous circuitry. He sniggered nastily as his long-fingered hands weaved binary magic, rewriting reality with applied description theory and insane mathematics, and the angels couldn't get anywhere near him. King of Skin slouched into the Square, his eyes bright with glory, undoing probabilities with his terrible glamour. And Bloody Blades, reeking of sweat and musk and awful appetites, snorted and stamped his great hooves impatiently as he waited for one of the others to bring something down in reach of his great spurred hands.

And all through Time Tower Square there was a terrible sound of angels crying out in pain and rage, as magic moved in the night, denying them their rightful prey.

The angels flew in great spirals overhead, moving faster and faster, spreading wider and wider as they gathered in ever greater numbers. Soon there would be so many of them that no amount of magics would be enough to hold them back, then they would descend. One had clearly been impatient, and had paid the price. It had ventured too low, too soon, and one of the major players had snatched it out of the air and crucified it against the side of the Time Tower. Dozens of cold iron nails pierced its outstretched arms and legs, pinning it to the wall like a frog in a science lab, ready for dissection. But the angel was still alive, its light flickering feebly like a fallen star. Its golden eyes wept slow, mystified tears, unable to understand what had brought it so low. It was finding out the limitations of the material world the hard way. Its severed wings lay on the ground beneath its broken feet.

Further off in the night, in a direction that could not be named or pointed to, there was a sound like a great engine slowly turning, as older, darker, more powerful presences began to wake, to defend the Nightside. They stirred in ancient vaults, or long-forgotten graves, creatures and beings of power and legend, some of them almost as old as angels, and as dreadful.

The Nightside is an old, old place.

Suzie and I eased around the edges of the Square, scurrying from one place of relative safety to the next. The air was full of the stresses of great forces clashing, like icebergs grinding together in the night sea. I had no intention of getting involved. I knew when I was out of my depth, and for once Suzie had enough sense to follow my lead. There were powers abroad in the night now that could crush both of us like bugs and never even notice. It seemed to take forever to creep around two sides of the Square, my heart hammering painfully fast in my chest all the way, but finally we were able to slip away into a blessedly anonymous side street and run for our lives. Behind us someone was screaming, but we didn't pause to look back. We weren't far from Big Sergei's Warehouse now.

And, of course, Razor Eddie. Punk God of the Straight Razor. Possibly. Sometimes a friend, sometimes not. Saint *and* sinner, all wrapped up in one enigmatic and distinctly unhygienic bundle. Your connection to minor deities and divinity wannabes, and as much trouble as you can handle. An extremely disturbing agent for the good, and no, the good didn't get any say in the matter. He lived a life of violent penance for earlier misdeeds. Lots of them. The last time I'd seen Eddie was in a possible future I'd accessed through a Timeslip, and I'd ended up having to kill him. It had been a mercy killing, made necessary at least partly because of the time-travelling Collector, but even so it wasn't the kind of thing that came up easily in the conversation. I was still trying to decide just how much, if any, of this I should tell Eddie. The situation was complicated by Eddie's future self blaming me for the eventual destruction of the world. If I told Eddie that, I could quite easily see him killing me on the spot, on general principle. Of course, the future I'd visited wasn't inevitable. Nothing is set in stone where Time is concerned.

As in so many things, I decided the best thing to do was wait and see what happened, and decide then, if at all. I'd always had a real talent for putting things off till later. Hell, I could dither for the Olympics.

Suzie and I stopped at the edge of the warehouse district and looked cautiously about us. Fires were burning all around, some of them seriously out of control. The shadows danced and leapt, but the area seemed abandoned by mortals and angels. The fighting was over, and the struggle had moved on, leaving only flames and devastation behind. The air was tight and hot as a summer's day, and twice as sweaty. I could see Big Sergei's Warehouse at the end of the street, just another anonymous building among many. It seemed to have survived pretty much intact. The way to it seemed clear enough, but still I hung back, taking my time. Razor Eddie wasn't above luring me into a trap if he felt it served a higher purpose. Suzie growled restlessly at my side, hefting her pump-action shotgun and looking frustrated because she didn't have anyone to use it on.

"This whole situation stinks, Taylor." Her voice was as cold and calm as ever, but her knuckles were white from holding the shotgun too tightly. I should really have insisted she go home, and rest and recover, but I didn't because I needed her. She sniffed at the smoky air as though she could smell trouble, and perhaps she could, at that. "Think about it. Why would the Collector tell Eddie his most preciously guarded secret, the location of his collection? Eddie's spooky, but the Collector would slit his own granny's throat for a bargain. I can't see him putting his hoard at risk without a hell of a good reason. And everyone knows the Collector never gives away anything he can sell."

"True," I said. "But on the other hand, Razor Eddie isn't an easy person to say no to. More to the point, if the Collector really has been forced to reveal the location of his warehouse, you can bet he's already making plans to move his hoard to a new location. If we take too long getting the information from Eddie, it might well turn out to be worthless."

"It'll take the Collector time to move," said Suzie. "If he really does have everything he's supposed to have, it'll take him ages to shift it all. Particularly if he doesn't want to draw attention. And that's assuming he has an alternative safe site ready to move his collection to. No, we've got time. I'm more concerned with how much longer we can afford to spend standing around here. I'm beginning to feel like I've got a target painted on me. Find me something I can shoot."

She was right, of course. In times like these, doing nothing can be just as dangerous as doing the wrong thing. So I started off down the street, heading straight for Big Sergei's Warehouse, as though I didn't have a care in the world. Suzie rather spoiled the effect by slinking along beside me, gun at the ready, glaring about her like a junkyard dog. No-one shot at us, or swooped down out of the sky on glowing wings.

The front of Big Sergei's Warehouse was a long blank wall, with no name or sign anywhere. Big Sergei didn't believe in advertising. Either you knew his reputation, or you weren't big-league enough to do business with him. I kept my eyes open as we headed for the front door, ready to duck and weave and run as necessary. The warehouse was supposed to be protected by all kinds of state-of-the-art defences, everything from tailored curses to anti-aircraft guns. No-one stole from Big Sergei and lived to boast of it. Didn't stop people trying, though. This was the Nightside, after all. The front door was said to be six inches of solid steel, protected by the very finest electronic locks, and all the windows had bulletproof glass and steel shutters. Big Sergei believed in feeling secure.

Not that any of that would stop Razor Eddie, of course.

"If Big Sergei's got any sense, he'll have sealed this place up tighter than a duck's arse and gone into hiding," said Suzie. "In which case, how are we going to get in?"

"We'll just have to improvise," I said, trying hard to sound confident.

"Ah yes," said Suzie. "Improvise. Suddenly and violently and without remorse. I feel better already."

"Unfortunately," I said, slowing thoughtfully as we approached the front door, "it would appear someone else has beaten us to that."

Up close, it was clear the warehouse had taken a battering. Several of the windows had been smashed, which couldn't have been easy with bulletproof glass, and their steel shutters were buckled, hanging crookedly, or completely missing. There was a hole in the wall up by the first floor, as though it had been hit by a cannon-ball. Or a very angry fist. And the celebrated front door, six inches of solid steel protected by all kinds of heavy-duty defences, had been ripped right out of its frame and was currently lying in the street some distance away, in a severely crumpled condition. I gave it plenty of room as I cautiously approached the opening where the door had been. Suzie stuck close to me, shotgun at the ready. I peered in, satisfied myself that there was no movement or sounds of life, then stepped warily forward into the reception lobby. Suzie crowded past me, sweeping her gun back and forth, eager for a target. The possibility of imminent violence had cheered her up considerably.

The lobby was a mess. Every stick of furniture had been wrecked or overturned, and in some cases reduced to little more than kindling. The expensive carpeting had been torn and rucked up, as though whole armies had trampled across it. There were signs of bullet and bomb damage on some of the walls, and a tall potted plant in the corner had been pretty much shredded. The sheer extent of the destruction might almost have been funny, if it hadn't been for the blood. There was spilled blood everywhere, gallons of it. The torn carpeting was soaked from wall to wall, most of still so wet it squelched under our feet. There was more blood splashed across the walls, in thick red swatches and spatters, and the occasional handprint. It dripped from the shattered furniture, and from a wide wet stain on the ceiling. I didn't even want to think about what could have caused blood to jet almost a dozen feet into the air. I stepped around the dripping ceiling and advanced slowly across the lobby. I glanced at Suzie.

"If I didn't know better, I'd swear you'd been here."

She sniffed unhappily. "No, this is Razor Eddie's work. I'm a professional, he's . . . enthusiastic. You know what worries me the most about this? Lots of blood . . . but no bodies. What the hell has he done with the bodies? And what's with all this religious stuff on the walls?"

She gestured at the paintings hanging crookedly on the walls. They all depicted extremely detailed scenes from the deaths of Christian martyrs, with the emphasis very much on blood and gore and suffering. There were large crucifixes too. Extremely graphic crucifixes. And there were signs in ugly block lettering; *Pray for mercy while you still can. Every day, God is judging you. No mercy for the ungodly. The Church's way is the only way. Have you killed an unbeliever today?*

"Hard-core," said Suzie.

"None of that was here the last time I had occasion to have words with Big Sergei," I said. "He believed in profits, not prophets. I can only assume that the Warriors of the Cross wanted to buy so much from him that it was easier for him to rent them the whole warehouse, for as long as they were here. And they . . . made themselves at home. Just how many guns were the Warriors buying, I wonder?"

Suzie scowled. "Didn't he realise they were planning an invasion of the Nightside?"

I shrugged. "If he had, he wouldn't have cared. As long as they paid in advance. Someone was going to make a profit anyway, so why not him?" I looked around at all the blood and destruction. "The Unholy Grail has a lot to answer for. Jude said it attracted evil."

Suzie looked at me. "Jude?"

"Our client."

"Oh yeah. So much has happened, I'd almost forgotten about him. So, where do we go now, Taylor?"

"I think I may have spotted a clue," I said. She looked where I pointed. By a door marked STAIRS, someone had drawn a large arrow, painted in blood. "The stairs lead up to the offices on the third floor. We'd better get a move on. Razor Eddie's waiting for us."

"Wonderful," said Suzie.

● ● ●

We made our way up the stairs, following bloody arrows on the walls. Suzie took the lead with gun at the ready, checking every shadowed corner before she committed herself. There were no nasty surprises, only more damage and even more blood. A hell of a lot of people had to have died here, and recently, given how wet the blood still was. But there was never any sign of a body. The smeared scarlet arrows eventually led us to a small office at the back of the third floor. The door had been kicked in and was hanging drunkenly from one hinge. Suzie and I ducked past it, into the office. The cheap but practical furniture was still intact, but there was a long splash of blood across one wall. Not far away, there was a wall safe, with its heavy steel door torn away and left discarded on the floor. And sitting behind the office desk, slowly working his way through a pile of papers he'd taken from the safe, was Razor Eddie. He didn't look up as we came in.

"Hello, John. Suzie. Come on in. Make yourselves at home. Be with you in a minute."

Suzie headed straight for the open safe, grinned widely on finding it still packed with bundles of cash, and immediately set about transferring as many of them as she could into the many pockets of her leather jacket. Suzie had always been a deeply practical person.

The Punk God of the Straight Razor looked much the same as always, a painfully thin presence in an oversized grey coat that had seen better days, a really long time ago. It was torn and ragged, and apparently only held together by accumulated filth and grease. His long gaunt face was unhealthily pale, all dark hollows and fever-bright eyes. His voice was low, controlled, almost ghostly. And he smelled really bad, all the time. There are sewer rats dying of the Black Death that smell better than Razor Eddie. The only reason he didn't attract flies was because they tended to drop dead if they got too close to him. His slender pale hands moved slowly and methodically through the papers before him, now and again setting one aside in a separate pile.

"The Warriors of the Cross are an extreme, far-right Christian sect," Eddie said finally, still not looking up from what he was doing. "Widespread, very well funded, and very much into fire and brimstone and Crusades against . . . well, anything with even the faintest hint of fun about it. This particular branch of the Warriors was planning a full-scale invasion of the Nightside, in search of the Unholy Grail. Big Sergei apparently sold them everything from left-over Tiger Tanks to shoulder-mounted rocket launchers, and more guns and ammunition than the mind can comfortably comprehend, then disappeared sharpish before the shit could hit the fan. Nasty bastards, the Warriors. According to what I've found here, they were planning to set the Nightside on fire, then shoot everything that moved until someone handed over the Unholy Grail. But they got lucky. Someone just walked in here and offered to sell them the bloody thing. They, of course, tortured its location out of the poor bastard, then went and got it.

"And then I came here and took it from them. After a certain amount of unpleasantness.

"The Warriors of the Cross have done a lot of really nasty things in the past, and I had been looking for an excuse to make clear how displeased I was with them. It's extremists like this who give religion a bad name. They were only a small branch, of course, but I like to think I've sent a message."

"A message?" I said.

"Stay out of the Nightside, for starters." He looked up for the first time, and a smile moved briefly over his pale lips. "Wish I'd known the angels were coming. They'd probably have been even more unpleasant to the Warriors than I was. Not that I like the angels much better."

Suzie came back to join me, her jacket bulging with accumulated cash. She gave Eddie a hard look. "What did you do with the bodies, Eddie?"

He smiled again, just as briefly. "I sold them. Got a good price, too."

There are some conversations you know you don't want to pursue any further. I coughed politely, to draw Eddie's attention back to me. "You said you knew where we could find the Collector, Eddie. I really do need to see him rather urgently."

"Ah yes. The great mystery of the Nightside; the location of the Collector's secret lair. I've been there. No doubt you've been wondering why he should chose to reveal his greatest secret to the likes of me. Simple really. I didn't give him any choice. A quick tour of his collection was part of the price I demanded for retrieving the Unholy Grail from the Warriors and handing it over to him." Eddie laughed softly, a thin ghostly sound, like the wind gusting through dead branches. "I had him over a barrel, and he knew it. He was desperate at the thought of losing out on such a unique item, and I wanted to see his collection. I hadn't known he possessed the Speaking Gun, until he told me he'd lost it. Nasty weapon. I understand you have it now. If you're sensible, you'll get rid of it. The Speaking Gun has never made anyone happy or wealthy or wise. It was made to destroy, and that's all it does. Anyway, it occurred to me that if the Collector had one such weapon, he might well have others, and I wanted to know what. After all someday he might try to use them against me."

There were many things I might have said, but I chose not to. "We did try to use the Speaking Gun," I said. "It wasn't a success."

"Bloody thing's alive," said Suzie. "And vicious."

"In which case, I'm amazed you're still alive," said Eddie. "Hell, I'm impressed you're still sane."

"What was the Collector's place like?" said Suzie, sticking to the point as always.

"Big," said Eddie. "Bigger than the human mind can comfortably conceive. Floors and floors of it, packed to saturation point, including a whole load of crates he hasn't even got around to unpacking yet. He has so much stuff now, even he can't be sure of everything he's got. And, of course, he'd die before he brought in any assistance." Eddie considered for a moment. "I'll tell you this; he must have been collecting for a lot longer than any of us thought. He has some items you wouldn't believe . . ."

"Where is his lair, Eddie?" I said patiently. "And how do we get in?"

Eddie produced a computer card out of nowhere and laid it carefully on the desk before me. It was made of brass and studded with precious gems. "This card is programmed to open all his locks. The

Collector shouldn't know it's missing yet, but I wouldn't wait too long before using it."

"Eddie," I said, "Where . . ."

"On the Moon," said Razor Eddie. "In a series of caverns and tunnels, dug out deep under the Sea of Tranquility. Complete with power, atmosphere, and artificial gravity. I don't know whether he had it made for him, or simply inherited it . . . Either way, he's filled it with all the comforts of home, and all kinds of defence systems, including some he apparently looted from the future. You have to admire the man's nerve . . . How you two get to the Moon, and into his lair, is unfortunately your problem. I can't help. The Collector teleported me there and back. Any questions?"

"Yes," I said. "Know any good travel agents?"

"Ah, Taylor," said a calm, familiar voice behind me. "Always ready with an inappropriate quip."

I took my time turning around. I knew that voice. It was Walker, standing magnificently at ease in the open doorway, as always every inch the cultivated city gent. Suzie had already spun round and was covering him with her shotgun. Walker tipped his bowler hat to her, then to me. He glanced at Razor Eddie, and his mouth made a brief moue of distaste before he looked back at me.

"Well, Taylor, still keeping bad company, I see. You could do so much better for yourself."

"By working for you, and the Authorities?" I gave him my best cold, menacing smile. "Walker, I wouldn't piss on the Authorities if they were on fire. They, and you, stand for everything I despise. I have my pride. Not to mention scruples."

"Yes," said Walker. "Best not to. I'm afraid I have some bad news for you, Taylor. It seems that the angels have made direct contact with my superiors in the Authorities. Which came as something of a shock, I understand. My superiors were apparently under the impression that they had made themselves unreachable . . . In any case, the angels have made it very clear that either the Authorities cooperate fully in locating and handing over the Unholy Grail, or the angels will raze the Nightside to the ground. Slaughter every living being, and leave not one stone left standing upon another. Angels aren't the most subtle of creatures, but then, I suppose they don't have to be."

"Which angels are we talking about here?" said Suzie. "The ones from Above, or Below?"

"I don't know," said Walker. "Either. Both. Does it really matter? The point is that the Authorities have far too much invested in the Nightside to allow such a threat to their interests, so they have agreed to assist the angels. To be exact, they ordered me to come and get you, Taylor. I will take you in, we'll all have a nice chat and a cup of tea, and perhaps the good biscuits, and then you will use your special gift to track down and locate the Unholy Grail. And no, you don't get a choice in the matter. Your presence is required. Don't scowl, Taylor. You get to save the Nightside from utter annihilation, and put yourself in the Authorities' good books, for once. Some people would be flattered and grateful. Now come along, dear boy. Time is of the essence."

"You think we're going to just let you walk in here and take him?" Suzie's voice was very flat and very dangerous, and her shotgun didn't waver an inch, trained on the second button of Walker's waistcoat. "I've never trusted the Authorities before, and I'm not about to start now. The angels already tried to screw with Taylor's head once, so they could get their hands on the Unholy Grail. This is the Nightside, Walker. We don't bow down to Heaven or Hell."

Walker looked at her dispassionately. "I don't have any orders about you, or Eddie. You're both free to leave and go your own ways. Unless you choose to interfere with this, in which case I really can't speak for your safety."

The tension in the room cranked up a whole other notch. Suzie was grinning unpleasantly, and Eddie was looking at Walker in a disturbingly thoughtful manner. Anyone else would have turned and run, but not Walker. He was the Authorities' voice, with the power to back it up. There were a lot of stories about Walker, and the things that he'd done, and none of them had a happy ending. I took a step forward, to bring his attention back to me. He smiled charmingly, but it didn't reach his eyes.

"Well done, Taylor. I knew I could rely on you to do the right thing, eventually."

"You assured me earlier that you trusted me to sort this one out," I said. "You said it would be best for everyone if I got to the Unholy Grail first and put it out of everyone's reach."

"Times change," Walker said calmly. "The wise man bows to the inevitable. I have my orders, and now so do you. Come along, Taylor. I don't want to have to get testy with you."

"Do you really want to go one-on-one with me, Walker?" I said, and something in my voice made his eyes narrow. "Maybe we should, just for the hell of it. Haven't you ever wondered . . . haven't you ever wanted to know if either of us is really everything our reputations make us out to be?"

Walker looked at me thoughtfully for a long moment, and I met his gaze unflinchingly. I could feel Suzie poising for action, tense as a coiled spring. And then Walker smiled his charming smile again, and shrugged. "Perhaps another time, Taylor. Are you sure I can't persuade you to come with me? There are forces at my beck and call that you really don't want to meet. And surely you wouldn't want to risk your friends being hurt?"

Suzie sniggered offensively. "Yeah, right. That'll be the day."

"Good-bye, Walker," I said. "I'm sure you can find your own way out."

Walker shook his head. "You know your father wouldn't approve of behaviour like this, John. He understood about duty and responsibility."

"You leave my father out of this! What did working for the Authorities ever do for him? And where were you when he needed you? You were supposed to be his friend! Where were you when he married my mother? Perhaps we should talk about my mother. Would you like that?"

"No," said Walker. "I wouldn't."

"No . . . no-one ever does," I said, cold and flat and bitter. "Funny, that."

Razor Eddie stood up behind his desk, and all eyes immediately went to him. He never looked like much, but just then his presence seemed to fill the room. He looked at Walker, and Walker inclined his head slightly, respectfully.

"John doesn't have to go anywhere he doesn't want to," said Razor Eddie, in a voice like a death sentence. "And don't think you can threaten me, Walker. I have known worse things than Authorities or angels."

"And I'm just plain mean," said Shotgun Suzie.

"I have seen the Unholy Grail," said Razor Eddie. "The Collector wasn't fit to have it, and neither are you, or the angels. It is a thing that doesn't belong here, and the only person I trust to get rid of it is Taylor. Go now, John, Suzie. I'll keep Walker occupied."

Walker looked at me almost sadly. "You didn't really think I'd come here alone, did you?"

A gaudily coloured blur swept past him and into the office, blasting through the open doorway almost too fast to be seen. Something buffeted me in passing, almost knocking me off my feet, and rushed on to slam into Razor Eddie. The sheer force of the impact lifted him off his feet, smashed him clean through the closed window behind him, and sent him tumbling helplessly through the smoky air to the ground three stories below. Suzie was only just turning round, and trying to bring her gun to bear, when the blur turned and swept back, and a single horribly clawed hand slapped the shotgun out of Suzie's hand, then whipped back to tear out her guts. The black leather jacket blew apart in an explosion of tatters, and Suzie cried out once, in shock and pain, as her stomach opened up like a great mouth, and her intestines fell out in a rush of blood. She collapsed to her knees, grabbing with shaky hands at the thick purple ropes spilling out of her. More blood gushed out, soaking her lap and legs, and pooling on the floor around her.

It only took a few steps before I was kneeling beside her and holding her in my arms, but it seemed to take forever. I held her shoulders tightly, trying to stop her shaking. Her face was bone white, and already wet with sweat. She rolled her eyes at me and tried to say something, but her mouth was loose and ugly and wouldn't work properly. There was no fear in her eyes, only something that might have been a terrible resignation. One bloody hand groped around for her shotgun, but it was on the other side of the room. Her other hand was still trying to stuff severed bits of intestines back into her stomach. The stench of blood and guts was almost overwhelming. Suzie was breathing clumsily now, great heaving gasps, as though every breath was an effort.

She was dying, and both of us knew it.

And then the blur came to a sudden halt before me, solidifying into a familiar shape, one I hadn't seen in years. I should have known; it had to be her. She struck an elegant pose before me and smiled a happy contented smile. She always did like to show off. In one white-gloved hand she held the Speaking Gun's case, taken from Suzie even as she ripped out her guts. She waggled the case a few times before me, as a trophy, then slipped it casually under one arm.

"A little extra, I think, on top of my exorbitant fee. You don't object, do you, Walker darling?"

Walker started to say something, then stopped himself.

"Hello, Belle," I said, in a voice I didn't recognise. "It's been a while, hasn't it?"

"Oh, years and years, darling. But you know me. Always happy to bump into old friends."

Belle. Short for *La Belle Dame Sans Merci.* Tall and elegant, beautiful and sophisticated, supernaturally slender. She had poise and style and vicious charm, and an aristocratic disdain for small-minded things like ethics or morality, good or evil. She was what she was, and delighted in it. Her face had a marvelous bone structure, a broad forehead, purple eyes and a heavy, sulky mouth. Belle was a freelancer—intrigue, murder, theft, and conspiracy, or anything else you might desire, as long as you could pay for it. She'd done it all in her time, and always on her own terms. She drifted from one European capital to another, leaving a trail of broken hearts and broken bodies behind her, and never once looked back. Mostly she stayed out of the Nightside. Said the place was beneath her. I think she just felt happier away from any real competition.

To give her her due, she'd always been ready to take on anyone, anywhere, and she'd never been known to lose. Mainly because Belle had armoured herself in trophies taken from her many victims. On her back she wore a werewolf's pelt, thick and grey and shaggy. She skinned the hide off him herself, and now she wore the pale grey fur all the way down her back, with the emptied head pulled forward over her head like a hood. The skull's long canines dented her forehead, above her purple eyes. It wasn't just a garment; her magics kept the pelt alive and plugged into her own system. It was her skin now, her fur, and as a result she had a werewolf's ability to regenerate. Her burnished golden breastplate was made from a dragon's hide, and it formed utterly impenetrable armour. Her shimmering white elbow-length gloves were in fact a vampire's lily white skin, flayed from the undead victim by Belle's own fair hand. On one of her hands, heavy claws pushed through the white glove; claws taken from a ghoul and fused onto her own fingers. The thigh-high leather boots were new. I didn't know who she'd got them from. Belle's magics made her various armours a part of her, made her, for all practical purposes, unkillable.

Belle was very much a self-made woman.

Most strikingly, the two halves of her face didn't match. The left half was a distinctly darker shade than the rest of her body. One victim had got close enough to rip half of Belle's face away. So after she was dead, Belle took half the victim's face as a replacement. The new skin was younger, tighter, and a perfect fit.

Belle would go anywhere, and do anyone, as long as the cheque cleared. Or as long as the enemy was a challenge, or had something Belle wanted.

I clutched Suzie to me, cradling her shaking body in my arms. She was trembling violently now, as shock took hold. Blood ran in sudden spurts from her slack mouth, and dripped off her chin. I could almost feel the life going out of her. Part of me wanted to throw myself at Belle and tear her throat out, make her pay for what she'd done. But I couldn't do that. I had to be smarter, sharper, than that. Belle was armoured against all attacks, physical or magical. Or so she thought. My only hope was to keep cool and talk calmly with Belle. Keep her mind occupied, distracted, while I slowly and very surreptitiously focussed my gift on her. Do it right, and she'd never even notice. As long as I narrowed my concentration right down, into a single cold needle, I should be able to slip my gift past her mental and magical defences just long enough to do what I had to do. It was dangerous. If Belle even suspected what I was planning, she'd have my throat out in a second, and to hell with her mission. And even so small a use of my gift would still blaze like a beacon in the night, revealing my presence to those who were always hunting me. So I had to be careful, and focussed, and utterly underhanded.

Luckily, I was good at that.

"Been a long time, Belle," I said, in something very like a normal voice. "What is it, six, seven years since we worked together on that Hellstorm business? I thought we made a good team."

"Don't try to appeal to my better nature, darling," Belle said in her marvelously cool and smoky voice. "You know very well I don't have one. We made good partners, John, but we were never more than that."

"I heard the Walking Man got you, stalking you through the catacombs under Paris."

"Oh he very nearly did, darling, but I'm so very hard to kill. Unlike your little sweetie there. Poor Suzie. Never did know what you saw in her."

"You're a lot faster than you used to be, Belle. Been taking vitamins?"

"See these new boots, darling? Aren't they simply super? I skinned a minor Greek deity to get them, so I could have his speed."

"Give it up, John," said Walker. "Come with me now, and I promise you I'll see Suzie gets help. No-one has to die here. Don't let your pride get in the way. I'm the good guy, this time. I'm saving the Nightside from destruction."

"I've been told," I said, still looking at Belle, "that if either set of angels gets their hands on the Unholy Grail, Armageddon could come early."

"You say that like it's a bad thing," said Walker. "The dark chalice doesn't belong among people, John. It's always been trouble. Let it pass to others more suited to control it."

"Ah, Walker," I said. "Always ready with an inappropriate homily." I smiled sadly at Belle. "You must know you can't trust him, or the Authorities."

"I don't trust anyone, darling. But Walker paid in advance, so I'm all his, for as long as the money lasts. And after this unfortunate business is over, and they're finished with you, I've been promised that I can root through your living brains until I find the source of your special gift. Then I'll rip it out and stick it in my own head. And your gift will become mine. Isn't that sweet? It means you'll always be with me. Now put Suzie down, dear, and come with me. Or do you want to dance a little first?"

I put Suzie carefully to one side, laying her tenderly on the bloody floor. Her eyes stayed locked on mine. I stood up and faced Belle. The whole front of my coat was soaked in Suzie's blood. More of it dripped from my clenched hands. I grinned at Belle, cold as ice. "Let's dance, darling."

She laughed in my face. "You wouldn't hit a lady, would you?"

"Sure," I said. "Know any?"

And while she was still laughing, I hit her with my sharply focussed gift, driving it right past all her defences. I can find anything, with my gift. This time, I found the single small magic that Belle used to hold all her acquisitions together, that made it possible for her to access all their various attributes. And it was the easiest thing in the world for me to tear that magic away from her and crush it with my mind. Belle screamed once as the magic vanished, and her control over her various armours disappeared with it. The werewolf pelt fell away from her back and head, revealing only bare meat showing, red and glistening, with no skin left to cover it any more. The long gloves and boots cracked and rotted and fell apart, leaving bare muscles and tendons showing on her arms and legs. And half her face, the younger half, slipped away from her head, disintegrating into dust. Belle shrieked horribly, half her face a horror show.

I stepped forward and hit her once, breaking her neck. She was dead before she hit the floor.

I leaned over her and grabbed the werewolf pelt. It started to come apart in my hands, but I thought it would hold together long enough for what I had in mind. I looked around for Walker, but he was gone. Presumably in search of reinforcements. I knelt down beside Suzie. She was lying ominously still, scarcely even breathing. I pushed her guts back into the tear in her stomach, then held the werewolf pelt over the gaping wound. I crushed the pelt with both hands, wringing the last of its blood out of the pelt so that it dripped into the open wound. Werewolf blood, with all its regenerative properties. For a moment I couldn't breathe, then the edges of Suzie's wound slowly crept together, and vanished, as though it had never been there at all.

The pelt crumbled and fell apart, and I threw it away. It had done its job. I sat Suzie up again and cradled her in my arms, rocking her slowly back and forth. Her breathing became stronger, and more regular, and suddenly her eyes snapped open, wide and questioning. For a moment she just breathed steadily, as though it was a new thing and not to be trusted, and then her bloody hands went to her stomach, where the wound had been. Finding nothing, she looked at the unmarked flesh for a while. Then she smiled tremulously and turned her head back to look at me. I nodded and smiled, and she smiled back.

She slowly raised one hand and touched my face with her fingertips. I sat very still, afraid to do anything that might break the moment. Her fingertips moved slowly, hesitantly, across my cheek, my lips, delicate as the breath of a butterfly's wing. And then she pushed herself away from me, almost throwing me away. She knelt on all fours, with her back to me, breathing heavily and shaking her head back and forth.

"Suzie . . ." I said.

"No. I can't *do* this!" she said, in a voice so harsh it must have hurt her throat. "I *can't*. Not even with you."

"It's all right," I said.

"No it isn't! It'll never be all right. No matter how many times I kill him."

She rose unsteadily to her feet, looked around for her shotgun, and snatched it up from the floor. And then she shot Belle in the face three times, until there was hardly anything left above the neck.

"Just in case," said Suzie. "Besides, look what the bitch did to my best jacket."

I got to my feet and looked at her resolutely turned back, and for once in my life I didn't have a damned clue what to say. There was the sound of hurrying feet outside in the corridor, and Suzie and I both turned quickly to face the door. I think right then both of us would have been happy to see Walker with reinforcements. We could have used something to hit. But it was only Razor Eddie, appearing abruptly in the open doorway with his pearl-handled straight razor in his hand. He saw Belle's body, and relaxed a little.

"Where the hell were you?" said Suzie, lowering her shotgun.

"It will take more than a three-storey drop to kill me," said Eddie, in his pale ghostly voice. "But there's a limit to how fast even I can take three flights of stairs. Still, you seemed to have coped quite well in my absence. Where's Walker?"

"He made himself scarce when the trouble started," I said. "No doubt he'll soon return, with backup."

"Someone's coming," said Eddie. "I can feel it. Someone's coming, but it isn't Walker."

And we all looked round sharply as we suddenly realised we weren't alone in the office any more. Standing by the desk was a grey man in a grey suit. Up close, even his face looked grey. The angels had found me.

"Get out of here, John," said Razor Eddie. "There are more coming. Lots of them." He moved forward to put himself between the angel and Suzie and me. "Move! I'll hold them off."

He raised his left hand, and in it was the Speaking Gun, poisoning the air with its presence. The angel began to glow, a light so bright it seemed to come from another place entirely. Suzie and I ran for the open door. We clattered down the stairs at full speed, a terrible pressure building on the air behind us. It felt like a storm was coming. It felt like thunder in the blood, and lightning in the soul. We hit the lobby together and kept running. And from far away and close at hand, we heard the awful sound of a single backwards spoken Word. Something screamed, so loudly I thought my head would burst. Suzie and I ran out into the street and kept going, and the whole damned warehouse exploded behind us. The shock wave almost blew us off our feet, but somehow we kept going, and didn't stop running until we were at the end of the street.

We finally stumbled to a halt and looked back, breathing harshly. The walls of Big Sergei's Warehouse collapsed slowly inwards, and disappeared in a great outrushing of black smoke. In a moment, there was nothing left of the building except a great pile of rubble.

"Think Eddie got out in time?" said Suzie.

"I think so," I said. "Razor Eddie's always been very hard to kill."

"Isn't that what they used to say about Belle?"

"We'd better get moving," I said. "More angels will be on the way."

"Terrific. Where can we go that will be safe from angels?"

"Strangefellows," I said, trying hard to sound confident. "I've got an idea."

"Oh, that's always dangerous."

"Shut up and run."

SEVEN

Manifesting Merlin

Suzie Shooter and I ran through the Nightside, with Heaven and Hell close behind. Angels circled overhead in a narrowing gyre, riding the night skies on widespread wings, closing in remorselessly as Suzie and I sprinted down one deserted street after another. The night was full of fires and explosions, death and destruction. All the power and sleazy majesty of the Nightside, brought low in a single night, crushed under celestial heels. I looked quickly about me, trying to get my bearings. I didn't know the warehouse district that well, and I was so turned around now that the only thing I was still sure of was that I was a long way from home and safety. I chose another street at random and plunged down it, Suzie pounding away at my side. I had a stitch in my side that was killing me, and she wasn't even breathing hard.

Something moved in the street ahead, and I stumbled to a halt. Suzie saw it too, and crashed to a halt just ahead of me, automatically bringing her shotgun to bear. Two dim figures came running down the street towards us, silhouetted against the fires burning behind them. They both looked . . . wrong, somehow. And then the skin of Count Video came flapping down the street, raw and empty, with his flayed body running weeping after it. Suzie and I drew back to let them pass. There was nothing we could do.

"I don't think the city resistance is faring too well," I said, trying hard to sound calm.

"Just when you think you've seen everything . . ." said Suzie. "These angels are hard-core. We have got to get off the street, Taylor. But I am fresh out of ideas. Think of something. Fast."

From up above came the sound of great wings, beating on the night. Hundreds, maybe thousands of them, sounding lower all the time. I glared about me, looking for inspiration. We had the street pretty much to ourselves. Everyone else had either gone to ground or was waiting to be buried under it. Dark, hulking, anonymous buildings lined the street to either side. Some of them were more damaged than others, but none of them had lights in their windows. Suzie and I were on our own, surrounded by the enemy, and miles and miles from friendly territory. Business as usual, really, only more so. And just when things couldn't get any worse, they did.

Grey figures appeared out of nowhere, blocking off the street ahead of us. A dozen grey men in grey suits, watching us, unnaturally still and focussed. I looked behind me, and, sure enough, there were more grey figures there. The angels had found us. I looked up at the sky, half-expecting to see winged figures plunging down, to snatch us out of the street and carry us away, but there was no sign of any attack. Presumably they thought we still had the Speaking Gun. Once they figured out we didn't, we were dead in the water.

The figures up ahead pulsed suddenly with a bright and brilliant light, pushing back the night. Suzie and I both cried out, dazzled, and had to raise our arms to shield our faces. We'd grown too accustomed to the gloom. Widespread wings blazed like the sun. I looked back, eyes smarting, only to see grey figures disappear inside a sea of darkness that rolled slowly up the street towards us. A complete and unrelenting shadow, far darker than any mere absence of light could ever be. Unbearable light ahead, and a merciless dark behind.

"Oh shit," said Suzie.

"My thoughts exactly," I said. "Please don't shoot at the angels, Suzie. If you do, and they notice, they'll get even more annoyed with us."

"What do you mean us, white man?" Suzie flashed me a brief smile. "These bastards really do want you, don't they, Taylor?"

"They want my gift, my ability to find things. Whichever side controls that is pretty much guaranteed to get to the Unholy Grail first."

"Well," said Suzie, "given that we are outclassed, outnumbered, and almost certainly out-gunned, might this be a good time to strike some kind of deal?"

"No," I said immediately. "I don't work for free. And I don't trust extremes, of whatever kind."

"I really don't think they're in the mood to take no for an answer."

"And there is the very real possibility that either side would be willing to destroy me, rather than lose my gift to the enemy." I looked at Suzie. "They only want me. You could . . ."

"No I couldn't," said Suzie. "I'm not leaving you. That much I can do for you."

The light swept slowly down the street, while the darkness advanced from behind. It would have been a close bet which was the most disturbing to look at. Such pure manifestations didn't belong in the material world. And I really didn't want to be still standing here when the two forces met. I looked about me while Suzie hefted her shotgun unhappily.

"All this, just for you, Taylor? Haven't these creeps ever heard of overkill?"

"They're angels, Suzie. I think they invented the concept. Remember Sodom and Gomorrah? And we're facing agents from Above and Below . . . The light and the dark, and us caught right in the middle."

"Story of my life," Suzie said briskly. "Come on, Taylor, I'm waiting. What are we going to do? What can we do?"

"I'm thinking!"

She sniffed. "You always did freeze in the clinch, Taylor."

Suzie turned her shotgun on a recessed door in the wall beside us and let fly with one blast after another, as fast as she could work the pump. The door collapsed and blew inwards in a cloud of smoke and splinters, blown right off its hinges. Suzie dived through the jagged gap into the gloom beyond, with me crowding her heels all the way.

Once inside, we moved to either side of the open doorway and pressed our backs against the wall, while we waited for our eyes to adjust to the dim light. The wall felt comfortably thick and solid, even though I knew it wouldn't even slow the angels down. I felt as much as saw a huge, echoing space before and around me. A little light came through slit windows set high up on the walls, and I began to make out a series of narrow aisles between towering stacks of piled-up merchandise. Outside in the street, inhuman voices rose in rage and frustration. The sound was pure and primal and painfully loud. The two forces swept down the street and slammed together with a sound like mountains crashing. The floor shook underfoot, and the walls of the warehouse trembled. Flashes of blinding light flared through the slit windows, illuminating the warehouse like lightning going to war. And above it all, the sound of giant wings beating furiously. The air was heavy with significance, with the feeling of vital matters being decided by forces far above Humanity. I snorted, and shook my head. Like I was going to let that happen. *This is the Nightside, you bastards. We do things differently here . . .*

"Any idea where the hell we are?" said Suzie. "All I can see is crates, and all I can smell is sawdust and cat's pee."

"If we're where I think we are, they manufacture lucky charms here. Let's hope some of it will rub off. This way, I think."

I pushed myself away from the wall and strode off into the gloom, Suzie padding along beside me. We threaded our way through the piles of stacked crates, heading for the far end of the warehouse. We hadn't made twenty feet before what was left of the doorway was blown inwards by a blast of concentrated light. The gloom was banished in a moment, every part and content of the warehouse thrown into sharp relief. I ran like hell, and Suzie was right there beside me. The floor shook under our feet like an earthquake as angels punched through the warehouse wall like it was made of paper. I put my head down and kept running.

The floor broke open right in front of me, a jagged crack that widened in an instant into a gaping crevice. I tried to jump it, but didn't even come close. My stomach lurched as my kicking feet found nothing beneath them, and I fell into a darkness that seemed to fall away forever. At the last moment I caught the far edge of the crevice with one flailing hand, and fastened on to it with a death grip. My shoulder exploded with pain as my fall was suddenly halted, all my weight hanging from the one arm. I scrambled for the edge with my other hand, but I couldn't quite reach. The ground was still shaking, and the edge under my hand didn't feel at all secure. I looked up, and there was Suzie, on the far side of the gap, looking down at me. I should have known she'd make it. She knelt, studying my situation, her face entirely blank.

"Get out of here," I said. "They don't want you. And I think I'd rather fall than let them use me."

"I can't let you fall, Taylor."

"You can't touch me, remember?"

"Hell with that shit," said Suzie Shooter.

She reached down with one hand, and I reached up with my free hand and grabbed it. Suzie's face set into cold, determined lines, and her grip was as sure as death, sure as life, sure as friendship. She hauled me up out of the crevice, and we both fell sprawling on the far side of the gap. She let go of me the second I was safe, and we both scrambled to our feet on our own.

"You'd be surprised what I can do, when I have to," said Suzie.

"No I wouldn't," I said. "I've tasted your cooking, remember?"

Sometimes humour is all we have to say the things that can't be said.

Angels came crashing through the warehouse wall as though it was nothing more than heavy mist. As though the angels were more solid, more real than anything in the material world they currently moved in. And perhaps they were, at that. Brilliant light and pitch-darkness invaded the warehouse, consuming everything they touched. Suzie glared at me.

"Tell me you've come up with an idea, Taylor. Any idea. Because I think we've run as far as we're going."

"I do have an idea," I said. "But I'm reluctant to use it."

"It's a wonderful idea," Suzie said immediately. "Whatever it is, it's a marvelous idea. I am in love with this idea. What is it?"

"I have a short cut that can take us straight to Strangefellows. Sometime back, in a weak moment, Alex Morrisey gave me a special club membership card, for use in emergencies. Once activated, the magic in the card will transport us right into the bar. Alex heard about a rather unpleasant experience I had with the Harrowing, outside his club . . ."

Suzie was staring at me ominously. "You've had it all along, and you haven't used it?"

"There's a catch."

"Why am I not surprised?"

"Magic like this leaves a trail," I said patiently. "The angels will know immediately where we've gone. I was still hoping we might shake them off . . . but that doesn't seem to be an option any more."

"Use the card," said Suzie. "Trust me, this is the right time to use it. Morrisey's always boasted his place had major-league protections. I say it's well past time we put that to the test."

"He won't be pleased to see us."

"Is he ever? Use the card!"

I already had it in my hand. A simple embossed card, with the name of the club in dark Gothic script, and the words *You Are Here* in blood red lettering. I pressed my thumb against the crimson words, and the card activated, thrumming with stored energy. It leapt out of my hand and hung in mid-air before me, pulsing with light and bubbling with strange energies. Alex always liked his magics showy. The angels sensed what was happening, and both sides surged forward. The card grew suddenly in size and became a door, which opened before me. Comfortable light and convivial sounds spilled out into the warehouse. Suzie and I ran through the opening into Strangefellows, and the door slammed shut behind us, cutting off the frustrated screams of thwarted angels.

• • •

I suppose I must have made more impressive entrances into Strangefellows, but I can't think when. Certainly the two of us appearing out of nowhere, crying *Run for your lives! The angels are coming!* made one hell of an impression. The crowd of assorted suspects and dubious types drinking in the club all suddenly remembered they had urgent appointments somewhere else and left the bar in an extreme hurry. Some used the doors, some used the windows. A few vanished in impressive puffs of black smoke, while others opened their own doors to less immediately threatening locations, and disappeared into them. One thoroughly panicked shapeshifter turned himself into a barstool, and hoped not to be noticed. And one guy (there's always one) took advantage of the general confusion to vault over the bar top and make a grab for the cash register. But Alex's bouncers, Betty and Lucy Coltrane, got him before he'd taken a dozen steps. Betty took the register away from him, Lucy kicked his arse up around his ears; then they let the dumb bastard run (or more properly limp) away. The Coltranes were both pretty sure they were going to have more important things to worry about. Alex stood behind the bar, watching it all and looking even more bitter and put upon than usual. As the last of his patrons vanished, and the place fell unusually quiet, he threw his mopping-up rag onto the bar top and glared at me.

"Thanks a whole bunch, Taylor. There go my profits for the evening. I knew I should never have given you that bloody card."

Suzie and I leaned on the bar, breathing heavily, and Alex grudgingly pushed a bottle of brandy towards us. I took a good swallow, then passed the bottle to Suzie, who drank the rest of it. Alex winced.

"Why do I even bother giving you the good stuff? You never appreciate it. Now what's this about angels coming here?"

"They're right behind us," I said. "And in a really bad mood."

"Tell us this place is protected," said Suzie, wiping her mouth with the back of her hand. "I really need to hear this dump is seriously protected."

"It is protected," said Alex. "But possibly . . . not *that* protected."

"Be specific," I said. "What have you got?"

Alex sighed heavily. "I hate giving away trade secrets, but . . . Basically, this whole building is protected by wards, shaped curses and genetic-level booby-traps laid down by various magicians down the centuries, all of them pretty powerful and vicious as all hell. Grandfather put a really nasty curse on people who miss the urinals in the toilet. And, of course, my ancestor Merlin's still buried somewhere under the wine cellar. More than enough to keep the flies off, even in the Nightside, but no-one ever said anything about bloody angels! I don't suppose anyone ever thought the possibility would arise. Of course, they didn't know about you, Taylor."

"You could always turn me over to the angels," I said. "I'd understand."

"This is my bar!" Alex snapped immediately. "No-one messes with my patrons, even if it's you. And no-one tells me what to do in my own bar, not even a bunch of celestial storm troopers. Should I lock all the doors and barricade the windows?"

"If you like," I said.

"Won't it help?"

"Not really, no."

"You're a bundle of fun to be around, Taylor, you know that?"

Suzie had her back to the bar, her shotgun in her hands, glowering warily about her. "Taylor, how long before the angels get here?"

"Not long," I said.

"Am I at least allowed to ask why both of you are soaked in what looks revoltingly like fresh blood?" said Alex. "Not that I care if you're hurt, of course. I ask only for information, in the interests of hygiene."

"I met up with an old friend," I said.

"Anyone I know?"

"Belle."

"Oh," said Alex. "Her. Is she . . . ?"

"She rests in pieces."

"Good," said Alex. "Snooty bitch. Never liked her. Always putting on airs and looking down her nose at my bar snacks. And she always ordered the best champagne and never paid for it."

"You wouldn't happen to have a really, really big gun stashed away behind your bar, would you?" Suzie said hopefully.

Alex sneered in her face. "Even if I did, I'm not stupid enough to annoy an angel by pointing it at him. Anyway, last I heard, you and Taylor had the Speaking Gun . . . Tell me you still have the Speaking Gun."

"We lost it," I admitted.

Alex really looked like he was about to have a fit. His fists clenched, his teeth clenched, and he actually shuddered for a moment with frustration and outrage. He grabbed two tufts of spiky hair sticking out from under his beret and tugged at them dangerously.

"That is typical of you, Taylor! As long as I thought you had the Speaking Gun, I thought we might actually have a chance. But no! You get your hands on one of the most powerful weapons in the Nightside, and you lose it! You're a jinx, Taylor, you know that? You are nothing but bad news, and always have been! I can feel one of my heads coming on . . . How are we supposed to defend ourselves now? Buy the angels a round and spike their drinks? Lucy, Betty, emergency measures! Right now!"

The Coltranes fell to with a will, moving all the furniture away from in front of the bar, and opening up a large clear space. (The shapeshifted barstool yelped quietly at the rough handling, but refused to turn back.) Once the Coltranes had created a big enough space, they laid out a large pentacle, using salt cellars from behind the bar to mark the lines. They made a really professional job of it, considering they were drawing it free-hand. Bouncers have to know many special skills, especially in the Night-side. We all took our places inside the pentacle, then Lucy and Betty sealed and activated the design by scrawling disturbing signs in the vales between the five points. Betty drew the last sign with a flourish, and the salt lines blazed with blue-white energies. Properly constructed pentacles drew their power from ley lines, the living nervous system of the material world. Unfortunately, angels drew their power from somewhere even more impressive.

Betty and Lucy Coltrane sat down together and held each other tightly. They'd done all they could. Suzie and I stood back-to-back, watching and waiting. Alex muttered darkly to himself while trying to look in all directions at once. At least when he wasn't shooting dark glances at me that clearly said *This is all your fault. Do Something. And you'd better have a really good plan.* As it happened, I did. But I wasn't going to tell him about it just yet. Because he really wasn't going to like it.

Upstairs, the front door to the club blew in. There was the sound of great wings beating, followed by the tread of heavy feet. A blindingly bright light spilled out of the foyer but stopped abruptly at the top of the stairs leading down into the bar proper. A heavy tension built on the air, oppressive and threatening like a storm about to break, as the angels pressed against Strangefellow's ancient defences. All of the windows shat-tered at once, vicious shards of glass flying through the air, only to fall just short of the pentacle's glowing lines. A blackness far darker than the night oozed through the windows, swallowed them up, then crept slowly across the walls.

"They're here," said Suzie. "Heaven and Hell."

"And poor Humanity caught in the middle, just like always," I said. I turned to Alex. "And now, it's up to you. We need your ancestor, Alex. We need Merlin."

"No," he said. "No way. I won't do it."

"He's the only one powerful enough to make a stand against angels, Alex."

"You don't know what you're asking, John. I can't do it."

"That's your big plan?" said Suzie. "Call up Merlin? What's he but another dead sorcerer who won't lie down?"

"According to some Arthurian legends, his full name was Merlin Satanspawn," I said. "Because his father was supposed to be the devil."

"Just when you think things can't get any worse . . ." Suzie scowled unhappily. "I can see a rock and a hard place moving into position around us. If you like, I could just shoot us all now. It might be less painful."

"Relax, Suzie," I said. "I'm on the case. Alex . . ."

"Don't make me do this, John," he said quietly. "Please. You don't know what it's like, what it does to me. When I call him up, he manifests through me. He takes my place in the world. I have to cease to exist, so he can be real. It feels like dying."

"I'm sorry, Alex," I said. "Really. But we don't have the time for me to be kind."

I pushed my gift into his head, found the connection that still existed between Alex and his most ancient ancestor, and pushed it hard.

"Merlin Satanspawn; come forth!"

Alex cried out, in pain and shock and horror, and ran out of the pentacle before any of us could stop him. He got as far as the bar before the change hit him. The whole world seemed to shudder, as reality shifted and changed . . . and where Alex had been, suddenly someone new, or rather very old, came into the world. He sat in state upon a great iron throne, the heavy black metal carved and scored with crawling, unquiet runes. He was naked, his corpse-pale body decorated from throat to toes with curving Celtic and Druidic tattoos. Many were unpleasant and actually disturbing to look upon. Between the ancient designs, his skin was blotchy and discoloured and visibly decayed in places. He'd been dead a long time, and it showed. His hair was long and grey, falling past his shoulders in convoluted knots, and stiffened here and there with clay and woad. Upon his heavy brow he wore a crown of mistletoe. His face was heavy-boned and ugly, and two fires leapt and danced in the sockets where his eyes should have been. There was an ancient wound in the centre of his chest, where skin and muscle and bone had been torn apart, leaving a gaping hole. His heart was gone, torn out, long and long ago. He was Merlin, dead but not departed, powerful beyond hope or sanity. Merlin, sitting on his ancient throne and smiling horribly.

They say he has his father's eyes . . .

He only still existed through an awful act of will. Life and death and reality itself bowed down to his magics. Though there were those who said he was only still around because neither Heaven nor Hell would take him.

"Who disturbs me at this time?" Merlin's voice was deep and dark, and grated on the ear like fingernails dragged across the soul.

"I'm John Taylor," I said, politely. "I called you. Angels have come to the Nightside, from Above and Below, in search of the Unholy Grail. They threaten this place, and your current descendant."

"Damn," said Merlin. "If it isn't one thing, it's another."

A voice spoke from the top of the stairs; a choir of voices speaking in a harmony so perfect it was inhuman. "We are the Will of the Most High. We are the soldiers of the shimmering plains, and the Courts of the Holy. Give us the mortal, for we have need of him."

Another voice spoke, from out of the darkness that had enveloped the windows and was spreading slowly across the walls. Its harmonies were dissonant and disturbing, but still inhumanly perfect. "We are the Will of the Morningstar. We are the soldiers of the Pit, and the Inferno. Do not stand in our way. The mortal is ours."

"Typical angels," said Merlin, sitting utterly at ease and unmoved on his iron throne. "All bluff and bluster. Bullies, then and now. The Hereafter's attack dogs, only with less manners. Guard your tongues, all of you. I am the Son of the Morningstar, and I will not be spoken to in such a fashion. I could have been the Anti-Christ, but I declined the honour. I was determined to be free, from both Heaven and Hell. I gave birth to Camelot, and the song that never ends. I made a Golden Age for Mankind, an Age of Reason. And then the Holy Grail came to England's fair shores, and no-one could think of anything else. They all went riding off on their stupid quests, abandoning their duty to the people. And, of course, it all fell apart. What is Reason, in the face of dreams? I still miss Arthur. He was always the best of them. Arthur, my once and future King."

"Did you really get to see the Holy Grail?" said Suzie, who would interrupt anybody. "What was it like?"

Merlin's smile softened, just for a moment. "It was . . . wonderful. A thing of beauty, and of joy. Almost enough to be worth losing the world for. Almost beautiful enough . . . to shame me for the shallowness of my vision. Man cannot live by Reason alone."

"And now the Unholy Grail's come here," I said. "I've been told it would be a really bad thing if either set of angels gets their hands on it. Judgement Day was mentioned, and not in a good way."

"The sombre chalice . . ." Merlin raised one rotting hand to the gaping hole in his chest. "I suppose it was inevitable the ugly thing should turn up here. The Nightside was created to be the one place where neither Heaven nor Hell could intervene directly. A place apart, free from the tyrannies of fate and destiny. In the Nightside, even the Highest and the Lowest can only work through agents. Which is why the angels are so much weaker here."

Suzie and I exchanged a glance. If these were angels in a weaker form . . . "Excuse me, Sir Merlin," I said, with all the politeness at my command, "Did you just say the Nightside was created for a specific purpose? Who created it, and why?"

Merlin looked at me with his flame-filled eyes, and smiled unpleasantly. "Ask your mother."

Somehow, I'd known he was going to say that.

"If some of these angels are agents of Heaven," said Suzie, in the manner of someone who had a problem bone, and was determined to worry at it until she got an answer that satisfied her, "why have they been killing people, and turning them to salt, and blowing up perfectly good buildings?"

"We only punish the guilty," said the chorused voice in the light. "And so many here are guilty of something."

Suzie looked at me. "They have a point."

"Of course," said Merlin, "here, all the angels are cut off from their Masters. Poor things, they're not used to having to think for themselves. Which is why they've made such a mess. Decision-making isn't really what you do best, is it, boys?"

"We are here for the Unholy Grail," said the light.

"Do you dare stand against us?" said the dark.

"Why not?" said Merlin. "It wouldn't be the first time, would it? Now back off, all of you, or I'll fry your pinfeathers."

The light faded back a little, and the darkness stopped spreading, but the sense of surrounding presences was as strong as ever.

"Taylor," Suzie said urgently. "Tell me there was more to your plan than just this . . ."

"Not even half of it," I murmured. "Hang in there. Sir Merlin, with your leave I think I can sort out this whole mess in a way that will please . . . well, nobody really, but it'll be a solution we can all live with. *Live* being a relative term, of course. I don't know where the Unholy Grail is, but I'm pretty sure I know someone who does. You see everywhere, Sir Merlin, so could you please grab the Collector and bring him here?"

Merlin gestured languidly with a heavily tattooed hand, and suddenly the Collector was standing right there in the pentacle with us. He looked around, startled, and his eyes all but popped out of their sockets with outrage. He started to say something, then saw Merlin sitting on his throne and shut his mouth quickly before it could get him into even more trouble. The Collector was a podgy, middle-aged man with a thick neck and a florid face, wearing a white jumpsuit and cape, as popularised by Elvis in his later days. It didn't suit him at all.

"Wow," said Suzie, sticking the barrel of her shotgun in the Collector's ear. "Now that's what I call service."

"Oh shit," said the Collector.

"Language!" said Suzie. "There are angels present."

"Hello, Collector," I said calmly. "How's the leg?"

"Taylor! I might have known you were behind this!" The Collector started to say something else, but Suzie shoved her gun a little further into his ear, and he stopped himself again. He glowered at me. "I had to grow a new leg, thanks to your interference all those years ago. Put me right off time-travelling. Never was cost-effective. And besides, I kept bumping into myself, and I kept giggling at me, which was unnerving, to say the least. Now will someone please tell me why I have been transported here against my will!" .

"Because you're needed," I said, and then hesitated, because I just had to know. "Is that outfit you're wearing the real thing?"

The Collector pulled himself up to his full, not particularly impressive, height, and preened. It wasn't a pretty sight. "Of course it's real! Graceland hasn't even noticed it's missing yet."

I grinned. "Are you wearing the authentic nappy under it?"

The Collector's eyes narrowed so much they almost disappeared. "What . . . do you want, Taylor?"

"The Unholy Grail. You've got it."

"Yes, and I'm keeping it. The dark chalice is a totally unique piece. It's going to be the pride of my collection. The rest of the collecting fraternity will just die when they hear I've got it!"

"We could all die if we don't get this mess sorted out right now," I said.

"Starting very definitely with you," Suzie growled, applying a little more pressure to the gun barrel in the Collector's reddening ear.

He slapped the gun aside and glared right back at her. "Don't you threaten me, Shooter. I'm protected in ways you can't even imagine."

"Unfortunately, he probably is," I said. "So ease off a little, Suzie. Collector, in case it's slipped your attention, we are currently surrounded by whole armies of angels, all of whom would be quite willing to take you apart, right down to the molecular level, while still keeping you alive and aware and screaming horribly if that's what it takes to get you to hand over the Unholy Grail. Only Merlin's power is holding them back, for the moment. You really think your protections are good enough to hold off a whole bunch of really angry angels?"

He sniffed, but he was visibly weakening. "They don't even know where my collection is."

"It's on the Moon," said Suzie, smiling smugly. "Under the Sea of Tranquility."

The Collector actually stamped his foot, he was so angry, and he waved his pudgy fists in the air. "I knew I couldn't trust Razor Eddie . . . but he had me over a barrel, the bastard. It doesn't matter. Let the angels try and take my prize away from me. They'll discover I can summon up worse things than angels!"

"You're not fooling anyone, little man," said Merlin, and his cold, rasping voice dismissed the Collector's confidence in a moment. "Give up the sombre chalice, while you still can. It's already corrupting your mind."

"It's mine!" said the Collector. "You can't have it! You just want it for yourself!"

Merlin laughed briefly, and everyone winced at the awful sound. "Hardly, little man. I once held the true cup of the Christ in my hands. The Sangreal itself. Nothing less will ever tempt me again."

"I won't give up the Unholy Grail!" the Collector shouted. His face was an unhealthy shade of purple. "I won't, and you can't make me! Not even you, Merlin Satanspawn. Not as long as you still want me to find your missing heart for you someday. Everyone else has failed you. I'm your last hope."

Suzie looked at me, and I sighed. "Okay, very quick précis of a *very* long and complicated story. Merlin lost his heart to a young witch called Nimue, back when the world was a lot younger. She then lost it in a card game. Without his heart, Merlin's power is only a fraction of what it once was. The heart's been through almost as many hands as the Unholy Grail, down the centuries, and is currently . . . missing in action."

"Couldn't you find it for him, with your gift?" said Suzie.

"Perhaps. That's why Merlin's helping us now. Right, Sir Merlin?"

He smiled and nodded, the flames leaping in his eye sockets. What I didn't tell Suzie was that I had absolutely no intention of ever trying to find Merlin's heart. Nobody in their right mind wanted Merlin to regain his full powers. Even dead, he'd be more trouble than the angels . . .

"You can't keep the Unholy Grail," I said bluntly to the Collector. "You don't have anything strong enough to hold off angels, and you can bet they'd be ready and willing to destroy your entire collection, fighting each other over possession of the Unholy Grail."

The Collector pouted sullenly. "They would too, wouldn't they? Bloody winged philistines. All right, you can have it! Ugly damned thing anyway. Merlin? Back to the Moon. Please."

"With a little company, to keep you honest," said Merlin.

I looked at Suzie resignedly. "Hang on to your aura," I said. Suddenly Suzie and I and the Collector were somewhere else.

EIGHT

Cats and Robots and One Last Vicious Truth

Every time I get teleported anywhere, I end up watching my whole life flashing before my eyes. Or at least, edited highlights. Most of it seemed to make some kind of sense at the time. I live in fear that someday Some-one will find a way to slip in commercials.

Suzie and the Collector and I materialised out of nowhere, surrounded by thick clouds of noxious black smoke. Merlin learned his magic in the Old School, and still believed in traditional effects. Suzie batted at the smoke with her hand, swearing harshly in between racking coughs, while I checked to make sure I still had two of everything I should have. You can't be too careful with other people's teleport spells. Hidden extractor fans soon sucked most of the black smoke away, and we were able to take a clear look at our surroundings. We'd arrived in an almost blindingly technicolour reception area, with bright hanging silks for walls, dyed in every colour of the rainbow, and twice as gaudy, while thick chequerboard padding covered the floor and the ceiling. My feet sank deeply into the cushioned floor, and walking across it I rose and fell so suddenly that I al-most felt seasick. The air smelled strongly of something very like pine. Suzie glared about her suspiciously, the shotgun in her hands, but there were no obvious threats.

The Collector brushed aside one hanging silk to reveal a small high-tech console, all gleaming steel and crystal displays. He stabbed at the controls with his podgy fingers, ignoring everything else, while muttering something to his console that sounded suspiciously like *Daddy's home.* I was more concerned with the fact that I couldn't see a door anywhere. Suzie finished her coughing by hacking up what sounded like half a lung, and then spat viciously on the padded floor.

"I wish Merlin would get over his need for flashy special effects," she growled. "That smoke always plays hell with my sinuses."

"Boys and their toys," I said. "We have to allow Merlin his little eccentricities. Because if we don't, he'll probably turn us into frogs. Collector, what are you doing?"

"Shutting down some of my internal security systems," he snapped, without looking round. "I have all kinds of hidden protections here, and I don't want them all opening fire on you the moment you enter my warehouse. Some of my collection might get damaged. I have to be careful. There are always people trying to break in and steal my precious things. Bastards!"

"The nerve of some people," I murmured. "Thinking they could steal some of the many things you've stolen."

The Collector said nothing, still hunched over his console. I bounced a few times on the padded floor, checking my weight. If we really were somewhere under the Sea of Tranquility on the Moon, someone had gone to a lot of trouble to make things feel like home. The gravity, air, and temperature all seemed perfectly normal. Which suggested that the Collector must have a lot more high-tech hidden away somewhere else. Suzie prowled restlessly back and forth in the confined space, poking at the hanging silks with the barrel of her gun. She jabbed at the padded floor with one bootheel and sniffed loudly.

"I always said you belonged in a padded cell, Collector."

"I believe in being comfortable and indulging myself," he said, finally turning away from his console. "The padding is there to protect me in the event of sudden, unexpected fluctuations in the artificial gravity. Most of the tech that keeps this place running comes from a possible future I visited, and I have to admit I'm not fully sure how all of it works. I know which buttons to push, but the minute anything goes wrong, I have to fall back on trial and error. Mostly I let my robots run things. You'll meet them later."

"That's the trouble with looting," I said. "There's so rarely enough time to grab the instruction manual as well."

"I do not loot! I collect and preserve!"

"So where is this famous collection?" said Suzie. "Don't tell me we came all this way to hang around what looks suspiciously like a tart's boudoir? We are on something of a tight schedule, remember?"

"Right through here," said the Collector, a little sullenly. "Follow me."

He ducked past a deep puce hanging silk and opened a concealed door. He gestured for Suzie and me to go first, but neither of us was having any of that. We made him go first, then followed quickly on his heels as he led us into the biggest damned warehouse I have ever seen. It seemed to stretch away forever, the walls so far off I couldn't even see them. There was no ceiling, just a bright unfocussed glow from somewhere up above. And filling this gigantic warehouse; thousands upon thousands of wooden crates, in every size you could think of. They were stacked in towering piles, each marked with a stencilled number. Narrow aisles ran between them. I looked around, trying to get some idea of the size of the collection, but the sheer number of crates numbed my brain. There was nothing on display, nothing to admire or examine. Just crates.

"This is *it*?" said Suzie, wrinkling her nose.

"Yes it is, and *don't touch anything!*" the Collector said severely. "I've shut down the hidden guns, but my robots are still programmed to protect my collection from any and all harm. I may have to allow your presence for a while, but that's as far as I'll go. You're here for one object only, and I will get that for you. Luckily I was only just packing it up when Merlin grabbed me. I can see I'm going to have to upgrade my security again."

"Somehow, I'd always pictured something more impressive," said Suzie. "Don't you ever put any of the good stuff out, so you can play with it?"

The Collector winced. "It's much safer this way. I don't encourage visitors, and for me, owning an item is everything. All right, when I first obtain a piece, I do get a certain satisfaction out of holding it, examining it, enjoying all its many qualities . . . I do like to examine every detail . . . close-up . . ."

"If he starts to drool, I may puke," said Suzie, and I had to nod in agreement.

The Collector scowled at both of us. "*But*, once the initial thrill is over, I immediately pack it safely away in here. It's the thrill of the chase I really enjoy. That, and the knowledge that I've done my rivals dirt, that I've got my hands on something, and they haven't. I do so love to crow and preen in all the best newsgroups . . . And, of course, everything is computer-scanned before it's put into storage, so I can visit it again at my leisure in virtual mode. After all, some of the more delicate items aren't up to too much . . . handling. And it's so much easier to find an item on a computer menu than try to dig through all this lot looking for one particular item."

That was when the first of the robots made its appearance, and Suzie and I immediately lost all interest in what the Collector was saying. The metal figure came striding down the narrow aisle towards us on impossibly slender legs, a tall and spindly thing of shining steel and brass, its clean lines the very definition of art deco. It advanced on us smoothly, unhurriedly, its every movement impossibly graceful. The robot was vaguely humanoid in shape, though the squarish head had been cast to resemble a stylised cat's features, right down to jutting steel whiskers and glowing slit-pupilled eyes. The long-fingered hands ended in vicious claws. More robots appeared silently out of the many interconnecting aisles, until we were faced by a small army of cat-faced automatons. I thought I could detect a faint humming from them, so high it was only just in the range of my hearing. They seemed to be talking to each other. The Collector smiled on them fondly. Suzie's shotgun moved restlessly back and forth in her hands, seeking a target.

"Relax, Suzie," said the Collector. "They're only looking you over. Getting used to your presence. Strangers make them nervous. I had them programmed that way. Nothing like a spot of paranoia to keep a guard on his toes. I picked this lot up in a particularly good deal from another possible future. They have basic limited AIs, built around polymerised cat's brains. Simple, obedient, and marvelously malicious when they have to be. They do so enjoy a good chase . . . and the torture afterwards. The purrfect protectors for my collection. They built this whole place for me and run it in my absence. Far better than any fallible human guards, and besides, I don't care for company these days. I prefer to be alone, with my things. My lovely things."

"No offence, Collector," said Suzie, "but you are seriously weird, even for the Nightside."

"For someone who wasn't trying to offend, I thought you did awfully well," I said.

"Is all well, master?" said one of the cat-faced robots, in a thrilling female contralto that made Suzie and me look at the Collector in a whole new way.

"All is well," the Collector said grandly. "You may all return to your regular duties. My guests will not be staying long. I'll call if I have need of you."

"As you wish, master," said the robot, then they all turned smoothly on their steel heels and disappeared back into the many narrow aisles of the warehouse. Suzie watched carefully until they were all gone, then turned back to the beaming Collector.

"Do they all have to call you master?"

"Of course."

"Doesn't that get creepy after a while?"

"No. Why should it?"

"Don't go there, Suzie," I said. "We really don't have the time."

The Collector led the way down a narrow aisle that to the untrained eye looked exactly like all the others, and Suzie and I followed after him, pulling faces behind his back. We stuck close; the hundreds of interconnecting passageways made up a maze it would clearly be only too easy to get thoroughly lost in. I let my eyes drift over the many crates and cases we passed; a few were labelled as well as numbered. One label said *Antarctic Expedition 1936; Do not open till the Elder Ones return*. The exterior of the crate was covered in frost, despite the uncomfortable warmth of the warehouse. A much larger crate was labelled simply *Roswell 1947*. It had air holes. Something inside the crate was growling, in a thoroughly pissed off way. And one crate standing on its own levitated proudly a few inches off the floor. I don't know what was inside that crate, but it smelled awful. Suzie drew my attention to a smaller box that was juddering fiercely, almost shaking itself apart. I tapped the Collector politely on the shoulder, and indicated the box.

"What the hell have you got in there?"

"Perpetual motion machine," said the Collector. "Can't figure out how to turn the damned thing off."

"You have so much amazing stuff here," I said. "Who do you share it with? Who else gets to see all the marvels and wonders you've acquired?"

"No-one, of course," he said, looking at me as though I was crazy.

"But . . . doesn't half the fun of collecting lie in showing off your treasures to someone else?"

"No," said the Collector firmly. "It's all to do with ownership. With knowing it's mine, all mine. I do like to rub my rivals' noses in it, now and again; show them proof that I have some hotly contested item that we've all been after. I drive them crazy with jealousy, then laugh in their faces. But in the end it wouldn't matter to me if no-one knew what I had but me. It's enough to know that I've won. That I'm the best."

"That's all this is?" said Suzie. "Whoever dies with the most toys wins?"

The Collector shrugged. "I don't give a damn what happens to any of this stuff once I'm dead and gone. Let it rot, for all I care. I collect because . . . it's what I'm good at. The only thing I've ever been good at. And things . . . possessions . . . can't hurt you. Can't leave you."

For a moment there, he actually looked human, and vulnerable. It didn't suit him.

"Do you want us to keep quiet about the things we've seen here?" I asked.

"Hell no!" he said immediately, all his usual obnoxiousness returning in a moment. "Tell everyone! Drive them mad with curiosity and envy! My problem has always been that I can't prove how big my collection is without bringing people here to see it, and, of course, I can't do that. They'd only betray me and try to steal something. There are people who've spent their whole lives plotting how to get in here . . ."

"You weren't always the Collector," I said. "I've seen photos of you, with my father, from when you were both younger. What were you . . . before this?"

He looked at me, not bothering to hide his surprise. "I thought you knew. I worked for the Authorities, along with Walker and your father. Protecting the Nightside. We were all such friends, in those days. We had such plans, such hopes . . . but in the end it turned out we all had different plans and different hopes. I retired, before they could fire me, and set up on my own. One day I'll own the whole damned Nightside. And then I'll make them listen to me."

I was so fascinated by what he was saying and its implications that I didn't notice all the robots sneaking up on us. Suzie did. Nothing gets past her. She realised I was mesmerised by the Collector's hints and allusions, and elbowed me firmly in the ribs. I looked up and found we were surrounded by ranks and ranks of the the cat-faced robots, standing perfectly still and silent, watching coldly with their glowing cat's eyes. There were hundreds of the damned things. The Collector realised that I'd finally noticed and stopped talking in mid sentence to laugh cheerfully in my face. He was well out of reach, and I had more sense than to try and make a grab for him. The robots looked decidedly . . . menacing.

"I had to keep going until enough of my boys arrived," he said, almost giggling with self-satisfaction. "You didn't really think you could see my collection and my home, with all its secrets, and live, did you? To hell with Merlin, and the angels; nothing can touch me here. I'm protected by spells and tech beyond your imagination, and Merlin won't catch me napping twice. The Unholy Grail is my greatest prize, the jewel of my collection, and I won't give it up! I'll never give it up! I'll just stay here, safe on the Moon, until all this nonsense has blown over. And long before then, you'll be in no condition to betray my secrets to anyone. Perhaps I'll have what's left of you stuffed and mounted. Something to brighten up the reception area."

"You'd kill the son of an old friend?" I said.

"Of course," said the Collector. "Why not?"

He gestured to the waiting robots, and they surged forward in perfect unison. Suzie opened fire with her shotgun, blasting robots as fast as she could work the pump action. The robots shattered under the bullets' impact, flying apart in showers of steel and brass shrapnel that had us all ducking for cover. Suzie kept firing, grinning fiercely as robots blew apart before her. Either she'd found a whole new kind of ammunition for her gun, or they didn't build robots to last in the future.

It helped that the narrow aisles meant the robots could only come at us a few at a time. Suzie and I put our backs to the wall of crates, while the Collector danced back and forth in the background, crying out miserably as some of his crates were inevitably damaged or destroyed by the exploding robots. Suzie pulled grenades from her belt, and lobbed half a dozen where they'd do the most good. Robots and crates blew apart in bowel-churning explosions, and for a while it seemed to be raining machine parts. The Collector cried out for Suzie to stop, and when she didn't, he ran from crate to crate, prying them open and looking inside, searching for some weapon or device he could use against us. He didn't seem to be having much luck. Suzie reloaded the shotgun from her bandoliers and went back to blowing robots apart like metal ducks in a shooting gallery. She was grinning widely now, her eyes hot and happy.

But the robots kept pressing forward, forward, and there didn't seem to be any end to their numbers. The Collector must have got a job lot. One of them got close enough to take a swipe at me with a clawed hand, and I decided enough was enough. This far from the Nightside, I didn't have to worry about the angels seizing my soul again. So I opened my third eye, my private eye, and used my gift to locate the automatic shutdown commands in the robots' minds. I knew they had to be there. The Collector didn't trust anyone, not even his own creatures. He had to have a way to shut down the robots in case they ever turned against him. I hit the commands I'd found in those clever polymerised cat's brains, and all the robots froze suddenly in mid motion. A few of them had got worryingly close. Suzie slowly lowered the smoking shotgun, took a deep breath, and turned to look at me.

"You could have done that at any time, couldn't you?"

"Actually, yes."

"Then why did you wait so long!"

"You looked like you were having fun."

Suzie considered that for a moment, then smiled and nodded. "You're right. I was. Thank you, Taylor. You always did know how to show a girl a good time."

"All vicious gossip, rumours and lies," I said. "Collector . . . Collector? Where are you?"

We found him not far away, slumped exhausted and weeping over another open crate. Whatever it held was buried in plastic packing pieces. The Collector stirred them miserably with one hand, then looked up at us. He spat at me, but his heart wasn't in it.

"Look at what you've done . . . so many lovely things destroyed . . . It'll take me weeks just to find out how much I've lost. Bullies, both of you. No respect for art, for the treasures of centuries . . . And I have weapons here! Great weapons, that would stop even you! I have the Horn of Jericho, Grendel's Bane, even the legendary lost Sword of the Daun. But I can't find them!"

"Show us the Unholy Grail," I said, not unkindly. "The sooner you hand it over, the sooner we'll be gone."

The Collector nodded a few times, sniffing back tears, and finally dug his hands deep into the packing pieces before him.

"I was packing it away when Merlin grabbed me. It is my greatest prize, but . . . the dark chalice is too disturbing to have around. The air's always cold, the shadows have eyes, and I hear voices, whispering . . . things. Ah. Here."

He brought out a small beaten copper bowl, gleaming dully in the subdued lighting. It was dented and dull and not at all impressive. We all looked at it for a long moment, then the Collector offered it to us. I hesitated to touch the thing.

"That's *it*?" said Suzie. "*That*'s the dark chalice, the Unholy Grail? The cup Judas drank from at the Last Supper? That miserable-looking thing?"

"What were you expecting?" said the Collector, smiling just a little at one last chance to show off his expertise. "You thought perhaps it would be some great silver chalice, studded with jewels? Romantic medieval claptrap. The Disciples were a bunch of poor fishermen. This is the kind of thing they drank out of."

"It's the real deal," I said. "I can feel it from here. It's like every bad thought you ever had, wrapped up in one never-ending nightmare."

"Yeah," said Suzie. "Like it's poisoning the air, just by existing."

The Collector looked at me slyly. "You could keep it for yourself, Taylor. You could. This simple cup is powerful beyond all your wildest fantasies. It could make you rich, worshipped, adored. It can satisfy every dirty little yearning in your soul. It has the answer to every question you ever had. The truth about your past, your enemies . . . even your mother."

I looked at the Unholy Grail, and it was like looking into the heart of temptation. Suzie watched me carefully, but said nothing. She trusted me to do the right thing. And in the end, perhaps it was that trust that gave me the strength to turn away.

"Put it in a bag, Collector. I wouldn't dirty my hands by touching it."

The Collector pulled an airline carry-on bag out of the packing pieces and stuffed the Unholy Grail into it. He almost seemed relieved. I took the bag and slung the strap over my shoulder.

"Merlin!" I said, raising my voice. "I know you're listening. We've got it. Bring us home."

Merlin's magic gathered about us, preparing to teleport Suzie and me back to Strangefellows, and the waiting angels. And in the last possible moment, when the Collector was sure the teleport spell had been activated and couldn't be stopped, he stepped forward and shouted one last vicious hurt.

"You're not the only one who can find things, Taylor! There was a time I used to take commissions, in return for help in establishing my collection. I found your father for your mother! I put them together. Everything you are is because of me!"

I went for his throat with furious hands, but Suzie and I were already fading away. The last thing I heard on the Moon was the Collector laughing, loud and bitterly, as though his heart would break.

NINE

For the Remission of Sins

Strangefellows sprang into being around us again, and Suzie braced herself for the thick black smoke, but there wasn't any this time. She looked suspiciously about her, and there was Merlin, no longer sprawled on his dark iron throne but leaning casually against the long wooden bar, a bottle of the good whiskey in one tattooed hand. He smiled unpleasantly and took a long drink from the bottle. I glanced at the gaping hole in Merlin's chest, where his heart used to be, half-expecting to see the swallowed whiskey come running out of it.

"Welcome back, far travellers," said Merlin. "In deference to your delicate feelings, I dispensed with the smoke this time. Typical of youngsters today. No respect for tradition. Probably wouldn't know what to do with a newt's eye if I slapped it in your hand."

I stepped forward, and he stopped talking. "Send us back!" I said, my hands clenched into fists, so angry it was all I could do to get the words out. "Send us back, right now. Better still, grab the Collector again and haul his nasty arse back down here, so I can beat the truth out of him with my bare hands."

"Easy, tiger," said Suzie, moving in close beside me. Her voice was surprisingly gentle. "I'm the violent one in this partnership, remember?"

"Things change," I said, not taking my eyes off Merlin. "I want the Collector here, right now. He knows things. Things about my mother, and my father. And I will break his bones one by one, and make him eat every last piece, until he tells me what I need to know."

"Wow," said Suzie. "Hard-core, Taylor."

"I'm sorry," said Merlin, still leaning against the bar, entirely unmoved by the raw fury in my voice and eyes. "The Collector has disappeared from his lair under the Moon's surface, taking his collection with him. I can't see him anywhere. Which ought to be impossible, but that's the modern age for you. No doubt I'll track him down eventually, but that will take time. For a mere mortal, he's surprisingly elusive."

I was so angry and frustrated I could hardly breathe, ready to lash out at anyone, even Merlin. Suzie moved as close to me as she could without actually touching me, calming me with her presence, and slowly the red haze began to lift from my thoughts. It's always thoughts of family that drive me crazy, and it's always my friends who bring me back.

"Let it go, John," Suzie said calmly, reasonably. "There'll be other times. He can't hide from us forever. Not from us."

"And now it's time for me to go," said Merlin. "You have the sombre chalice in that bag. I can feel its awful presence from here. I can't be this close to it. Too many bad memories . . . and far too much temptation. I may be dead, but I'm not stupid."

"Thanks for your help," I made myself say, in an almost normal tone. "We'll meet again, I'm sure."

"Oh yes," said Merlin. "We have unfinished business, your mother and I."

And before I could pursue that any further he was gone, disappearing back into his ancient grave somewhere deep under the wine cellar. The arrogant bastard always had to have the last word. Reality flexed and shuddered, and Alex Morrisey was suddenly back among us again, sitting slumped in the middle of the pentacle. He groaned loudly and shook his head slowly. He realised he had a bottle of whiskey in his hand and took a stiff drink. He almost choked getting the stuff down, but he was determined.

"I should have known he'd get into the good stock," he said bitterly. "Damn. I hate it when he manifests through me. My head will be full of corrupt Latin and Druidic chants for days." He shuddered suddenly, unable to continue with his usual facade. He looked at me, and I knew that behind his ubiquitous shades, his eyes were full of betrayal. "You bastard, Taylor. How could you do that to me? I thought we were friends."

"We are friends," I said. "I know that can be difficult, sometimes. I'm sorry."

"You're always sorry, John. But it never stops you screwing up people's lives."

I didn't say anything, because I couldn't. He was right. He struggled to his feet. I offered him a hand, but he slapped it aside. Lucy and Betty Coltrane moved quickly in and got him on his feet again, supporting him between them until his legs were firm again. He looked at the airline bag slung over my shoulder and gestured jerkily at it with his whiskey bottle.

"Is that it? Is that what you risked my sanity and soul for? Get the damned thing out and let me take a look at it. Haven't I earned the right? I want to see it."

"No you don't," I said. "It's vile. Poisonous. Your eyes could rot in your head just from looking at it for too long. It's dark and it's evil and it corrupts all who come into contact with it. Just like its original owner."

Alex sneered at me. "You always were a frustrated drama queen, Taylor. *Show me.* I've a right to see what I suffered for."

I opened the airline bag and took out the copper bowl, holding it carefully by the edges. It was feverishly hot to the touch, and my skin crawled at the contact. It felt as though someone new had entered the bar, someone terribly old and horribly familiar. Part of me wanted to throw the thing away, and part of me wanted to clutch it to my breast and never give it up. Alex leaned forward for a better look, but didn't try to touch it. Just as well. I wouldn't have let him.

"*That's* it?" said Alex. "I wouldn't serve a cheap claret in that."

"You're not going to get the chance," I said, trying to keep my voice normal. I stuffed the bowl back into the bag, though the effort brought beads of sweat to my brow. "This nasty little thing is going straight to the Vatican, where hopefully they will have the good sense to lock it up somewhere extremely safe, until the End of Time."

"If only it was that simple," said Walker.

We all looked round sharply as the Authorities' chief voice in the Nightside came strolling unhurriedly down the metal stairs into the bar. He still looked every inch the city gent out on his lunch break. Calm and sophisticated, and very much the master of the moment. He glanced at the pitch-darkness filling the bar's shattered windows, but didn't seem in the least perturbed by it, as though he saw something like it every day. And perhaps he did. This was Walker, after all. Alex scowled at him.

"Perfect. What the hell are you doing here, Walker? And how did you get in?"

"I'm here because the angels want me to be here," said Walker easily, striding across the floor to join us and stopping just short of the pentacle's salt lines. He glanced at it briefly and looked away, managing to imply that he'd seen much better workmanship in his day. Walker could say a lot with a look and a raised eyebrow. He tipped his bowler hat to us and smiled pleasantly. "The angels contacted the Authorities and made a deal, and the Authorities sent me here to implement it. And while this club's defences are more than adequate to keep out the usual riffraff, they're no barrier to me. I have been empowered by the Authorities to go wherever I have to go, to carry out their wishes. And right now, they want the Unholy Grail. They intend to hand it over to the angels, in return for . . . certain future considerations. And an end to all violence and destruction in the Nightside, of course."

"Which set of angels?" I asked.

Walker shrugged and smiled charmingly. "Yet to be determined, I believe. Whoever makes the better offer. I understand it could go either way. Still, that isn't really any of your business, is it? Give me the Unholy Grail, and we can all get on with our lives again."

"You know that isn't going to happen," I said. "Angels can't be trusted with the dark chalice, and neither can the Authorities. None of you have Humanity's best interests at heart. So, do you think you can take it from me, Walker? I don't see any backup, this time. Are you really ready to go head to head with me?"

Walker looked at me thoughtfully. "Perhaps. I'd really hate to have to kill you, John. But I do have my orders."

Suzie pushed past me suddenly, standing at the edge of the pentacle so she glared right into Walker's face. "You set your pet on me. Set Belle on me. I could have died."

"Even I just have to do what I'm told, sometimes," said Walker. "However much I might regret the necessity."

"Wouldn't stop you doing it again, though, would it?"

"No," said Walker. "My position doesn't allow me to play favourites."

"I ought to shoot you dead where you stand," said Suzie, in a voice that was cold as ice, cold as death.

Walker didn't even flinch. "You'd be dead before you could pull the trigger, Suzie. I told you, I'm protected in ways you can't even imagine."

I moved quickly to stand between them. "Walker," I said, and something in my voice made him turn immediately to look at me. "There are things we need to talk about. Things you should have told me long ago. The Collector had some very interesting information about the old days, when you and he and my father were such very close friends."

"Ah yes," said Walker. "The Collector. Poor Mark. So many possessions, and none of them enough to make him happy. Haven't talked to him in years. How is he?"

"Well down the road to full on crazy," I said. "But there's nothing much wrong with his memory. He still remembers finding my mother, and putting her together with my father. If the three of you were as tight as he says, you had to know all about it. So who commissioned him to go out and find my mother, and why? What part did you play in it all? And how come you never told me anything about this before, Walker? What else do you know about my parents that you've never seen fit to share with me?"

By the end I was shouting right into his face, almost spitting out the words, but he held his ground, and the calm expression on his face never once changed. "I know all kinds of things," he said finally. "Comes with the territory. I told you all you needed to know. But there are some things I can't talk about, not even with old friends."

"Don't just think of us as old friends," said Suzie. "Think of us as old friends with a pump-action shotgun. Tell him what he needs to know, Walker, or we'll see how good your precious protections really are."

He raised a single eyebrow. "The consequences could be very unfortunate."

"To hell with consequences," said Suzie. Her smile was really unpleasant. "When have I ever given a damn for consequences?"

And perhaps he saw something in her eyes, heard something in her voice. Perhaps he knew Suzie Shooter's shotgun wasn't just any shotgun. So he smiled regretfully and used one of his oldest tricks. The Authorities had given him a Voice that could not be denied, by the living or the dead or anything in between. When he spoke in that Voice, gods and monsters alike would bow down to him.

"Put down the shotgun, Suzie, and step back. Everyone else, stand still."

Suzie put down her gun immediately and stepped back from the edge of the pentacle. Nobody else moved. Walker looked at me.

"John. Give me the bag. Now."

But what was in the bag burned against my side like a hot coal, fanning the anger within me, feeding the fury that blazed within me. I could feel the power of the Voice, but it couldn't get a hold on me. I stood my ground and smiled at Walker, and for the first time his certainty seemed to slip a little.

"Go to hell, Walker," I said. "Or better yet, stay right where you are while I come and beat the truth out of you. I'm in a really bad mood, and

I could just use someone like you to take it out on. Can you still use the Voice when you're screaming, Walker?"

I stepped out of the pentacle, crossing the salt lines, and nothing could touch me. I could feel myself smiling, but it didn't feel like my smile at all. I was ready to do awful things, terrible things. I was going to enjoy doing them. Walker backed away from me.

"Don't do this, John. To attack me is to attack the Authorities. They won't stand for that. You don't want them on your trail, as well as your enemies."

"Hell with you," I said. "Hell with them."

"That isn't you talking, John. It's the Unholy Grail. That's why you're shielded from me. Listen to me, John. You don't know how much I've done to protect you, down the years, using my position in the Authorities."

I stopped advancing on him, though part of me didn't want to. "You protected me, Walker?"

"Of course," he said. "How else do you think you've survived, all these years?"

"Oh, you'd like me to think that, wouldn't you? But I know better. You belong to the Authorities, Walker. Body and soul. And now you're scared, because the Voice they gave you doesn't work on me. Perhaps it's the Grail, perhaps it's something I inherited from my mother or my father. You tell me. Are you ready to talk about my parents now?"

"No," said Walker. "Not now. Not ever."

I sighed, shrugged the airline bag off my shoulder, and let it fall onto the floor. Something cried out, in shock and rage, or maybe that was only in my mind. I stirred the bag with the toe of my shoe, and sneered at it. I'm my own man, now and always. I looked at Walker. "Why is it that everyone seems to know all about my parents except me?"

"The truth is, no-one really knows it all," said Walker. "We're all just guessing, and whistling in the dark."

"You're not getting the Unholy Grail," I said. "I don't trust you."

"Me, or the Authorities?"

"Is there a difference?"

"Now that was cruel, Taylor. Quite unnecessarily cruel."

"You hurt Suzie."

"I know."

"Get out of here," I said. "You've done enough damage for one day."

He looked at me, then at Suzie and the others, still standing rigidly inside the pentacle. He nodded to them, and they all relaxed as the paralysis disappeared. Walker nodded once to me, then turned and walked briskly out of the bar and back up the metal steps. Suzie dived for her shotgun, but by the time she had it levelled he'd already disappeared. She scowled at me, her lower lip pouting in disappointment.

"You let him go? After everything he did? After what he did to me?"

"I couldn't let you kill him, Suzie," I said. "We're supposed to be better than that."

"Well done," said the man called Jude. "I'm really very impressed, Mr. Taylor."

We all looked round sharply, and there was my client, the undercover priest from the Vatican, standing patiently by the bar, waiting for us to notice him. Short and stocky, dark-complected, long, expensive coat. Dark hair, dark beard, kind eyes. Alex glared at him.

"Its getting so just anyone can walk in . . . All right, how did *you* get in here, past two sets of homicidal angels and my supposedly state-of-the-art defences that I'm beginning to think I wasted a whole bunch of my money on?"

"No-one can prevent me from going where I must," Jude said calmly. "That was decided where all the things that matter are decided. In the Courts of the Holy."

"You aren't just an emissary for the Vatican, are you?" I said.

"No. Though the Vatican doesn't know that. I want to thank you for bringing me the Unholy Grail, Mr. Taylor. You've done me a great service."

"Hey, I helped," said Suzie.

Jude smiled at her. "Then thank you too, Suzie Shooter."

"Look," I said, a bit sharply, "this is all very civilised and pleasant, but whoever the hell you really are, how do you intend to get the Unholy Grail past the supernatural brigades surrounding this place? They've already destroyed half the Nightside trying to get their hands on it. How can you keep it from them?"

"By making it worthless to them," Jude said simply. "May I have the cup, please?"

I hesitated, but only for a moment. Bottom line, he was the client. I never betray a client. And he had paid me a hell of a lot to find the Unholy Grail for him. I handed him the airline bag, and he reached in and took out the copper bowl. He dropped the bag on the floor and studied his prize, turning it back and forth. It was hard to read the expression on his face, but I thought it might be a kind of tired amusement.

"It's smaller than I remembered. But then, it's a long time since I last held it," he said quietly. "Almost two thousand years." He looked up and smiled at us all. "My name, in those long-ago days, was Judas Iscariot."

I think we all gasped. None of us doubted him. Alex and the Coltranes retreated to the far end of the pentacle. Suzie turned her shotgun on the client. I stood my ground, but I could feel a terrible chill creeping through my bones. Jude. Judas. Of course I should have made the connection . . . but you don't expect to encounter two Biblical myths in one day, not even in the Nightside.

"Taylor," Suzie said tightly, "I think there is a distinct possibility that we have screwed up royally."

"Relax," said Jude. "Things aren't as bad as they may appear. Yes, I am that Judas Iscariot who betrayed the Christ to the Romans, and afterwards hanged myself in shame. But the Christ forgave me."

"He forgave *you*?" I said.

"Of course. That's what he does." Jude smiled down at the cup in his hands, remembering. "He was my friend, as well as my teacher. He found me and cut me down, brought me back from the dead and told me I was forgiven. I knelt at His feet, and said, *You must go, but I will stay, until you return.* And I've been here, doing penance, ever since. Not because He required it, but because I do. Because I do not forgive me."

"The Wandering Jew," I said softly.

"I've been with the Vatican for years," said Jude. "Under one name or another. Working quietly in the background, doing my best to keep them honest. And now, at long last, I have a chance to purge the last remaining vestige of my ancient sin. Bartender, some wine, if you please."

Outside, the voices in the dark rose in protest. Voices from the light answered them, then the two angelic armies slammed together again, two unimaginable forces continuing a conflict almost as old as Time itself. The whole bar shook, as though in the grip of an earthquake. Jagged cracks opened in the walls, and the dark pulsed at the windows while the light flared in the foyer above. Angelic voices rose, singing battle songs, as they trampled the world beneath their uncaring feet. Jude ignored it all, standing patiently by the bar with his old cup in his hands. Alex looked at me.

"He's your client; you go and get him some wine. I'm not leaving this pentacle."

"It's your bar," I said. "You serve him. I don't think the angels will bother with you now. They sound distinctly preoccupied."

Alex stepped gingerly over the salt lines, and when nothing immediately awful happened to him, he made a run for the bar. He dug at a bottle of house red, pulled the cork, and presented the bottle to Jude with only slightly shaking hands. Jude nodded and held out his cup. Alex poured a measure of wine into it, and Jude made the sign of the cross over it.

"And this . . . is His blood, shed for us all, for the remission of sins."

He raised the cup to his mouth, and drank. And in that moment, the war between the angels stopped. Everything grew still. The darkness slowly withdrew from the shattered windows, and the light faded away from the top of the stairs. Somewhere, a choir of perfect voices was singing something almost unbearably beautiful in perfect harmony. Jude drank the last of the wine and lowered the cup with a satisfied sigh. The song reached a ringing climax, and faded away. There was the sound of great wings beating, departing, fading away into an unimaginable distance.

"They've gone . . ." said Suzie, finally lowering her shotgun.

"They have no business here any more," said Jude. "It's only a cup now. Made pure again, in His name. Blessed, like me."

"So," I said, just a little breathlessly. "What happens now?"

Jude picked up the airline bag and stuffed the cup into it. "I take it back to the Vatican with me, put it on a shelf somewhere, and let it fade into obscurity. Just another old cup, of no particular importance or significance to anyone."

He smiled on us all, like a benediction.

"No charge for the wine," said Alex. "On the house."

Suzie snorted. "Who said the age of miracles was over?"

"You have done all of Humanity a great service," said Jude, bowing slightly to me. "And enabled me to right an old wrong. Thank you. Now I really must be going."

"I hate to spoil the moment," I said. "But . . ."

"The Vatican will pay the rest of your fee, Mr. Taylor. With a substantial bonus."

"Pleasure doing business with you," I said. "Even if it was a little hard on the Nightside."

He smiled. "I think you'll find the angels of the light have repaired all the damage they caused, and put right as much as they can. They are the good guys, after all, if somewhat limited in their thinking."

"What about all the people who got hurt?" said Suzie.

"The injured will be healed and made whole again. The dead, however, must remain dead. Only one man could ever raise the dead to life again."

Suzie walked across the pentacle lines to approach him. Her shotgun was back in its holster. She stopped directly before him and looked him in the eye.

"Are you ever going to forgive yourself?"

"Perhaps . . . When He finally returns, so I can say I am sorry to His face once again."

Suzie nodded slowly. "Sometimes, you have to forgive yourself. So you can move on."

"Yes," said Jude. "And sometimes it was never your fault in the first place."

He leaned forward and kissed her gently. On the brow, not the cheek. And Suzie didn't flinch away.

"Hey, Jude," I said. "Can *you* tell me the truth about my mother?"

He looked at me. "I'm afraid not. Have faith in yourself, Mr. Taylor. In the end, that's all any of us can do."

He turned and walked away, back up the metal stairs, towards the night. At the last moment, Alex called after him.

"Jude, what was He really like?"

Jude stopped, considered for a moment, and then looked back over his shoulder. "Taller than you'd think."

"God speed you on your way," I said. "But please, don't come back. You guys are just too disturbing. Even for the Nightside."

NIGHTINGALE'S LAMENT

ONE

The Hanged Man's Beautiful Daughter

There are all kinds of Powers running loose in the Nightside, but its power sources have to be rather more reliable, as well as completely divorced from outside interference. Someone's got to pump out the electricity to keep all that hot neon burning. The Nightside, being a city within a city, draws its energies from many sources—some of them illegal, some of them unnatural. Power is generated by blood sacrifices and imprisoned godlings, gestalt minds and tiny black holes held captive inside stasis fields. And there are other sources, so vast and awful, so alien and unutterably *other*, that just to glimpse their secret workings would drive a man insane. Not that anyone cares about such things in the Nightside, not as long as the lights are bright and the trains keep running. But the only really dependable source for *electricity* used to be the futuristic power plant of Prometheus Inc. Magic may be more flashy, but there's always been as much super-science as sorcery in the Nightside.

Prometheus Inc. was a fairly recent success story. Not quite six years old, it had a reputation for dependability and savagely undercutting prices, which made it the company that supplied some twelve per cent of the Nightside's electricity. So the recent sudden outbreak of sabotage and destruction inside the closely guarded power plant could not be allowed to continue. Walker made that very clear. Walker represents the Authorities, the shadowy people who run things here, inasmuch as anyone does, or can. He sends the occasional job my way, when it suits him, because I am quiet, dependable, and entirely expendable.

I stood in the shadows at the end of the street, quietly studying the hulking edifice that was Prometheus Inc. It wasn't much to look at—just another great tower block of glass and steel. The top floors were offices, administration and the like. Middle floors were laboratories, for research and development. And the bottom floor was public relations. The power plant itself, that modern wonder of efficiency and incredible output, was supposedly somewhere underground. I say supposedly, because as far as I knew, only a handful of people had ever seen it. The whole thing was automated, run from a single control centre, and even after six years no-one had any idea of what it was or how it worked. And it's not easy, keeping secrets in the Nightside.

The whole Prometheus Inc. success story had happened while I was away, trying—and failing—to live an ordinary life in the ordinary world. Now I was back, and I was quite keen to see what was being hidden under the surface of Prometheus Inc. I like knowing things that no-one else does. It's helped me keep alive, down the years. I strolled out of the shadows and headed for the office building. There was a small army of security men and rent-a-cops surrounding the place, and those nearest the main door lifted their heads and paid attention as they spotted me approaching. An awful lot of guns zeroed in on me, and the sound of safeties clicking off was almost deafening. If I'd been anyone else, I might have been worried.

I came to a halt before the main door and smiled at the rent-a-cops arrayed before me, in their wonderfully striking uniforms of midnight blue with silver piping. I nodded to the officer in charge, a tall and somewhat overweight man with cold, careful eyes. He held his ground, and his gaze didn't waver, though behind him we could both hear his men whispering my name. Some of them crossed themselves or made ancient warding signs. I let my smile widen just a little, because I could see it upset them. Ever since I tracked down the Unholy Grail and stood off two armies of angels to do it, my reputation had been going through the roof. Mostly nonsense, of course, but I did nothing to discourage the rumours, particularly the nasty ones. Nothing like a good—or more properly speaking a bad—reputation to keep the flies off.

"I'm supposed to ask for identification," said the officer. "And shoot anyone who isn't on the approved list."

"You know who I am," I said calmly. "And I'm expected."

The officer relaxed a little. "First good news I've had all night. Hello,

Taylor. I'm actually glad to see you. This whole business has my people seriously spooked."

"Has anyone been killed?" I asked, frowning. "I understood this was just a sabotage case."

"No deaths as yet, but a hell of a lot of casualties." The officer scowled. "Whoever's tearing this place apart doesn't give a damn about anyone who gets in his way. I've lost forty of my people in the last three nights, and I still haven't got a clue as to who's behind it all. No-one ever sees anything, until it's too late. I've had this place closed up tighter than a duck's arse, and still the bastard keeps getting in."

"Inside job?" I asked, to show I was paying attention.

"That was my first thought, but there hasn't been anyone in there for a week. The boss sent them all home when the problems started. He's the only one left in the building. I ran the usual security checks on the staff anyway, just in case, but nothing showed up. Most of them haven't been around long enough to work up a serious grudge."

"So what's freaking your men?" I asked quietly. "If they were any more on edge, they'd be shooting each other."

The officer snorted. "I told you. No-one ever sees *anything*. I've got saturation coverage around the building, CCTV inside, and infrared and motion sensors working. And whoever it is comes and goes without setting off any of them."

"There are a lot of things in the Nightside that come and go as they please," I pointed out.

"Don't I know it. But this is supposed to be a high-tech, low-magic area. If any heavy-duty magic-user had appeared here, he'd have set off all kinds of alarms. Whoever or whatever's trying to shut this place down, it's outside anything I've ever experienced, in science or magic."

I nodded easily, doing my best to exude casual confidence. "That's why they sent for me. Because I find the answers other people can't. See you later."

I stepped past the officer and headed for the main door, only to stop abruptly as one of the rent-a-cops moved suddenly forward to block my way. He was a big lad, with muscles on his muscles, and his huge hands made the semi-automatic in his grasp look like a toy. He scowled at me in what he obviously imagined was an intimidating way.

"Everyone gets frisked for guns," he snapped. "That's the rules. No exceptions. Even for jumped-up ambulance chasers like you, Taylor."

The officer started to say something, but I stopped him with a quick gesture. The day I couldn't deal with a constipated rent-a-cop, I'd retire. I gave him my best nasty smile.

"I don't use guns. Never have. They have too many limitations."

I slowly raised my hands, opened them, and the rent-a-cop's eyes widened as a steady stream of bullets fell from my hands to bounce and rattle on the ground at his feet.

"Your gun is empty," I said. "Now get out of my way before I decide to do something unpleasantly similar to your insides."

He pulled the trigger anyway, and made a small unhappy sound in the back of his throat when nothing happened. He swallowed hard and stepped back. I walked past him as though he didn't exist. I could hear the officer chewing him out as I passed through the heavy main door into the lobby beyond.

I strolled into the luxurious reception area as though I owned the place, but the effect was wasted, because there was no-one there. I heard electronic locks closing behind me. Someone knew I was there. I looked around the lobby and quickly spotted the security cameras tucked away in the ceiling corners. All the little red lights were on, so I just stood there and let the cameras get a good look at me. I thought I looked pretty good. My white trench coat was actually a little cleaner than usual, and I was almost sure I'd remembered to shave. Appearances can be so important. There was a brief burst of static from an unseen speaker, then a familiar voice whispered in the great empty lobby.

"John, I'm so glad you're here. Come on through to the manager's office and join me. Take the blue door at the end of the lobby, and follow the arrows. Don't go wandering. I've got booby-traps set up everywhere. And watch your back. We never know when the saboteur's going to strike next."

I passed through the blue door and followed the glowing arrows that appeared on the wall beyond. After the luxurious reception lobby, the inner workings of Prometheus Inc. turned out to be decidedly functional. Narrow corridors with bare walls, numbered doors, and scuffed carpeting. It was all very quiet, as though the whole building was tense, waiting for something bad to happen. The arrows finally led me to a door with the Prometheus company logo on it, and there waiting to greet me was the manager-owner himself, Vincent Kraemer.

He nodded and smiled and shook my hand, but it was clear his thoughts were somewhere else. The man was seriously worried, and it showed. He ushered me into his office, looked quickly down the corridor, and shut and locked the door. He waved me to the visitor's chair and seated himself behind the magnificent mahogany desk. The office looked comfortable, lived in. Nice prints on the walls, deep deep carpet, and a high-tech drinks cabinet in the corner. All the usual signs of success. But the desk top was covered in papers that had overflowed and almost buried the In and Out trays, and one whole wall of the office was covered in CCTV monitor screens, showing ever-shifting views of the power plant interior. I studied them for a while, to show I was taking an interest, but it was all just machinery to me. I couldn't tell a turbine from a teapot, unless one of them had a tea cosy on it. Everything seemed to be working okay for the moment, and the walkways were deserted. I turned my attention back to the manager, and he flashed me another preoccupied smile.

I knew him vaguely, from several years back. Vincent Kraemer was one of those people who was always running around like a mad thing, trying to put far-fetched and precarious deals into motion, chasing after the one Big Score that would make him horribly wealthy. He finally made it, with Prometheus Inc. Vincent was tall, buff, immaculately dressed, with a prematurely lined face and no hair left to speak of. His suit probably cost more than I used to make in a year.

"Good to see you again, John." His voice was steady, cultivated, and artificially calm. "Been hearing interesting things about you since you got back."

"And you've done very well," I said courteously. "Is wealth and success everything you thought it would be?"

He laughed briefly. "Pretty much. What do you think of my pride and joy, John?"

"Impressive, but I'm not really equipped to appreciate it. Technology has always been a mystery to me. I have to get my secretary to work the timer on my video."

He laughed dutifully. "It's your other areas of expertise I need, John. I need you to find out who's trying to drive me out of business."

And then he stopped, because he saw I was looking at the only photo on his desk. A wedding scene, in a simple silver frame. Bride, groom, best man, and me. Six years ago, and still as fresh in my memory as though it had happened yesterday. It should have been the happiest day in the lives of two wonderful young people, but it instead it became a tragedy that everyone still talked about. Mostly because no-one had ever been found to blame it on.

The bride was Melinda Dusk, also known as the Hanged Man's Beautiful Daughter. The groom was Quinn, also known as the Sunslinger. She wore a wedding gown of brilliant white, with a long creamy train. He wore his best cowboy outfit, all black leathers studded with dazzling displays of steel and silver. And standing on either side of the happy couple, doing our best to look at ease in our rented tuxedos, Vincent Kraemer as best man, and me as the bride's oldest friend. Melinda and Quinn—scions of the two oldest and most powerful families in the Nightside. Married and murdered in the same day.

There aren't many happy endings in the Nightside. Even the greatest celebrities and the most powerful people aren't immune to tragedy. Melinda was of the dark, her powers those of shadow and sorcery. Quinn was of the light, the deadly energies he controlled derived from the power of the sun itself. Their ancestors, the original Hanged Man and the original Sunslinger, had been deadly enemies hundreds of years ago, and all the generations since then had continued the feud, polishing their hatred with years of constant use. And Melinda and Quinn, the two latest avatars in this ongoing struggle, raised to hate and fight each other to the death, happened to meet during one of the rare truces. And it was love at first sight.

They continued to meet in secret for months, but finally went public. Their families went berserk and almost went to war. But Melinda and Quinn stood firm, secure in the powers they wielded, and threatened to disown their families and elope if they weren't given permission to marry. It was a magnificent wedding in the end, attended by absolutely every member of both families, partly as a show of strength and partly to make sure neither side tried to pull a fast one. There were famous faces and celebrities everywhere, and Walker himself turned up to run security. It should have been the safest place in the Nightside.

Vincent and I also worked as ushers, showing people to their seats, frisking them for weapons, keeping everyone in order, always ready to jump on anyone who even looked like doing anything funny. We were both young men then, still building our reputations. They called Vincent the Mechanic, because he could build or fix anything. Magic was good for short cuts, he was fond of saying, but technology was always going to be the more dependable in the long run. He'd built an automatic confetti-thrower, especially for the wedding, and kept dashing off to tinker with it when he wasn't needed. He and Quinn had been friends since they were kids, and he had risked his life many times to act as go-between for the two lovers. Melinda was one of the few friends I had left from childhood, one of the few powerful enough in her own right that my enemies didn't dare mess with her.

The wedding ceremony went fine, the families behaved themselves, and no-one got the words wrong or dropped the ring. And when it was all over, everyone cheered and applauded and some of us dared to think that just maybe the long war was over at last. Bride and groom left the church together, looking radiant. As though they belonged together. As though they completed each other. The automatic confetti-chucker worked first time.

Everyone posed for photographs, drinks circulated, snacks were consumed, and old enemies nodded to each other from a safe distance, even exchanging a few polite words. Bride and groom accepted the bridal cup, full to the brim with the very best champagne, and toasted their families and the bright future ahead. Ten minutes later, they were both dead. Poison in the bridal cup. It was all over so quickly that neither magic nor science could save them. Whoever had chosen the poison had known what they were doing. There wasn't even a sign of symptoms until Quinn suddenly fell dead to the ground. Melinda lived long enough to hold her dead husband in her arms, her tears dropping onto his dead face, then she collapsed across him and was gone.

If Walker and his people hadn't been there, the wedding party would have turned into a massacre. Both families went crazy, blaming each other. Somehow Walker kept the sides separated until they all left, swearing vengeance, then he organised a full investigation, using all his considerable resources. He never found anything. There was no shortage of suspects, of people in both families who'd spoken out loudly against the wedding and the truce, but there was no proof, no evidence. Meanwhile, the two families fought running battles in the streets, mercilessly slaughtering anyone foolish enough to be caught out on their own. Finally, the Authorities stepped in and shut it down, threatening to banish both families from the Nightside. A slow, sullen armed truce prevailed, but only just. That was six years ago. Melinda and Quinn were cold in their separate family graves, and still no-one had any idea of the who or why of it. There are loads of conspiracy theories, but then, there always are.

I would have done my best to find the killer, but shortly after the wedding my own life went to hell in a hurry, and I ended up running from the Nightside with Suzie Shooter's bullet in my back, vowing never to return.

"Such a terrible tragedy," said Vincent. He picked up the photo and studied it. "I still miss them. Like part of me died with them. Sometimes I think I keep this photo on my desk as a reminder of the last time I was really happy." He put the photo down and smiled briefly at me. "I wish they could have seen this place. My greatest achievement. And now someone, or something, is trying to shut it down. Which is why I asked Walker to contact you, John. Can you help me?"

"Perhaps," I said. "I'm still trying to get a feel for what's going on here. Talk me through it, from the beginning."

Vincent leaned back in his manager's chair and linked his fingers together across his expansive waistcoat. While he talked, his voice was calm and even, but his gaze kept flickering to the CCTV monitors.

"It started two weeks ago, John. Everything normal, just another day. Until one of the main turbines suddenly stopped working. My people investigated and found it had been sabotaged. Not a professional job—the whole interior had simply been . . . ripped apart. My people repaired it and got it back on-line in under an hour, but by then systems were breaking down all through the plant. And that's been the pattern ever since. As fast as we fix things, something else goes wrong. It's costing us a fortune in spare parts alone. There's nothing sophisticated about the sabotage, just brutal, senseless destruction.

"No-one ever sees the saboteur. You've seen the security I've hired, but they haven't made a blind bit of difference. I've got cameras everywhere, and they never see anything either. I've had the videotapes checked by experts, but there's no trace of anything. We can't even tell how the bastard gets in or out! The destruction's getting steadily worse. Repairs and reconstruction are starting to fall behind. It's only a matter of time before it starts affecting our power output. And a whole lot of people depend on the electricity we produce here."

And if Prometheus Inc. goes down, so do you, I thought, but I was still being polite, so I didn't say it aloud.

"How about rivals?" I said. "Perhaps someone in the same line of business, looking to profit at your expense?"

"There are always competitors," said Vincent, frowning. "But there's no-one else big enough to take over if we go under. Prometheus Inc. supplies 12.4 per cent of the Nightside's electricity needs. If we crash, there'll be power outages and brownouts all across the Nightside, and no-one wants that. The other companies would have to push themselves almost to destruction to take up the slack."

"All right," I said. "How about people who just don't like you? Made any new enemies recently?"

He smiled briefly. "A month ago, I would have said I didn't have an enemy in the world. But now . . ." He looked at the wedding photo on his desk again. "I've been having dreams . . . about Melinda and Quinn, and the day they died. And I have to wonder . . . if the bastard who killed them is coming after me."

I hadn't seen that twist coming. "Why you? And why wait six years?"

"Maybe the killer thinks I know something, though I'm damned if I know what. And just maybe it's all started up again because you're back,

John. An awful lot of old grudges and feuds have bubbled to the surface since you returned to the Nightside."

He had a point there, so I decided to change the subject. "Let's talk about the actual damage here. You said it was . . . unsophisticated."

"Hell yes," said Vincent. "It's clear the saboteur has no real technical knowledge. There are a dozen places he could have hit that would shut the whole plant down if they were even interfered with. But none a layman could hope to recognise. And, of course, there's the secret process at the heart of Prometheus Inc. that makes this whole operation possible. I invented it. But that's kept inside a steel vault, protected by state-of-the-art high-tech defence systems. Even the Authorities would have a hard time getting to it without the right pass codes." Vincent leaned forward across the desk and fixed me with a pleading gaze. "You've got to help me, John. It's not only my livelihood we're talking about here. If Prometheus Inc. is forced off-line, and power levels drop all across the Nightside, people are going to start dying. Hundreds of thousands of lives could be at risk."

I should have seen what was coming. But I always was a sucker for a sob story.

• • •

Vincent took me on a tour through the plant, the underground section that outsiders never got a chance to see. It was all spotlessly clean and eerily quiet. The actual generators themselves turned out to be much smaller than I expected, and made hardly a sound. There were panels and gauges and readouts and any amount of gleaming high tech, none of which meant anything to me, though I was careful to make impressed sounds at regular intervals. Every bit of it had been designed by Vincent, back when he was the Mechanic, rather than the Manager. He kept up a running commentary throughout the tour, most of which went right over my head, while I nodded and smiled and kept an eye out for the saboteur. Eventually Vincent ran out of things to point at, and we stopped at the end of a cavernous hall, before a large, closed, solid steel door. He looked at me, clearly expecting me to say something.

"It's all . . . very clean," I said. "And very impressive. Though it's hard to believe you produce so much of the Nightside's electricity with . . . just this. I was expecting something ten times the size."

Vincent grinned. "None of the power comes from *this*. All the machinery does is convert the power produced in there into electricity. The secret lies in my own special process, behind this sealed door. A scientific marvel, if I do say so myself."

I glared suddenly at the steel door. "If you're about to tell me you've got a nuclear pile in there . . ."

"No, no . . ."

"Or a contained singularity . . ."

"Nothing so crude, John. My process is perfectly safe, with no noxious by-products. Though I'm afraid I can't show it to you. Some things have to remain secret."

And then he broke off, and we both looked round sharply as we heard something. A harsh juddering began in one of the machines at the far end of the hall, and black smoke billowed suddenly from a vent, before an alarm shrilled loudly and the machine shut itself down. Vincent shrank back against the steel door.

"He's here! The saboteur . . . he's never got this far before. He must have been following us all this time . . . Are you armed, John?"

"I don't use guns," I said. "I've never felt the need."

"Normally I don't, either, but ever since this shit began happening, I've felt a lot more secure knowing I've got a little something to even out the odds." Vincent produced a gleaming silver gun from inside his jacket. It looked sleek and deadly and very futuristic. Vincent hefted it proudly. "It's a laser. Amplified light to fight the forces of darkness. Another of my inventions. I always meant to do more with it, but the power plant took over my life. I can't see anyone, John. Can you see anyone?"

A machine a little further down the hall exploded suddenly. More black smoke, and the hum of the other machines rose significantly, as though they were having to work harder. A third machine blew apart like a grenade, throwing sharp-edged steel shrapnel almost the length of the hall. Some of the overhead lights flickered and went out. There were shadows everywhere now, deep and dark. Some of the other machines began making unpleasant, threatening noises. And still there was no sign of the saboteur anywhere.

Vincent's face was pale and sweaty, and his hand trembled as he swept his laser gun back and forth, searching for a target. "Come on, come on," he said hoarsely. "You're on my territory now. I'm ready for you."

Something pale flashed briefly at the corner of my eye. I snapped around, but it was already gone. It appeared again, just a glimpse of white in the shadows between two machines. It flashed back and forth, appearing and disappearing in the blink of an eye, darting up and down the length of the hall. Glimmers of shimmering white as fleeting as moonlight, but I thought I was beginning to make out an impression of a pale, haunted face. It moved in the shadows, never venturing out into the light. But it was gradually drawing nearer. Heading for us, or perhaps for the steel door behind us and the secret vulnerable heart of Prometheus Inc.

My first thought was that it had to be a ghost of some kind, maybe a poltergeist. Which would explain why the CCTV cameras hadn't been able to see anything. Ghosts could operate in science- or magic-dominated areas, provided their motivation was strong enough. In which case, Vincent needed a priest or an exorcist, not a private eye. I suggested as much to Vincent, and he shrugged angrily.

"I had my people do a full background check on this location before we began construction; and they didn't turn up anything. The whole area was supposed to be entirely free from magical or paranormal influences. That's why I built here. I'm the Mechanic, I build things. It's a talent, just like your talent for finding things, John. I don't know about ghosts. You're the expert on these matters. What do we do?"

"Depends what the ghost wants," I said.

"It wants to destroy me! I would have thought that was obvious. *What was that?*"

The white figure was flashing in and out of the shadows, on every side at once, drawing steadily closer all the time. Shimmering white, ragged round the edges, with long, reaching arms and a dark malevolent glare in an indistinct face. It gestured abruptly, and suddenly all the shrapnel scattered across the floor rose and hammered us like a metallic hailstorm. I put my arms over my head and did my best to shield Vincent with my body. The rain of objects ended as suddenly as it began, and we looked up to see something pale and dangerous squatting on one of the machines, tearing it apart with unnatural strength. Vincent howled with rage and fired his laser, but the figure was gone long before the light beam could reach it. I glared about me, my back pressed hard against the steel door. There were no other exits, no way to escape. So I did the only thing I could. I used my talent.

I don't like to use it too often, or for too long. It helps my enemies find me.

I reached inside, concentrating, and my third eye, my private eye, slowly opened. And just like that, I could see her clearly. As though my psychic gaze had focussed her, made her plain at last, she walked out of the shadows and into the light, standing openly before us. She nodded to me, then glared at Vincent with her deep dark eyes. I knew her immediately, though she looked very different from her wedding photo. Melinda Dusk, dead these six years, still wearing her wonderful white wedding dress, though it hung in tatters about her corpse-pale body. Her raven black hair fell in thick ringlets to her bare shoulders. Her lips were a pale purple. Her eyes . . . were black on black, like two deep holes in her face. She looked angry, haunted, vicious. The Hanged Man's Daughter, mistress of the dark forces, still beautiful in a cold, unnatural way. She raised one hand to point accusingly at Vincent, her fingernails grown long in the grave. I glanced at Vincent. He was breathing fast, his whole body trembling, but he didn't look particularly surprised.

I shut down my talent, but she was still there. I took a step forward, and the ghost turned her awful unblinking gaze upon me. I held up my hands to show they were empty.

"Melinda," I said. "It's me, John."

She looked away. I wasn't important. All her attention, all her rage, was focussed on Vincent.

"Talk to me, Vincent," I said quietly. "What's going on here? You knew who and what it was all along, didn't you? Didn't you! Why is she so angry with you, angry enough to pull her up out of her grave after six years?"

"I didn't know," he said. "I swear I didn't know!"

"He knew," said Melinda. Her voice was clear but quiet, like a whisper in my ear, as though it had to travel impossible distances to reach me. "You chose this place well, Vincent. As far as you could get from my family plot, and still be in the Nightside. And the sacrifices you made here in secret, before construction began, the innocent blood you spilled, and the promises you made . . . they would have kept out anyone else but me. I am an avatar of the dark, and every shadow is a doorway to me. Six years it took me, to track you down. But you could never hope to keep me out, not when the only thing that matters to me is still here. I will have my revenge, Vincent. Dear good friend Vincent. For what you did, to me and to Quinn."

And that was when I finally understood. I looked at Vincent, too shocked even to be angry, for the moment.

"You killed them," I said. "You murdered Melinda and Quinn. But you were their friend . . ."

"Best friends," said Vincent. He'd stopped shaking, and his voice was steady. "I would have done anything for you two, Melinda, but when the time came, you let me down. So I poisoned the bridal cup. It was necessary. And surprisingly easy. Who'd ever suspect the best man? No-one ever did, not even Walker himself." He looked at me suddenly, and he was smiling. "I was pretty sure my little problem had to be Melinda, but I needed you here to make certain. That's why I asked Walker to contact you, on my behalf. Because your talent to find things holds her in one place, one shape. All you have to do is hold her here, and my laser light will disrupt her, take her apart so thoroughly she'll never be able to put herself back together again. Do this for me, John, and I'll make you a partner in Prometheus Inc. You'll be wealthy and powerful beyond your wildest dreams."

"They were my friends, too," I said. "And there isn't enough money in the Nightside to turn me against a friend."

"Be my friend, John," said Melinda. She'd drifted very close now, and I could feel the cold of the grave radiating from her. "Be my friend and Quinn's, one last time. Find the source of Vincent's power. His secret source."

Vincent fired his laser at her. The light beam punched right through her shimmering form, but if it hurt her she didn't show it.

I called up my talent again, focussing my inner eye, my private eye from which nothing can be hidden, and immediately I knew where the secret was, and how to get to it. I turned to the steel door and punched in the correct entry codes. The heavy door swung slowly open. Vincent shouted something, but I wasn't listening. I walked through the opening, Melinda drifting after me, and there in the underground chamber Vincent had made specially for him, was the reason Vincent had been able to produce power so easily. It was Quinn, the Sunslinger.

He still looked a lot like he had in his wedding photo, but like Melinda, he had been through some changes. Quinn still wore his black leathers, though the steel and silver were dirty and corroded. His body was contained in a spirit bottle, a great glass chamber designed to contain the souls of the dead. Electricity cables penetrated the sides of the bottle, plugging into Quinn's eye sockets, his wedged-open mouth, and holes cut in his torso. Quinn, the Sunslinger, whose power had been to channel and direct energies from the sun, had been made into a battery. The spirit bottle trapped his soul with his dead body and made him controllable. The cables leached his power, and Vincent's machines turned it into electricity to feed the Nightside.

Ingenious. But then, the Mechanic had never been afraid to think big.

Melinda hovered beside the spirit bottle, staring at what had been done to her dead love with yearning eyes, unable to touch him for all her ghostly power. I ran my fingertips down the glass side of the spirit bottle, testing its strength.

"Get away from that, John," said Vincent.

I looked round to see Vincent stepping through the doorway, his laser gun trained on me. He laughed, a little shakily.

"Ordinary guns are no use against you, John. I know that. I know all about that clever trick you do with bullets. But this is a laser, and it will quite definitely kill you. It's a clever little device. Draws its power directly from Quinn. So you're going to do exactly what I tell you to do. You're going to use your talent to fix and hold Melinda in one place, one shape, while I kill her. Or I'll kill you. Slowly and very nastily."

"How will you stop Melinda without me?" I said.

"Oh, I'm sure I'll be able to think of something, now I know for sure it's Melinda. Maybe I'll build another spirit bottle, just for her."

"What happened?" I said, careful to keep my voice calm and my hands still. "You three were friends for years, closer than family. So what happened, Vincent? What turned you into a murderer?"

"They let me down," he said flatly. "When I needed them most, they weren't there for me. I dreamed up this power station, you see. A way at last to provide dependable electricity for the Nightside. A licence to print money. My big score, at last. And all I needed to make it work was Quinn. I was sure studying his powers under laboratory conditions would enable me to build something that would power the plant. But when I told him, he turned me down. Said his secrets were family secrets and not for sharing. After all the things I'd done for him! I talked to Melinda, tried to get her to persuade him, but she didn't want to know either. She and Quinn were planning a new life together, and there was no room in it for me.

"But I'd already sunk all my money into this project, and a hell of a lot more I'd borrowed from some really unpleasant people. It had never occurred to me that Quinn would turn me down. The project was already under way. It had to go on. So I killed Quinn and Melinda. It was their own fault, for putting their own selfish happiness ahead of my needs, my success. I would have made them partners. Made them rich. After they were dead, my financial associates retrieved Quinn's body from his grave, leaving a duplicate behind, and brought him here. Where he ended up working for me anyway. My . . . silent partner, if you like."

Melinda looked at me, silently pleading. The spirit bottle was full of light, with no shadows she could use. I looked at the bottle thoughtfully. Vincent aimed the laser at my stomach.

"Don't even think it, John. If you break the bottle, that breaks the connection between Quinn and my machines, and that would shut down the whole plant. No more of my electricity for the Nightside. Power cuts everywhere. Thousands of people could die."

"Ah well," I said. "What did they ever do for me?"

It was the easiest thing in the world for my talent to find the entry point into the spirit bottle and nudge it open just a crack. That was all Quinn needed. His dead body convulsed and suddenly blazed with light. Brilliant sunlight, too bright for mortal eyes to look upon. Vincent and I both had to turn away, shielding our eyes with our arms. The spirit bottle exploded, unable to contain the released energies of the Sunslinger. Glass fragments showered down. I made myself turn back and look through dazzled eyes as Quinn strode out of the wreckage, pulling the cables out of his face and his body. They fell to twitch restlessly on the floor, like severed limbs.

The dead man looked upon the ghost, and they smiled at each other, together again for the first time since their wedding day. And Vincent stumbled forward with his laser gun. His eyes weren't really clear yet, and I wasn't entirely sure who he was trying to point the gun at, but I didn't feel like taking any chances. So I reached down, grabbed one of the twitching cables from the floor, and lunged forward to jam one end of the cable into Vincent's eye. It plunged into his eye socket, burrowing beyond, and Vincent screamed horribly as his own machines sucked the life energies out of him. He was dead before his twitching body hit the floor.

Melinda Dusk and Quinn—the Hanged Man's Beautiful Daughter and the Sunslinger—dead but no longer separated, were already gone, too wrapped up in each other to care about lesser needs like vengeance. Quinn's body lay still and empty on the floor beside that of his old friend Vincent. I looked at Quinn's body and thought about whether I should take it back to his family, for a proper burial. But I had no proof of what had happened here, and as long as the armed truce between the two families continued, it was better not to stir things up. After all, who would Vincent have gone to first for financial backing? Who did he know, who would still lend him money after all his failures, except for certain factions in the two families?

I walked out of the secret vault, leaving the dead past behind, and used my talent one last time to find the self-destruct mechanism for the power plant. I knew there had to be one. Vincent was always very jealous about guarding his secrets. I allowed myself enough time to get clear, then set the clock ticking. I told the security men outside to start running, and something in my voice and my gaze convinced them. I was three blocks away when the whole of Prometheus Inc. went up in one great controlled explosion. I kept walking and didn't look back.

Not exactly my most successful case. My client was dead, so I wasn't going to get paid. Walker was probably going to be pretty mad that the power plant was gone, and God alone knew how much damage its loss was going to cause the Nightside. But none of that mattered. Melinda Dusk and Quinn had been my friends. And no-one kills a friend of mine and gets away with it.

TWO

Between Cases

Everyone needs somewhere to go, when it all goes pear-shaped. A bolt-hole to shelter in, till the shitstorm passes. I usually end up in Strangefellows, the oldest bar in the world. A (fairly) discreet drinking establishment, tucked away in the back of beyond, at the end of an alley that isn't always there, Strangefellows is a good place to booze and brood and hide from any number of people, most of whom wouldn't be seen dead in such a dive. It was run with malice aforethought by one Alex Morrisey, who didn't allow any trouble in his bar, most especially from me.

I found a table in a corner, so I wouldn't have to watch my back, and indulged myself with a bottle of wormwood brandy. It tastes like a super-model's tears and is so potent it can catch alight if someone at the next table strikes a match. I kept my head well down and looked about me surreptitiously. If anyone had noticed me come in, they were keeping their excitement well under control. Certainly no-one was rushing for the exit to tell on me. Perhaps word hadn't got around yet as to how royally I'd screwed up this time. There were any number of people who weren't going to be at all pleased with me for knocking out twelve per cent of the Nightside's electricity supply. Not least Walker, who'd got me the job in the first place. I faked a careless shrug. If they couldn't take a joke, they shouldn't hire me.

It was a quiet night at Strangefellows, for once. All the lights were out, and the whole place was illuminated by candles, hurricane lamps, and the occasional hand of glory. It gave the place a pleasant golden haze, like an old photo of better times. Alex explained when I got my drink that the power was down in various spots all over the Nightside, and I just nodded and grunted. Alex was severely pissed off by the inconvenience and loss of takings, but that was nothing new. Strangefellows's owner and bartender was a thin pale streak of misery who only wore black because no-one had come up with a darker colour yet. He wore a snazzy black beret to hide his bald patch and designer shades to tone down the perpetual glare with which he regarded the world.

He's a friend of mine. Sometimes.

Music was playing from a portable CD player, rising easily over the bare murmur of conversation from the few regulars nursing their drinks in the back booths. Most of the bar's usual crowd were probably out and about in the Nightside, taking advantage of the blackouts to do unto others and run off with the takings. It would be a busy time for the Nightside's fences, before the lights went on again. Alex's pet vulture was perched over the till, cackling to itself and giving the evil eye to anyone who looked like getting too close. The bar's muscular bouncers, Betty and Lucy Coltrane, were occupying themselves with a flex-off at the end of the bar, frowning seriously as muscles distended and veins popped up all over their sculpted bodies. Pale Michael was running a book as to which one would pass out first.

And my teenage secretary, Cathy Barrett, was dancing wildly on a tabletop, to the music of Voice of the Beehive's "Honey Lingers." Blonde, bubbly, and full of more energy than she knew what to do with, Cathy ran the business side of my life. I'd rescued her from a house that tried to eat her, and she adopted me. I didn't get a say in the matter. Dancing opposite her on the tabletop, in a leather outfit, cape, mask, and six-inch stiletto heels, was Ms. Fate, the Nightside's very own transvestite superhero, a man who dressed up as a superheroine to fight crime and avenge injustice. He was actually pretty good at it, in her own way. Cathy and Ms. Fate danced their hearts out, pounding their heels on the table to "Monsters and Angels," and I had to smile. They were the brightest things in the whole bar.

I topped up my glass with the murky purple liquor and drank to the memory of Melinda Dusk and Quinn. It was good to know they were finally at rest, together, their murders avenged. I don't have that many friends. Either my enemies kill them, or I do. Morality can be a shifting, treacherous thing in the Nightside, and both love and loyalty have a way of getting drowned in the bigger issues. My few longtime friends have all tended to be dangerous as hell in their own right, and more than a little crazy. People like Razor Eddie and Shotgun Suzie . . . both of whom have tried to kill me in the past. I don't hold it against them. Much. It's a hard life in the Nightside, and a harder death, usually. I sipped my drink and listened to the music. I wasn't in any hurry. I had the rest of the bottle to get through.

I've never found it easy to mourn, though God knows I've had enough practice.

I looked around the bar, searching for something to distract myself with. A sailor had passed out at the main bar, and the tattoos on his back were quietly arguing matters philosophical over the low rumble of his snores. A mummy at the other end of the long wooden bar was drinking gin and tonics while performing necessary running repairs on his yellowed bandages. Roughly midway between the two, an amiable drunk in a blood-stained lab coat was endeavouring to explain the principles of retro-phrenology to a frankly disinterested Alex Morrisey.

"See, phrenology is this old Victorian science, which claimed you could determine the dominant traits of a man's personality by studying the bumps on his head. The size and position of these bumps indicated different personality traits. See? Now, *retro-phrenology* says, why not change a man's personality by hitting him on the head with a hammer, till you raise just the right bumps in the right places!"

"One of us needs a lot more drinks," said Alex. "That's starting to make sense."

Cathy suddenly slammed down into the chair opposite me, breathing harshly and radiating happy sweat. She flashed me a cheerful grin. She'd picked up a fresh flute of champagne from somewhere and drank from it thirstily. Cathy always drank "champers," and nearly always found a way to stick me with the bill.

"I love to dance!" she said cheerfully. "Sometimes I think the whole world should be put to music and choreographed!"

"This being the Nightside, someone somewhere is undoubtedly working on that very thing, right now," I said. "Where's your partner, the Dancing Queen?"

"Oh, he's nipped off to the loo, to freshen her make-up. You know, John, I could see you brooding from right across the room. Who died this time?"

"What makes you think someone died?"

"You only drink that wormwood muck when you've lost someone close to you. I wouldn't use that stuff to clean combs. I thought the Prometheus gig was a straightforward deal?"

"I really don't want to talk about it, Cathy."

"No, you'd rather sulk and be miserable and pollute the atmosphere for everyone else. If you're not careful, you'll end up like Alex."

Cathy could always make me smile. "There's no danger of that. I'm not in Alex's class. That man could brood for the Olympics, and pick up a bronze in self-pity while he was at it. He's why there's never been a Happy Hour in Strangefellows."

Cathy sighed, leaned forward, and gave me her best exasperated look. "Get another case going, John. You know you're really only happy when you're working. Not that that's much healthier, given the cases you specialise in. You need to get out more and meet people, preferably people who aren't trying to kill you. You know, I found this really great new dating site for professional singles on the Net the other day . . ."

I shuddered. "I've seen some of those. *Hi! I'm Trixi, and I've got diseases so virulent you can even catch them down a phone line! Just give me your credit card number, and I guarantee to make your eyes water in under thirty seconds!* No, Cathy! I'm quite happy with my solitary brooding. It builds character."

Cathy pouted, then shrugged. She never could stay unhappy for long. She finished off the last of her champagne, hiccuped happily, and looked hopefully round the bar for another dancing partner. I'd never admit it to her, but she was mostly right. My work was all I had to give my life meaning. But since my last successful case earned me a quarter of a million pounds, plus bonuses, I could afford to be more particular about what work I chose to take on. (I located the Unholy Grail for the Vatican, and faced down Heaven and Hell in the process. I'd *earned* that money.) Maybe I should start looking for a new case, if only to take the taste of Prometheus Inc. out of my mouth.

"I'm bored," Cathy announced, slapping both hands on the table to prove it. "Bored of sitting around your expensive new office with nothing to do. It's all very comfortable, I'm sure, and I love all the new equipment, but a growing girl can't spend all her life surfing dodgy porn sites on the Internet. Like you, I need to be doing. Earning my keep and smiting the ungodly where it hurts. There must be something in all the messages I've taken that appeals to you. What about the case of the missing shadows? Or the guy who lost his adolescence in a rigged card game?"

"Hold everything," I said sternly. "A disturbing thought has just occurred to me. Who's looking after things in my expensive new Nightside office, while you're out cavorting and carousing in dubious drinking establishments?"

"Ah," said Cathy, grinning. "I got a really good deal on some computers from the future. They practically run the whole business on their own, these days. They can even answer the phone and talk snotty to our creditors."

"Just how far up the line did these computers come from?" I said suspiciously. "I mean, are we talking Artificial Intelligence here? Are they going to want paying?"

"Relax! They're data junkies. The Nightside fascinates them. Why don't we ask them to find something that would interest you?"

"Cathy, I only took on the Prometheus case to keep you quiet . . ."

"No you didn't!" Cathy said hotly. "You took that on because you wanted Walker to owe you a favour."

I scowled and addressed myself to my drink. "Yes, well, that didn't actually work out as well as I'd hoped."

"Oh God," said Cathy. "Am I going to have start locking the doors and windows and hiding under the desk again, when he comes around?"

"I think it would be a better idea if we both stayed away from the office completely, just for a while."

"That bad?"

"Pretty much. Let Walker argue with the computers and see how far it gets him."

There was a sudden flare of brilliant light, and a man fell out of nowhere into Strangefellows. He crashed to the floor just in front of the bar, his New Romantic silks in shreds and tatters. Static sparks discharged from every metal object in the bar, and the air was heavy with the stench of ozone—the usual accompanying signs of time travel. The newcomer groaned, sat up, and wiped at his bloody nose with the back of his hand. He'd clearly been through a hell of a fight recently, and just as clearly lost. I knew him, though if I met him in the street, I tried very hard not to. He was Tommy Oblivion, a fellow private investigator, though he specialised in cases of an existential nature. He lurched to his feet, leaned his back against the bar for support while he pulled his ragged silks around him, then saw me watching him. His battered face purpled with rage, and he stabbed a shaking finger at me.

"You! Taylor! This is all your fault! I'll have your balls for this!"

"I haven't seen you in months, Tommy," I said calmly.

"No, but you will! In the future! Only this time I'll be ready for you, and better prepared! I'll have guns! Big guns!"

He continued to spit abuse at me, but I couldn't be bothered. I looked at Alex, and he gestured at his two bouncers. Betty and Lucy hurried forward, glad of an excuse for a little action. Tommy made the mistake of threatening them, too, and the two girls briskly knocked him to the floor, kicked him somewhere painful, and then frog-marched him out of Strangefellows. Cathy gave me a hard look.

"What was that all about?"

"Beats the hell out of me," I said honestly. "Presumably I'll find out. In time."

"Excuse me," said a voice with a cultured French accent. "Have I the honour of addressing Mr. John Taylor?"

Cathy and I both looked round sharply. Standing right before us was a short, comfortably padded, middle-aged man in an expertly cut suit. He looked supremely elegant, not a hair out of place, and his smile was sophisticated charm itself. There was no way he could have entered the bar and approached my corner table without being seen, but there he was, large as life and twice as French. He nodded courteously to me, smiled at Cathy, and kissed her proffered hand. She gave him a dazzling smile in return. I decided not to like him, on general principles. I really don't like being sneaked up on. It's bad for my health. I gestured for the Frenchman to pull up a chair. He studied the empty chair solemnly for a moment, then produced a blindingly white handkerchief from an inner pocket and flicked the seat of the chair a few times before deigning to sit on it. I gave him my best intimidating glare, to remind him who was boss around here.

"I'm John Taylor," I growled. "You're a long way from home, *m'sieu*. What can I do for you?"

He nodded easily, entirely unimpressed. "I am Charles Chabron, for many years one of the most respected bankers in Paris. And I have come a very long way to meet with you, Mr. Taylor, and inquire whether I might hire your professional services."

"Who recommended me to you?" I said carefully.

He flashed his charming smile again. "An old friend of yours who does not wish to be identified."

He had me there. "I get a lot of that," I admitted. "What is it you want, Mr. Chabron?"

"Please, call me Charles. I am here because of my daughter. You may have heard of her. She is currently the new singing sensation of the Nightside. She calls herself Rossignol, though that is of course not her real name. Rossignol is merely French for nightingale. She first came to London, then the Nightside, some five years ago, determined to make for herself a career as a singer. And this last year she has been singing very successfully to packed houses in nightclubs all over the Nightside. I understand there's even talk of a recording contract with one of the major companies. Which is all well and good.

"However, since she took up with her new management, a Mr. and Mrs. Cavendish, she only sings at one nightclub, Caliban's Cavern, and she has . . . changed. She has broken off all contact with her old friends and family. She does not answer phone calls or letters, and her new management won't let anyone get near her. They say they do this at her explicit request and justify it in the name of protecting her from over-zealous fans of her new fame. But I am not so sure. Her mother is frantic with worry, convinced that the Cavendishes have poisoned our daughter's mind against her family, and that they are, perhaps, taking advantage of her. And so I have come here, to you, Mr. Taylor, in the hope that you can establish the truth of the matter."

I looked at Cathy. The music scene was her speciality. There wasn't a club in the Nightside she hadn't drunk, danced, and debauched in at one time or another. She was already nodding.

"Yeah, I know Rossignol. And the Caliban club, and the Cavendishes. They run Cavendish Properties. They have a collective finger in practically every big deal in the Nightside. They were big in real estate, until the market crashed just recently, after the angel war. Lot of people lost a lot of money in that disaster. Mr. and Mrs. Cavendish moved sideways into entertainment, representing clubs, groups, people . . . nothing really mega yet, but they've quickly made themselves a power to be reckoned with. Other agents cross themselves when they see the Cavendishes coming."

"What sort of people are they?" I asked.

Cathy frowned. "If the Cavendishes have first names, no-one knows or uses them. They don't get out much, preferring to work through intermediaries. Not at all averse to playing hardball during negotiations, but then, nice people don't tend to last long in show business. There are rumours they're brother and sister, as well as husband and wife . . . Cavendish Properties is based on *old* money, going back centuries, but there's a lot of gossip going round that says the current owners are hungry for money and not too fussy about how they acquire it. There's also supposed to be a scandal about their last attempt at building Sylvia Sin into a singing sensation. But they spent a lot of money to cover it up. But there's always gossip in the Nightside. They could be on the level with Rossignol. I just hope her agent checked the small print in their contract carefully."

"She has no agent," said Chabron. "Cavendish Properties represents Rossignol. You can understand why I am so concerned."

I looked at him thoughtfully. There were things he wasn't telling me. I could tell.

"What brought your daughter all the way to London, and the Nightside?" I said. "Paris has its own music scene, doesn't it?"

"Of course. But London is where you have to go to be a star. Everyone knows that." Chabron sighed. "Her mother and I never took her singing seriously. We wanted her to take up a more respectable occupation, something with a future and a pension plan. But all she ever cared about was singing. Perhaps we pressured her too much. I arranged an interview for her, with my bank. An entry-level position, but with good prospects. Instead, she ran away to London. And when I sent people to track her down, she disappeared into the Nightside. Now . . . she is in trouble, I am sure of it. One hears such things . . . I wish for you to find my daughter, Mr. Taylor, and satisfy yourself on my behalf that she is well and happy, and not being cheated out of anything that is rightfully hers. I am not asking you to drag her back home. Just to assure yourself that everything is as it should be. Tell her that her friends and her family are concerned for her. Tell her . . . that she doesn't have to talk to us if she doesn't want to, but we would be grateful for some form of communication, now and then. She is my only child, Mr. Taylor. I need to be sure she is happy and safe. You understand?"

"Of course," I said. "But I really don't see why you want me. Any number of people could handle this. I can put you onto a man called Walker, in the Authorities . . ."

"No," Chabron said sharply. "I want you."

"It doesn't seem like my kind of case."

"People are dying, Mr. Taylor! Dying, because of my daughter!" He took a moment to calm himself, before continuing. "It seems that my Rossignol sings only sad songs these days. And that she sings these sad songs so powerfully that members of her audience have been known to go home and commit suicide. Already there are so many dead that not even her management can keep it quiet. I want to know what has happened to my daughter, here in your Nightside, that such a thing is possible."

"All right," I said. "Perhaps it is my kind of case after all. But I have to warn you, I don't come cheap."

Chabron smiled, back on familiar ground. "Money is no problem to me, Mr. Taylor."

I smiled back at him. "The very best kind of client. My whole day just brightened up." I turned to Cathy. "Go back to the office and get your marvelous new computers working on some background research. I want to know everything there is to know about the Cavendishes, their company, and their current financial state. Who they own, and who they owe money to. Then see what you can find out about Rossignol, before she went to work for the Cavendishes. Where she sang, what kind of following she had, the usual. Mr. Chabron . . ."

I looked around, and he was gone. There was no sign of him anywhere, even though there was no way he could have made it to any of the exits in such a short time.

"Damn, that's creepy," said Cathy. "How does he *do* that?"

"There's more to our Mr. Chabron than meets the eye," I said. "But then, that's par for the course in the Nightside. See what you can you can find out about him, too, while you're at it, Cathy."

She nodded quickly, blew me a kiss, and hurried away. I got up and wandered over to the bar. I shoved the cork back into the bottle of wormwood brandy and handed it over to Alex. I didn't need it any more. He made it disappear under the bar and gave me a smug smile.

"I used to know Rossignol. Bit skinny for my tastes, but a hell of a set of pipes on her. I hired her a few years back to provide cabaret, to add some class to the place. It didn't work, but then this bar is a lost cause anyway. You couldn't drive it upmarket with a chair and a whip."

"Were you eavesdropping again, Alex?"

"Of course. I hear everything. It's my bar. Anyway, this Rossignol was pretty enough, with a good if untrained voice, and more importantly, she worked cheap. In those days she'd sing anywhere, for peanuts, for the experience. She had this need, this hunger, to sing. You could see it in her face, hear it in her voice. And it wasn't just your usual singer's ego. It was more like a mission with her. I wouldn't say she was anything special back then, but I always knew she'd go far. Talent isn't worth shit if you haven't got the determination to back it up, and she had that in spades."

"What kind of songs did she sing, back then?" I asked.

Alex frowned. "I'm pretty sure she only sang her own material. Happy, upbeat stuff, you know the sort of thing, sweet but forgettable. There were definitely no suicides when she sang here, though admittedly this is a tougher audience than most."

"So she was nothing like the deadly diva her father described?"

"Not in the least. But then, the Nightside can change anyone, and usually not for the better." Alex paused and gave the bar top a polish it didn't need, so he wouldn't have to look me in the eye as he spoke. "Word is, Walker's looking for you, John. And he is not a happy bunny."

"Walker never is," I said, carefully casual. "But just in case he shows up here, looking for me, you haven't seen me, right?"

"Some things never change," said Alex. "Go on, get out of here, you're lowering the tone of the place."

I left Strangefellows and walked out into the night. One by one the neon signs were flickering on again, like road signs in Hell. I decided to take that as a good omen and kept walking.

THREE

Downtime in Uptown

If you're looking for the real nightlife in the Nightside, you have to go Uptown. That's where you'll find the very best establishments, the sharpest pleasures, the most seductive damnations. Every taste catered for, satisfaction guaranteed or your soul back. They play for keeps in Uptown, which is, of course, part of the attraction. It was a long way from Strangefellows, so I took my courage in both hands, stepped right up to the very edge of the passing traffic, and hailed a sedan chair.

The sedan chair was part of a chain I recognised, or I wouldn't have got in it. The traffic that runs endlessly through the rain-slick streets of the Nightside can be a peril to both body and soul. I settled myself comfortably on the crimson padded leather seat, and the sedan chair moved confidently out into the flow. The tall wooden walls of the box were satisfyingly solid, and the narrow windows were filled with bulletproof glass. They were proof against a lot of other things, too. There was no-one carrying the chair, front or back. This particular firm was owned and run by a family of amiable poltergeists. They could move a lot faster than human bearers, and even better, they didn't bother the paying customers with unwanted conversation. Poltergeist muscle was also handy when it came to protecting their chairs from the other traffic on the roads. The Nightside is a strange attractor for all kinds of traffic, from past, present, and future, and a lot of it tended towards the predatory. There are taxis that run on deconsecrated altar wine, shining silver bullets that run on demons' tears and angels' urine, and things that only look like cars but are always hungry.

A pack of headless bikers tried to crowd the sedan chair with their choppers, but the operating poltergeist flipped them away like poker chips. The roaring traffic gave us a bit more room after that, and it wasn't long at all before we were cruising through Uptown. You could almost smell the excitement, above the blood, sweat, and tears. Nowhere does the neon blaze more brightly, neon noir and Technicolor temptation, the sleazy signs pulsing like an aroused heartbeat. You can bet the lights here never even dimmed during the recent power outages. Uptown would always have first call on whatever power was available. But even so, it's always that little bit darker here, in the world of three o'clock in the morning, where the pleasures of the night need never end, as long as your money holds out.

You can find the very best restaurants in Uptown, featuring dishes from cultures that haven't existed for centuries, using recipes that would be banned in saner places. There are even specialised restaurants, offering meals made entirely from the meats of extinct or imaginary animals. You haven't lived till you've tasted dodo drumsticks, roc egg omelettes, Kentucky-fried dragon, kraken sushi surprise, chimera of the day, or basilisk eyes (that last entirely at your own risk). You can find food to die for, in Uptown.

Bookshops contain works written in secret by famous authors, never intended to be published. Ghostwritten books, by authors who died too soon. Volumes on spiritual pornography, and the art of tantric murder. Forbidden knowledge and forgotten lore, and guide-books for the hereafter. One shop window boasted a new edition of that infamous book *The King in Yellow*, whose perusal drove men mad, together with a special pair of rose-tinted spectacles to read it through.

People bustled through the streets, following the lure of the rainbow neon. Scents of delicious cooking pulled at the nose, and snatches of beguiling music spilled from briefly opened doors. Long lines waited patiently outside theatres and cabaret clubs, and crowded round newsstands selling the latest edition of the *Night Times*. More furtive faces disappeared into weapons shops, or brothels, where for the right price you could sleep with famous women from fiction. (It wasn't the real thing, of course, but then it never is, in such places.) Uptown held every form of entertainment the mind could conceive, some of which would eat you alive if you weren't sharp enough.

And nightclubs, of every form and persuasion. Music and booze and company, all just a little hotter than the consumer could comfortably stand. Some of the clubs go way back. Whigs and Tories argue politics over cups of coffee, then sit down to wager on demon-baiting matches. Romans recline on couches, pigging out on twenty-course meals, in between trips to the vomitorium. Other clubs are as fresh as today and twice as tasty. You'd be surprised how many big stars started out singing for their supper in Uptown.

The streets became even more thickly crowded as the sedan chair carried me deep into the dark heart of Uptown. Flushed faces and bright eyes everywhere, high on life and eager to throw their money away on things they only thought they needed. In and among the fevered punters, the people who earned their living in the clubs and nightspots of Uptown rushed from one establishment to another, working the several jobs it took to pay their rent or quiet their souls. Singers and actors, conjurers and stand-up comedians, strippers and hostesses and specialist acts—all of them thriving on a regular diet of buzz, booze, and bennies. And walking their beats or standing on corners, watching it all go by, the ladies of the evening with their kohl-stained eyes and come-on mouths, the twilight daughters who never said no to anything that involved hard cash.

This still being the Nightside, there were always hidden traps for the unwary. Smoke-filled bars where lost week-ends could stretch out for years, and clubs where people couldn't stop dancing, even when their feet left bloody marks on the dance floor. Markets where you could sell any part of your body, mind, or soul. Or someone else's. Magic shops that offered wonderful items and objects of power, with absolutely no guarantee they'd perform as advertised, or even that the shop would still be there when you went back to complain.

There were homeless people, too, in shadowed doorways and the entrances of alleyways, wrapped in shabby coats or tattered blankets, with their grubby hands held out for spare change. Tramps and vagabonds, teenage runaways and people just down on their luck. Most passersby have the good sense to drop them the odd coin or a kind word. Karma isn't just a concept in the Nightside, and a surprising number of street people used to be Somebody once. It's always been easy to lose everything, in the Nightside. So it was wise to never piss these people off, because they might still have a spark of power left in them. And because it might just be you there, one day. The wheel turns, we all rise and fall, and nowhere does the wheel turn faster than in Uptown.

The sedan chair finally dropped me off right outside Caliban's Cavern. I checked the meter, added a generous tip, and dropped the money into the box provided. No-one ever cheats the poltergeists. They tend to take it personally and reduce your home to its original components while you're still in it. The chair moved off into the traffic again, and I studied the nightclub before me, taking my time. People flowed impatiently around me, but I ignored them, concentrating on the feel of the place. It was big, expensive, and clearly exclusive, the kind of place where you couldn't get in, never mind get a good table, unless your name was on someone's list. Caliban's Cavern wasn't for just anybody, and that, of course, was part of the attraction. Rossignol's name blazed above the door in Gothic neon script, giving the times of her three shows a night. A sign on the closed front door made it clear the club was currently in between shows and not open for business. Even the most upmarket clubs have to take time out to freshen the place up in between sets. A good time for someone like me to do a little sneaking around. But first, I wanted to make sure this wasn't a setup of some kind.

I have enemies who want me dead. I don't know who or why, but they've been sending agents to try and kill me ever since I was a child. It has something to do with my absent mother, who turned out not to be human. She disappeared shortly after my father discovered that, and he spent what little was left of his life drinking himself to death. I like to think I'm made of harder stuff. Sometimes I don't think about my missing mother for days on end.

I studied the crowd bustling around and past me, but didn't spot any familiar faces. And the sedan chair would have let me know if someone had tried to follow us. But the case could be nothing more than a way of bringing me here, so that I could be ambushed. It's happened before. The only way to be sure there were no hidden traps was to use my Sight, my special gift that lets me find anything, or anyone. And that was dangerous in itself. When I open up my third eye, my private eye, my mind burns very brightly in the endless night, and all kinds of people can see me and where I am. My enemies are always watching. But I needed to know, so I opened up my mind and Saw the larger world.

Even in the Nightside there are secret depths, hidden layers, above and below. I could See ghosts all around me, running through their routines like shimmering video loops, moments trapped in Time. Ley lines blazed so brightly even I couldn't look at them directly, criss-crossing in brilliant designs, plunging through people and buildings as though they weren't really there. In the passing crowds, dark and twisted things rode on people's backs—obsessions, hungers, and addictions. Some of them recognised me and bared needle teeth in defiant snarls to warn me off. Giants walked in giant steps, towering high above the tallest buildings. And flitting here and there, the Light People, forever bound on their unknowable missions, occasionally drawn to this person or that for no obvious reason, but never interfering.

But what really caught my third eye were the layers of magical defences surrounding Caliban's Cavern. Intersecting strands of hexes, curses, and anti-personnel runes covered every possible way in and out of the club, all of them positively radiating maleficent energies. This was heavy-duty, hard-core protection, way out of the range of even the most talented amateurs. Which meant someone had paid a pro a small fortune, just to protect an up-and-coming singing sensation. However, none of those defences were targeted specifically at me, which argued against this being a trap. I shut down my Sight and looked thoughtfully at the closed door before me. As long as I didn't use magic, the defences couldn't see me, so . . . I'd just have to think my way past them.

Luckily, most magical defences aren't very bright. They don't have to be. I grinned, stepped forward, and knocked firmly on the door. A staggeringly ugly face rose before me, forming itself out of the wood of the door. The varnish cracked loudly as the face scowled at me. Wooden lips parted, revealing large jagged wooden teeth.

"Forget it. Go away. Push off. The club is closed between acts. No personal appearances from the artistes, no autographs, and no, you don't get to hang around the stage door. If you want tickets, the booking office will be open in an hour. Come back then, or not at all. See if I care."

Its message over, the face began to subside back into the door again. I knocked again on the broad forehead, and the face blinked at me, surprised.

"You have to let me in," I said. "I'm John Taylor."

"Really? Congratulations. Now piss off and play with the traffic. We are very definitely closed, not open, and why are you still standing there?"

There's nothing easier to outmanoeuvre than a pushy simulacrum with a sense of its own self-importance. I gave the face my best condescending smile. "I'm John Taylor, here to speak with Rossignol. Open the door, or I'll do all kinds of horrible things to you. On purpose."

"Well, pardon me for existing, Mr. *I'm going to be Somebody someday.* I've got my orders. No-one gets in unless they're on the list, or they know the password, and it's more than my job's worth to make exceptions. Even if I felt like it. Which I don't."

"Walker sent me." That one was always worth a try. People were even more scared of Walker than they were of me. With very good reason.

The face in the door sniffed loudly. "You got any proof of that?"

"Don't be silly. Since when have the Authorities ever bothered with warrants?"

"No proof, no entry. Off you go now. Hop like a bunny."

"And if I don't?"

Two large gnarled hands burst out of the wood, reaching for me. There was no way of dodging them, so I didn't try. Instead, I stepped forward inside their reach and jabbed one hand into the wooden face, firmly pressing one of my thumbs into one of its eyes. The face howled in outrage. I kept up the pressure, and the hands hesitated.

"Play nice," I said. "Lose the arms."

They snapped back into the wood and were gone. I took my thumb out of the eye, and the face pouted at me sullenly.

"Big bully! I'm going to tell on you! See if I don't!"

"Let me in," I said. "Or there will be . . . unpleasantness."

"You can't come in without saying the password!"

"Fine," I said. "What's the password?"

"You have to tell me."

"I just did."

"No you didn't!"

"Yes I did. Weren't you listening, door? What did I just say to you?"

"What?" said the face. "What?"

"What's the password?" I said sternly.

"Swordfish!"

"Correct! You can let me in now."

The door unlocked itself and swung open. The face had developed a distinct twitch and was muttering querulously to itself as the door closed behind me. The club lobby looked very plush, or at least, what little of it I could see beyond the great hulking ogre that was blocking my way. Eight feet tall and almost as wide, he wore an oversized dinner jacket and a bow tie. The ogre flexed his muscled arms menacingly and cracked his knuckles loudly. One look at the low forehead and lack of chin convinced me there was absolutely no point in trying to talk my way past this guardian. So I stepped smartly forward, holding his eyes with mine, and kicked him viciously in the unmentionables. The ogre whimpered once, his eyes rolled right back in their sockets, and he fell over sideways. He hit the lobby floor with a crash and stayed there, curled into a ball. The bigger they are, the easier some targets are to hit. I walked unchallenged past the ogre and all the way across the lobby to the swinging doors that led into the nightclub proper.

Most of the lights were turned down here, and the cavern was all gloom and shadows. Bare stone walls under a threateningly low stone ceiling, a waxed and polished floor, high-class tables and chairs, and a raised stage at the far end. The chairs were stacked on top of the tables at the moment, and there were multi-coloured streamers curled around them and scattered across the floor. The only oasis of light in the club was the bar, way over to the right, open now just for the club staff and the artistes. A dozen or so night-time souls clustered together at the bar, like bedraggled moths drawn to the light.

I stepped out across the open floor towards them. Nobody challenged me. They just assumed that if I'd got in, I was supposed to be there. I nodded politely to the cleaning staff, busy getting the place ready for the next shift—half a dozen monkeys in bellhop uniforms, hooting mournfully as they pushed their mops around, passing a single hand-rolled back and forth between them. Lots of monkeys doing menial work in the Nightside these days. Some still even have their wings.

At the bar, the ladies in their faded dressing gowns and wraps didn't even look up as I joined them. The smell of gin and world-weariness was heavy on the air. Come showtime, these women would be all dolled up in sparkly costumes, with fishnet tights and high heels and tall feathers bobbing over their heads, hair artificially teased, faces bright with gaudy make-up . . . but that was then, and this was now. In the artificial twilight of the empty club, the chorus line and backup singers and hostesses wore no make-up, had their hair up in curlers, and as often as not a ciggie protruding grimly from the corner of a hardened mouth. They looked like soldiers resting from an endless war.

The bartender was some kind of elf. I can never tell them apart. He looked at me suspiciously.

"Relax," I said. "I'm not from Immigration. Just a special investigator, hoping to spread a little bribe money around where it'll do the most good for everyone concerned."

The ladies gave me their full attention. Cold eyes, hard mouths, ready to give away absolutely nothing without seeing cold cash up front. I sighed inwardly, pulled a wad of folding money out of an inner pocket, and snapped it down on the bar top. I kept my hand on top of it and raised an eyebrow. A short-haired platinum blonde leaned forward so that the front of her wrap fell open, allowing me a good look at her impressive cleavage, but I wasn't that easily distracted. Though it really *was* impressive . . .

"I'm here to see Rossignol," I said loudly, keeping my eyes well away from the platinum blonde. "Where can I find her?"

A redhead with her hair up in cheap plastic curlers snorted loudly.

"Best of luck, darling. She won't even speak to me, and I'm her main backing vocalist. Snotty little madam, she is."

"Right," said the platinum blonde. "Too good to mix with the likes of us. Little Miss Superstar. Speak to Ian, that's him up there on the stage. He's her roadie."

She nodded towards the shadowy stage, where I could just make out a short sturdy man wrestling a drum kit into position. I nodded my thanks, took my hand off the wad of cash, and walked away from the bar, letting the ladies sort out the remuneration for themselves. There was the sound of scuffling and really bad language by the time I got to the stage. I knocked on the wood with one knuckle, to get the roadie's attention. He came out from the drum kit and nodded to me. He seemed quite cheerful, for a hunchback. He swayed slightly from side to side as he came forward to join me, and I pulled myself up onto the stage. Up close, he was only slightly stooped on his bowed legs, with massive arms. He wore a T-shirt bearing the legend *Do Lemmings Sing the Blues?*

"How do, mate. I'm Ian Auger, roadie to the stars, travelling musician, and good luck charm. My grandfather once smelled Queen Victoria. What can I do for you, squire?"

"I'm looking to speak with Rossignol," I said. "I'm . . ."

"Oh, I know who you are, sunshine. John bloody Taylor, his own bad and highly impressive self. Private eye and king-in-waiting, if you believe the gossip, which I mostly don't. You're here about the suicides, I suppose? Thought so. Word was bound to get out eventually. I warned them, I said they couldn't hope to keep a lid on it for long, but does anyone here ever listen to me? What do you think?" He grinned cheerfully and lit up a deadly little black cigar with a battered gold lighter. "So, John Taylor. You here to make trouble for my little girl?"

"No," I said carefully. Behind the cheerful conversation, Ian's blue eyes were as cold as ice, and he had the look of someone who had very straight forward ideas on how to deal with problems. And the ideas probably involved blunt instruments. "I'm just interested in what's happening here. Maybe I can find a solution. It's what I do."

"Yeah, I've heard of some of the things you do." He considered the matter for a long moment, then shrugged. "Look, mate, I've been with Ross a long time. I'm her roadie, I set up the equipment and do the sound checks, I play her music, I take care of all the shit work so she doesn't have to. I look after her, right? I do the work of three men, and I don't begrudge a moment of it, because she's worth it. I've roadied for all sorts in my time, but she's the real thing. She's going to be big, really big. I was her manager, originally. The first one to see what she had and what she could be. I took her here and there in the Nightside, got her started, but I always knew she'd leave me behind. It doesn't matter. A voice like hers comes along once in a lifetime. I just wanted to be part of her legend."

"I thought Rossignol was managed by the Cavendishes," I said.

He shrugged. "I always knew she'd move on. I couldn't open the doors for her that the Cavendishes could. They're big, they're *connected*. But . . ."

"Go on," I prompted him, when he paused a little too long. He scowled and took his cigar out of his mouth and looked at it so he wouldn't have to look at me.

"This should have been Ross's big break. Caliban's Cavern; biggest, tastiest nightspot in the whole of Uptown. Just the right place to be seen, to be heard, to be *noticed*. But it's all gone wrong. She's changed since she came here. All she ever sings now are sad songs, and she sings them so powerfully that people in the audience go home and kill themselves. Sometimes they don't make it all the way home. God knows how many there've been . . . The Cavendishes are doing their best to cover it up, at least until the recording contract's signed, but word's getting out. They do so love to gossip in the music biz."

"Doesn't it put people off coming to see her?" I said.

Ian almost laughed. "Nah . . . that's all part of the thrill, innit? Makes her even more glamourous, to a certain type of fan. This is the Nightside, after all, always looking for the next new sensation. And Russian roulette is so last week . . ."

"What are the Cavendishes doing to investigate the phenomenon?"

"Them? Naff all! They never even show their faces down here. Just send the bullyboys around, to keep an eye on things, and put the wind up any investigative journalists that might come sniffing around." He smiled briefly. "They don't much care for private eyes either, mate. You watch yourself."

I nodded, carefully unimpressed. "Where can I find Rossignol?"

"She's still my girl," said Ian. "Even if she doesn't have much time for me these days. Are you here to help her, or are you just interested in the bloody *phenomenon*?"

"I'm here to help," I said. "Stopping innocent people dying has got to be in everyone's best interests, hasn't it?"

"She's in her dressing room, round the back." He gave me directions, then looked away from me, his gaze brooding and strangely sad. "I wish we'd never come here, her and me. This wasn't what I wanted for her. If it was up to me, I'd say stuff the money and stuff the contract, something's *wrong* here. But she doesn't listen to me any more. Hardly ever leaves her dressing room. I only get to see her when I'm onstage playing for her to sing to."

"Where does she go when she isn't here?"

"She's always here," Ian said flatly. "Cavendishes arranged a room for her, upstairs. Very comfortable, all the luxuries, but it's still just a bloody room. I don't think Ross has left the club once since she got here. Doesn't have a private life, doesn't care about anything but the next show, the next performance. Not healthy, not for a growing girl like her, but then, there's nothing healthy about Ross's career, since she took up with the bloody Cavendishes."

I started to turn away, but Ian called me back.

"She's a good kid, but . . . don't expect too much from her, okay? She's not herself any more. I don't know who she is, these days."

• • •

I found Rossignol's dressing room easily enough. The two immaculate gentlemen guarding her door weren't everyday bodyguards. The Cavendishes had clearly spent some serious money on internal security. These bodyguards wore Armani suits, and each bore a tattooed ideogram above his left eyebrow that indicated they were the property of the Raging Dragon Clan. Which meant they were magicians, martial artists, and masters of murder. The kind of heavy-duty muscle who usually guarded emperors and messiahs-in-waiting. A sensible man would have turned smartly about and disappeared, at speed, but I just kept going. If I let myself get intimidated by anyone, I'd never get anything done. I came to a halt before them and smiled amiably.

"Hi. I'm John Taylor. I do hope there's not going to be any unpleasantness."

"We know who you are," said the one on the left.

"Private eye, con man, boaster, and braggert," said the one on the right.

"King-in-waiting, some say."

"A man of little magic and much bluff, say others."

"We are combat magicians, mystic warriors."

"And you are just a man, full of talk and tricks."

I stood my ground and said nothing, still smiling my friendly smile.

The bodyguard on the left looked at the one on the right. "I think it's time for our coffee break."

The one on the right looked at me. "Half an hour be enough?"

"Three-quarters," I said, just to show I could play hardball.

The two combat magicians bowed slightly to me and walked unhurriedly away. They just might have been able to take me, but they'd never know now. I've always been good at bluffing, but it helps that most people in the Nightside aren't too tightly wrapped, at the best of times. I knocked on the dressing room door, and when no-one answered, I let myself in.

Rossignol was sitting on a chair, facing her dressing room mirror, studying her reflection in the mirror. She didn't even look round as I shut the door behind me. Her face was calm, and quietly sad, lost in the depths of her own gaze. I leaned back against the closed door and looked her over carefully. She was a tiny little thing, only five feet tall, slender, gamine, dressed in a blank white T-shirt and washed-out blue jeans.

She had long, flat, jet-black hair, framing a pale pointed face that was almost ghostly in the sharp unforgiving light of the dressing room. She had high cheekbones, a long nose, pale pink lips, and not a trace of make-up. If she was thinking anything, it didn't show in her expression. Her hands were clasped loosely together in her lap, as though she'd forgotten they were there. I said her name aloud, and she turned slowly to face me. I did wonder for a moment whether she might have been drugged, given a little something to keep her calm and manageable, but that thought disappeared the moment I met her gaze. Her eyes were large and a brown so dark they were almost black, full of fire and passion. She smiled briefly at me, just a faint twitching of her pale mouth.

"I don't get many visitors these days. I like it that way. How did you get past the two guard dogs at my door?"

"I'm John Taylor."

"Ah, that explains many things. You are perhaps the only person in the Nightside with a more disturbing reputation than mine." She spoke English perfectly, with just enough of a French accent to make her effortlessly charming. "So now, why would the infamous John Taylor be interested in a poor little nightclub singer like me?"

"I've been hired to look into your welfare. To make sure you're all right and not being taken advantage of."

"How nice. Who hired you? Not the Cavendishes, I assume."

I gave her a brief smile of my own. "My client wishes to remain confidential."

"And I do not get a say in the matter?"

"I'm afraid not."

"It is my life we are discussing, Mr. Taylor."

"Please. Call me John."

"As you wish. You may call me Ross. You still haven't answered my question, John. What makes you think I need your assistance? I assure you, I am perfectly safe and happy here."

"Then why the heavy muscle outside your door?"

Her mouth made a silent moue of distaste. "They keep the more obsessive fans at bay. The over-enthusiastic and the stalkers. Ah, my audience! They would fill every moment of my life, if they could. I need time to myself, to be myself."

"What about friends and family?"

"I have nothing to say to them." Ross folded her arms across her chest and gave me a hard, angry stare. "Where were they when I needed them? For years they didn't want to know me, never answered my letters or my pleas for but a little support, to keep me going until my career took off. But the moment I became just a little bit famous, and there was the scent of real money in the air, ah then, suddenly all my family and my so-called friends were all over me, looking for jobs and hand-outs and a chance to edge their way into the spotlight, too. To hell with them. To hell with them all. I have learned the hard way to trust no-one but myself."

"Not even your roadie, Ian?"

She smiled genuinely for the first time. "Ian, yes. Such a sweet boy. He believed in me, even during the bad times when I was no longer sure myself. There will always be a place for him with me, for as long as he wants it. But at the end of the day, I am the star, and I will decide what his place is." She shrugged briefly. "Not even the closest of friends can always climb the ladder at the same pace. Some will always be left behind."

I decided to change the subject. "I understand you live here, in the club?"

"Yes." She turned away from me and went back to looking at herself in the mirror. She was looking for something, but I didn't know what. Maybe she didn't either. "I feel safe here," she said slowly. "Protected. Sometimes it seems like the whole world wants a piece of me, and there's only so much to go round. It's not easy being a star, John. You can take lessons in music, and movement, and how to get the best out of a song, but there's no-one to teach you how to be a success, how to deal with suddenly being famous and in demand. Everybody wants something . . . The only ones I can trust any more are my management. Mr. and Mrs. Cavendish. They're only interested in the money I can make for them . . . and I can deal with that."

"There have been stories, of late," I said carefully. "About mysterious, unexplained suicides . . ."

She looked back at me, smiling sadly. "You of all people should know better than to believe in such gossip, John. It's all just publicity stories that got out of hand. Exaggerations, to put my name on everyone's lips. Everyone claims to have heard the story direct from a friend of a friend, but no-one can ever name anyone who actually died. The Nightside does so love to gossip, and it always prefers bad news to good. I'm just a singer who loves to sing . . . Talk to the Cavendishes, if you're seriously worried. I'm sure they will be able to reassure you. And now, if you will be so good as to excuse me, I need to prepare myself. I have a show to do soon."

And she went back to staring at her face in the mirror, her chin cupped in one hand, her eyes lost in her own thoughts. I let myself out, and she didn't even notice I was gone.

FOUR

Cavendish Properties

I made my way back to the club bar, the tune from "There's No Business Like Show Business" playing sardonically in the back of my head. My encounter with Rossignol hadn't been everything it might have been, but it had been . . . interesting. My first impressions of her were muddled, to say the least. She'd seemed sharp enough, particularly her tongue, but there was no denying there was something *wrong* about Rossignol. Some *missing* quality . . . as though some vital spark had been removed, or suppressed. All the lights were on, but the curtains were a little too tightly closed. It didn't seem to be drugs, but that still left magical controls and compulsions. Not to mention soul thieves, mindsnakes, and even possession. There's never any shortage of potential suspects in the Nightside. Though what major players like that would want with a mere up-and-coming singer like Rossignol . . . Ah hell, maybe she was just plain crazy. No shortage of crazies in the Nightside either. In the end, it all came down to her singing. I'd have to come back again, watch her perform, listen to what she did with her voice. See what it did to her audience. After taking certain sensible precautions, of course. Certain defences. There are any number of magical creatures, mostly female, whose singing can bring about horror and death. Sirens, undines, banshees, Bananarama tribute bands . . .

Back at the bar I used their phone to call my new Nightside office and see how Cathy was getting on with her research into the Cavendishes. The elf bartender didn't raise any objections. He saw me coming and retreated quickly to the other end of the bar, where he busied himself cleaning a glass that didn't need cleaning. The chorus in their wraps and dressing gowns now had a bottle of gin each and were growing definitely raucous, like faded birds of paradise with a really bad attitude. One of them had produced a copy of the magazine *Duelling Strap-ons*, and they were all making very unkind comments about the models in the photos. I looked deliberately in the opposite direction and pressed the phone hard against my ear.

I don't use a mobile phone in the Nightside any more. It makes it far too easy for anyone to find me. Besides, signals here have a tendency to go weird on you. You can end up connected to all kinds of really wrong numbers, talking to anyone or anything, from all kinds of dimensions, in the past, present, and future. And sometimes in between calls, you can hear something whispering what sounds like really awful truths . . . I had my last mobile phone buried in deconsecrated ground and sowed the earth with salt, just to be sure.

My secretary answered the phone before the second ring, which suggested she'd been waiting for my call. "John, where the hell are you?"

"Oh, out and about," I said cautiously. "What's the matter? Problems?"

"You could say that. Walker's been by the office. In his own calm and quiet way he is really not happy with you, John. He started with threats, escalated to open menace, and demanded to know where you were. Jail was mentioned, along with excommunication, and something that I think involves boiling oil and a funnel. Luckily, I was honestly able to say I hadn't a clue where you were, at the moment. You don't pay me enough to lie to Walker. He once made a corpse sit up and answer his questions, you know."

"I know," I said. "I was there. Where's Walker now?"

"Also out and about, looking for you. He says he's got something with your name on it, and I'm pretty sure it's not a warrant. Did you really black out half the Nightside? Do you need backup? Do you want me to contact Suzie Shooter or Razor Eddie?"

"No thank you, Cathy. I'm quite capable of handling Walker on my own."

"In your dreams, boss."

"Tell me what you've found out about the Cavendishes. Anything useful? Anything tasty?"

"Not much, really," Cathy admitted reluctantly. "There's very little direct information available about Mr. and Mrs. Cavendish. I couldn't even find out their first names. There's nothing at all on them in any of the usual databases. They believe very firmly in keeping themselves to themselves, and their business records are protected by firewalls that even my computers from the future couldn't crack. They're currently sulking, by the way, and comforting themselves by sending abusive e-mails to Bill Gates. I've been ringing round, tapping all my usual sources, but once I mention the Cavendishes, most of them clam up, too afraid to speak, even on a very secure line. Of course, this being the Nightside, you can always find someone willing to talk . . . It's up to you how much faith you want to put in people like that."

"Just give me what you've got, Cathy."

"Well . . . Current gossip says that given the kind of deals the Cavendishes have been making recently—sales of property, calling in debts, grabbing at every short-term deal that's going—it's entirely possible they have an urgent need for money. Liquid cash, not investment. There are suggestions that either a Big Deal went seriously wrong, and won't be paying off as hoped, or that they need the money to support a new Big Deal. Or both. There are definite indications that the Cavendishes have recently moved away from their usual conservative investments in favour of high-risk/high-yield options, but that could just be the market."

"When did they make the move into show business?"

"Ah," said Cathy. "They've spent the last couple of years establishing themselves as big-time agents, managers, and promoters of up-and-coming new talent. They've thrown around a lot of money, without much to show for it so far. And again there's gossip that something went seriously wrong with their earlier attempt to promote a new singing sensation at Caliban's Cavern. Sylvia Sin really looked like she was going places for a time. Her face was all over the covers of the music and lifestyle magazines last year, but she went missing very suddenly, and no-one's seen her since. Sylvia Sin has completely disappeared, which isn't an easy thing to do, in the Nightside."

"Give me the bottom line, Cathy."

"All right. Cavendish Properties is an important, respectable, and wide-ranging business, with most of its money still in property and shares. Their showbiz ventures are backed up by serious capital investment, but though they've got dozens of acts on their books, Rossignol is the only potential big breakout. There's a lot of money riding on her being a big success. They can't afford for her to be another Sylvia Sin."

"Interesting," I said. "Thanks, Cathy. I'll look by later, when I get a chance. If Walker should show up again . . ."

"I know, hide in the loo and pretend no-one's home."

"Got it in one," I said. "Now, tell me where to find the Cavendishes."

● ● ●

Clearly the next logical step was to go and brace the Cavendishes in their lair and ask a few impertinent questions, so I left Caliban's Cavern and went walking through the long night, heading through Uptown towards the Business Area. It wasn't a long walk, and the crowds thinned away appreciably as I left show behind and headed towards business. In the end, it was like crossing a line between tinsel and glamour, and stark reality. Bright and gaudy clubs and restaurants were replaced by sober, stern-faced buildings, and the clamour of the Nightside at play was replaced by the thoughtful quiet of the Nightside at work. The Business Area was right on the edge of Uptown, and as close to respectable as the Nightside got. All City Gents in smart suits, with briefcases and rolled umbrellas. But it still payed to be wary—in the Nightside, business people aren't always people. Beings from higher and lower dimensions were always setting up shop here, hoping to make their fortune, and the battles were no less vicious for being waged in boardrooms.

The Cavendishes' building was right where Cathy had said it would be—an old Victorian edifice, still defiantly old-fashioned in aspect, with no name or number anywhere. Either you had business there, and knew where to find it, or the Cavendishes didn't give a damn. They weren't supposed to be easy to find. The Cavendishes weren't just successful, they were exclusive, like their club. I stood some distance away from the front door and looked the place over thoughtfully. The Cavendishes had surrounded their own private little kingdom with a hell of a lot of magical protection, most of it so strong I didn't even need to raise my Sight to detect it. I could feel it, like insects crawling over my skin. There was a tension on the air, of some terrible unseen watching presence, of immediate and dreadful danger. The building was definitely protected by Something, either from Above or Below. The feelings weren't strong enough to scare off anyone who had proper business in the building, but it was more than enough to put the wind up casual visitors or even innocent passersby. And certainly enough to keep most visitors cautious, and maybe even honest.

There was nothing subtle about this building's defences. The Cavendishes wanted everyone to know they were protected.

I approached the front door confidently, as though I had every reason to be there, and pushed it open. Nothing happened. I strode into the lobby like I owned the place, trying hard to ignore the feeling that I had a target painted on my forehead. The lobby was large, plush, very comfortable. Pictures on the walls, fresh flowers in vases, business men sitting in upholstered chairs, reading the *Night Times* and waiting to be called. I headed for the reception desk, and a young man and a young woman moved immediately forward to intercept me. It seemed I was expected. The two combat magicians at the nightclub must have phoned home. I smiled at the man and the woman heading my way, started to say something clever, and stopped. There was no point. They were both Somnambulists. Dressed in basic black, their faces were pale and calm and empty, their eyes tight shut. They were both fast asleep. Somnambulists rent out their sleeping bodies for other people to use. Usually they're indentured servants, paying off debts. They have no say in what's done with their bodies, and any resulting damage is their problem. Their owners, or more properly their puppet masters, can do anything they want, indulge any appetite or fantasy, for as long as the contract lasts. Or until the body wears out. That's the deal.

The real problem, for people like me, is that Somnambulists can't be bluffed or fooled or distracted by clever words. Which meant I was in real trouble. So I just shrugged and smiled and nodded to them, and said, "Take me to your leader."

The man punched me in the head. He moved so quickly I didn't even see it coming. I fell to the floor, and the woman kicked me in the ribs. I tried to scramble away, but in a moment they were all over me, both of them kicking me so hard I could feel ribs cracking. They kept in close, leaving me no room to escape, so I curled into a ball, protecting my head as best I could. The attack had been so sudden and so brutal I couldn't get my thoughts together to try any of my usual defences. All I could do was take it, and promise myself revenge later.

The beating went on for a long, long time.

Occasionally I'd get a glimpse of the other people in the lobby, but none of them even looked my way. They knew better than to get involved. They had their deals with the Cavendishes and absolutely no intention of putting them at risk. And I knew better than to call for help. I curled up tight, my body shuddering with every blow, damned if I'd give my enemies the satisfaction of hearing me cry out. And then one boot connected solidly with my head, and everything went fuzzy for a while.

• • •

The next thing I knew I was in an elevator, going up. The Somnambulists were standing on either side of my slumped body, faces empty, eyes closed. I lay still, doing nothing that might attract their attention. I hurt everywhere I could feel, pain so bad it made me sick. My thoughts were slow and drifting. I flexed my fingers slowly, then my toes, and they all worked. Breathing hurt, which suggested cracked and maybe even broken ribs. My mouth was full of blood. I let it drool out one side and tested my teeth with my tongue. A few felt worryingly loose, but at least I hadn't lost any. I hoped I hadn't wet myself. I hate it when that happens. It had been a long time since I took a beating this bad. Probably piss blood for a week. I'd forgotten the first rule of the Nightside—it doesn't matter how bad you think you are, there's always someone nastier. Still, this visit wasn't a total loss. I'd come looking for evidence that the Cavendishes were guilty of something, and this would do just fine.

The elevator stopped with a jerk that rocked my body, and the pain almost made me cry out. The doors opened, and the Somnambulists bent down, picked me up and carried me out. I didn't try to fight them. Partly because I wasn't in any shape to, but mostly because I was pretty sure they were taking me where I wanted to go—to meet their masters, the Cavendishes. They carried me across an office and dropped me like a rubbish bag before the reception desk. The thick carpet absorbed some of the impact, but it still hurt like hell, and I went away for a few moments.

When I came back, the Somnambulists were gone. I turned my head slowly, cautiously, and saw the door to an inner office closing. I relaxed a little and slowly forced myself up onto my hands and knees. New pains flared up with every move, and I spat mouthfuls of thick and stringy blood onto the luxurious carpet. I ended up sitting awkwardly, favouring the ribs on my left side, leaning the other side carefully against the reception desk for support. Someone was going to pay for this.

I was hurt, shaken, sick, and dizzy, but I knew I had to get my wits back together before the Somnambulists returned, to drag me before the Cavendishes. They didn't want me dead, or at least, not yet. The beating had been to soften me up, before the interrogation. Well, bad luck for them. I don't do soft. I had to wonder what they thought I knew . . . I eased a handkerchief out of my pocket with a shaking hand and gently mopped the worst of the blood from my bruised and beaten face. One eye was already so swollen and puffy that I couldn't see out of it. The handkerchief was so much a mess when I'd finished that I just dropped it on the expensive carpet. Let someone else worry about it.

I peered up and over the reception desk, and saw one of those icily gorgeous secretaries who are de rigueur in all the better offices. The kind who would bite their own limbs off before letting you past without an appointment. She studiously ignored me. The phone rang, and she answered it in a cool and utterly business-like way, as though there wasn't a half-dead private eye bleeding all over her lousy carpet. It could have been just another day in any office, anywhere.

I turned around slowly, gritting my teeth against the shooting pains, and put my back against the desk. After I'd got my breath back from the exertion, I realised there were other people in the office apart from me. In fact, there was quite a crowd of them, filling all the chairs, sitting cross-legged on the carpet, and leaning against the walls. Young, slim, fashionable and Goths to a boy and a girl, they lounged bonelessly, flipping through music and lifestyle magazines, chatting quietly and comparing tattoos, and checking out their elaborate make-up in hand mirrors. They all had the same uniform of black on black, pale faces and heavy dark eye make-up. Skin like chalk, eyes like holes—Death's clowns. Piercings and purple mouths and silver ankhs on chains. A spindly girl curled up in a chair noticed me watching and put aside her copy of *Bite Me* magazine to consider me dispassionately.

"Damn, they really put a world of hurt on you. What did you do to make them mad?"

"I was just being me," I said, trying hard to keep my voice sounding light and effortless. "I have this effect on a lot of people. What are you doing here?"

"Oh, we're all just hanging out. We run errands, sign fan photos for the stars, do a bit of everything really, just to help out. In return, we get to hang, hear all the latest gossip first. And sometimes we even get to meet the stars, when they show up here. Our favourite's Rossignol, of course."

"Of course," I said.

"Oh, she is just the best! Sings like a dark angel, love and death all wrapped up in one easy-on-the-eyes package. She sings like she's been there, and it's all going to end tomorrow . . . we all just adore Rossignol!"

"Yeah," said a skull-faced boy, in his best sepulchral growl. "We all love Rossignol. We'd die for her."

"What makes her so special?" I asked. "Worth dying for?"

They all looked at me like I was mad.

"She is just so *cool*, man!" a barely legal girl said finally, tossing her long black hair angrily, and I knew that was all the answer I was going to get.

"So," said one of the others. "Are you, you know, anyone?"

"I'm John Taylor," I said.

They all looked at me blankly and went back to their magazines and their conversations. If you weren't in the music biz, you weren't anyone.

And none of them gave a damn about my condition or predicament. They wouldn't risk doing anything that might get them banned from the office and their chance to meet the stars. Fans. You have to love them.

The door to the inner office swung open, and the Somnambulists reappeared. They headed straight for me, and I tried not to wince. They picked me up with brutal efficiency and half carried, half dragged me into the inner office. They dumped me on the floor again, and it took me a moment to get my breath back. I heard the door close firmly shut behind me. I forced myself up onto my knees, and then two hands slapped down hard on my shoulders to keep me there. Two stern figures were standing before me, wearing matching frowns, but I deliberately looked away. The inner office was surprisingly old-fashioned, almost Victorian in its trappings—all heavy furniture and solid comforts. Hundreds of identical books lined the walls, looking as old and well used as the furniture. No flowers here. The room smelled close and heavy, like clothes that had been worn too long.

Finally, I looked at my hosts. The Cavendishes resembled long spindly scarecrows clad in undertakers' cast-offs. Even standing still, there was something awkward and ungainly about them, as though they might topple over if they lost concentration. Their clothes were City Gent, both the man and the woman—characterless, anonymous, timeless. Their faces were unhealthily pale, the skin unnaturally perfect, without flaw or blemish, with that tight, taut look that usually comes from too many face-lifts. I didn't think so, in their case. The Cavendishes' faces were unlined because they'd probably never experienced an honest emotion in their lives.

They both stepped forward suddenly, to stand right in front of me, and their movements were eerily synchronised. Mr. Cavendish had short dark hair, a pursed pale mouth, and a flat, almost emotionless glare, as though I was less an enemy than a problem that needed solving. Mrs. Cavendish had long dark hair, good bone structure, a mouth so thin there were hardly any lips to it, and exactly the same eyes.

They made me think of spiders, contemplating what their web had brought them.

"You have no business here," the man said suddenly, the words cold and clipped. "No business. Isn't that right, Mrs. Cavendish?"

"Indeed it is, Mr. Cavendish," said the woman, in a very nearly identical voice. "Up to no good, I'll be bound."

"Why do you interfere in our business, Mr. Taylor?" said the man.

"You must explain yourself," said the woman.

Their manner of speech was eerily identical, almost without inflection.

Their gaze bored into mine, stern and unblinking. I tried a friendly smile, and a thin rill of blood spilled down my chin from a split lip.

"Tell me," I said. "Is it really true you're brother and sister as well as husband and wife?"

I braced myself for the beating, but it still hurt like hell. When the Somnambulists finally stopped, at some unseen signal, it was only their grip on my shoulders that kept me upright.

"We always use Somnambulists," said the man. "The very best kind of servants. Isn't that so, Mrs. Cavendish?"

"Indeed yes, Mr. Cavendish. No back talk, and no treacherous independence."

"Good help is so hard to find these days, Mrs. Cavendish. A sign of the times, I fear."

"As you have remarked before, Mr. Cavendish, and quite rightly." The woman and the man looked at me all the time they were speaking, never once even glancing at each other.

"We know of you, John Taylor," said the man. "We are not impressed, nor are we disposed to endure your famous insolence. We are the Cavendishes. We are Cavendish Properties. We are people of substance and of standing, and we will suffer no intrusions into our affairs."

"Quite right, Mr. Cavendish," said the woman. "You are nothing to us, Mr. Taylor. Normally, you would be utterly beneath our notice. You are only one little man, of dubious parentage. We are a corporation."

"The singer Rossignol is one of our Properties," said the man. "Mrs. Cavendish and I own her contract. Her career and life are ours to manage, and we always protect what's ours."

"Rossignol belongs to us," said the woman. "We own everything and everyone on our books, and we never let go of anything that's ours."

"Except to make a substantial profit, Mrs. Cavendish."

"Right you are, Mr. Cavendish, and I thank you for reminding me. We don't like anyone taking an unhealthy interest in how we manage our affairs, Mr. Taylor. It is no-one's business but ours. Many would-be heroes have tried to meddle in our concerns, down the years. We are still here, and mostly they are not. A wise man would deduce a useful lesson from these facts."

"How are you planning to stop me?" I said, not quite as distinctly as I would have liked. My lower lip was swelling painfully. "These sleeping beauties can't follow me around all the time."

"On the whole, we deplore violence," said the man. "It's so . . . common. So we have others perform it for us, as necessary. If you annoy us again, if you so much as approach Rossignol again, you will be crippled. And if you choose not to heed that warning, you will be killed. In a sufficiently unpleasant manner to discourage any others who might presume to interfere in our business."

"Still," said the woman, "we are reasonable people, are we not, Mr. Cavendish?"

"Business people, Mrs. Cavendish, first and foremost."

"So, let us talk business, Mr. Taylor. How much do you require to work for us, and only us?"

"To become one of our people, Mr. Taylor."

"A valued part of Cavendish Properties, and thus entitled to enjoy our goodwill, remuneration, and protection."

"Not a chance in hell," I said. "I'm for hire, not for sale. And I already have a client."

The Somnambulists stirred on either side of me, and I flinched despite myself, expecting another beating. A sensible man would have played along, but I was too angry for that. They'd taken away my pride—all I had left was my defiance. The Cavendishes sighed in unison.

"You disappoint us, Mr. Taylor," said the woman. "I think we will let the proper Authorities deal with you, this time. We have already contacted Mr. Walker, to complain about your unwanted presence, and he was most interested to learn of your present location. It seems he is most anxious to catch up with you. He is on his way here now, in person, to express his displeasure with you and take you off our hands. Whatever can you have done, Mr. Taylor, to upset him so?"

"Sorry," I said. "I never kiss and tell."

The Somnambulists started to move again, and I reached into an inside pocket of my trench coat and grabbed one of the packets I kept there for emergencies, recognising it immediately by shape and texture. I pulled the packet out as the Somnambulists leaned over me, tore it open, and threw the pepper into their faces. The heavy dark powder hit them squarely in the nose and eyes, and they both breathed it in before they could stop themselves. And then they were both sneezing, loud, vicious sneezes that made their whole bodies convulse. Tears rolled out from under their closed eyes, and they fell back from me, sneezing so hard and so often they could hardly stay upright. And still the sneezing went on as the pepper did its unrelenting work.

Both Somnambulists bent forward from the waist, tears forcing themselves from their closed eyes, and in a moment they were both wide awake. The shock to their systems had been too much, the sheer strength of the involuntary physical reactions had been enough to overcome their enforced sleep. They were both wide awake, and hating every moment of it. They clutched at each other for support and looked around through watering eyes. I lurched to my feet and glared at them both.

"I'm John Taylor," I said, in my very best Voice of Doom. "And I am really upset with you."

The two awakened Somnambulists looked at me, looked at each other, in between sneezes, then turned and ran. They practically fought each other over who got to go through the door first. I grinned, despite my split and swollen lips. There are times when a carefully cultivated bad reputation can come in very handy. So can pepper, and salt. I always keep packets of both in my pockets. Salt is very good for dealing with zombies, for tracing protective circles and pentacles, and as a general purifier. Pepper has many practical uses, too. I carry other things in my pockets, some of them potentially quite viciously nasty, and right then I was in a mood to use every single one of them on the Cavendishes.

I'd like to say I waited till I'd learned all I could before I used the pepper. But the truth is, it had taken me until then to find the strength of will to use it.

I fixed the Cavendishes with a heavy glare. They stared back, apparently unmoved, and the man turned abruptly, picked up a silver bell from his desk, and rang it loudly.

A transport pentacle flared into life in one corner of his office, the pentacle's design shining suddenly in bright actinic lines as it activated, and in a moment there was someone else in the room with us. Someone I knew. He was dressed very formally, in a midnight blue tuxedo, a blindingly white shirt and bow tie, and a sweeping opera cloak, complete with scarlet lining. His carefully styled hair was jet-black, as was his neatly trimmed goatee. His eyes were an icy blue, and his mouth was set in a supercilious sneer. Anyone else would have been impressed, but I knew better.

"Hello, Billy," I said. "Like the outfit. How long have you been a waiter?"

"You look a mess, John," the newcomer said, stepping elegantly out of the transport pentacle, which flickered away into nothing behind him. He checked his cuffs were straight and looked me over disapprovingly. "Nasty. I always said that someday you'd run into trouble your rep couldn't get you out of. And don't call me Billy. I am Count Entropy."

"No you're not," I said. "You're the Jonah. Count Entropy was your father, and a far greater man than you. I remember you, Billy Lathem. We grew up together, and you were a useless little tit then, too. I thought you wanted to be an accountant?"

"I decided there was no money in it. Real money is to be made working for people like the Cavendishes. They keep me on a very handsome retainer, just for such occasions as this. And since my father is dead, I have inherited his title. I am Count Entropy. And I'm afraid I'm going to have to kill you now, John."

I sniffed. "Don't try and impress me, Billy Lathem. I've sneezed scarier-looking objects than you."

Why do bad things happen to good people? Because people like Billy Lathem profit from them. Essentially, he had the power to alter and control probabilities. The Jonah could see all the intertwining links of destiny, the patterns in the chaos, and reach out to choose the one-in-a-million chance for everything to go horribly wrong, and make that single possibility the dominant one. He caused bad luck and delighted in disasters. He destroyed lives and brought down in a moment what it had taken others a lifetime to build. When he was a kid, he did it for kicks—now he did it for money. He was the Jonah, and the misfortunes of others were his meat and drink.

"You're not fit to be Count Entropy," I said angrily. "Your father was a mover and a shaker, one of the Major Powers, revered and respected in the Nightside. He redirected the great energies of the universe."

"And what did it get him, in the end?" said Billy, just as angrily. "He made an enemy of Nicholas Hob, and the Serpent's Son killed him as casually as he would a fly. Forget the good name and the pats on the back. I want money. I want to be filthy, stinking rich. The title's mine now, and the Nightside will learn to fear it."

"Your father . . ."

"Is dead! I don't miss him. He was always disappointed in me."

"Well gosh," I said. "I wonder why."

"I'm Count Entropy!"

"No. You'll only ever be the Jonah, Billy. Bad luck to everyone, including yourself. You'll never be the man your father was, and you know it. Your dreams are too small. You're just the Bad Luck Kid, a small-time thug for hire."

He was breathing hard now, his face flushed, but he controlled himself with an effort and gave me his best disdainful sneer.

"You don't look like much right now, John. Those Somnambulists really did a job on you. You look like a passing breeze would blow you away. It shouldn't be too difficult to find a blood clot in your heart, or a burst blood vessel in your brain. Or maybe I'll start with your extremities and work inwards. There are so many nasty things I can do to you, John, so many bad possibilities."

I smiled back at him, showing him my bloody teeth. "Don't you mess with me, Billy Lathem. I'm in a really bad mood. How would you like me to use my gift, and find the one thing you're really afraid of? Maybe if I tried really hard . . . I could find what's left of your daddy . . ."

All the colour fell out of his face, and suddenly he looked like a child dressed up in an adult's clothes. Poor Billy. He really was very powerful, but I've been playing this game a lot longer than he has. And I have this reputation . . . I nodded to the Cavendishes, turned my back on them, and walked out of their office. And then I got the hell out of their building as fast as my battered body could manage.

No-one tried to stop me.

FIVE

The Singer, Not the Song

I must be getting old. I don't take beatings as well as I used to. By the time I got out of the Cavendishes' building, my legs were barely holding me up, and a cold sweat was breaking out all over my face. Every breath hurt like someone had stabbed me, and a rolling blackness was moving in and out at the edges of my vision. There was fresh blood in my mouth. Never a good sign. I still kept moving, forcing myself on through sheer effort of will. I needed to be sure I was far enough away from the Cavendishes that they couldn't send the building's defence spells after me. And even when I was sure, I kept going, though I was having to stamp my feet down hard to feel the pavement beneath me. I might look a sight, with my swollen face and blood-stained trench coat, but I couldn't afford to appear weak and vulnerable. Not in the Nightside. There are always vultures hovering, ready to drop on anything that looked like prey. So, stare straight ahead and walk like you've got a purpose. I caught a glimpse of myself, reflected in a window, and winced. I looked almost as bad as I felt. I had to get off the streets.

I needed healing and general repairs, and time out to get my strength back. But I was a long way from home, and I couldn't go to any of my usual haunts. Walker would have his people staking them all out by now. Even the ones he wasn't supposed to know about. And if I called any of my friends or allies, you could bet Walker would have someone listening in. The man was nothing if not thorough.

Well, when you can't go to a friend, go to an enemy.

I dragged my battered, aching body down the street, glaring at everyone to keep them from bumping into me, and finally reached a public phone booth. I hauled myself inside and leaned heavily against the side wall. It felt so good to be able to rest for a moment that I briefly forgot why I'd come in there, but I made myself pick up the phone. The dial tone was loud and reassuring. There tends to be very little vandalism of public phone booths in the Nightside. The booths defend themselves, and have been known to eat people who venture inside for reasons other than making a call.

I didn't know Pew's current number. He's always on the move. But he always makes sure to leave cards in phone booths so that people can find him in an emergency. I peered blearily at the familiar card (bright white with an embossed bloodred crucifix) and stabbed out the numbers with an unsteady hand. I was pretty much blind in one eye by then, and my hands felt worryingly numb. I relaxed a little as I heard the number ringing. I studied the other cards plastered across the glass wall in front of me. The usual mixture—charms and potions and spells, love goddesses available by the hour, transformations and inversions, and how to do horrible things to a goat for fun and profit.

Someone picked up the phone at the other end and said, "This had better be important."

"Hello, Pew," I said, trying hard to sound natural through my puffed-up mouth. "It's John Taylor."

"What the hell are you doing, calling me?"

"I'm hurt. I need help."

"Things must really be bad if I'm your best bet. Why me, Taylor?"

"Because you're always saying you're God's servant. You're supposed to help people in trouble."

"People. Not abominations like you! None of us in the Nightside will be safe until you're dead and buried in unconsecrated ground. Give me one good reason why I should put myself out for you, Taylor."

"Well, if charity won't do it, Pew, how about this? In my current weakened state, I am vulnerable to all kinds of attack, including possession. You really want to face something from the Pit in my body, with my gift?"

"That's a low blow, damn you," said Pew. I could practically hear him thinking it over. "All right, I'll send you a door. If only because I'll never really be sure you're dead unless I've finished you off myself."

The phone went dead, and I put it down. There's no-one closer, outside of family and friends, than an old enemy.

I turned around, slowly and painfully, pushed the booth door open and looked outside. A door was standing right in front of me, in the middle of the pavement. Just a door, standing alone, old and battered with the paint peeling off in long strips, and a rough gap showing bare wood where the number had once been. Probably stolen. Pew lived by choice in the rougher neighbourhoods, where he felt his preaching was most needed. I left the phone booth and headed for the door with the last of my strength. Luckily everyone else was giving it plenty of room, probably because it was so obviously downmarket as to be beneath their notice. I hit the door with my shoulder, and it swung open before me, revealing only darkness. I lurched forward, and immediately I was in Pew's parlour. The door slammed shut behind me.

• • •

I headed for the bare table in front of me and leaned gratefully on it as I got my breath back. After a while, I looked around me. There was no sign of Pew, but his parlour seemed very simple and neat. One table, bare wood, unpolished. Two chairs, bare wood, straight-backed. Scuffed lino on the floor, damp-stained wallpaper, and one window smeared over with soap to stop people looking in. The window provided the only illumination. Pew took his vows of poverty and simplicity very seriously. One wall was covered with shelves, holding his various stock in trade. Just useful little items, available for a very reasonable price, to help keep you alive in a dangerous place.

The door at the far end of the parlour slammed open, and Pew stood there, his great head tilted in my general direction. Pew—rogue vicar, Christian terrorist, God's holy warrior.

"Do no harm here, abomination! This is the Lord's place! I bind you in his word, to bring no evil here!"

"Relax, Pew," I said. "I'm on my own. And I'm so weak right now, I couldn't beat up a kitten. Truce?"

Pew sniffed loudly. "Truce, hellspawn."

"Great. Now do you mind if I sit down? I'm dripping blood all over your floor."

"Sit, sit! And try to keep it off the table. I have to eat off that."

I sat down heavily and let out a loud, wounded sigh. Pew shuffled forward, his white cane probing ahead of him. He wore a simple vicar's outfit under a shabby and much-mended grey cloak. His dog collar was pristine white, and the grey blindfold covering his dead eyes was equally immaculate. He had a large head with a noble brow, a lion's mane of grey hair, a determined jaw, and a mouth that looked like it never did anything so frivolous as smile. His shoulders were broad, though he always looked like he was several meals short. He found the other chair and arranged himself comfortably at the opposite end of the table. He leaned his cane against the table leg so he could find it easily, and sniffed loudly.

"I can smell your pain, boy. How badly are you injured?"

"Feels pretty bad," I said. My voice sounded tired, even to me. "I'm hoping it's mostly superficial, but my ribs are holding out for a second opinion, and my head keeps going fuzzy round the edges. I took a real beating, Pew, and I'm not as young as I once was."

"Few of us are, boy." Pew got to his feet and moved unerringly towards the shelves that held his stock. Pew might be blind, but he didn't let it slow him down. He pottered back and forth along the wall, running his hands over the various objects, searching for something. I just hoped it wasn't a knife. Or a scalpel. I could hear him muttering under his breath.

"Wolfsbane, crows' feet, holy water, mandrake root, silver knives, silver bullets, wooden stakes . . . could have sworn I still had some garlic . . . dowsing rods, pickled penis, dowsing rod made from a pickled penis, miller medallions . . . Ah!"

Pew turned back to me, triumphantly holding up a small bottle of pale blue liquid. And then he stopped, his mouth twisted, and his other hand fell to the rosary of human fingerbones hanging from his belt. "How has it come to this? You, alone and helpless in my home, in my power . . . I should kill you, damnation's child. Bane of all the chosen . . ."

"I didn't get to choose my parents," I said. "And everyone said my father was a good man, in his day."

"Oh, he was," Pew said unexpectedly. "Never worked with him myself, but I've heard the stories."

"Did you ever meet my mother?"

"No," said Pew. "But I have seen the auguries taken shortly after your birth. I wasn't always blind, boy. I gave up my eyes in return for knowledge, and much good it's done me. You will be the death of us all, John. But my foolish conscience won't let me kill you in cold blood. Not when you come of your own free will, begging my help. It wouldn't be . . . honourable."

He shook his great head slowly, came forward, and stopped just short of the table. He placed the phial of blue liquid on the table before me. I considered it, as he shuffled back to his chair. There was no identifying label on the phial, nothing to tell whether it was a cure or a poison or something else entirely. Pew collected all kinds of things on his travels.

"Hard times are coming," he said suddenly, as he sat down again. "The Nightside is very old, but it is not forever."

"You've been saying that for years, Pew."

"And it's still true! I know things. I See more without my eyes than I ever did with them. But the further ahead I look, the more unclear things become. By saving you here today, I could be damning every other soul in the Nightside."

"No-one's that important," I said. "And especially not me. What's in the phial, Pew?"

He snorted. "Something that will taste quite appalling, but should heal all your injuries. Knock it back in one, and you can have a nice sweetie afterwards. But magic has its price, John, it always does. Drink that, and you'll sleep for twenty-four hours. And when you wake up, all your injuries will be gone, but you'll be a month older. The price you pay for such accelerated healing will be a life one month shorter than it would otherwise have been. Are you ready to give that up, just to get well in a hurry?"

"I have to," I said. "I'm in the middle of a case, and I think someone needs my help now, rather than later. And who knows, maybe I'll find a way to get the lost month back again. Stranger things have happened, in the Nightside." I paused and looked at Pew. "You didn't have to help me. Thank you."

"Having a conscience can be a real bastard sometimes," said Pew solemnly.

I unscrewed the rusted metal cap on the phial and sniffed the thick blue liquid within. It smelled of violets, a sweet smell to cover something fouler. I tossed down the oily liquid in one and just had time to react to the truly awful taste before everything went black. I woke up lying on my back on the table. My first feeling was relief. Although I'd tried hard to sound confident, there was a real chance Pew might have decided to finish me off while he had the chance. He'd tried often enough in the past. I sat up slowly. I felt stiff, but there was no pain anywhere. Pew had taken off my trench coat and folded it up to make a pillow for my head. I swung my legs down over the side of the table and stretched slowly. I felt good. I felt fine. No pain, no fever, and even the taste of blood was gone from my mouth. I put my hand to my face and was startled to encounter a beard. A month of my life had flown by while I slept . . . I got to my feet, went over to the wall shelves, and scrabbled among Pew's stock until I came up with a hand mirror. My reflection was a surprise, if not a shock. I had a heavy ragged beard, already showing touches of grey, and my hair was long and straggling. I looked . . . wild, uncivilised, intimidating. I didn't like the new look. I didn't like to think I could look like that. Like someone Pew would have a right to hunt down and kill.

"Vanity, vanity," said Pew, entering the room. "I knew that would be the first thing you'd do. Put the mirror back. They're very expensive."

I held on to it. "I look a mess!"

"You just be grateful I remembered to dust you once in a while."

"Have you got a razor, Pew? This beard has to go. It's got grey in it. It makes me look my age, and I can't have that."

Pew grinned nastily. "I have a straight razor. Want me to shave you?"

"I don't think so," I said. "I don't trust anyone that close to my throat with a sharp blade."

He chuckled and handed me a pearl-handled straight razor. One dry shave later, with the help of the hand mirror, and I looked like myself again. It wasn't a very good or even a very close shave, but I got tired of nicking myself. I handed back the razor, then did a few stretches and knee bends. I felt fit to take on the world again. Pew sat on his chair like a statue, ignoring me.

"Once you leave here," he said suddenly, "you're fair game again."

"Of course, Pew. You wouldn't want people to think you were getting soft."

"I will kill you one day, boy. The mark of the beast is upon your brow. I can See it."

"You know," I said thoughtfully, changing the subect, "I could use one last piece of help . . ."

"God save us all, haven't I done enough? Out, out, before you ruin my reputation completely!"

"I need a disguise," I said firmly, not moving. "I have to get back on my case, and I can't afford to be recognised. Come on, you must have something simple and temporary you can let me have . . ."

Pew sniffed resignedly. "Let this be a lesson to me. Never help the stranger upon his way, because he'll only take advantage, the bastard. Where is it you have to go next?"

"A nightclub called Caliban's Cavern."

"I know it. A den of iniquity, and the bar prices are an outrage. I'd better make you a Goth. There are so many of the grubby little heathens around that place, one more shouldn't be noticed. I'll put a seeming on you, a simple overlay illusion. It won't last more than a couple of hours, and it certainly won't fool anyone with the Sight . . ." He was pottering along the shelves again, picking things up and putting them down until finally he came up with an Australian pointing bone. He jabbed it twice in my direction, said something short and aboriginal, and put the bone back on the shelf again.

"Is that it?" I said.

Pew shrugged. "Well, you can have all the chanting and gesturing if you want, but I usually save that for the paying customers. It's really nothing more than window dressing. When you get right down to it, magic's never anything more than power and intent, no matter what the source. Look in the mirror."

I did so, and again someone else looked back at me. My face was entirely hidden under a series of swirling black tattoos, thick interlocking lines that made up a series of designs of ancient Maori origin. Along with the shaggy hair, the new look made me completely unrecognisable.

"You'll need another coat, too," said Pew. "Your trench coat's a mess." He held up a battered black leather jacket with *God Give Me Strength* spelled out on the back with steel studs. "You can have this instead."

I tried on the jacket. It was a bit on the large side, but where I was going they wouldn't care. I made my good-byes to Pew, and the parlour door opened before me, revealing a familiar blackness. I walked into the dark, and immediately I was back in Uptown again, only a few minutes' walk from Caliban's Cavern. I heard the door close firmly behind me and knew it would be gone before I could turn to look. I smiled. Pew probably thought he'd put one over on me, by keeping my trench coat. A personal possession like that, liberally stained with my own blood, would make a marvelous targeting device for all kinds of magic. Certainly Pew could use it to send all kinds of nastiness my way. Which was why I'd taken out a little insurance long ago, in the form of a built-in destructive spell for the trench coat. Once I was more than an agreed distance away, the coat would automatically go up in flames. As Pew should be finding out, right about now.

Of course, I'd been careful to transfer all my useful items from the coat to my nice new jacket before I left.

Pew was good, but I was better.

• • •

By the time I got back to Caliban's Cavern, the queue was already forming for Rossignol's next set. I'd never seen so many Goths in one place.

All dark clothes and brooding faces, like a gathering of small thunder-clouds. They were all talking nineteen to the dozen, filling the night with a clamour of anticipation and impatience. Every now and again someone would start chanting Rossignol's name, and a dozen others would take it up until it died away naturally.

Ticket touts swaggered up and down beside the queue, fighting each other to be the first to target latecomers, offering scalped tickets at outrageous prices. There was no shortage of takers. The growing crowd wasn't just Goths. There were a number of celebrities, complete with their own entourages and hangers-on. You could always recognise celebrities from the way their heads swivelled restlessly back and forth, on the lookout for photographers. After all, what was the point of being somewhere fashionable if you weren't seen being there?

The queue stretched all the way down the block, but I didn't let that bother me. I just walked to the very front and took up a position there like I had every right to be there. Nobody bothered me. You'd be amazed what you can get away with if you just exude confidence and glare ferociously at anyone who even looks like questioning your presence. One of the ticket touts was rude enough to make sneering comments about my tattoos, though, so I deliberately bumped into him and pickpocketed one of his best tickets. I like to think of myself sometimes as a karma mechanic.

Caliban's Cavern finally opened its doors, and the queue surged forward. The Cavendishes had hired a major security franchise, Hell's Neanderthals, to man the door and police the crowd, but even they were having trouble handling the pressure of so many determined Rossignol fans. They pressed constantly forward, shouting and jostling, and the security Neanderthals quickly realised that this was the kind of crowd that could turn into an angry mob if its progress was thwarted. They were there to see Rossignol, and no-one was going to get in their way. So, the Hell's Neanderthals settled for grabbing tickets and waving people through. I would have given them strict orders to frisk everyone for weapons and the like, but it was clear any attempt to slow the fans down now would have risked provoking a riot. The fans were close to their goal, their heroine, and they were hungry.

Inside the club, all the tables and chairs had been taken out to make one great open space before the raised stage at the far end of the room. The crowd poured into it, gabbling excitedly, and quickly filled all the space available, packing the club from wall to wall. I was swept along and finally ended up right in front of the stage, with elbows digging into my sides, and someone's hot breath panting excitedly on the back of my neck. The club was already overpoweringly hot and sweaty, and I looked longingly across at the bar, with its extra staff, but it would have taken me ages to fight my way through the tightly packed crowd. No-one else seemed interested in the bar. All the crowd cared about was Rossignol. Their diva of the dark.

There were far too many people in the club, packed in like cattle in their stalls. It didn't surprise me. The Cavendishes hadn't struck me as the type to care about things like safety regulations and keeping fire exits clear. Not when there was serious money to be made.

Set off by a single bright spotlight, a huge stylised black bird (presumably someone's idea of a nightingale) covered most of the wall behind the stage. It looked threatening, wild, ominous. Looking around, I could see the design everywhere on the fans, on T-shirts, jackets, tattoos, and silver totems hanging on silver chains. I could also see the celebrities jammed in the crowd like everyone else, their hangers-on struggling to form protective circles around them. There were no real movers or shakers, but I could see famous faces here and there. Sebastian Stargrave, the Fractured Protagonist; Deliverance Wilde, fashion consultant to the Faerie; and Sandra Chance, the Consulting Necromancer. Also very much in evidence were the supergroup Nazgul, currently on a comeback tour of the Nightside with their new vocalist. They looked just as freaked and excited as everyone else.

And yet, for all the excitement and passion in the air, the overall mood felt decidedly unhealthy. It was the wrong kind of anticipation, like the hunger of animals waiting for feeding time. The hot and sweaty air had the unwholesome feel of a crowd gathered at a car wreck, waiting for the injured to be brought out. These people weren't just here to hear someone sing—this was a gathering throbbing with erotic Thanatos. The mood was magic. Dark, reverent magic, from all the wrong places of the heart.

The crowd was actually quietening down, the chanting dying out, as the anticipation mounted. Even I wasn't immune to it. Something was going to happen, and we could all feel it. Something big, something far out of the ordinary, and we all wanted it. We needed it. And whether what was coming would be good or bad didn't matter a damn. We were a congregation, celebrating our goddess. The crowd fell utterly silent, all our eyes fixed on the stage, empty save for the waiting instruments and microphone stands. Waiting, waiting, and now we were all breathing in unison, like one great hungry creature, like lemmings drawn to a cliff edge by something they couldn't name.

Rossignol's band came running onto the stage, smiling and waving, and the crowd went wild, waving and cheering and stamping their feet. The band took up the instruments waiting for them and started playing. No introductions, no warm-up, just straight in. Ian Auger, the cheerful hunchbacked roadie, played the drums. And the bass and the piano. There were three of him. I felt he might have mentioned it earlier. Next a quartet of backing singers came bounding onstage, wearing old-fashioned can-can outfits, with teased high hairstyles, beautiful and glamorous, with bright red lips and flashing eyes. They joined right in, belting out perfect harmonies to complement the music, stamping their feet and flashing their frills, singing up a storm. And then Rossignol came on, and the massed baying of the crowd briefly drowned out the music. She wore a chic little black number, with long black evening gloves that made her pale skin look even more funereal. Her mouth was dark, and so were her eyes, so that she seemed like some old black-and-white photograph. Her feet were bare, the toenails painted midnight black.

She grabbed hold of the mike stand at the front of the stage with both hands and clung to it like it was the only thing holding her up. As the show progressed, she rarely let go of it, except to light a new cigarette. She stood where she was, her mouth pressed close to the mike like a lover, swaying from side to side. She had a cigarette in one corner of her dark mouth when she came on, and she chain-smoked in between and sometimes during her songs.

The songs she sang were all her own material; "Blessed Losers," "All the Pretty People," and "Black Roses." They had good strong tunes, played well and sung with professional class, but none of that mattered. It was her voice, her glorious suffering voice that cut at the audience like a knife. She sang of lost loves and last chances, of small lives in small rooms, of dreams betrayed and corrupted, and she sang it all with utter conviction, singing like she'd been there, like she'd known all the pain there ever was, all the darknesses of the human heart, of hope valued all the more because she knew it wasn't real, that it wouldn't help; and all the loss and heartbreak there ever was filled her voice and gave it dominion over all who heard it.

There were tears on many faces, including my own. Rossignol had got to me, too. I'd never heard, never felt, anything like her songs, her voice. In the Nightside it's always three o'clock in the morning, the long dark hour of the soul—but only Rossignol could put it into words.

And yet, despite all I was feeling, or was being made to feel, I never entirely lost control. Perhaps because I'm more used than most to the dark, or simply because I had a job to do. I tore my eyes away from Rossignol, reached inside my jacket pocket, and pulled out a miller medallion. It was designed to glow brightly in the presence of magical influence, but when I held it up to face Rossignol, there wasn't even a glimmer of a glow. So Rossignol hadn't been enchanted or possessed or even magically enhanced. Whatever she was doing, it came straight from her, and from her voice.

The audience was utterly engrossed, still and rapt and silent, drinking their diva in with eyes and ears, immersing themselves in emotions so sharp and melancholy and compelling that they were helpless to do anything but stand there and soak it up. It was all they could do to come out of it to applaud her in between songs. The three Ian Augers and the quartet of backing singers were looking tired and drawn, faces wet with sweat as they struggled to keep up with Rossignol, but the crowd only had eyes for her. She hung on to her microphone stand as though it was a lifeline, smoking one cigarette after another, blasting out one song after another, as though it was all she lived to do.

And then, as she paused at the end of one song to light up another cigarette, a man not far from me pressed right up against the edge of the stage, a man who'd been staring adoringly at Rossignol from the moment she first appeared, smiled at her with tears still wet on his cheeks and drew a gun. I could see it happening, but I was too far away to stop it. All I could do was watch as the man put the gun to his head and blew his brains out. All over Rossignol's bare feet.

At the sound of the gun, the Ian Augers looked up sharply from their instruments. The backing singers huddled together, eyes and mouths stretched wide. Rossignol stared blankly down at the dead man. He was still standing there, because the press of the crowd wouldn't allow him to fall, even though half his head was missing. And in the echoing silence, the crowd slowly came back to themselves. As though they'd been shocked awake from a deep dark dream where they'd all been drifting towards . . . something. I knew, because I'd been feeling it too. Part of me recognised it.

Then the crowd went crazy. Screaming and shouting and roaring in what might have been shock or outrage, they all surged determinedly *forward*. They wanted, they needed, to get to the stage, get to *her*. They fought each other with hands and elbows, snapping like animals. People were crushed, dragged down and trampled underfoot. Those nearest the dead man at the front tore him apart, literally limb from limb, scattering the bloody body parts among them like sacrificial offerings. There was an awful feeling of . . . celebration in the crowd. As though this was what they'd all been waiting for, even if they didn't know themselves.

I'd already vaulted up onto the stage and out of the way. Rossignol snapped out of her horrified daze, turned, and ran from the stage. The crowd saw her disappear and howled their rage and disapproval. They started to scramble up onto the stage. The backing singers ran forward to the edge of the stage and kicked viciously at people trying to pull themselves up. The three Ian Augers came forward and reinforced the singers with large, bony fists. But they were so few, and the crowd was so large, and so determined. Hell's Neanderthals waded into the crowd from the rear, slapping people down and throwing them in the direction of the exit, whether they wanted to go or not. I started after Rossignol. One of the Ian Augers reached out to grab me, but I've had a lot of practice at dodging unfriendly hands. I headed backstage, just as the first wave of the crowd boiled up over the edge.

• • •

Backstage, no-one tried to stop me. Everyone there had their own problems, and once again as long as I moved confidently and like I had a purpose and a right to be there, no-one even looked at me. I saw the two combat magicians coming and ducked through a side door for a moment. They hurried past, dark sparks already sputtering around their fists as they prepared themselves for some magical mayhem. They should be able to hold off the crowd, assuming Stargrave and Chance didn't get involved. If they did, there could be some serious unpleasantness. I waited until I was sure the combat magicians were gone, then headed for Rossignol's dressing room.

She was sitting there alone, again, with her back to the mirror this time. Her eyes were wild, unfocussed, as she struggled to cope with what had just happened. She was trying to scrub the blood and gore off her bare feet with a hand towel. And yet, for all her obvious distress, it seemed to me that this was the most alive I'd ever seen her. She looked up sharply as I came in and shut the door behind me.

"Get out! Get out of here!"

"It's all right, Ross," I said quickly. "I'm not a fan." I concentrated and shrugged off the seeming Pew had placed on me. It was only a small magic, after all. Rossignol recognised me as the tattoos disappeared from my face, and she slumped tiredly.

"Thank God. I could use a friendly face."

She suddenly started to tremble, her whole body shuddering, as the shock caught up with her. I took off my leather jacket and wrapped it gently round her shoulders. She grabbed my hands, squeezing them hard as though to draw some of my strength and warmth into her, then suddenly she was in my arms, holding me like a drowning woman, her tear-stained face pressed against my chest. I held her and comforted her as best I could. We all need a little simple human comfort, now and again. Finally, she let go, and I did, too. I knelt, picked up the hand towel, and cleaned the last of the blood off her feet to give her a moment to compose herself. By the time I'd finished and was looking around for somewhere to dump the towel, she seemed to have calmed down a little.

I straightened up, sat on the dressing room table, and dropped the towel beside me. "Has anything like this ever happened to you before, Ross?"

"No. Never. I mean, there have been rumours, but . . . no. Never right in front of me."

"Did you recognise the guy?"

"No! Never saw him before in my life! I don't mix with my . . . audience. The Cavendishes insist on that. Part of building the image, the mystique, they said. I never really believed the rumours . . . I thought it was just publicity, stories the Cavendishes put about to work up some excitement. I never dreamed . . ."

"As if we would ever do such a thing, dear Rossignol," said a cold, familiar voice behind me. I got to my feet and looked round, and there in the dressing room doorway were Mr. and Mrs. Cavendish. Tall and aristocratic, and twice as arrogant. They glided in like two dark birds of ill omen, ignoring their property Rossignol to consider me with a cold, thoughtful gaze.

"You do seem in very rude health, Mr. Taylor," said the man. "Does he not, Mrs. Cavendish?"

"Indeed he does, Mr. Cavendish. Quite the picture of good health."

"Perhaps some of the stories about you are true after all, Mr. Taylor."

I just smiled and said nothing. Let them wonder. It all added to the reputation.

"We did think you'd learned your lesson, Mr. Taylor," said the woman.

"Afraid not," I said. "I'm a very slow learner."

"Then we shall just have to try harder," said the man. "Won't we, Mrs. Cavendish?"

Rossignol was looking back and forth, confused. "You know each other?"

"Of course," said the man. "Everyone in the Nightside comes to us, eventually. Do not concern yourself, my dear. And most of all, do not worry yourself about the unfortunate incident during the show. Mrs. Cavendish and I will take care of everything. You must allow us to worry for you. That is what you pay us our forty per cent for."

"*How much?*" I said, honestly outraged.

"Our hard-won expertise does not come cheaply, Mr. Taylor," said the woman. "Not that it is any of your business. Isn't that correct, dear Rossignol?"

She seemed to shrink under their gaze, and she looked down at the floor like a scolded child. "Yes," she said, in a small voice. "That's right."

"What's happening out in the club?" I said.

"The club is being cleared," said the man. "It is a shame that the show had to be cut short, but we did make it clear on the tickets that there would be no refunds, under any circumstances."

"I am sure they will be back again, for the next show," said the woman. "Everyone is so desperate to hear dear Rossignol sing."

"You expect her to go on again, after what just happened?" I said.

"Of course," said the man. "The show must go on. And our dear Rossignol only lives to sing. Isn't that right, dear child?"

"Yes," said Rossignol, still staring at the floor. "I live to sing."

"People are dying!" I said loudly, trying to get a reaction from her. "Not just here, not just right now. This is only the most recent suicide, and the most public. People are taking their own lives because of what they hear when Rossignol sings!"

"Rumour," said the woman. "Speculation. Nothing more than tittle-tattle."

"And there will always be fanatics," said the man. "Poor deranged souls who fly too close to the flame that attracts them. You are not to concern yourself, dear Rossignol. The club will be cleared soon, and all will be made ready for your next performance. We will have extra security in place and take all the proper precautions to ensure your safety. Leave everything to us."

"Yes," said Rossignol. Her voice was heavy now, almost half-asleep. Just the presence of the Cavendishes had reduced her to the same dull state in which I'd first found her. There was no point in talking to her any more. So I shrugged mentally and took my jacket back from around her shoulders. She didn't react. I put it on, and the Cavendishes stepped back to make room for me to leave. I headed for the door like it was my decision, and the Cavendishes glided smoothly aside to let me pass. I was almost out of the room when Rossignol's voice stopped me. I looked back. She had her head up again, and her voice was quiet but determined.

"John, find out what's happening. I need to know the truth. Do this for me. Please."

"Sure," I said. "Saving damsels in distress is what I do."

SIX

All the News, Dammit

Every good guest knows better than to outstay his welcome. Especially if he's an uninvited guest, and his hosts want his head on a platter. So I slipped quietly away, passing unnoticed in the general chaos and hysteria backstage, and finally made my exit by a sinfully unguarded back door. The back alley was surprisingly clean and tidy, not to mention well lit, though I did surprise half a dozen of the cleaning monkeys caught up in a red-hot dice game. I murmured my apologies and hurried past them. Monkeys can get really nasty if you interrupt their winning streak.

I moved quietly round the corner of the club and peered down the side alley that led back to the main street. It was empty, for the moment, but there were clear sounds of trouble and associated mayhem out on the street. I padded cautiously forward, sneaking the occasional quick look over my shoulder, and eventually eased up to the front corner of Caliban's Cavern. Someone had already smashed the street-light there, so I stood and watched from the shadows as a riot swiftly put itself together outside the nightclub.

Out in front of Caliban's Cavern, a loud and very angry crowd was busily escalating a commotion into an open brawl. The recently ejected audience was feeling distinctly put upon and out of sorts at being cheated out of their show, and even more upset at the management's firm *no refunds* policy. A few of the crowd, most definitely including the various celebrities, were not at all used to being manhandled in such a peremptory manner, and many had taken it upon themselves to express their displeasure by tearing apart the whole front edifice of the club. Windows were smashed, facia torn away, and anything at all fragile ended up in small pieces all over the pavement. The outnumbered security staff retreated back inside the club and locked the front doors. The increasingly angry crowd took that as a challenge and set about kicking the doors in. Some even levered up bits of the pavement to use as missiles or battering rams.

An even larger crowd gathered, to watch the first crowd. Free entertainment was always highly valued in the Nightside, especially when it involved violence and the chance of open mayhem. On learning the reason for the riot, some of the new arrivals expressed their solidarity by joining in, and soon an army of angry faces were attacking the front of Caliban's Cavern with anything that came to hand. And it's surprising how many really destructive things can just come to hand, in the Nightside.

A roar of rabid motorcycles announced the arrival of security reinforcements. The outer edges of the huge seething mob looked round to see a pack of almost a hundred Hell's Neanderthals slamming to a halt on their stripped-down chopper bikes. They quickly dismounted and surged forward, howling their pre-verbal war cries and brandishing all sorts of simple weaponry. The mob turned to face them, happy and eager for a chance to have living targets to take out their fury on. The two sides joined battle with equal fervour, and soon half the street was a war zone, with bodies flying this way and that, and blood flowing thickly in the gutters. The watching crowd retreated to a safe distance and booed the newly arrived security for the spoil-sports they were.

It seemed to me that this was a good time to make myself scarce, while the Cavendishes' attention would be focussed on more immediate problems. I skirted round the edges of the boiling violence, firmly resisting all invitations to become involved, and walked briskly back towards the business area of Uptown. I'd thought of someone else to go to in search of answers. When in doubt, go to the people who know everything, even if they can't prove any of it. Namely journalists, gossip columnists, and all the other nosey parkers employed by the *Night Times*, the Nightside's very own newspaper.

• • •

It didn't take long to reach Victoria House, the large and comfortably rundown building that housed the *Night Times*. It was a big and bulky building because it had to be. Within its heavy grey stone walls the paper was written, edited, published, printed, and distributed every twenty-four hours, all under the guardianship of its remarkable owner and editor, Julien Advent. The legendary Victorian Adventurer himself. Advent had to keep everything under one roof because that was the only way he could ensure the paper's safety and independence. I paused outside the front door to look up at the gargoyles sneering down from the roof. One of them was scratching itself listlessly, but otherwise they showed no interest in me. I took that as a good sign. The gargoyles were always the first to make it clear when you were out of favour with the paper, and some of them had uncanny aim and absolutely no inhibitions when it came to bodily functions.

The *Night Times* has prided itself throughout its long history in telling the truth, the whole truth, and as much gossip as it could get away with it. This had not endeared it to the Nightside's many powerful movers and shakers, and they had all made attempts, down the years, to shut the paper down by magic, muscle, political and business pressure. But the *Night Times* was still going strong, over two centuries old now, and as determined as ever to tell the general populace where the bodies were buried. Sometimes literally. It helped that the paper had almost as many friends and admirers as enemies. The last time some foolish soul tried to interfere with the *Night Times*'s distribution, by sending out a small army of thugs to intimidate the news vendors, the Little Sisters of the Immaculate Chain Saw had made one of their rare public appearances to deal with the matter and made such a mess of the thugs it was three days before the gutters ran freely again.

I stepped up to the front door very carefully, ready to duck and run at a moment's notice. I was usually welcome at the *Night Times* offices, but it paid to be cautious. Victoria House had really heavy-duty magical defences, of a thorough and downright vicious nature that would have put the Cavendishes' defences to shame. They'd been built up in layers over two hundred years, like a malevolent onion. A subsonic avoidance spell ensured that most people couldn't even get close to the building unless they were on the approved list, or had legitimate business there. I'm not saying I couldn't get in if I really had to, but nothing short of a gun at the back of my head would convince me to try. The last time some idiot tried to smuggle a bomb into Victoria House, the defences turned him into something. No-one was quite sure what, because you couldn't look at him for more than a moment or two without projectile vomiting everything you'd ever eaten, including in previous lives. I'm told he, or more properly it, works in the sewer systems these days, and the rat population is way, way down.

I pushed the front door open, tensed, then relaxed as nothing awful happened to me. I counted my fingers anyway, just in case, and then strode into the lobby, smiling like I didn't have a care or guilty secret in the world. It's important to keep up appearances, especially in front of journalists. It was a wide-open lobby, to allow for a clean line of fire from as many directions as possible, and the receptionist sat inside a cubicle of bulletproof glass, surrounded by a pentacle of softly glowing blue lines. It was said by many, and believed by most, that you could nuke the whole building and the receptionist would still be okay.

The old dear put down her knitting as she saw me coming, studied me over the top of her granny glasses, and smiled sweetly. Most people thought of her as a nice old thing, but I happened to know that her knitting needles had been carved from human thigh-bones, and if she smiled widely enough, you could see that all her teeth had been filed to points.

"Ah, hello there, Mr. Taylor. So nice to see you back again. You're looking very yourself. Would I be right in thinking you're here to have a wee word with the man himself?"

"That's right, Janet. Could you ring up and ask Julien if he'll see me?"

"Oh, there's no need for that, you wee scamp. News of your latest exploits has already reached Mr. Advent, and he is most anxious to get all the details from you while they're still fresh in your mind." She shook her grey head and tut-tutted sadly. "Such a naughty boy you are, Mr. Taylor, always getting into trouble."

I just smiled and nodded, though I wasn't all that sure what she was talking about. Surely Julien couldn't know about my part in the destruction of Prometheus Inc. already? Janet hit the concealed switch that opened the elevator doors at the back of the lobby. She was the only one who could open the doors from this side, and she took her responsibility very seriously. There were those who said she never left her cubicle. Certainly no-one else had ever been seen in her place. I walked across the lobby, carefully not hurrying in case it made me look too anxious, and stepped into the waiting elevator. The steel doors closed silently, and I hit the button for the top floor.

Top floor was Editorial. I'd been there often enough before that my unexpected appearance shouldn't ring too many alarm bells. I used to do occasional legwork for the editor, in my younger days, before I had to leave the Nightside in a hurry. My gift for finding things came in very handy when Julien Advent needed to track down witnesses or people in hiding. I hadn't done anything for him recently, but he did still owe me a couple of favours . . . Not that I'd press the point. In the past, I'd always been careful to keep our relationship strictly business, because the great Victorian Adventurer had always been a man of unimpeachable and righteous morality, and such people have always made me very nervous. They tend not to approve of people like me, once they get to know me.

I'd never been sure how much Julien knew about my various dubious enterprises. And I've never liked to ask.

The elevator doors opened with a bright and cheerful chiming sound, and I stepped out into the plain, largely empty corridor that led to Editorial. The only decoration consisted of famous front pages from the *Night Times*'s long history, carefully preserved behind glass. Most were from way before my time, but I glanced at some of the more recent examples as I headed for the Editorial bullpen. *Angel War Ends in Draw, Beltane Blood Bonanza, New Chastity Scare, Who Watches the Authorities?* And, from its brief tabloid incarnation, *Sandra Chance Ate My Haploids!* (Julien Advent had been on vacation that month.) I stopped outside the bullpen to consider the *Night Times*'s famous motto, proudly emblazoned over the door.

ALL THE NEWS, DAMMIT.

The solid steel door had a wild mixture of protective runes and sigils engraved into its surface. It was sealed on all kinds of levels, but it recognised me immediately and opened politely. The general bedlam from within hit my ears like a thunderclap, and I braced myself before walking in like I had every right to be there. The long room was full of people, working at desks and shouting at each other. A few people ran back and forth between the desks, carrying important memos and updates, and the even more important hot coffee that kept everybody going. The bullpen ran at full blast, non-stop, in three eight-hour shifts, to be sure of covering everything as it happened. The computers were never turned off, and the seats were always warm. A few people looked round as I entered, smiled or grimaced, and went straight back to work. This wasn't a place for hanging around watercoolers—everyone here took their work very seriously.

The place hadn't changed at all in the five years I'd been away. It was still a mess. Desks groaned under the weight of computer equipment, tottering stacks of books, and assorted magical and high-tech paraphernalia. Piles of paper overflowed the In and Out trays, and the phones never stopped ringing. Ever-changing displays on the far wall showed the current times and dates within all the Timeslips operating within the Nightside, while a large map showed the constantly contracting and expanding boundaries of the Nightside itself. Occasional details within the map flickered on and off like blinking eyes, as reality rewrote itself. Slow-moving ceiling fans did their best to move the cigarette smoke around. No-one had ever tried to ban smoking here—journalism in the Nightside was a high-stress occupation.

I breezed down the central aisle, nodding and smiling to familiar faces, most of whom ignored me. Junior reporters brushed past me as they scurried back and forth, trying to outshout each other. A zone of magical silence surrounded the communications section, cut off from the rest of the room as they chased up the very latest stories on telephones, crystal balls, and wax effigies. I stopped as the copyboy came whirling towards me. Otto was an amiable young poltergeist who manifested as a tightly controlled whirlwind. He bobbed up and down before me like a miniature tornado, tossing the papers he carried inside himself towards In trays and waiting hands with uncanny accuracy.

"Hello, hello, Mr. Taylor! So nice to have you back among us. Love the jacket. You here to see the gaffer, are you?"

"Got it in one, Otto. Is he in?"

"Well, that's the question, isn't it? He's in his office, but whether he's in to you . . . Hang on here while I nip in and check."

He shot off towards the soundproofed glass cubicle at the end of the bullpen, singing snatches of show tunes as he went. I could just make out Julien Advent sitting behind his editor's desk, making hurried last-minute corrections to a story, while his sub-editor hovered frantically before him. Julien finally finished, and the sub snatched the pages from the desk and ran for the presses. Julien looked up as Otto swirled into his office, then looked round at me.

I looked around the bullpen. Hardly anyone looked back. Despite all my previous hard work for the *Night Times*, they didn't consider me one of them. I didn't share their holy quest for pursuing news. And as far as newsies were concerned, it was always going to be them versus everyone else. You couldn't afford to get close to someone you might have to do a story on someday.

Not all of the staff were human. The editor operated a strictly equal opportunity employment programme. A semi-transparent ghost was talking to the spirit world on the memory of an old-fashioned telephone. Two ravens called Truth and Memory fluttered back and forth across the room. They were moonlighting from their usual job, working as fact-checkers. A goblin drag queen was working out the next day's horoscopes. His fluffy blonde wig clashed with his horns. It probably helped in his job that he was a manic depressive with a nasty sense of humour. His column might be occasionally distressing, but it was never boring. He nodded casually to me, and I wandered over to join him. He adjusted the fall of his bright green cocktail dress and smiled widely.

"See you, John! Who's been a naughty boy, then? That creep Walker was here looking for you earlier, and he was not a happy bunny."

"When is he ever?" I said calmly. "I'm sure it's all a misunderstanding. Any idea why the editor wants to see me?"

"He hasn't said, but then he never does. What have you been up to?"

"Oh, this and that. Anything in the future I should know about?"

"You tell me, pet. I just work here."

We shared a laugh, and he went back to scowling over his next column, putting together something really upsetting for tomorrow's Virgos. I strolled down the central aisle towards the editor's cubicle, as slowly as I thought I could get away with. There was no telling what Julien knew, or thought he knew, but I had no intention of telling him anything I didn't have to. Knowledge was power here, just as in the rest of the Nightside. A lot of the staff were affecting not to notice my presence, but I'm used to that. The haunted typewriter clacked busily away to my left, operated by a journalist who was murdered several years ago, but hadn't let a little thing like being dead interfere with his work. One of the *Night Times*'s few real ghost writers.

I'd almost reached the editor's cubicle, when the paper's gossip columnist pushed his chair back to block my way. Argus of the Thousand Eyes was a shapeshifter. He could be anyone or anything, and as a result was able to infiltrate even the most closely guarded parties. He saw everything, overheard all, and told most of it. He had an endless curiosity and absolutely no sense of shame. The number of death threats he got every week outnumbered those of all the rest of the staff put together. Which was probably why Argus had never been known to reveal his true shape or identity to anyone. Rumours of his complicated sex life were scandalous. For the moment he was impersonating that famous reporter Clark Kent, as played by Christopher Reeve in the *Superman* movies.

"So tell me," he said. "Is it true, about Suzie Shooter?"

"Probably," I said. "Who's she supposed to have killed now?"

"Oh, it's something much more juicy than that. According to a very reliable source, dear Suzie has been hiding some really delicious secrets about her family . . ."

"Don't go there," I said flatly. "Or if Suzie doesn't kill you, I will."

He sneered at me and changed abruptly into an exact copy of me. "Maybe I should go and ask her yourself."

I gripped him firmly by the throat and lifted him out of his chair, so I could stick my face right into his. Or, rather, mine. "Don't," I said. "It isn't healthy to be me at the best of times, and I don't need you muddying my waters."

"Put him down, John," said Julien Advent. I looked round, and he was standing in the open door of his cubicle. "You know you can't kill him with anything less than a flamethrower. Now get in here. I want a word with you."

I dropped Argus back into his chair. He stuck out my tongue at me and changed into an exact copy of Walker. I made a mental note to purchase a flamethrower and went over to join Julien in his office. He shut the door firmly behind me, then waved me to the visitor's chair. We both sat down and considered each other thoughtfully.

"Love the jacket, John," he said finally. "It's so not you."

"This from a man who hasn't changed his look since the nineteenth century."

Julien Advent smiled, and I smiled back. We might never be friends, or really approve of each other, but somehow we always got along okay. It probably helped that we had a lot of enemies in common.

Julien Advent was the Victorian Adventurer, the greatest hero of his age. Valiant and daring, he'd fought all the evils of Queen Victoria's time and never once looked like losing. He was tall and lithely muscular, impossibly graceful in an utterly masculine way, with jet-black hair and eyes, and an unfashionably pale face. Handsome as any movie star, the effect was somewhat spoiled by his unwaveringly serious gaze and grim smile. Julien always looked like he didn't believe in frivolous things like fun or movie stars. He still wore the stark black-and-white formal dress of his time, the only splash of colour a purple cravat at his throat, held in place by a silver pin presented to him by Queen Victoria herself. And it had to be said, Julien looked a damn sight more elegant than the Jonah. Julien had style.

There were any number of books and movies and even a television series about the great Victorian Adventurer, most of them conspiracy theories as to why he'd disappeared so suddenly, at the height of his fame, in 1888. And then he astonished everyone by reappearing out of a Timeslip into the Nightside in 1966. It turned out he'd been betrayed by the only woman he ever loved, who lured him into a trap set by his greatest enemies, the evil husband-and-wife team known as the Murder Masques. The three of them tricked him into a pre-prepared Timeslip, and the next thing he knew he'd been catapulted into the future.

Being the great man that he was, Julien Advent soon found his feet again. He went to work as a journalist for the *Night Times* and made a great investigative reporter—partly because he wasn't afraid or impressed by anyone and partly because he had an even scarier reputation than the villains he pursued so relentlessly. Julien still fought evil and punished the guilty—he just did it in a new way. He was helped in adjusting to his new time by his newfound wealth. He'd left money in a secret bank account, when he disappeared from 1888, and the wonders of compound interest meant he'd never have to worry about money ever again. Eventually Julien became the editor, then the owner, of the *Night Times*, and that great crusading newspaper had become the official conscience of the Nightside and a pain in the arse to all those who liked things just fine the way they were.

Still, everybody read the *Night Times*, if only to be sure they weren't in it.

Julien Advent was in every way a self-made man. He hadn't started out as a hero and adventurer. He was just a minor research chemist, pottering away in a small laboratory on a modest stipend. But somehow he created a transformational potion like no other, a mysterious new compound that could unlock the secret extremes of the human mind. A potion that could make a man absolute good or utter evil. He could have become a monster, a creature that lived only to indulge itself with all manner of violence and vice, but being the good and moral man that he was, Julien Advent took the potion and became a hero. Tall and strong, fast-moving and quick-thinking, courageous and magnificent and unwaveringly gallant, he became the foremost adventurer of his time.

A man so perfect, he'd be unbearable if he wasn't so charming. He had tried to re-create his formula over the years, but to no success. Some unknown ingredient escaped him, some unknown impurity in one of the original salts . . . and Julien Advent remained the only one of his kind.

He never did discover what happened to the Murder Masques. That terrible husband-and-wife team, who ran all the organised crime in the Victorian Nightside, their faces hidden behind red leather masks, were long gone . . . no more now than a footnote in history. Only really remembered at all as the main adversaries of the legendary Victorian Adventurer. Some said progress changed London and the Nightside so quickly that they couldn't keep up, or they were brought down by others of their vicious kind. And some said they just got old and tired and slow, and younger wolves dragged them down. Julien had tried to determine their fate, using all the considerable resources of the *Night Times*, but the Murder Masques were lost in the mists of history and legend.

The woman who betrayed Julien to his mortal enemies hadn't even made it into the legends, her very name forgotten. Julien had been known to say that that was the best possible punishment he could have wished for her. Otherwise, he never spoke of her at all.

And now he sat behind his editor's desk, studying me intently with his dark eyes and sardonic smile. Julien was still a man who saw the world strictly in black and white, and despite all his experience of life in the current-day Nightside, he still would have no truck with shades of grey. As a result, he was often not at all sure what to make of me.

"I'm putting together a piece on the recent unexpected power cuts," he said abruptly. "You wouldn't know anything about them, of course."

"Of course."

"And Walker's appearance here looking for you with fire and brimstone in his eyes was nothing but a coincidence."

"Couldn't have put it better myself, Julien. I'm all tied up with a new case at the moment, investigating the Cavendishes."

Julien frowned briefly. "Ah yes, the reclusive Mr. and Mrs. Cavendish. A bad pair, though always somehow just on the right side of the law. For all their undoubted influence in the Nightside, all I have on them are rumours and unsubstantiated gossip. Probably time I did another piece on them, just to see what nastiness they're involved with these days. They haven't sued me in ages. But don't change the subject, John. Why is Walker after you?"

"Don't ask me," I said, radiating sincerity. "Walker's always after me for something, you know that. Are you going to tell him I was here?"

Julien laughed. "Hardly, dear boy. I disapprove of him even more than I do of you. The man has far too much power and far too little judgement in the exercising of it. I honestly believe he has no moral compass at all. One of these days I'll get the goods on him, then I'll put out a special edition all about him. I did ask him if he knew what was behind the blackouts, but he wouldn't say anything. He knows more than he's telling . . . but then, he always does."

"How bad were the blackouts?" I asked cautiously.

"Bad. Almost half the Nightside had interruptions in their power supply, some of them disastrously so. Millions of pounds' worth of damage and lost business, and thousands of injuries. No actual deaths have been confirmed yet, but new reports are coming in all the time. Whoever was responsible for this hit the Nightside where it hurt. We weren't affected, of course. Victoria House has its own generator. All part of being independent. You were seen at Prometheus Inc., John, just before it all went bang."

I shrugged easily. "There'd been some talk of sabotage, and I was called in as a security consultant. But they left it far too late. I was lucky to get out alive."

"And the saboteur?"

I shrugged again. "We'll probably never know now."

Julien sighed tiredly. "You never could lie to me worth a damn, John."

"I know," I said. "But that is my official line as to what happened, and I'm sticking to it."

He fixed me with his steady thoughtful gaze. "I could put all kinds of pressure on you, John."

I grinned. "You could try."

We both laughed quietly together, then the door banged open suddenly as Otto came whirling in, his bobbing windy self crackling with energy. An eight-by-ten shot out of somewhere within him and slapped down on the table in front of Julien. "Sorry to interrupt, sir, but the pictures sub wants to know whether this photo of Walker will do for the next edition."

Julien barely glanced at the photo. "No. He doesn't look nearly shifty enough. Tell the sub to dig through the photo archives and come up with something that will make Walker look actually dishonest. Shouldn't be too difficult."

"No problem, chief."

Otto snatched the photo back into himself and shot out of the office, slamming the door behind him.

I decided Julien could use distracting from thoughts about Prometheus Inc., so I told him I'd been present at Caliban's Cavern when one of Rossignol's fans had shot himself right in front of her. Julien's face brightened immediately.

"You were there? Did you see the riot as well?"

"Right there on the spot, Julien. I saw it all."

And then, of course, nothing would do but I sit down with one of his reporters immediately and tell them everything while the details were still fresh in my mind. I went along with it, partly because I needed to keep Julien distracted, and partly because I was going to have to ask him a favour before I left, and I wanted him feeling obligated towards me. Julien's always been very big on obligation and paying off debts. I tend not to be. Julien used his intercom to summon a reporter to his office, a young up-and-comer called Annabella Peters. I tried to hide my unease. I knew Annabella, and she knew far too much about me. She'd already published several pieces on my return to the Nightside, after five years away, and she had speculated extensively about the reasons for my return, and all the possible consequences for the Nightside. Some of her guesses had been disturbingly accurate. She came barging into Julien's office with a mini tape recorder at the ready, a bright young thing dressed in variously coloured woollens, with a long face, a horsey smile and a sharp, remorseless gaze. She took my offered hand and pumped it briskly.

"John Taylor! Good to see, good to see! Always happy to have a little sit down and chat with you."

"Really?" I said. "In your last piece, you said I was a menace to the stability of the whole Nightside."

"Well, you are," she said reasonably. "What were you doing at Prometheus Inc., John?"

"We've moved on from that," I said firmly. "This is about the riot at Caliban's Cavern."

"Oh, the Rossignol suicide! Yes! Marvelous stuff, marvelous stuff! Did she really get his brains all over her feet?"

"Bad news travels fast," I observed. Annabella sat down opposite me and turned her recorder on. I told her the story, while downplaying my own involvement as much as possible. I suggested, as strongly as I could without being too obvious about it, that I was only there as part of my investigation of the Cavendishes, and not because of Rossignol at all. I never discuss my cases with journalists. Besides, putting the Cavendishes in the frame as the villains of the piece would make it easier for me when I had to ask Julien for that favour. The two of us had worked together in the past, on a few cases where our interests merged, but it never came easily. I finished my story of the riot by telling how I'd been swept outside along with the rest of the ejected audience and only saw the resulting mayhem from a safe distance. Julien nodded, as though he'd expected nothing else from me. Annabella turned off her mini recorder and smiled brightly.

"Thanks awfully, John. This will make a super piece, once I've chopped it down to a reasonable length. Pity you weren't more personally involved with the violence, though."

"Sorry," I said. "I'll try harder next time."

"One last question . . ." She surreptitiously turned her recorder back on again, and I pretended I hadn't noticed. "There are rumours circulating, suggesting the Nightside was originally created for a specific purpose, and that this is somehow connected with your missing mother's true nature and identity. Could you add anything to these rumours?"

"Sorry," I said. "I never listen to gossip. If you do find out the truth, let me know."

Annabella sighed, turned off her recorder, and Julien held the door open for her as she left. She trotted off to write her piece, and Julien shut the door and came back to join me.

"You're not usually this cooperative with the press, John. Would I be right in assuming you're about to beg a favour from me?"

"Nothing that should trouble your conscience too much, Julien. It wouldn't break your heart if I was to bring the Cavendishes down, would it?"

"No. They're scum. Parasites. Their very presence corrupts the Nightside. Just like the Murder Masques in my day, only without the sense of style. But they're very big and very rich, and extremely well connected. What makes you think you can hurt them?"

"I may be onto something," I said carefully. "It concerns their new singer, Rossignol. What can you tell me about her?"

Julien considered for a moment, then used his intercom to summon the gossip columnist Argus. The shapeshifter breezed in, looking like Kylie Minogue. Dressed as a nun. She sat down beside me, adjusting her habit to show off a perfect bare leg. Julien glared at Argus, and she sat up straight and paid attention.

"Sorry, boss."

"Rossignol," said Julien, and that was all the prompting Argus needed.

"Well, I heard about the suicides, of course, everybody has, all of them supposedly linked to Rossignol's singing, but nobody's come forward with any real proof yet. For a long time we all thought it was just a publicity stunt. And, since no-one famous, or anyone who really matters, has died yet, the Authorities don't give a damn. They never do, until they're forced to. But . . . the word is that the Cavendishes have a lot riding on Rossignol's success. They need her to make it big. Really big. Their actual financial state is a lot dodgier than most people realise. A lot of their money was invested in property in the Nightside, most of which was thoroughly trashed during the recent Angel War. And of course insurance doesn't cover Acts of God. Or the Adversary. Or their angels. It was in the small print; the Cavendishes should have looked.

"Anyway, Rossignol is all set to be their new cash cow, and they can't afford to have anything go wrong with her big launch onto the music scene. Especially with what happened to their last attempt at creating a new singing sensation, Sylvia Sin. You wouldn't remember her, John. This was while you were still away. Sylvia Sin was going to be the new Big Thing. A marvelous voice, a face like an angel, and breasts to die for. She could whip up a crowd like no-one I ever saw. But she vanished, very mysteriously, just before her big opening night. Her current whereabouts are unknown. Lots of rumours, of course, but no-one's seen anything of her in over a year."

"She could have had it all," said Julien. "Fame, money, success. But something made her run away and dig a hole so deep no-one can find it. Which isn't easy, in the Nightside."

And that was when all hell broke loose out in the bullpen. All the supernatural-threat alarms went off at once, but it was already too late. Julien and I were immediately on our feet, staring out through the office's glass walls as a dark figure roared through the bullpen, throwing desks and tables aside, casually overturning and smashing computer equipment. Journalists and other staff dived for cover. Truth and Memory flew round the room, screeching loudly. Argus peered past my shoulder, her Kylie eyes wide. The dark figure paused for a moment, looking around for new targets, and it was only then that I realised it was Rossignol. She looked small and compact in her little black dress, and extremely dangerous. The expression on her face was utterly inhuman. She saw Julien and me watching, picked up a heavy wooden desk, and threw it the length of the bullpen. We scattered out of the way as the desk smashed through the cubicle's glass wall and flew on to slam against the opposite wall, before finally dropping to the floor with a crash.

Julien and I were quickly back at the shattered glass wall. Argus hid under the editor's desk.

"How the hell did she get in here, past all our defences?" Argus yelled.

"Language, please," Julien murmured, not looking round. "Only one answer—someone must have followed you here from the club, John. You brought her in with you."

"Oh come on, Julien. I think I would have noticed."

"That isn't Rossignol," Julien said firmly. "No-one human is that strong. That is a sending, probably from the Cavendishes, guided by something they planted on your person."

"No-one planted anything on me!" I said angrily. "No-one's that good!"

I searched my pockets anyway, paying special attention to the jacket Pew had given me, but there was nothing anywhere on me that shouldn't have been there. The fake Rossignol advanced menacingly on a group of journalists trying to build a barricade between themselves and her, and Julien decided he'd had enough. He strode out of his office and into the bullpen, heading straight for Rossignol. He might be an editor these days, but he was still every inch a hero. I hesitated, then went after him. I couldn't see how I might have brought that creature here, but Julien had made me feel responsible. He's good at that. Argus stayed in her hiding place.

Rossignol raged back and forth across the bullpen, smashing computer monitors with flashing blows of her tiny fists. The staff scattered back and forth, trying to keep out of her way. The ones that didn't got hurt. Her strength was enormous, impossible, as though she moved through a world made of paper. Her smile never wavered, and her eyes didn't blink. One journalist didn't move fast enough, and she grabbed him by the shoulder with one hand and slammed him against a wall so hard I heard his bones break. Julien was almost upon her. She dropped the limp body and turned suddenly to face him. She lashed out, and Julien only just dodged a blow that would have taken his head clean off his shoulders. Julien darted forward and hit her right on the point of the chin, and her head hardly moved with the blow.

Otto the poltergeist came bobbing over to join me, as I moved cautiously forward. "You've got to stop her, Mr. Taylor, before she destroys everything!"

"I'm open to suggestions," I said, wincing as another vicious blow only just missed Julien's head. "I'm a bit concerned that if we hurt or damage whatever the hell that thing is, we might hurt or damage the real thing."

"Oh, you don't have to worry about that," said Otto. "She's not real. Well, she is, in the sense that she's very definitely kicking the crap out of our revered editor right now, but that thing isn't in any way human. It's a tulpa, a thought form raised up in the shape of whatever person it's derived from. You must have brought something with you that came from the real Rossignol, something so small you didn't even notice."

I thought hard. I was sure Rossignol hadn't actually given me anything, which meant whatever it was must have been planted on me after all. I checked all my pockets again, and again came up with nothing. Julien was bobbing and weaving, snapping out punches that rocked the fake Rossignol back on her heels without actually hurting her. The goblin drag queen suddenly tackled Rossignol from behind and pinned her arms to her sides. Julien picked up a desk with an effort and broke it over her head. Rossignol didn't even flinch. She freed herself from the goblin's grasp with a vicious back elbow that left him gasping, and went after Julien again. She wasn't even breathing hard from her exertions. I decided, very reluctantly, that I was going to have to get involved.

I circled behind Rossignol, picked up a heavy paperweight, and bounced it off the back of her head. She spun round to face her new enemy, and Julien kicked her neatly behind her left knee. She staggered, caught off-balance, and Julien and I hit her together, putting all our strength into our blows. She just shrugged us off. We both backed away and circled her. She turned smoothly to keep us both in view. I looked around for something else to use and spotted a large bulky object with satisfyingly sharp points. Perfect. I reached for it, then hesitated as Annabella hissed angrily at me from behind an overturned table.

"Don't you dare, you bastard! That's my journalist of the year award!"

"Perfect," I said. I grabbed the ugly thing and threw it with all my strength. Rossignol snatched it out of mid air and threw it straight back, and it only just missed my head as I dived for cover. Julien yelled back at his office.

"Argus! Get your cowardly self out here! I've got an idea!"

"I don't care if you've got a bazooka, I'm not budging! You don't pay me enough to fight demons!"

"Get your miserable self out here, or I'll cut off your expenses!"

"Bully," said Argus, but not too loudly. He came slouching out of the editor's office, trying to look as anonymous as possible. His face was so bland as to be practically generic. He edged towards the ongoing battle, while Julien glared at him.

"Look like Rossignol! Do it now!"

Argus shapeshifted and became an exact copy of Rossignol. The tulpa looked at the new fake Rossignol and paused, bewildered. Julien caught my attention and gestured at an overturned table. I quickly saw what he had in mind, and we picked it up between us. The tulpa Rossignol had just started to come out of her trance when we hit her from behind like a charging train. Caught off-balance, she fell forward, and we threw our combined weight onto the table, pinning the tulpa to the ground. She struggled underneath us, trying to find the leverage to free herself. And I used my gift and found just what it was that the tulpa was using as its link. On the shoulder of my jacket was a single black hair from Rossignol's head, almost invisible against the black leather. It must have happened when I held her in my arms to comfort her. No good deed goes unpunished, especially in the Nightside. I held up the hair to show it to Julien, while the table bucked beneath us. He produced a monogrammed gold lighter and set fire to the hair. It burned up in a moment, then the table beneath us slammed flat against the floor. There was no longer anything underneath it.

Julien and I helped each other to our feet. We were both breathing hard. He looked about his devastated bullpen, as journalists and other staff slowly emerged from the wreckage. Somebody found a phone that still worked and called paramedics for the injured. Julien looked at me, and his dark eyes were very cold.

"This has to be the Cavendishes' work. And that makes this personal. No-one attacks the *Night Times* and gets away with it. I think I'll send the arrogant swine a bill for damages and repairs. Meanwhile, I'm starting a full-scale investigation into what they're up to, using all my best people. And John, I suggest you go and see Dead Boy. If anyone knows where Sylvia Sin is hiding, it will be he."

I nodded. That was the favour I'd been hoping for.

Julien Advent looked back at his wrecked bullpen. "No-one attacks my people and gets away with it."

SEVEN

Death and Life, Sort Of

I left the *Night Times* riding in Julien Advent's very own Silver Ghost Rolls-Royce. He wanted to make sure I got where I was going and not die anywhere near him or the *Night Times*'s offices. I considered this a thoughtful gesture and left him and the rest of the staff to clean up the extensive mess and damage caused by Rossignol's tulpa. My chauffeuse was a slender delicate little flower in a full white leather outfit, right down to the peaked chauffeur's hat pulled firmly down over her mop of frizzy golden hair. She asked me where she was to take me, then refused to say another word. I have that effect on women sometimes. Either that, or Julien had warned her about me. I sprawled happily on the polished red leather seat and indulged myself with a very good brandy from the built-in bar. It does the heart and soul good to travel first-class once in a while. The Rolls purred along, sliding smoothly through the packed and snarling traffic of the Nightside, where the only rule of the road is survival. Most of the other vehicles had enough sense to give the Rolls plenty of room—they knew that a vehicle that expensive had to have state-of-the-art defences and weaponry.

But there's always one, isn't there? I was peering vaguely out the side window, not really thinking about anything much, except trying to remember whether Dead Boy and I had parted on good terms the last time we'd met, when I gradually became aware of a battered dark saloon car of unfamiliar make easing in beside us. It didn't take me long to realise it wasn't a proper car. I sat up straight and paid attention. All the details were wrong, and when I looked closely, I could see that the car's wheels weren't turning at all. I looked at the chauffeuse. She was staring straight ahead, apparently not at all concerned. I looked at the black car again. The outlines of the doors were just marks on the chassis, with no depth to them, and though the back windows were opaque, I could see the driver through the front side window. He wasn't moving at all. I was pretty sure he was a corpse, just put there to add verisimilitude and fool the casual eye.

The Rolls was moving pretty fast, and so was the thing that wasn't a car. It really was getting very close. A split appeared in the side facing me, stretching slowly to reach from one end to the other. It opened like a mouth, revealing rows of bloodred cilia within, thrashing hungrily. They sprouted vicious barbs and lashed out at the Rolls's windows. I retreated to the opposite side of the seat, as the cilia scratched futilely at the bulletproof glass. The chauffeuse reached for the weapons console on the dashboard.

And then the fake car lurched suddenly, as huge feet slammed down from above, burying long claws in the fake roof. Blood spurted thickly from the wounds the claws made. The thing surged back and forth across the road, trying to break the claws' hold, and couldn't. Its wide mouth screamed shrilly as it was lifted suddenly up and off the road. There was the sound of very large leathery wings flapping, and the thing that only looked like a car was gone, snatched up into the night skies. It had made a very foolish mistake—in becoming so fascinated by its prey it forgot the first rule of the Nightside. No matter how good a predator you are, there's always something bigger and stronger and hungrier than you, and if you let yourself get distracted, it'll creep right up behind you.

The Rolls-Royce purred on its way, the traffic continued as though nothing had happened, and I drank more brandy.

• • •

It took about half an hour to reach the Nightside Necropolis, site of Dead Boy's current assignment. The Necropolis takes care of all funerals for those who die in the Nightside and is situated right out on the boundary, because no-one wanted to be too close to it. Partly because even the Nightside has some taboos, but mostly because on the few occasions when things go wrong at the Necropolis, they go *really* wrong.

It is the management's proud claim that they can provide every kind of service, ritual, or interment you think of, including a few best not thought of at all if you like sleeping at night. Their motto: It's *Your* Funeral. In the Nightside, you can't always be sure that the dear departed will rest in peace, unless the proper precautions are taken, so it pays to have professionals who specialise in such matters. They charge an arm and a leg, but they can work wonders, even when there isn't an actual body for them to work with.

So when things do go wrong, as they will in even the best regulated firms, they tend to go spectacularly wrong, and that's when the Necopolis management swallows its considerable pride and calls in the Nightside's very own expert in all forms of death—the infamous Dead Boy.

The chauffeuse brought the Rolls to a halt a respectful distance away from the Necropolis. In fact, I could only just make out the building at the end of the street. I'd barely got out of the car and slammed the door shut behind me before the Rolls was backing away at speed, heading back to the more familiar dangers of Uptown. Which if nothing else solved the nagging problem of whether I was supposed to tip the chauffeuse. I've never been very good at working out things like that. I set off down the street, which was very quiet and utterly deserted. All the doors and windows were shut, and there were no lights on anywhere. My footsteps sounded loud and carrying, letting everyone know I was coming.

By the time I got to the Necropolis building itself, my nerves were absolutely ragged, and I was ready to jump right out of my skin at the first unexpected movement. The huge towering edifice before me was built of old brick and stone, with no windows anywhere, and a long sharp-edged gabled roof. It had been added to and extended in all directions, down the long years, and now it sprawled over a large area, the various contrasting styles not even trying to get along with each other. It was a dark, lowering, depressing structure with only one entrance. The massive front door was solid steel, rimmed with silver, covered with deeply etched runes, sigils, and other dead languages. I pitied the poor sod who had to polish that every morning. Two huge chimneys peered over the arching roof, serving the crematorium at the back, but for once there was no black smoke pumping up into the night sky. There was also supposed to be a hell of a graveyard in the rear, but I'd never seen it. Never wanted to. I don't go to funerals. They only depress me. Even when my dad died, I only went to the service. I know too much about pain and loss to take any false comfort from planting people in the ground. Or maybe I've just seen too many people die, and you can't keep saying good-bye.

Dead Boy's car was parked right outside the front entrance, and I strolled over to it. Gravel crunched loudly under my feet as I approached Dead Boy's one known indulgence—his brightly gleaming silver car of the future. It was long and sleek and streamlined to within an inch of its life, and it had no wheels. It hovered a few inches above the ground and looked like it ran on liquid starlight. Probably had warp drive, deflector shields, and, if pushed, could transform itself into a bloody great robot. The long curving windows were polarized so you couldn't see in, but the right-hand front door was open. There was one leg protruding. It didn't move as I drew near, so I had to bend over and peer into the driving seat. Dead Boy smiled pleasantly back at me.

"John Taylor. So good to see you again. Welcome to the most popular location in the Nightside."

"Is it really?"

"Must be. People are dying to get into it."

He laughed and took a long drink from his whiskey bottle. Dead Boy was seventeen. He'd been seventeen for over thirty years, ever since he was murdered. I knew his story. Everybody did. He was killed in a random mugging, because such things do happen, even here in the Nightside. Clubbed to death in the street, for his credit cards and the spare change in his pockets. He bled to death on the pavement, while people stepped over and around him, not wanting to get involved. And that should have been it. But he came back from the dead, filled with fury and unnatural energies, to track down and kill the street trash who murdered him. They died, one by one, and did not rise again. Perhaps after all the awful things Dead Boy had done to them, Hell seemed like a relief. But though they were all dead and gone long ago, Dead Boy went on, still walking the Nightside, trapped by the deal he made.

Who did you make your deal with? He was often asked. *Who do you think?* he always replied.

He got his revenge, but nothing had ever been said in the deal he made about being able to lie down again afterwards. He really should have read the small print. And so he goes on, a soul trapped in a dead body. Essentially, he's possessing himself. He does good deeds because he has to. It's the only chance he has of breaking the compact he made. He's a useful sort to have on your side—he doesn't feel pain, he can take a hell of a lot of damage, and he isn't afraid of anything in this world.

He's spent a lot of time researching his condition. He knows more about death in all its forms than anyone else in the Nightside. Supposedly.

He got up out of his car to greet me, all long gangling legs and arms, then leaned languidly against the side of the car. He was tall and adolescent thin, wearing a long, deep purple greatcoat over black leather trousers and shining calfskin boots. He wore a black rose in one lapel. The coat hung open, revealing his bare scarred torso. Being the revived dead, his body doesn't decay, but neither does it heal, so when he gets damaged on a case, as he often does, having no sense of self-preservation, Dead Boy stitches, staples, and superglues his corpse-pale flesh back together again. Occasionally, he has to resort to duct tape. It's not a pretty sight. There were recent bullet holes in his greatcoat, but neither of us mentioned them.

His long pale face had a weary, debauched, pre-Raphaelite look, with burning fever-bright eyes and a sulky pouting mouth with no colour to it. He wore a large floppy black hat over long dark curly hair. He drank whiskey straight from the bottle and munched chocolate biscuits. He offered me both, but I declined.

"I don't need to eat or drink," Dead Boy said casually. "I don't feel hunger or thirst, or even drunkenness any more. I just do it for the sensations. And since it's hard for me to feel much of anything, only the most extreme sensations will do." He produced a silver pill-box from inside his coat, spilled half a dozen assorted pills out onto his palm, and knocked them back with more whiskey. "Marvelous stuff. Little old Obeah woman makes them for me. It's not easy getting drugs strong enough to affect the dead. Please don't look at me like that, John. You always were an overly sensitive soul. What brings you to this charmless spot?"

"Julien Advent said you were working a case here. If I help you out, would you be willing to work with me on something?"

He considered the matter, eating another biscuit and absently brushing the crumbs off his lapels. "Maybe. Does your case involve danger, gratuitous violence, and kicking the crap out of the ungodly?"

"Almost certainly."

Dead Boy smiled. "Then consider us partners. Assuming we survive my current assignment, of course."

I nodded at the silent, brooding Necropolis. "What's happened here?"

"A good question. It seems the Necropolis suffered an unexpected power cut, and all hell broke loose. I've been telling them for years they should get their own generator and hang the expense, but . . . Anyway, the cryonics section was very badly hit. I warned them about setting that up, too, but oh no, they had to be up to date, up to the moment, ready to meet any demand their customers might come up with." He paused. "I did try it out myself, once, wondering whether I could sleep it out in the ice until someone found an answer to my predicament, but it didn't work. I didn't even feel the cold. Just lay there, bored . . . Took me ages to get the icicles out of my hair afterwards, as well."

I nodded like I was listening, but inside I was cursing silently. Another consequence of my actions at Prometheus Inc. No good deed goes unpunished . . .

If the cryonics section was the problem here, we were in for a really rough ride. Bodies have to be dead before they can be frozen and preserved, which means the soul has already departed. However, since some people have a firm suspicion of where their souls might be headed, they see cryonics as their last hope. Get a necromancer in after the body dies, and have him perform the necessary rituals to tie the soul to the body. Then freeze it, and there they are, all safe and sound till Judgement Day. Or until the power cuts out. There were supposed to be all kinds of safe-guards, but . . . Once the power failed, all the frozen bodies would start defrosting, and the spell holding the souls to them would be short-circuited. So you'd end up with a whole bunch of untenanted thawing bodies, every one of them a ripe target for possession by outside forces.

"So," I said, trying hard to sound calm and casual and not all worried. "Do we know what's got into them?"

"Afraid not. Facts are a bit spotty. About two hours ago, everyone who worked here came running out screaming and refused to go back. Most just kept running. And given the appalling things they deal with here every day as a matter of course, I think we can safely assume the *oh shit* factor is way off the scale. According to the one member of the Necropolis management I talked to who wasn't entirely hysterical, we have five newly thawed bodies to deal with, all of them taken over by *Something From Outside*. Doesn't exactly narrow the field down, does it? The only good news is that the magical wards surrounding the Necropolis are still intact and holding. So whatever's in there is still in there."

"Can't we just turn the power back on?" I said hopefully.

Dead Boy gave me a pitying smile. "Try and keep up with the rest of us, John. Power was reconnected some time back, but the damage had been done. The corpsicles' new tenants have made themselves at home, and their influence now extends over the whole building. The Necropolis's own tame spellslingers have tried all the usual techniques for putting down unwanted visitors from Beyond, from a safe distance, of course, but it seems the possessors are no ordinary imps or demons. We're talking extra-dimensional creatures, elder gods, many-angled ones—the right bastards of the Outer Dark. Not the sort to be bothered by your everyday expulsions or exorcisms. No, something really nasty has taken advantage of the situation to wedge open a door into our reality, and if we don't figure out a way to slam it shut soon, there's no telling what might come howling through. So we get to go in there and serve the extradition papers in person. Aren't we the lucky ones?"

"Luck isn't quite the word I was going to use," I said, and he laughed, entirely unconcerned.

I looked down at the ground before me. A narrow white line crossed the gravel, marking the boundary of the protective wards surrounding the Necropolis. It had been laid down in salt and silver and semen centuries before, to keep things in and keep things out. It remained unbroken, which was a good sign. Those old-time necromancers knew their business. I crouched down and touched the white line with a tentative fingertip. Immediately I could feel the presence of the force wall, like an endless roll of thunder shaking the air. I could also feel a great pressure, pushing constantly from the other side. Something wanted out bad. It was raging at the wall that held it imprisoned, and it was getting stronger all the time. I snatched my hand back and straightened up again.

"Oh yes," said Dead Boy, draining the last of his whiskey and throwing the bottle aside. "Nasty, isn't it?" The bottle smashed on the gravel, but the sound seemed very small. Dead Boy fixed the front door of the Necropolis with a speculative look. "Any ward will go down, if you hit it hard enough and long enough. So it's up to thee and me to go in there and clean their extra-dimensional clocks, while there's still time. Ah me, I do so love a challenge! Stop looking at me like that, it's going to be fun! Stick close to me, John. The charm the management gave me will get us past the wards, but it won't let you out again if we get separated."

"Don't worry," I said. "I'll be right behind you. Hiding."

Dead Boy laughed, and we crossed the barrier together.

• • •

It hit us both at the same time, a psychic assault so powerful and so vile we both staggered and almost fell. Something was watching us, from behind the blind, windowless walls of the Necropolis. A presence permeated the atmosphere, hanging on the air like an almost palpable fog, something dark and awful and utterly alien to human ways of thinking. It felt like crying and vomiting and the smell of your own blood, and it throbbed with hate. Approaching the Necropolis was like wading through an ocean of shit while someone you loved thrust knives into your face. Dead Boy just straightened his shoulders and took it in his stride, heading directly for the front door. I suppose there's nothing like having already died to put everything else in perspective. I gritted my teeth, hugged myself tightly to keep from falling apart, and stumbled forward into the teeth of the psychic assault.

We got to the door without anything nasty actually turning up to rip chunks off us, and Dead Boy rattled the door handle. From his expression, I gathered it wasn't supposed to be locked. He pushed at it with one hand,

and it didn't budge. Dead Boy pulled back his hand and looked at it thoughtfully. I put my hand against the solid steel door, and it gave spongily, as though the substance, the reality of it, was being slowly leached out of it. My skin crawled at the contact, and I snatched my hand back and rubbed it thoroughly against my jacket. Dead Boy raised one booted foot and kicked the door in. The great slab of steel and silver flew inwards as though it were weightless, torn away from its hinges. It fell forward and slapped against the floor inside, making a soft, flat sound. Dead Boy strode over it into the entrance hall beyond. I hurried in after him as he struck a defiant pose, hands on hips, and glared into the gloom ahead of him.

"Hello there! I am Dead Boy! Come out here so I can kick your sorry arse! Go on, give me your best shot! I can take it!"

"You see?" I said. "This is why other people don't want to work with you."

"Bunch of wimps," he said, indifferently.

The smell was really bad. Blood and rot and the scent of things that really belonged inside the body. The only light in the great open hall came from a thin, shifting mist that curled slowly on the air, glowing blue-silver like phosphorescence. My eyes slowly adjusted to the dim light, then I wished they hadn't as for the first time I saw the walls, and what was on them. All around us, the walls were covered with a layer of human remains. Corpses had been stretched and flattened and plastered over the walls from floor to ceiling, layering the hall with an insulating barrier of human skin and guts and fractured bones. There were hundreds, thousands of distorted faces, from bodies presumably torn from the graveyard out back. The human remains had been given a kind of life. They stirred slowly as they became aware of us. Eyes rolled in tightly spread faces, tracking the two of us as we advanced slowly across the great open hall. Hands and arms stretched out from the walls as though to grab us, or appeal for help. I could see hearts and lungs, pulsing and swelling in a mockery of life. I was just glad I didn't recognise any of the faces.

At least the floor was clear. Dead Boy strode forward, not even glancing at the walls, and I went with him. I felt somebody sane should be present when push inevitably came to shove. The sound of our feet on the bare floor was strangely muffled, and the shadows around us were very dark and very deep. It felt like walking down a tunnel, away from our world and its rules into . . . somewhere else.

We were almost half-way across the hall before we got our first glimpse of what was waiting for us. At the far end, in the darkest of the shadows, barely illuminated by the light of the swirling mists, were five huge figures. The corpsicles. Thawed from unimaginable cold, revived from the dead, reanimated by abhuman spirits from Outside, they didn't look human any more. The forces that possessed the vacant bodies were too strong, too furious, too *other* for merely human frames to contain. They had all grown and expanded, forced into unnatural shapes and configurations by the pressures within, and now they were changed and mutated in hideous ways. It hurt to look at them. Their outlines seethed and fluctuated, trying to contain more than three dimensions at once. Mere flesh and blood and bone should have broken down and fallen apart, but the five abominations were held together by the implacable will of the creatures possessing them. They needed these bodies, these vacant hosts. The corpsicles were their only means of access to the material world. I kept wanting to look away. The shapes the bodies were trying to take were just too complex, too intricate for simple human minds to deal with.

We were getting too close. I grabbed Dead Boy by the arm and made him stop. He glared at me.

"We need information," I murmured. "Talk to them."

"You talk to them. Find me something useful I can hit."

One of the shapes leaned forward. It was twice as tall as a man, and almost as wide, its pale, sweating skin stretched painfully tight. A head craned forward on the end of a long, extended neck. Bloody tears fell constantly, to hiss and steam on the hall floor. Bone horns and antlers thrust out of the distorted face, and, when it spoke, its voice was like a choir of children whispering obscenities.

"We are The Primal. Purely conceptual beings, products of the earliest days of creation, before the glory of ideas was trapped and diminished in the narrow confines of matter. Kept out of the material worlds, to protect its fragile creatures of meat and mortality. Ever since Time was, we were. Waiting and watching at the Edge of things, searching eternally for a way in, to finally show our contempt and hatred for all the lesser creations, that dare to dream of being more than they are. We are The Primal. We were here first. And we will be here when all the meat that dares to think has been stamped back into the mud it came from."

"Typical bloody demons," said Dead Boy. "Created millennia ago, and still sulking because they didn't get better parts in the story. Let's get this over with. Come on, let's see what you can do!"

"Can you at least try for a more rational attitude?" I said sharply. And then I broke off, as the head turned suddenly to look at me.

"We know you, little prince," said the choir of whispering voices. "John Taylor. Yes. We know your mother, too."

"What do you know about her?" My mouth was painfully dry, but I fought to keep my voice steady.

"She who was first, and will be first again, in this worst of all possible worlds. She's coming back. Yes. Soon, she will come back."

"But who is she? What is she?"

"Ask the ones who called her up. Ask the ones who called her back. She is coming home, and she will not be denied."

"You're scared of her," I said, almost wonderingly. *And you're scared of me, too,* I thought.

"We are The Primal. There is still time to play in the world, before she comes back to take it for her own. Time to play with you, little prince."

"This is all terribly interesting," said Dead Boy. "But enough of the chit-chat. Back me up, John. I have a plan."

And he ran forward and threw himself at the nearest shape.

"That's your idea of a plan?" I shrieked, and plunged after him, because there was nothing else to do. It's times like this I wish I carried a gun. A really big gun. With nuclear bullets.

Dead Boy reached out to grab the extended head of the speaking Primal, and its whole body surged suddenly forward to engulf and envelop him, holding him firm like an insect in amber. It wanted to possess him, but Dead Boy was already possessing his body, and his curse didn't allow room for anyone else. The Primal convulsed and spat him out, repulsed by his very nature. Dead Boy hit the floor hard, but was back on his feet in a moment, looking around for something he could hit. The Primal raised their voices in a terrible harmony, chanting something in a language full of higher things than words. And the reanimated dead plastered across the walls heard them. They slipped slowly down the walls and slid across the floor towards Dead Boy and me, a sea of body parts oozing and undulating towards us from all directions, spitting and seething and sprouting distorted limbs like weapons. Stomach acids burned the wooden floor. Eyeballs rose up on wavering stalks. Hands flexed fingers with nails long as knives, sharp as scalpels.

I grabbed two handfuls of salt from my jacket pocket and scattered it in a wide circle around Dead Boy and myself, yelling to him to stay inside it. I wasn't sure even his legendary invulnerability would stand up to being torn apart and digested in a hundred undead stomachs. The oozing biomass hesitated at the salt, then formed itself into high, living arches to cross over it. I glared about me, while Dead Boy slapped and punched at the nearest extensions of the biomass. He was shouting all kinds of spells, from elvish to corrupt Coptic, but none of them had any obvious effect. The reanimated tissues were charged with the energies of The Primal, forces old when the world was new, and even Dead Boy had never come across anything like this before.

I looked at The Primal. They were watching me, rather than Dead Boy, and I remembered my original insight, that they'd seemed almost afraid of me. Why me? What could I do to hurt them? I didn't even have the few battle magics Dead Boy had. There was my gift of finding, but I didn't see it being much use just then. *Think, think!* I looked hard at the five distorted bodies possessed by The Primal. They looked horrible, yes, but also . . . strained, stretched thin, unstable. Human bodies weren't meant to hold Primal essences. Maybe all the pressure within needed was a little extra nudge . . .

I was off and running even while the thought was still forming in my mind, my feet slapping and sliding on the slippery rotting organs beneath me. I headed straight for the nearest shape, the speaking Primal, shouting, "YOU THINK YOU'RE SO HARD, POSSESS ME, YOU BASTARDS!" while at the same time thinking, *I really hope I'm right about this.* I hit the first Primal even as it tried to draw back, and I slammed right into the heart of it. The body sucked me in like a mud pool, and I clapped a hand over my mouth and nose to keep it out. I felt cold, impossibly cold, like the dark void between the stars, but even worse than that, I could feel a vast and unknowable mind in there with me, in the cold and the dark, pressing upon me from all sides. And then suddenly there was screaming, an awful sound of outrage and betrayal, as the possessed body exploded.

I'd been too much for The Primal to manage. My body was still tenanted, soul intact, and The Primal couldn't cope. Something had to give, and it turned out to be the possessed body. It blew apart in a wet, sticky explosion, like a grenade inside a small furry creature, and the violence of the explosion ruptured the integrity of the four other bodies, setting them off like a row of firecrackers. It was all over in a moment, and Dead Boy and I stood looking around us, drenched in blood and gore, surrounded by a sea of unmoving body parts, already rotting and falling apart. Dead Boy looked at me.

"And people say I'm impulsive and hard to get along with. What did you just do to them?"

"I think I gave them indigestion. And, possibly, I am a bit special, after all."

Dead Boy sniffed. "God, I'm a mess. So are you. I really hope they've got some showers here somewhere. And a really good laundry."

• • •

Two long and very thorough showers later, Dead Boy and I climbed back into our very thoroughly laundered clothes. The Necropolis staff returned in dribs and drabs once it was clear the danger was over, and, with many a sigh and muttered oath, they began cleaning up the mess. A slow process that involved body bags, strong stomachs, not a little use of buckets and mops, and a *really* big bottle of Lysol. The Necropolis management made a brief appearence, to shake our hands and assure Dead Boy the cheque was in the post. They meant it. Absolutely no-one wanted Dead Boy mad at them. He tended to come round to where you lived and pull it down around you. As Dead Boy and I were leaving the Necropolis, two young men were staggering in, carrying a very large crate with the words *Air Fresheners* stencilled on the side.

We headed for Dead Boy's car of the future, and the doors swung open without being asked. Dead Boy slipped in behind the wheel, and I sank carefully into the luxurious front seat. The doors closed by themselves. The dashboard had more controls and displays than the space shuttle. Dead Boy produced an Extra-large Mars bar from somewhere and ate it in quick, hungry mouthfuls. When he'd finished, he crumpled up the wrapper and dropped it on the floor, where it joined the rest of the junk. He stared moodily out the windscreen. He looked like he wanted to scowl, but couldn't work up the energy.

"I'm tired," he said abruptly. "I'm always tired. And I am so bloody tired of being tired. Everything's such an effort, whether it's fighting elder gods or just getting through another day. You have no idea what it's like, being dead. I can't feel the subtle things any more, like a breeze or a scent, or even hot and cold. I have no appetites or needs, and I never sleep. I can't even remember what it was like, to be able to put aside the cares of the day and escape into oblivion, and dreams. Even my emotions are only shadows of what I remember them being like. It's hard to care about anything, when the worst thing that can happen to you has already happened. I just go on, doing my good deeds because I have no choice, throwing myself into danger over and over again for the chance to feel *something* . . . You sure you still want me to partner you, John?"

"I could use your help," I said. "And your insights. It's not much of a case, but it is . . . interesting."

"Ah well," said Dead Boy. "I can make do with interesting. Where are we going?"

"That's rather up to you. I'm looking for an ex-singer called Sylvia Sin. Used to be managed by the Cavendishes. Julien Advent thought you might know where she's hidden herself."

Dead Boy gave me a look I didn't immediately recognise. "I'm surprised you're interested in someone like her, John. Not really your scene, I would have thought. Still, far be it for me to pass judgement . . ."

"She's part of the case I'm working," I said. "Do you know where she is?"

"Yes. And I know what she's doing these days. You're wasting your time there, John. Sylvia Sin doesn't care about anyone or anything except what she does."

"I still have to talk to her," I said patiently. "Will you take me to her?"

He shrugged. "Why not? If nothing else, it should be interesting to see your face when we get there."

• • •

Dead Boy's car of the future slid smoothly through the Nightside traffic, all of which gave it plenty of room. Probably afraid of phasers and photon torpedos. If the engine made a noise, I couldn't hear it, and the car handled like a dream. I couldn't feel the acceleration, even though we were moving faster than anything else on the road. All too soon we'd left the main flow of traffic behind and were cruising through the quiet back streets of a mostly residential area. We glided past rows of typically suburban houses and finally stopped in front of one that looked no different from any of the others. Even the Nightside has its quiet backwaters, and this was one of the quietest.

Dead Boy and I got out of the car, which locked itself behind us. I hunched inside my jacket against a slow sullen drizzle. The night had turned gloomy and overcast, with heavy clouds hiding the stars and the oversized moon. The yellow street-lights gave the scene a sick, sleazy look. There was no-one else around, and most of the houses had no lights showing. Dead Boy led the way through an overgrown garden and up to the front door, then stood aside and indicated for me to knock. Again, his expression was hard to read. There being no bell, I knocked, and the door opened immediately. As though someone had been watching, or waiting.

The man who opened the door might as well have had a neon sign hanging over his head saying *Pimp*. The way he looked, the way he stood, the way he smiled, all combined to make you feel welcome and dirty at the same time. He wore an oriental black silk wraparound, with a bright red Chinese dragon motif. He was short and slender, almost androgynous. There were heavy silver rings on all his fingers, and a silver ring pierced his left nostril. His jet-black hair was slicked back, and there was something subtly *wrong* about his face. Something in the angles, or perhaps in the way he held his head. He never stopped smiling, but the smile didn't touch his dark, knowing eyes.

"Always happy to see new faces," he said, in a light breathy voice. "All are welcome here. And such famous faces. The legendary Dead Boy, and the newly returned John Taylor. Honoured to make your acquaintance, sirs. My name is Grey, entirely at your service."

"We need to see Sylvia," said Dead Boy. "Or at least, John does."

"But of course," said Grey. "No-one ever comes here to see me." He turned his constant smile in my direction. "What's your pleasure, sir? Whatever you want, whoever you want, I can promise you'll find it here. Nothing is forbidden, and everything is encouraged. Dear Sylvia is always very accommodating."

"Don't I need an appointment?" I said. I shot Dead Boy a quick glare. He should have warned me.

"Oh, Sylvia always knows when someone is coming," said Grey. "As it happens, she's just finished with her last client. You can go straight up, once we've agreed on a suitable fee, of course. In an ideal world such vulgarity would be unnecessary, but alas . . ."

"I'm not interested in buying her services," I said. "I just need to talk to her."

Grey shrugged. "Whatever you choose to do with her, it all costs the same. Cash only, of course."

"Go on up, John," said Dead Boy. "I'll have a nice little chat with Grey."

He moved forward, and Grey fell back, because people do when Dead Boy comes walking right at them. Grey quickly recovered himself and put out a hand to stop Dead Boy. Magic sparkled briefly on the air between them, then sputtered and went out. Grey backed up against a wall, his eyes very large.

"Who . . . *what* are you?"

"I'm Dead Boy. And that's all you need to know. Get a move on, John. I don't want to be here all night."

I pulled the door shut behind me, strode past Dead Boy and Grey, and started up the narrow stairs. Sylvia was on the next floor. I could feel it. The house was cold and grim, and the shadows were very dark and very deep. The stairs were bare wood, without carpeting, but still my feet made hardly any sound as I climbed. It was like moving through one of those houses we find in nightmares. Familiar and yet horribly alien, where every door and every window is a threat, every sight heavy with terrible significance. Distances seemed to stretch and contract, and it took forever to get to the top of the stairs.

There was a door right in front of me. A terrible door, holding awful secrets behind it. I stood there, breathing hard, but whether from fear or anticipation I couldn't tell. It was Sylvia's door. I didn't need to be told that. I could feel her presence, like the pressure of a coming storm on the evening air. I pushed the door with the fingertips of one hand, and it swung smoothly open before me, inviting me in. I smelled something that made my nostrils flare, and I walked in.

In the room, in the red room, in the room of rose-petal light and shifting shadows, it was like walking into a woman's body. It was warm and humid, and the still air was heavy with sweat and musk and perfumed hair. There was no obvious source for the light, but there were shadows everywhere, as though the delights the room offered were too subtle to be exposed by bright light. I felt welcomed and desired, and I never wanted to leave.

It was like walking into an antechamber of Hell. And I loved it.

The woman lying at her ease on the oversized bed, naked and smiling and unashamed, was entirely horrible and horribly attractive, like a taste for rotting meat or Russian roulette. She squirmed slowly on the crimson covers like a single maggot in a pool of blood. The details of her face and shape were always moving, changing, shifting subtly from one moment to the next, and even her height and weight were never constant. She could have been one woman or a hundred, or a hundred women in one. Her movements were slow and languorous, and her skin was as white as the white of an eye. Her face was a hundred kinds of beautiful, even when it was unbearably ugly. Her bone structures rose and fell like the turning of the tide, her mouth pursed and widened and changed colour, and her dark, dark eyes promised the kind of pleasures that would make a man cry out in self-disgust as much as passion. I wanted her like I'd never wanted anyone. Her presence filled the room, overpoweringly sexual, awfully female.

And I wanted her the way you always want things you know are bad for you.

"John Taylor," said the woman on the bed. Her voice was soft and caressing, every woman's voice in one. "They thought you might come here. The Cavendishes. I've been so looking forward to having you. They're the ones who made me what I am, even if the result wasn't exactly what they intended. I was just a singer in those days, and a good singer, too, but that wasn't enough for the Cavendishes. They wanted a star who would appeal to absolutely everyone. And this is what they got, this is what their money bought. A woman transformed, a chimera of sex, everything anyone ever desired, and a joy forever."

She laughed, but there was little humour and less humanity in the sound. Her flesh pulsed and shifted in slow rolling movements, never the same twice. My skin crawled, and I couldn't look away to save my life. I had an erection so hard it hurt. Only sheer willpower held me where I was, just inside the doorway. I couldn't go any closer. I didn't dare. I wanted to do things to her, and I wanted her to do things to me.

And then she lazily brought one hand up to her ever-changing mouth. There was something red and sticky on her fingers, and she put it to her mouth and ate it, chewing slowly, savouring the taste. For the first time, as my eyes grew accustomed to the rose-petal light, I realised there was someone else in the room, lying on the floor beside the bed. A man, lying very still, mostly hidden in shadows. A dead man, with his skull caved in. There was a gaping hole in the side of his head, and, as I watched, Sylvia lowered her hand to the hole, dug around in it with her fingers, and pulled out some more brains.

Sylvia's just finished with her last client, Grey had said.

She saw the expression on my face and laughed again. "A girl has to live. There's a price that comes with being what I am, but luckily I'm not the one who has to pay it. They come to me, all the men and the women, drawn to me by desires they didn't even know they had, and I let them sink themselves in my flesh. And while they're busying themselves, I take my toll. I drain them of their desires, their enthusiasms, their faiths and their certainties, and eventually their lives. Though by that stage they usually don't care. And afterwards, I eat them all up. Their vitalities keep me alive, and their flesh helps me maintain my shape. A balance must be struck, between stability and chaos. You wouldn't like what I look like, when I can't get what I need. Oh don't look so shocked, John! The Cavendishes' magic made me all the women you could ever desire, and I love it. Those who come to me know the risks, and *they* love it. This is sex the way it should be, free from all restraints and conscience. Total indulgence, in this best of all possible worlds." She glanced down at the dead body on the floor. "Don't mourn him. He was all used up. No good to himself, or anyone else, except me. And he did die with a smile on his face. See?"

I couldn't speak, couldn't answer her.

She stretched slowly, voluptuous beyond reason. "Don't you want me, John? I can be anyone you ever wanted, and you can do things with me you wouldn't dare do with them. I live for pleasure, and my flesh is very accommodating."

"No." I made myself say it, even though the effort brought beads of sweat out on my face. I learned self-discipline early, just to stay alive. And I was used to not getting what I wanted. But it still took everything I had to stay where I was. "I need . . . to talk to you, Sylvia. About the Cavendishes."

"Oh, I don't think about them any more. I don't care about the out-side world. I have made my own little world here, and it is perfect. I never leave it. I glory in it. Have you come here to tell me of the Nightside? Is it still full of sin? How long has it been, since I came here?"

"Just over a year," I said, taking a step forward.

"Is that all? It feels like centuries to me. But then time passes so slowly, in Heaven and Hell."

I took another step forward. Her body called to my body, in a voice as old as the world. I knew it would cost me my life and my soul, and I didn't care. Except some small part of me, screaming deep within me, still *did* care. So I did the only thing I could do, to save myself. I called up my gift, my power, and looked at Sylvia Sin with my third eye, my private eye. I used my gift to find the woman she used to be, before the Cavendishes changed her, and brought her back.

Sylvia screamed, convulsing on the bed, her white flesh boiling and seething, then one shape snapped into focus, one body rising suddenly out of all the others, and the changes stopped. Sylvia lay on the bed, curled up into a ball, breathing hard. One woman, with flesh-coloured flesh and a pretty, ordinary face. I was breathing hard, too, like a man who'd just stepped back from the very brink of a cliff. The overpowering sexual pres-sure was gone from the room, though faint vestiges of its presence still lin-gered on the air. Sylvia sat up slowly on the bed, naked and normal, and looked at me with merely human eyes.

"What did you do? *What have you done to me?*"

"I've given you back yourself," I said. "You're free now. Entirely normal."

"I didn't ask to be normal! I liked who I was! What I was! The plea-sures and the hungers and the feeding . . . I was a goddess, you bastard! Give it back! Give it back to me!"

She threw herself at me, launching herself off the bed like a wildcat, going for my eyes with her hands, my throat with her teeth. I jumped to one side, and she missed me, betrayed by her unfamiliar, limited body. She crashed against the wall by the door, started to move away and found she couldn't. The wall wouldn't let her go. Her skin was stuck to the rose-petal surface. And that was when I realised at last where the rosy light came from, and why there was still that faint trace of a presence on the air. You do magical crazy things in a room long enough, and you get a magical crazy room. I'd brought Sylvia back, but the room still remained. She cried out and hit the wall with her fist, and the fist stuck to the wall. Already she was sinking into it, as though into a rosy pool, her body being absorbed the same way she'd engulfed so many others. She didn't even have time to work up a proper scream before she was gone, and the sexual presence was suddenly that much stronger, like the eyes of a hungry predator suddenly turning in my direction.

I ran out of the room, and all the way back down the stairs.

• • •

I stopped at the foot of the stairs and concentrated on slowing my breathing. My heart was pounding like a hammer in my chest. There's always temptation in the Nightside, and one of the first lessons you learn is that when you've got away, you don't ever look back. Sylvia Sin was gone, and the room should starve to death soon enough. As long as some poor damned fool didn't start feeding it . . . I looked around for Grey. He was crouching huddled in a corner, shaking and shuddering and crying his eyes out. I looked at Dead Boy, leaning casually against the front door.

"What happened to him?" I said.

"He wanted to know what it was like, being dead," said Dead Boy. "So I told him."

I looked at Grey and shuddered. His eyes were very wide and utterly empty.

"So," said Dead Boy. "All finished with Sylvia, are you?"

"She's finished," I said. "The Cavendishes did something to her. Made her a monster. Maybe they've done something to Rossignol, too. I have to go see her again."

"Mind if I tag along?" said Dead Boy. "At least around you death's never boring."

"Sure," I said. "Just let me do all the talking, okay?"

EIGHT

Divas!

Like most cities, there's never anywhere to park in the Nightside when you need it. There are high- and low-rise tesseract car parks and protected areas, but they're never anywhere useful. And cars left unattended on Nightside streets tend to be suddenly stolen, or eaten, or even evolve into something else entirely while your back's turned. But Dead Boy pulled his car of the future in to the curb, just down the street from Caliban's Cavern, got out, and walked away without even a backward glance. I went with him, but couldn't help looking back uncertainly. The shining silver car looked distinctly out of place in the steaming sleazy streets of Uptown. Already certain eyes were studying it with thoughtful intent.

"It will take more than automatic locks to protect your car here," I pointed out.

"My car can take care of itself," Dead Boy said easily. "The onboard computers have access to all kinds of defensive weaponry, together with an exceedingly nasty sense of humour and no conscience at all."

We strolled up the rain-slick street, and the crowds parted in front of us to let us pass. The blazing neon was as sharp and sleazy as ever, and hot saxophone music and heavy bass beats drifted out of the clubs we passed. A small group were sacrificing a street mime to some lesser god, while tourists clustered round with camcorders. A teddy bear with his eyes and mouth sewn shut was handing out flyers protesting animal experimentation. Cooking smells from a dozen different cultures wafted across the still night air. And more than one person saw Dead Boy coming and chose to walk in another direction entirely.

We finally stopped and studied Caliban's Cavern from a discreet distance. The exterior of the nightclub had been thoroughly trashed during the riot, and a team of specialist restorers were on the scene, clearing up the mess and making good with style and speed and uncanny precision. The Nightside has always had a tendency to mayhem and mass destruction, so there's never any shortage of firms ready and willing to undertake quick repairs and restoration, for the usual exorbitant prices. Most of the big concerns were still busy dealing with the chaos and devastation left behind after the recent Angel War, but it seemed the Cavendishes had been able to raise enough cash-in-hand to get some firm on the job straight away. Three builder magicians were using unification spells to put the facia back together. It was quite fun watching the broken and shattered pieces leaping up from the pavement to fit themselves neatly together again like a complex jigsaw. Some other poor sod had the unenviable task of putting the front door back on its hinges, while the simulacrum in the wood cursed him steadily as an unfeeling incompetent, in between lengthy crying jags.

A crowd had gathered to watch, Nightsiders always being interested in free entertainment, and other people had arrived to sell the crowd things it didn't need, like T-shirts, free passes to clubs no-one in their right mind would visit anyway, and various forms of hot food. This usually consisted of something nasty and overpriced in a bun, that only the most newly arrived tourists would be dumb enough actually to eat.

Dead Boy sniffed loudly as some fool in a grubby dressing gown handed over good money in return for something allegedly meat-based in a tortilla. "Proof if proof were needed," he said loudly, "that tourists will eat absolutely anything. Truth in advertising, that's what's needed here. See how well that stuff would sell if the vendors were obliged to shout the truth. *Something wriggling on a stick! Pies containing creatures whose name you couldn't even spell! Food so fast it will be out your backside before you know it!*"

"Buyer beware," I said easily. "That should be the Nightside's motto. Nothing's ever what it seems . . ."

We watched interestedly as one of the builder magicians used a temporal reverse spell to restore some damaged woodwork, then joined in the general jeering as he let the spell get away from him, and time sped back too far, so that the wood started sprouting branches and leaves again. Dead Boy looked the nightclub over with his professionally deceased eyes.

"There are new and really nasty magical wards all over the place," he said quietly. "They're well disguised, but there's not much you can hide from the dead. It's mostly shaped curses and proximity hexes, an awful lot of them keyed specifically to your presence, John. We're only just out of range here. The Cavendishes really don't want you anywhere near their club again."

"How nasty are we talking?" I said.

"Put it this way—if you were to trigger even one of these quite appalling little bear-traps, they'll be scraping your remains off the surroundings with a palette knife."

"Ouch," I said. "I still have to get in to see Rossignol. Any ideas?"

Dead Boy considered the matter. People saw him frowning and moved even further away, just in case. "I could walk in," he said finally. "Those defences are only dangerous to the living."

"No," I said. "First, Rossignol wouldn't talk to you, only me. And second, you'd be bound to set off all kinds of alarms. I really don't want to attract the Cavendishes' attention if I can help it. They've got a Power on their side. The Jonah."

"Ah yes, young Billy. Nasty piece of work. If he ever grew a pair, he could be really dangerous."

"The odds are, Rossignol is still in her room over the club, guarded by a couple of heavy-duty combat magicians. I bluffed them once, but twice would definitely be pushing it. And who knows what other surprises they've got set up in there . . ."

"So what do you want to do, John?" said Dead Boy, just a little impatiently. "We can't just stand around out there. Word will get around. How are we going to get to your deadly little songbird? Come on, think devious. It's what you do best."

"If we can't get in to her," I said slowly, "she'll have to come out to us. We'll send her a message. Most of the club's staff will be kicking their heels somewhere close at hand, keeping out of the way and waiting for the repairs to be finished. All we have to do is track them down and find someone we can bribe, convince, or intimidate into passing Rossignol our message."

"They could be anywhere," Dead Boy said doubtfully. "What are you going to do, use your gift to locate them?"

"No," I said. "I don't think so. I've been using my gift too much, too often, lately. And every time I open up my mind, my thoughts blaze like a beacon in the night. My enemies can use that to find me. And you know some of the things they've sent after me. No, I've pushed my luck as far as

I dare. It's time to be sensible and stick to simple deduction. All we have to do is check out the local bars, cafes, and diners, and we'll find the club. Theatricals never can go for long without their creature comforts."

• • •

We found them all just a short walk further up the street, at the Honey Bee, an overly lit but very clean theme coffee bar, where all the waitresses were obliged to wear puffy black-and-yellow-striped bee outfits, together with bobbly antennae and spiked heel stilettos. They didn't look too happy about it as they tottered unsteadily between the tables, reeling off the specials through practiced smiles. The chorus girls from Caliban's Cavern had wedged themsleves into a corner, nursing their cups of distressed coffee, chattering loudly and smoking up a storm. Also present was one Ian Auger, roadie and musician, and the only one who seemed at all pleased to see me as Dead Boy and I approached their table.

"Oh it's you again, is it?" said the platinum blonde backing singer, flicking her ash disdainfully onto the floor. "Trouble on legs and twice as unfortunate. Everything was fine until you turned up. Then you show your face, and we get a suicide in the front row and a riot in the house. The Authorities should ban you, on general principles."

"It's been tried," I said calmly. "And I'm still here. I need someone to take a message to Rossignol." I looked around, hoping for a sympathetic smile, but it was all glowering faces and curled lips. I couldn't really blame them. One of the problems of having a carefully cultivated bad reputation like mine is that I tend to get the blame for everything that goes wrong around me.

"Who's your pale friend with no fashion sense?" said the blonde.

"This is Dead Boy," I said, and the whole coffee-house went suddenly quiet. Ian Auger pushed back his chair and stood up.

"Let's talk outside," he said resignedly. "You mustn't mind the girls. They're never keen on anything that might put their jobs at risk." We moved over to stand in the doorway, while the other customers and staff studied us warily. Ian Auger looked at me, frowning. "I'm worried about Ross. The Cavendishes have been all over her since the suicide, telling her what to do, what to say, what to think. All they seem to care about is what spin they can put on the suicide for the music media. Ross is practically a prisoner at the moment, under armed guard. Are you still interested in helping her?"

"Of course," I said. "Can you get a message to her?"

"Maybe," said Ian. "At least, one of me might be able to."

"Which one of them are you?" I said.

"All of them," Ian Auger said cheerfully. "I'm a temporal triplet. One soul, three bodies, no waiting. Close-part harmonies a speciality. Me mum always said Destiny stuttered when I was born. Right now my other two selves are busy inside the club, putting the stage set back together again. They're listening to you through me. What's the message?"

"Nothing good," I said. "The Cavendishes tried to make one of their singers into a superstar before. They had a young girl called Sylvia Sin magically augmented, to make her even more popular, and it turned her into a monster. Quite literally. I've seen what they did to her, what she became, and I don't want anything like that to happen to Ross. I need her to sneak out of the club and join me somewhere safe, so we can work out what to do for the best. I don't trust the Cavendishes to have her best interests at heart. It shouldn't be too difficult for Ross to get out. Bodyguards are usually more interested in watching for people trying to sneak in."

Ian scowled fiercely. "Sylvia Sin. There's a name I haven't thought of in a while. Always wondered what happened to her. All right, one of me will talk to Ross. She might listen, now the Cavendishes have left the club. She always seems brighter and more independent when they're not around."

"They do seem to have an unhealthy hold over her," I said. "Could they already have done something to her?"

"I don't know," said Ian. "No-one's allowed to get too close when the Cavendishes are in private conference with Ross. And there's no denying she's not been acting like herself since she came to live in that room over the club. You think if the Cavendishes have done something, that's what's causing the suicides?"

"Could be," I said.

"All right," said Ian. "If I can get a message to her, and if I can get her out of the club, where do you want to meet? It has to be somewhere secure, somewhere she can feel safe, and somewhere she won't be noticed. She has got a pretty famous face now, you know."

"I know the perfect place to hide a famous face," said Dead Boy. "Hide her in a whole crowd of famous faces. Tell Rossignol to meet us at Divas!"

• • •

Divas! is one of the more famous, or possibly infamous, nightclubs in Uptown, where you can go to see and hear all the most famous female singers in the history of entertainment. Of course, none of them are real. They're not even female. The famous faces are in fact transvestites, men dressed up as the women they adore. But dressed in style and made up to the nines, the illusion is more than perfect, for these trannies have taken their obsession one step further than most—they have learned to channel the talents and sometimes the personalities of the divas concerned. Dead or alive, the greatest stars of show business all come to Divas!, in proxy at least.

Dead Boy had clearly been there before. The doorman held the door to the club open and bowed very low, and no-one asked us if we were members, or even to pay the cover charge. The hatcheck girl was a 1960s Cilla Black in a black bustier, and from the wink she dropped Dead Boy it was clear he was a regular. Cilla did her best to ignore me, but I'm used to that. Dead Boy is one of the Nightside's celebrities. I'm more of an anti-celebrity. We made our way into the club itself, which was all silks and flowers and bright colours. The furniture was all art deco, and everywhere you looked was every kind of kitsh fashion you ever shuddered at in disbelief. Chandeliers and disco balls hung side by side from the ceiling.

The main floor was crowded, and the noise level was appalling. The night is always jumping at Divas! Dead Boy and I edged between the tightly packed tables, following a waitress. All the waitresses were channeling Liza Minnelli tonight, dressed in her *Cabaret* outfit. We ended up at a table tucked away in a corner and ordered over-priced drinks from the Liza. I asked for a glass of Coke, and then had to go through my usual routine of *No, I don't want a Diet Coke! I want a real Coke! A man's Coke! And I don't want a bloody straw either!* Dead Boy ordered a bottle of gin and the best cigar they had. I made a note of the prices for my expenses sheet. You have to keep track of things like that, or you can go broke on some cases.

"What if Rossignol doesn't turn up?" said Dead Boy, raising his voice to be heard over the general clamour. "What if she can't get away?"

"Then we'll think of something else," I said. "Relax. Enjoy the show. It's costing us enough."

"What do you mean *us*, white man?"

Up on the stage at the far end of the room, an Elaine and a Barbara were dueting on a pretty accurate rendition of "I Know Him So Well." The channelling must be going well tonight. Other famous faces paraded across the floor of the club, there to see and be seen, stopping at tables to chat and gossip and show themselves off. Marilyn and Dolly, Barbra and Dusty. Elaine and Barbara were replaced on stage by a Nico, who favoured us with her mournful voice and presence as she husked "It Took More Than One Man to Change My Name to Shanghai Lily" into the microphone, accompanying herself on the accordion. I just hoped she wouldn't do the

Doors's "The End." There's only so much existential angst I can take before my ears start bleeding.

A few tables away, two Judys were having a vicious wig-pulling fight. Spectators cheered them on and laid bets.

And then Ian Auger came in, with Rossignol on his arm, and no-one in Divas! paid her any attention, because everyone assumed she was another trannie, perhaps a little more convincing than some. Ian escorted her over to our table, pulled out her chair for her, introduced her to Dead Boy, and politely but firmly refused to sit down himself.

"I can't hang about here. I've got to get back. There's still a lot of work to do in the club, and I don't want to be missed."

"Any trouble getting Ross here?" I asked.

"Surprisingly, no. I just told the bodyguards that John Taylor was somewhere on the loose in the building, and they all went running off to look for you. We strolled right out. Look, I really do have to go. Ross, remember you're due to go on again in just under an hour."

Rossignol let him kiss her on the cheek, and he hurried away, his hunchback giving him a weird rolling gait. The waitress Liza came back to take Rossignol's order. I looked Rossignol over as she studied the wine list. She looked different. Same pale face, dark hair, little black dress. But she seemed somehow sharper, brighter, more focussed. She looked up, caught me watching, and smiled broadly.

"Ah, John, it is so good to be out and about for a change. You know what I want? I want five whiskey sours. I want them all at once, all lined up in front of me so I can look at them while I'm drinking them. I'm never allowed to drink in Caliban's Cavern, by order of the Cavendishes, though strangely, mostly I don't want to. I stick to the healthy diet they provide, and I never complain, both of which are also very unlike me. Cake! I want cake! Bring me the biggest, gooiest chocolate gateau you have, and a big spoon! I want everything that's bad for me, and I want it right now!"

The waitress whooped with glee. "You go, girl!"

I indicated for the waitress to bring Rossignol what she wanted, and the Liza tottered away on her high heels. Rossignol beamed happily.

"The Cavendishes are always very strict about what I'm allowed to have, and do. They act more like my mother than my managers."

"I notice they didn't stop you smoking," I said.

She snorted loudly. "I'd like to see them try." She stopped smiling suddenly and gave me a hard look. "Ian tells me that you've been out and about on my behalf, speaking to people. And that you found out something concerning my predecessor with the Cavendishes. I remember her face being on all the magazine covers, then . . . nothing. What did happen to her, John? What did the Cavendishes do to her?"

I told her enough of the story to scare her, without dwelling on some of the nastier details. Dead Boy shot me the occasional glance as he realised what I was doing, but he kept his peace. He'd already drunk half his bottle of gin and had started eating his cigar. When I finally finished, Ross let out a long sigh.

"I had no idea. The poor thing. And the Cavendishes did that to her?"

"More likely had it done," I said. "Have they ever offered to . . . do anything for you?"

"No. Never." Rossignol's voice was firm and sharp. "I'd have told them where they could stick their magic. I don't need any of that shit to be a success. I'm a singer, and all I've ever needed are my songs and my voice." And then she stopped and frowned suddenly. "And yet, having said that . . . things have changed since I came to live in my little room over the club. My songs are always sad songs now. And there are some odd gaps in my memory. I feel cold, and tired, all of the time. And the way I act when the Cavendishes are around . . . doesn't feel like me at all. Could they have worked a magic on me, without my knowing?"

"It's possible," I said carefully. "They could have done something, then made you forget it. The Cavendishes don't strike me as being particularly burdened with professional ethics."

The waitress arrived with the five whiskey sours on a tray. Rossignol cooed happily as they were lined up in front of her, then knocked back the first two, one after the other. She breathed heavily for a moment, then giggled happily, like a small child who's just done something naughty and doesn't give a damn. "Yes! Oh yes! That hit the spot!" She smiled charmingly at me, then at Dead Boy. "So, what's it like, being dead?"

"Don't tell her!" I said sharply, then looked apologetically at the startled singer. "Sorry about that, but some questions are best left unanswered. Especially when it concerns him."

"Like why he's eating that cigar instead of smoking it?"

"Very probably."

She smiled at me again, a warm and embracing moment quite at odds with her earlier, somewhat distanced personality. "You've been known to avoid answering questions yourself on occasion, *monsieur* mystery man." Her French accent had become slightly more pronounced after the third whiskey sour. I couldn't get over how alive she seemed. She looked at me thoughtfully. "You don't really think the Cavendishes would do anything to harm me, do you? I mean, they're relying on me to make them a great deal of money."

"Maybe they thought they were helping Sylvia," I said. "But there's the suicides, Ross. The Cavendishes have to be connected to that somehow. I don't trust them, and you shouldn't either. You say the word, and Dead Boy and I will take you away from them right now. We'll find you somewhere safe to lie low while we get some lawyers in to check out your contract, and maybe a few experts to make sure you haven't been messed about with magically. You don't have to worry. I can guarantee your safety. I know any number of people who'd be only too happy to bodyguard you. Not very nice people, perhaps, but . . ."

"No," said Rossignol, kindly but firmly. "It's a very generous offer, John, and I do appreciate you're only trying to help, but . . ."

"But?"

"But this is my big break. My chance to be a star. No-one has connections like the Cavendishes. They really can get me a contract with a major recording studio. I have to do this. I have to sing. It's all I've ever wanted, all I've ever cared about. I can't back out now. I won't back out over what could be just a case of nerves. You don't have any proof they've done anything wrong, do you?"

"No," I said. "But the suicides . . ."

She grimaced. "Trust me, I haven't forgotten. I'll never forget the look on that poor man's face as he pulled the trigger right in front of me. He looked right into my eyes, and he was smiling . . . I can't let that go on. My singing was always supposed to make people feel good! I wanted to lift their hearts and comfort them, send them back out to face the world feeling renewed . . . If the Cavendishes really have done something to corrupt my songs, my voice . . ." She shook her head sharply. "Oh, I don't know! I don't know what to do!" She picked up the fourth whiskey sour and stared at it moodily.

We all sat and considered the matter for a while. Up on the stage, a Whitney was singing "I Will Always Love You." Rossignol sniffed loudly.

"Never cared for that. Far too strident."

"I prefer the Dolly Parton version," said Dead Boy, unexpectedly. "More warmth."

I looked at him. "You're just full of surprises, aren't you?"

"You have no idea," said Dead Boy.

Rossignol put the fourth whiskey sour to one side as the chocolate gateau arrived. It really was very big, with scrapings of dark and white chocolate sprinkled on the top. Rossignol made ooh- and aah-ing noises, and her eyes went very wide. She grabbed the spoon and stuck it in, and soon there were chocolate smears all round her mouth. I considered her thoughtfully. An unpleasant idea had suggested itself. Perhaps the reason why this Rossignol seemed so different from the one I'd encountered at Caliban's Cavern, was because this was an entirely different Rossignol. Another duplicate, like the tulpa who'd wrecked the *Night Times*'s offices. It would explain a lot, including how she'd been able to get out of the club so easily.

"I think I need to go to the little boy's room," I said loudly, giving Dead Boy a meaningful look.

"Fine," he said. "Thanks for sharing that with us, John."

"This is the first time I've been to this club," I said pointedly. "Why don't you show me where the Gents is?"

"I've never had to use it," said Dead Boy. "One of the few advantages of being dead."

I glared at him and made furious eyebrow gestures while Rossignol was busy making ecstatic chocolate-eating noises, and he finally got the point. We got to our feet, excused ourselves, and headed for the nearby door marked *Stand Up*. Once inside, the shiny-tiled expanse was empty apart from a Kylie standing at the urinal with his skirt hiked up. Dead Boy and I waited until he'd finished, taking a keen interest in the vending machines, and once the Kylie was gone, Dead Boy gave me a hard look.

"This had better be important, John. Just being in here alone with you is undoubtedly doing my reputation no good at all."

"Shut up and listen. The Cavendishes have already sent one duplicate Rossignol after me—a tulpa with supernatural strength and a really bad attitude. Is there any way you can tell whether that's the real Rossignol or not? You're always saying nothing can be hidden from the dead."

"Oh sure. I've already checked her out."

"And?"

"She is the original. And she's dead."

I looked at him for a long moment. "She's *what?*"

"She doesn't have an aura. It was the first thing I noticed about her."

"Well, why didn't you say anything?"

"It's none of my business if she's mortally challenged. You need to be more open-minded, John."

"You mean, she's dead, like you?"

"Oh no. I'm a special case. And she's far too bright and bubbly to be a zombie. But you can't be alive without an aura. Everyone has one."

"Really?" I said, momentarily distracted. "What does mine look like?"

"Lots of purple."

"How can she be dead and not know it?" I said, almost as angry as I was exasperated. "She's out there right now giving every indication of being very much alive. Dead people don't have orgasms over chocolate gateau."

"Denial isn't just a river in Egypt. Or perhaps it's something to do with the Cavendishes and their hold over her. Do you want me to break the news to her?"

"No, I think it should come from someone who's at least heard of tact. And she did say she wanted the truth, whatever it was." I scowled at the immaculately shining white tiles. "How do you tell someone they're dead?"

"With your mouth. After all, it could be worse."

"How?"

Dead Boy gave me one of his looks. "Trust me, John. You really don't want to know."

"Oh shut up."

• • •

By the time we got back to our table, Rossignol had demolished fully half of the gateau and drunk the other two whiskey sours. She waved happily at us the moment we reappeared and stopped to suck the chocolate smears off her fingers. Her face was flushed, and she kept lapsing into fits of the giggles. Dead Boy and I sat down facing her.

"I want more drinks!" she said cheerfully. "Everybody should have lots more drinks! Do you want some cake? I can ask them for another spoon. No? You don't know what you're missing. Some days, chocolate is better than sex! Well, some sex, anyway. What are you both looking so dour for? Did you find your phone number on a wall in there?"

I took a deep breath and told Rossignol what Dead Boy had discovered about her, and what it meant. I said it as simply and straightforwardly as I could, and then I sat there, waiting to see how she'd take it. All the bounce went out of her, but her face was set and calm. Her gaze was far away and thoughtful, as she slowly licked chocolate off the back of her spoon. She might have been considering a business proposition, or the loss of a distant relative. When she finally looked at me, her gaze was entirely steady, and when she spoke, her voice seemed more resigned than anything else.

"It would explain a lot," she said. "The gaps in my memory, why I'm always so cold, why I'm always so docile when the Cavendishes are around. They did this to me. The old me, the true me, would never have put up with the way they've been treating me. Being here, away from them, is like waking up from some dark, listless nightmare. Only I'm not going to wake up from this dream, am I? I'm dead."

I wanted to take her in my arms and comfort her, tell her everything was going to be all right, but I'd promised her I'd never lie to her. She worried her lower lip between her teeth for a while, then she looked from me to Dead Boy and back again.

"Is there anything you can do to help me? Or at least find out what these cochons did to me?"

"I can try," said Dead Boy, surprisingly gently. "I have learned to See all kinds of things that are hidden from the living. It helps that you and I are both dead. It gives me a link I can use." He took her hand in his and gestured for me to take his other hand. I did so, a little hesitantly. I still remembered what he'd done to Grey. Dead Boy smiled briefly. "Don't wet yourself, John. I'm just going to look into Rossignol's mind and call up a vision of her last moments alive. Her memory is probably blocked by the trauma of what happened. As long as both of you are linked to me, you'll be able to see what I See. But remember, it's just a vision of the past. We can't interfere or intervene. The past cannot be changed, no matter how much we might wish to."

His grip tightened on my hand, and suddenly we were somewhere else. No incantations, no objects of power—just the will of a man who'd been dead for thirty years and still wouldn't lie down. We were in the Cavendishes' inner office, the place to which I had been dragged, broken and bleeding. Mr. and Mrs. Cavendish were smiling at a preoccupied and scowling Rossignol. She was trying to tell them something, but they weren't listening. Mrs. Cavendish poured Rossignol a glass of champagne and said something soothing. Rossignol snatched the glass out of her hand, knocked it back in one, and threw the glass aside. Then she fell heavily to the floor, as her legs betrayed her. She lay there, convulsing and frothing at the mouth, while Mr. and Mrs. Cavendish looked on, smiling. Until, finally, she lay still. Then the Cavendishes looked at someone standing in the shadows, but I couldn't make out who the third person was.

We were suddenly back at our table again. Dead Boy had let go of our hands. Rossignol was trembling, but her mouth was a firm, flat line. She made herself be still with an effort of will.

"The Cavendishes poisoned me?" said Rossignol. "Why would they want to murder their meal ticket?"

"A good question," I said. "And one I think we should ask them, in a pointed and forcible manner."

"You could also ask them what they did to her afterwards," said Dead Boy. He looked at Rossignol speculatively. "You don't act like any kind of zombie I'm familiar with. You're quite definitely deceased, but there are still traces of life about you."

"Could the Cavendishes have made a deal like yours?" I said. "Presumably on her behalf, as her management."

"No," Dead Boy said firmly. "Such compacts can only be entered into willingly. That's the point. You can't just lose your soul—you have to sell it."

"Still," I said, "any kind of magic that can raise the dead is by definition the work of a major player. There was someone else in that office, even if we couldn't make out who it was. The only Power the Cavendishes have on their side that I know of is the Jonah. And while he may become a Power and a Domination eventually, like his father, he's no necromancer."

"How does any of this tie in to the people killing themselves after they've heard me sing?" said Rossignol. Her face was still calm and controlled, but her voice was becoming increasingly brittle.

"You went into the dark," said Dead Boy. "And when you came back, you brought some of it with you. It comes out in your songs, when you sing. That's what's killing people."

"*How could they?*" said Rossignol. "How could the Cavendishes do something like that? My songs were always about life and being positive, even when I wrote about sad things. My voice was meant to raise people up, not destroy them! The Cavendishes have ruined the one thing that gave my life meaning!" Her voice threatened to crack then, but still she held on with iron self-control. Her hands were clenched into fists on top of the table. "I won't let this go on. No more people dead because of me. I want my old voice back. I want my life back!" She glared at Dead Boy, then at me. "Can you help me? Either of you?"

"I can't even help myself," Dead Boy said quietly.

"Let's not give up all hope just yet," I said quickly. "Dead Boy, you said yourself she's not like any other revenant you've ever met. Let's find out exactly what was done to her. Some magical deaths can be reversed."

"You think the Cavendishes will agree to that?" said Dead Boy.

"I don't plan to give them any choice," I said, and my voice was so cold that even Dead Boy had to look away.

And that was when a wave of quiet swept across the club. The music and the singing cut off abruptly in mid number, and the chatter from the surrounding tables died swiftly away to nothing. We all looked around and found every diva in the place staring straight at us. Every trannie, every celebrity by proxy, was up on their feet and staring at us with dark, malignant eyes. Their painted faces were suddenly strange, twisted, shaped by new and deadly emotions. It was like being suddenly surrounded by a pack of wolves. Rossignol and Dead Boy and I rose slowly to our feet, and a frisson of anticipation moved through the menacing crowd. They all smiled at the same moment, a grimace that was all teeth and no humour. One of the Marilyns produced a knife from out of his puffed sleeve. As though that was a signal, dozens of other divas suddenly had weapons in their hands, everything from knives to razor blades to the occasional derringer. Several of them smashed bottles and glasses against tables to make jagged-edged weapons.

"They've been possessed," Dead Boy said quietly. "I know the signs. Their auras have changed. They were channelling the talents and even some of the personalities of their heroines, but that channel has been overridden by a stronger signal, imposed from outside. There's something new and a whole lot nastier in those bodies now."

"Could it be The Primal?" I said. "Back for another crack at us?"

"No," said Dead Boy. "The signs are still human."

A Dusty lurched suddenly forward to stare at Rossignol with unblinking eyes. "We are your greatest fans. We worship you. We adore you. We would die for you. You shouldn't be here. We have come to take you back where you belong."

"Bloody hell," I said. "It's that bunch of Goths and geeks the Cavendishes let hang around their outer office. The fan club from Hell. The Cavendishes must have put them in the divas' heads and sent them to bring Ross back."

"You can't stay here," the Dusty said to Rossignol, ignoring me. "These people are no good for you. You must come with us, back to the Cavendishes. They will make you the star you were born to be. Come with us, now."

"And if she doesn't?" I said.

Without any change of expression, the Dusty slashed at my throat with his knife. I jerked my head back, and he only just missed. The other divas surged forward, raising the weapons in their hands. All the Judys, Kylies, Marilyns, Nicos, and Blondies. Famous faces, marred and twisted by second-hand rage and envy. Someone was threatening to take their goddess away from them, and they would die or kill to prevent that. In their minds, they were rescuing their heroine. Dusty cut at me again. I caught his wrist, twisted it till the fingers reluctantly opened, dropping the knife, then I punched him out. Dead Boy was picking divas up and throwing them around like rag dolls. But there were always more, pressing remorselessly closer, some with improvised weapons like spiked stiletto heels, long hairpins, and clawed fingernails. A Kate Bush came at me shrieking, with a long dagger in his hand. I grabbed Dead Boy and pulled him between us, using his dead body as a shield. The knife slammed into his chest up to the hilt.

"You bastard, Taylor!" said Dead Boy, and then rather spoiled the effect by giggling. I heaved his dead body this way and that, deflecting attacks. It soaked up the punishment, and Dead Boy didn't object. I think he was getting a weird kind of kick out of it. Rossignol was beside me, fighting dirty, pulling trannies' wigs down over their eyes and kicking them in the nuts when she could get a clear target. My back slammed up against the wall behind me, and I yelled past Dead Boy's shoulder for Rossignol to overturn our table and make it a barricade. She broke away from shoulder-charging a Nico and pulled the table over, and soon all three of us were sheltering behind it.

"I'm bored with this," said Dead Boy. "I know a curse that will boil their brains in their heads."

"No!" I said quickly. "We can't kill any of them! The divas aren't responsible for this. They're the victims here."

"Oh hell," said Dead Boy. "It's good deeds time again, is it?"

The divas, all of them eerily silent, swarmed around us, trying to reach us with their weapons and clawed hands. We were safe for the moment, but we were trapped in our corner. There was nowhere left for us to go, and soon enough the divas would work together to pull the table away; and then . . . I swore regretfully, and reluctantly did what I do best. I concentrated and opened up my inner eye, my third eye, and used my gift to find the channel the fans were using to drive the divas. It was like suddenly seeing a shimmering latticework of silver strings, rising up from the divas' heads and sailing off into infinity. And having seen it, it was the easiest thing in the world to locate the single thread they all connected to, the focus for the overlaying signal. It turned out to be a single diva, a Whitney, standing watching from the stage. All I had to do was point the Whitney out to Dead Boy, and he made a swift crushing motion with his fist. The Whitney crumpled unconscious to the stage, and all of the silver lines snapped off.

The spell was broken in a moment, and the attacking divas were suddenly nothing more than disoriented men in frocks and make-up. They stopped where they were, shocked and confused, some clinging to each other for mutual support and comfort. Possession is a kind of violation, of the mind and the soul. For a moment, it actually seemed the danger was over. I should have known better.

The trannies suddenly screamed and scattered as a dozen dark and dangerous figures appeared out of nowhere. Tall menacing figures, with smart suits and no faces. I had used my gift once too often, burned too brightly in the night, and now my enemies had found me again. They had sent the Harrowing for me. The trannies quickly cleared the floor and disappeared out the exits. It had all been too much for them. I would have run, too, if I could. The Harrowing advanced slowly towards us, unstoppable figures of death and horror. They had human shapes, but they didn't move like people did, and the faces under their wide-brimmed hats were only stretches of blank skin. They had no eyes, but they could see. One of them raised its hand, showing me the hypodermic needles where its fingernails should have been. Thick green drops pulsed from the tips of the needles, and I shuddered. Rossignol was clutching my arm so hard it hurt. Dead Boy was frowning for the first time.

"Would I be right in thinking events have just taken a distinct turn for the worse?"

"Oh yes," I said. "They're the Harrowing. The hounds my enemies send after me. You can't hurt or kill them because they're not real. Just constructs. And there's nothing you or I can do to stop them."

"How do you normally deal with them?" said Rossignol.

"I run like hell. I've spent a lot of my life running from the Harrowing." I raised my gift again, desperately trying to find a way out, but there wasn't one. There was no exit close enough to reach, and the overturned table wouldn't slow them down for a second. The dozen vicious figures moved towards us, relentless as cancer, implacable as destiny. And then a female figure came howling out of nowhere and launched itself at one of the Harrowing. The attacker had been a Kylie once, but all traces of glamour and femininity had been torn away by recent traumas. All that mattered to the Kylie now was that there was a target for his rage. He stabbed the Harrowing in the chest, and its pliant body just absorbed the blow, taking no damage and trapping both the knife and the hand inside its unnatural flesh. The Harrowing made a brief slashing gesture with one hand, and the Kylie just fell apart into a hundred pieces, blood spurting and gushing all over the floor.

"Damn," said Dead Boy. "That is seriously nasty. You know, I have to wonder . . . how many pieces could you cut me into, and I'd still be able to put myself back together again?"

"Well, unless you fancy life as a jigsaw, stop wondering about it and bloody well do something," I said, stridently.

"Boys," said Rossignol. "They really are getting terribly close. Please tell me one of you has something resembling a plan."

"When you get right down to it," said Dead Boy, "I'm just a walking corpse who's picked up a few unpleasant stratagems along the way. There's nothing in my bag of tricks that could even slow those bastards down. You have really powerful enemies, John."

"Okay," I said, my mouth almost painfully dry. "That's it. Dead Boy, grab Ross and run like hell. As long as you're not a threat, they might not bother with you. They're only here for me."

"What will they do to you?" said Rossignol.

"If I'm lucky, they'll kill me quickly," I said. "But I've never been that lucky. The Harrowing are horror and despair. Please, get out of here."

"I can't leave you," said Dead Boy. "Good deeds, remember? Abandoning you now would set me back years."

"And I won't leave you," said Rossignol. "If only because you're my only hope of breaking free from the Cavendishes."

"Please," I said. "You don't understand. If you stay, they'll do . . . horrible things to you. I've seen it happen before."

"You'll think of something, John," said Rossignol. "I know you will."

But I didn't. I'd never been able to face the Harrowing, only run from them. My very own pursuing demons. The first of the Harrowing grabbed one edge of our barricading table with a puffy corpse-pale hand and threw it aside as though it were nothing. Dead Boy braced himself, and I pushed Rossignol behind me, sheltering her with my body. And then all the Harrowing stopped and turned their featureless faces, as though listening to something only they could hear. They started to shake and shudder, and then one by one they fell apart into rot and slime, slumping shapelessly to the floor. One moment a dozen menacing figures were closing in on us, and the next there was nothing but thick puddles of reeking ooze, spreading slowly. Dead Boy and I looked at each other, and then we both glared round sharply at the sound of soft, mocking laughter. And there, standing on the stage at the end of the room was Billy Lathem, the Jonah, in his smart, smart suit. He looked very pleased with himself. Standing on either side of him in their undertakers' clothes were Mr. and Mrs. Cavendish.

"I told you, John," said the Jonah. "I am far more powerful than you ever realised. I am entropy, the end of all things, and not even sendings like those ugly bastards can stand against me. Now, you have something that doesn't belong to you. And I have come to repossess it."

"Come along, dear Rossignol," said Mr. Cavendish. "You'll be late for your show."

"You don't want to be late for your show, do you?" said Mrs. Cavendish.

Rossignol was still gripping my arm tightly. "I won't go with them. Don't let them take me, John. I can't go back to being the half-asleep thing I was, nodding and smiling and agreeing to everything they said. I'd rather die."

"You don't have to go anywhere you don't want to," I said, but it didn't sound convincing, even to me. I was still stunned at how easily the Jonah had destroyed the Harrowing. He *had* become a Power and a Domination, like his late father, Count Entropy, and I was just a man with a gift. And a bad reputation . . . I raised my head and gave Billy Lathem one of my best enigmatic looks.

"We've done this dance before, Billy. Back off, or I'll use my gift . . ."

"You don't dare," said the Jonah, grinning nastily. "Not now your enemies know where you are. What do you think they'll send next, if you're dumb enough to open up your mind again? Something so appalling even I might not be able to deal with it. No, your only option now is to hand over the girl and skulk off out of here, before your enemies track you down anyway." He laughed suddenly. "You'll never be able to bluff anyone ever again, John. Not after I tell everyone how I saw you cringing and helpless, and hiding behind a table. And all from things I turned to rot and slime with just a wave of my hand. Now, you back off, John. Or I'll use my power to find the one piece of bad luck that will break you forever."

NINE

Seeing the Light, at Last

And so, one of the messiest and most messed-up cases of my career came to this—showdown at the Divas! saloon. The only trouble was, in the Jonah the Cavendishes had by far the biggest gun. His reducing of the Harrowing to so much multi-coloured mush had been truly impressive. Never thought the boy had it in him. Perhaps staring him down and humiliating him in front of his employers hadn't been such a great idea after all. Certainly something had put a rocket up his arse. You could practically see his power crackling on the air around him, writhing and coiling, bad luck waiting to be born and cursed on the living.

We stood there in our two groups, at opposite ends of the ballroom, separated by a sea of overturned tables and chairs, and the suppurating remains of the Harrowing. Mr. and Mrs. Cavendish in their shabby undertakers' outfits, and the Jonah in his smart, smart suit, standing by the entrance doors. And me, Dead Boy, and Rossignol, standing by our abandoned barricade. The good guys and the bad guys, face to face for the inevitable confrontation.

I was looking unobtrusively around for an exit. I've never been much of a one for this kind of confrontation if there's an exit handy.

"Kill them," said Mr. Cavendish, in his cold, clipped voice.

"Kill them all," said Mrs. Cavendish, in her sharp clear voice.

"No," said the Jonah, and both the Cavendishes looked at him, surprised. He smiled, unmoved. "I want to see them suffer first."

The Cavendishes looked at each other. Both of them started to say something, then stopped. They considered the Jonah thoughtfully. Something had just changed in their relationship with their hired gun, and they weren't sure what.

"Come up onstage, all of you," said Billy Lathem, the Jonah, son of Count Entropy. "I want you to know exactly how badly you've failed, John. I want to explain it all to you, so you can see you never really stood a chance."

"Why should I do anything you say, Billy?" I said, genuinely interested in what his answer would be.

"Because I'll tell you the truth about what we did to poor dear Rossignol," said the Jonah.

Just like that he had me where he wanted me, and we both knew it. So I shrugged casually and headed for the stage, with all my hackles stirring. Something bad was coming, I could feel it, and it was aimed right at me. Dead Boy and Rossignol came with me. The Jonah said a few low words to the Cavendishes, and they followed him up onto the opposite side of the stage. We all stopped a cautious distance apart, then we all looked at the Jonah, to see how he wanted to play this. He was smiling a happy cruel smile, a predator about to play with his prey, for a while.

"We allowed Rossignol to escape from Caliban's Cavern," the Jonah said easily, "in order that we could follow her, to you. We were waiting for someone to make contact with her, and it wasn't really any surprise when the go-between turned out to be the besotted and predictable and stupidly loyal Ian Auger. The Cavendishes wanted me to trail Rossignol, then . . . take care of things, but I persuaded them to come along. I wanted them to see me take you down, John, to watch and appreciate as I destroy you, inch by inch. They don't get out much these days. Well, you can tell that from their awful pallor, can't you? I've seen things crawl out from under rocks sporting better tans. And they really don't like to be out and about in public, but I wanted them to be here, so here they are. Isn't it marvelous how things can work out, if you just put your mind to it?"

"So the servant becomes the master," I observed to the Cavendishes. "Or the monster turns on his creator, if you prefer. Not for the first time, of course. You do remember Sylvia Sin, don't you?"

"Charming girl," said Mr. Cavendish. "Always said she'd go far, didn't I, Mrs. Cavendish?"

"Indeed you did, Mr. Cavendish." The woman looked at me thoughtfully. "Have you seen the dear girl recently?"

"Yes," I said. "She was a monster. So I put her out of the misery you put her into."

"Oh good," said the woman. "We do so detest loose ends. And as for the Jonah—why, he is our dear friend and ally, and we are very proud of him. We predict great things for him, in the future."

"Couldn't have put it better," said the man. "A person to be watched, and studied."

"What happened to Ian?" Rossignol said suddenly. "What did you do to him?"

"Ah yes," said the Jonah. "Never cared much for the shifty little runt. Let's just say that the trio . . . has now become a duet." He sniggered loudly at his own wit, while Rossignol turned her head away. The Jonah looked at the Cavendishes. "Tell them. Tell them everything. I want them to know it all, to know how badly they've failed, before I do terrible things to them. You can start by telling them who you really are."

"Why not?" said the man. "It's not as if they will be around to tell anyone else."

"You tell it, Mr. Cavendish," said the woman. "You have always had a way with words."

"But you have always been the better story-teller, Mrs. Cavendish, and I won't have you putting yourself down."

"And I thank you kindly for saying that, my dear, but . . ."

"Get on with it!" said the Jonah.

"We are older than we look," said the man. "We have assumed many names and identities, down the years, but we are perhaps still best known for our original nom de guerre, in the nineteenth century—the Murder Masques."

"Yes," said the woman, smiling for the first time as she took in our expressions. "That was us. Uncontested crime lords of old London, the greatest villains of the Victorian Age. No sin was ever practiced there, but we took our commission. We laughed at police and politicans. We even brought down the great Julien Advent himself."

"Or rather, you did," said the man. "Credit where credit is due, my very dear."

"But I couldn't have done it without you, dearest. Now, where was I? Ah yes. We became involved with corruption in business, along with everyone else, and discovered to our surprise that there was far more money to be made in business than in crime, if business was approached with the right attitude. So we put aside our famous masques, cut off our old contacts, and made new names for ourselves in Trade. We prospered, mostly at the expense of our more timid competitors, and soon enough we became a Corporation. And as corporations are immortal, so we became immortal. Such things happen, in the Nightside. As our business thrives, so do we. As long as it exists, so shall we. Money is power, power is magic. And, of course, when the well-being of Cavendish Properties is threatened, so are we."

"So we take all such threats very seriously," said the man. "And we take all necessary steps to defend ourselves."

"You're just vultures," said Dead Boy. "Profiting from the weaknesses of others, feeding on the carcasses of those you bring down."

"The very best kind of business," said Mrs. Cavendish. "Born of the Age of Capitalism, we now embody it."

"That's why you call yourself Mr. and Mrs. all the time," I said, just to feel I was contributing something. "Because you've had so many identities, you have to keep reminding yourselves who you are these days."

"True," said Mr. Cavendish. "But irrelevant."

"Julien Advent will track you down," I said. "He's never forgotten you."

The Cavendishes shared a warm smile. "And we have never forgotten him," said the woman. "Because there's one part of the story, that oft-told legend, which dear Julien has never got around to telling. The great love of his life, the one who betrayed him to the Murder Masques and their waiting Timeslip, was me. I shall never forget the look of shock and horror on his face when I took off my Masque. I thought I'd never be able to stop laughing."

"He cried," said the man. "Indeed he did. Real tears. But then Julien always was a sentimental sort."

"He really had no-one but himself to blame," said the woman. "I was working as a dancer in the chorus line when he met me. Just another pretty face with an average voice and a good pair of legs, but he took a fancy to me. Gentlemen often did, in those days. He introduced me to a better life, to all sorts of expensive tastes and appetites. Some of which he proved unwilling to provide. He thought he was saving me. He should have asked me whether I wanted to be saved.

"Since he wouldn't give me what I wanted, I went looking for someone who would, and at one of Julien's soirees, I made the acquaintance of the generous gentleman at my side. The Murder Masque himself. He showed me a whole new world of monies and pleasures, and I took to it as to the manner born. And so I took up a Masque, too, and I found far more thrills as a lord of crime than I ever did in poor Julien's arms. In the end, when I pushed him into the Timeslip to be rid of him, I didn't feel anything at all."

"Tell them," the Jonah said impatiently. "Tell John what we did to Rossignol. I want to see his face, once he realises there's nothing he can do to save her."

"Our Rossignol grew just a little too independent as she became more popular," said Mr. Cavendish. He sounded stiff and even bored, as though he was only saying this to satisfy the Jonah's wishes. "She started taking meetings on her own, without consulting us first. Executives at the record companies professed to be concerned by the terms of our deal, though Rossignol had been glad enough to sign it at the time, when no-one else would touch her. Those executives assured Rossignol she could do much better with them. They promised their lawyers would easily break the contract, if she would only transfer her allegiance to them. So she came to us and demanded a better deal, or she would leave."

"The impudence of the girl!" said Mrs. Cavendish. "Of course, we couldn't allow her to do any such thing. Not after all the money we'd already invested in her. And all the money we stood to make. We found her, we made her, we groomed her. We made Rossignol into a viable product. We had a right to protect our investment. Don't think you're fighting the good fight here, Mr. Taylor. This damsel in distress doesn't need rescuing. From what, after all? Fame and fortune? We promised we would make her a star, and so we shall. But she is our property, and no-one else's."

"What about freedom of choice?" I said.

"What about it?" said Mr. Cavendish. "This is business we're talking about. Rossignol signed away all such nonsense when she put her fate in our hands. Rossignol belongs to Cavendish Properties."

"Is that why you murdered her?" said Dead Boy. "Because she wanted to leave and run her own life?"

The Cavendishes didn't seem at all surprised by the accusation. If anything, they preened a little.

"We didn't actually kill her," said the woman.

"Not quite," said the man.

"She isn't entirely dead," said the woman. "The poison we gave her took her to the very edge of death, then the Jonah found and imposed the one chance in a million that held her there, at death's very door, in an extended Near-Death Experience. And when she came back from the edge, and we revived her, the profound shock had reduced her will and vitality to such a malleable state that she imprinted on us and accepted us as surrogate parents and authority figures. We had to keep her isolated, of course, to preserve this useful emotional connection. But even so, she persisted in displaying annoying signs of independence . . . perhaps we need to poison her again and repeat the process, to put her back in the right frame of mind."

"You bastards," said Rossignol.

"Oh hush, child," said the man. "Artistes never know what's best for them."

"But the best bit," said the Jonah, beaming happily, "the best bit is that only my will holds her where she is, on the very edge of death. My magic, my power. Her life is irrevocably linked to mine now. If you attack me, John, if you kill me, she goes all the way into the dark. Forever and ever. You don't dare threaten me."

"That's as may be," Dead Boy said mildly. "But what can you threaten me with? I only just met this girl, and her life and death are a small thing to me. You, on the other hand, have dared to meddle in my province, and I won't have that. I think I'll kill you anyway, Billy boy."

"Don't call me that! That's not my name any more! I'm . . ."

"The same irritating little tit you've always been, Billy."

"I'll . . ."

"You'll what? Kill me dead? Been there, done that, stole the T-shirt. And you're nowhere near powerful enough to break the compact I made."

"Perhaps not," said the Jonah, and suddenly he was smiling again. I stirred uneasily. I really didn't like that smile. The Jonah stepped forward to lock glares with Dead Boy. "You've done a really good job of stitching and stapling yourself together, down the years. All the wounds and damage you took, and never thought twice. Holding your battered and broken body together with superglue and duct tape. But . . . what if none of it had ever held? What if all your repairs just . . . failed?"

He made a short chopping gesture with one hand, and it was as though Dead Boy's body exploded. His back arched as black duct tape suddenly unwrapped and sailed away like streamers. Stitches and staples shot out, pattering softly to the stage, and his clothes were only tatters. No blood flew, or any other liquid, but all at once there were gaping wounds opening everywhere in Dead Boy's death-white flesh. He collapsed as his legs failed him, pale pink organs and guts falling out of him, and he hit the stage hard. One hand fell away entirely, the fingers still twitching. Dead Boy lay still, wounds opening slowly like flowers. I'd never realised how much damage he'd taken. Rossignol gripped my arm so hard it hurt, but didn't make a sound. And I just stood where I was, because I couldn't think of a single damned thing I could do to help my friend.

"Entropy," the Jonah said smugly, "means *everything* falls apart. Look at you now, Dead Boy. Not so big now, are you? Can you still feel pain? I do hope so. You must have made a hell of a deal, to be able to survive so much punishment . . . Not that it's done you any good, in the end. Tell you what, Mr. and Mrs. Cavendish, why don't you come over here and do the honours. Send him on his way. I wouldn't want to be accused of hogging all the fun."

The Cavendishes looked at each other, sighed quietly, then moved forward to indulge the Jonah. They stood over Dead Boy and studied his stubbornly existing body with thoughtful frowns.

"We could always feed him into a furnace," said Mr. Cavendish.

"Indeed we could," said Mrs. Cavendish. "I always enjoy it so much more when they're still alive to appreciate what's happening."

"But I think a more immediate end is called for here," said the man. "Major players like Dead Boy have a habit of escaping their fates, if given the slightest chance."

"And we haven't existed this long by taking unnecessary chances with our enemies, Mr. Cavendish."

"Quite right, my dear."

They both drew handguns from hidden holsters and shot Dead Boy in the heart and in the forehead. He jerked convulsively, pink-and-grey brains spraying out the back of his head. And then he lay back and was perfectly still, and his eyes looked at nothing at all. The Cavendishes turned to face me, and I gave them my best sneer.

"Your guns don't have bullets in them any more, you bastards."

The Cavendishes pulled the triggers anyway a few times, but nothing happened. They shrugged pretty much in unison and went back to stand behind their Jonah.

"We've always believed in delegation," said the man.

"You wanted him, dear Billy," said the woman. "He's all yours."

The Jonah stepped forward, smiling his cocky smile like he had all the time in the world and wouldn't have rushed this for anything. "Still got a few tricks left up your sleeve, eh, John? But then, tricks are all you ever really had. Your precious gift for finding things was never a real power, not like mine. There's nothing you can do to stop me killing you and taking Rossignol back where she belongs. How shall I kill you, John? Let me count the ways . . . The cancers that lie in wait, needing only a nudge to swell and prosper. The arthritis that lurks in every joint, the bacteria and viruses to boil in your blood . . . Perhaps all of them at once might be amusing. You might even explode like Dead Boy! Or maybe . . . I'll find that one-in-a-million chance where you were born horribly deformed and helpless, and leave you like that. So everyone can see what happens to anyone foolish enough to cross the Jonah."

He could do it. He had the power. And all I had was a gift I didn't dare use again. Now my enemies knew exactly where I was, if I opened my mind to use my gift, they'd attack my mind directly. They'd take control of my mind and my soul in a second, then . . . there are worse things than death, in the Nightside. But without my gift, I didn't have anything strong enough to stop the Jonah and save Rossignol. All I had . . . was myself. I smiled suddenly, and the Jonah's grin faltered.

"Billy, Billy," I said, calm and easy and utterly condescending, "you never did understand the true nature of magic. It's not based in the power we wield or the gifts we inherit. In the end, it all comes down to will and intent. And the mind and soul behind them."

I locked eyes with the Jonah, and he stood very still. The whole world narrowed down to just the two of us, eye to eye, will to will. All we were, brought out onto the brightly lit mental stage, peeling back the layers to show who and what we were at the core. And for all his power, and despite everything he'd done, Billy Lathem looked away first. He actually staggered back a few steps, breathing hard, his face pale and sweaty.

"Who the hell are you?" he whispered. "What are you? You're not human . . ."

"More human than you, you little prick," said Rossignol. She stepped past me, and when the Jonah looked at her, she sang right into his face. Her voice was strong and true and potent, and she aimed it like a weapon right at him. I fell quickly backwards, clapping my hands to my ears. Beyond the Jonah, the Cavendishes were retreating, too, and protecting their ears. Rossignol sang, face to face with the Jonah—a sad, sad song of love lost and lovers gone, and all the secret betrayals of the heart. She sang directly at him, and he couldn't look away, couldn't back away, like a mouse hypnotized by a snake, like a fish on a hook. She held him where he was, with a merciless song of violation and isolation and the corruption of talent. Everything that had been done to her, she threw back at him. And the more she sang, the more it was the story of his life, too. Of poor little Billy Lathem, who might have been a Power and a Domination like his father, but had never been anything more than a hired thug.

The Cavendishes huddled together for comfort, as far away as they could get. I had my hands pressed so tightly to my ears I thought my skull would collapse under the pressure, and still the edges of the song ripped and tore at me, till my heart felt it would tear loose in my chest. Tears were running down my face. And Billy Lathem, forced to face the truth at last, whispered, *Daddy, I only wanted you to be proud of me* . . . and disappeared. Air rushed in to fill the space his body had occupied, as Billy turned his power on himself and selected the one chance where he was never born.

Rossignol stopped singing, though the power of her voice still seemed to reverberate on the air. She swayed suddenly on her feet, then collapsed. I grabbed her before she hit the floor, but caught off-balance, her weight carried both of us down. I sat on the stage, holding her in my arms, and only then realised she was dying. Her breathing was slowing, and I could feel her heart counting down to zero. Only the Jonah's will had kept her from death's door, and with him gone her long-delayed destiny was finally catching up with her. Vitality drained out of her, as though someone had opened a tap. I held her to me fiercely, as though I could stop it going through sheer force of will, but that trick never works twice.

"I promised I'd save you," I said numbly.

"You promised me the truth," said Rossignol, with pale lips that hardly moved. "I'll have to settle for that. Not even the great and mighty John Taylor can keep all his promises."

And just like that, she was gone. She stopped talking, she stopped breathing, and all the life went out of her. I still held her in my arms, rocking her quietly, still trying to comfort her.

"Oh dear," said Mr. Cavendish. "What a pity. Now we'll have to start all over again, with someone else."

"Never mind, Mr. Cavendish," said the woman. "Third time lucky."

I looked up at them, and there was murder in my eyes. They started pushing bullets into their guns, but their hands were trembling. And then we all looked round, startled, as Dead Boy spoke. It was just a whisper, with most of his lungs gone, but it was still and quite clear in the quiet.

"It's not over yet," he said, staring blindly up at the ceiling. "Rossignol is dead, but not actually departed. Not yet. There's still time, John. Still time to save her, if you've got the will and the courage."

"How is it you're still with us?" I said, too numb to be properly surprised. "Half of your insides are scattered across the stage. They blew your brains out, for God's sake!"

He chuckled briefly. An eerie, ghostly sound. "My body's been dead for years. It doesn't really need its internal organs any more. They don't serve any purpose. This body is just a shape I inhabit. A habit of living. Like eating and drinking and all the other things I do to help me pretend I'm still alive. You can still rescue Rossignol, John. I can use your life force to power a magic, to send both of us after her. Into the dark lands, the borderlands we pass through between this life and the next. When I died and came back, the door was left open a crack for me. I can go after her, but only a living soul can bring her back again. I won't lie to you, John. You could die, doing this. We could all go through that final door and never return. But if you're willing to try, if you're willing to give up all your remaining years in one last gamble, I promise you, we have a chance."

"You can really do this?" I said.

"I told you," said Dead Boy. "I know all there is to know about death."

"Ah, hell," I said. "I never let a client down yet."

"An attitude like that will get you killed," said Dead Boy.

"What if the Cavendishes attack us while we're gone? Destroy our bodies, so there's nothing left to come back to?"

"We'll be back the same moment we left. Or we won't be back at all."

"Do it," I said.

Dead Boy did it, and we both died.

• • •

Powered by all the remaining years of my life, Dead Boy and I went into the dark together, and for the first time I discovered there is a darkness even darker than the Nightside. A night that never ends, that never knew stars or a moon. The coldest cell, the longest fall. It was the absence of everything, except for me and Dead Boy. I was just a presence, without form or shape, a scream without a mouth to limit it, but I calmed somewhat as I sensed Dead Boy's presence. We spoke without voices, heard though there was no sound.

There's nothing here. Nothing . . .

Actually there is, John, but you're still too close to life to be able to appreciate it. Think yourself lucky.

Where's Ross?

Think of the darkness as a tunnel, leading us to a light. A way out. This way . . .

Yes . . . How can there be a direction when there's nothing . . .

Stop asking questions, John. You really wouldn't like the answers. Now follow me.

You've been this way before.

Part of me is always here.

Is that supposed to make me feel better? You're a real spooky person, you know that?

You have no idea, John. This way . . .

And we were falling in a whole new direction. It did help to think of the darkness as a tunnel, leading somewhere. We were definitely approaching something, though with no landmarks it was impossible to judge our speed or progress. I should have been scared, terrified, but already my emotions were fading away, as though they didn't belong there. Even my thoughts were growing fuzzy round the edges. But then I began to feel there was something ahead of me, something special, calling me. A speck of light appeared, beautiful and brilliant, all the colours of the rainbow in a single sharp moment of light. It grew unhurriedly, a great and glorious incandescence, yet still warm and comforting, like the golden beam from a lighthouse, bringing ships safely home through the long lonely nights. And then there was another presence with us, and it was Rossignol.

Are you angels?

Hardly, Ross. I don't think they're talking to me any more. This is John, with Dead Boy. We've come to take you home.

But I can hear music. Wonderful music. All the songs I ever wanted to sing.

For her it was music, for me it was light. Like the warm glow from a window, the friendly light of home after a long hard journey. Or pehaps the last light of the day, when all work is over, all responsibilities put aside, and we can all rest at last. Day is done. Welcome home, at last.

Oh John, I don't think I want to go back.

I know, Ross. I feel it, too. It's like . . . we've been playing a game, and now the game's over, and it's time to go back where we belong . . .

There was a sense of taking her hand in mine, and we moved towards the light and the music. But Dead Boy had been there before. Kindly, remorselessly, he took us both by the hand and pulled us away, back to life and bodies and all the worries of the world.

• • •

I sat up sharply, dragging air deep into my lungs as though I'd been underwater for ages. The lesser light of the world crashed in around me. I'd never felt so clearly, starkly *alive*. My skin tingled with a hundred sensations, the world was full of sound, and Ross was right there beside me. She threw herself into my arms, and for a long moment we hugged each other like we'd never let go. But eventually we did and got to our feet again. We were back in the real world, with all its own demands and priorities. Dead Boy was standing before us, complete and intact again, resplendent in his undamaged finery. The only difference was the neat bullet hole in his forehead.

"Told you I know all there is to know about death," he said smugly.

"Oh, I used some of your life energy to repair the damage the Jonah did to my body, John. Knew you wouldn't mind. Trust me, you won't miss it."

I glared at him. "Next time, ask."

Dead Boy raised an eyebrow. "I hope very much there isn't going to be a next time."

"Just how much of my life force did we use up on this stunt anyway?"

"Surprisingly little. It seems there is more to you than meets the eye, John. Mind you, there would have to be."

"You were dead!" said Mr. Cavendish, just a little shrilly. He sounded like he might be going to cry. "You were all dead, and now you're alive again! It just isn't fair!"

"That's the trouble with the Nightside," Mrs. Cavendish said sulkily. "You can't rely on people staying dead. Next time, do remember to bring some thermite bombs with us."

"Quite right, Mrs. Cavendish. Still, they all look decidedly weakened by whatever unnaural thing it was they just did, so I think it's back to the old reliable bullet in the head. Lots of them, this time."

"Exactly, Mr. Cavendish. If we can't have Rossignol, no-one can."

They aimed their reloaded guns at her. I moved to put myself between her and the guns, but that was all I could do. My time in the dark had taken everything else out of me, for the moment. I looked at Dead Boy, who shrugged.

"Sorry, I'm running on empty, too. Rossignol, any chance of a song?"

"Darling, right now I couldn't even squeak out a note. There must be something we can do!"

"Oh, shut up and die," said Mrs. Cavendish.

The two of them approached us, guns extended, taking their time, enjoying seeing their enemies helpless before them. They were going to shoot us all, and I had no magics left to stop them. But I've never relied on magic to get me through the many and varied dangers of the Nightside. I've always found using my wits and being downright sneaky much more reliable. So I waited till the Cavendishes were right in front of me, then I dug a good handful of pepper out of my hidden stash and threw it right into their smug, smiling faces. They both screamed pitifully as the pepper ground into their eyes, and I slapped the guns out of their flailing hands and gave the two of them a good smack round the back of the head, just on general principles. Dead Boy kicked their feet out from under them, and they ended up sitting on the stage, huddled together and clawing frantically at their streaming eyes.

"Condiments," I said easily. "Never leave home without them. And once the Authorities get here, I'll rub salt into your wounds as well."

At which point, an unconscious combat magician came flying onto the stage from the wings, upside down and bleeding heavily. He'd barely hit the stage with a resounding thud before two more combat magicians were backing quickly onto the stage, retreating from an unseen foe. Zen magics spat and shimmered on the air before them, as their rapidly moving hands wove cat's cradles of defensive magics. But Julien Advent, the great Victorian Adventurer himself, was more than a match for them. He bounded onstage with marvelous energy, dodging the thrown spells with practiced skill, and proceeded to run rings around the bewildered combat magicians with breathtaking acrobatics and vicious fisticuffs. He moved almost too quickly to be seen, impossibly graceful, smiling all the time, smiting down the ungodly with magnificent ease.

Being an editor for thirty years didn't seem to have slowed him down at all.

He finally stood over three unconscious combat magicians, not even breathing hard, the bastard. Dead Boy and Ross and I applauded him because, you had to, really. Julien Advent actually was all the things they said he was. He shot me a quick grin as he took in the defeated Cavendishes.

"I see the cavalry probably wasn't needed after all. Good work, John. We were afraid we might be a little overdue."

I'd only just started to process the word *we* and get the beginnings of a really bad feeling, when Walker strolled on from the wings, and all I could think was *Oh shit. I'm really in trouble now.*

Walker strode over to consider the weeping, red-eyed Cavendishes, his face as always completely calm and utterly unreadable. Walker, in his neat city suit and bowler hat, representative of the Authorities, and quite possibly the most dangerous man in the Nightside. He had been given power over everyone and everything in the Nightside, and if you were wise, you didn't ask by whom. I would have run like hell, if I'd had any strength left.

The Cavendishes became aware of Julien's presence. They forced themselves up onto their feet and faced him defiantly. He studied their faces for a long moment, his smile gone, his eyes cold.

"I've always known who you were," he said finally. "The infamous Murder Masques, still villains, still unpunished. But I could never prove it, until now." He looked at me. "I knew if anyone could bring them down, it would be you, John. If only because you were too dumb to know it was impossible. So after you came to me, I contacted Walker, and we've been following you ever since. At a discreet distance, of course. We even stood in the wings and listened as the Cavendishes incriminated themselves with their gloating. It was all so very interesting I almost didn't hear the combat magicians until it was too late. I should have known the Cavendishes would bring backup."

"I speak for the Authorities," Walker said to the Cavendishes. "And I say you're history."

"It all began with them," said Julien. "They Timeslipped me because they wanted to sieze my transformational potion, as their first big business venture. Typical, really. They couldn't just earn their money. They had to cheat. Little good it did them, because it was only after I was gone, slammed eighty years into the future in a moment, that they discovered there was no formula anywhere among my notes. I'd kept all the details in my head."

He stopped then and looked directly at Mrs. Cavendish. She stood a little straighter, still knuckling tears from one eye. The legendary Victorian Adventurer and his legendary lost love, the betrayed and the betrayer, face to face for the first time in over a century.

"Irene . . ."

"Julien."

"You haven't changed at all."

"Oh, don't look at me. I look awful."

"I've always known it was you. Hidden behind your new names and identities."

"Then why did you never come for me?"

"Because even the greatest love will die, if you stick a sharp enough knife through its heart. I knew it was you, but I couldn't prove it. You and your husband were very well protected. And in the end, I just didn't care any more. It was all such a long time ago, and I never did believe in living in the past."

She gaped at him, almost horrified. "All those years we spent waiting for you to come after us. Spinning webs and layers of protections around us, always hiding . . . all those years of being afraid of you, and you didn't give a damn."

"I had a new life to build, Irene. And there were far worse things than you in the Nightside that needed fighting."

She looked away. "I thought, sometimes, that you might have held back . . . because of me."

"My love died a long time ago. I don't know you now, Irene."

"You never did, Julien."

Mr. Cavendish moved in possessively beside his wife. "Enough talk!

We all know why you're here! Have your precious revenge and be done with it! Kill us, for everything we did to you!"

"You never did understand me," said Julien. He looked at Walker. "Take them away. Destroy their business, dismantle it, and you destroy their power. Bring them to trial and send them down. Make them into little people, like all the ones they hurt. What better punishment, for such as these?"

"I'd be delighted," said Walker, tipping his bowler hat to Julien. "My people are already on their way."

Julien gave Walker a hard, thoughtful look. "These two probably know all sorts of top people and secrets. Don't let them wriggle out."

"Not going to happen," Walker said easily. "I've been looking for an excuse to bring the Cavendishes down. Trouble-makers, always rocking the boat, never playing well with others. They might even have become a threat to the Authorities, in time. And we can't have that, can we?"

He turned unhurriedly to look at me, and I braced myself. "Well, John," said Walker. "You've led me quite a chase. Who's been a bad boy, then? But . . . not to worry. Helping me put away two big fish like these goes a long way to making up for all the trouble you've caused the Night-side tonight. Only just, mind . . ."

Julien looked at me sharply, suddenly scenting a story. "John, what is he talking about?"

"Haven't a clue," I lied, cheerfully.

TEN

Coda, with a Dying Fall

A week later, I caught Rossignol's new set at Caliban's Cavern. It was a sell-out, she was singing up a storm, and the audience loved it.

A lot had changed in the past week. The Cavendishes had had to sell Caliban's Cavern, for quick cash, to help them pay their mounting legal bills. The charges against them were building all the time, with more and more people coming out of the woodwork to kick the Cavendishes while they were safely down. It was fast becoming the Nightside's favourite sport.

Rossignol was under new management. Some group of show business lawyers who knew a good thing when they heard it and were wise enough to present Rossignol with a reasonably fair contract. They were putting a lot of money behind her, and the word was she was going to break big. She was already recording her first album, with a respected big-name producer.

The club that night was really swinging. The audience packed the place from wall to wall and danced in the aisles. It was a more usual mix this time, with hardly any of the old Goth element. Rossignol was moving up-market with her new material. I was there on my own. Dead Boy was off working on another case, and Julien Advent had a paper to put out. I could have asked my secretary Cathy, but she'd lost interest in Rossignol once she'd gone mainstream. Cathy was strictly cutting-edge only.

Backed by two Ian Augers, a new drummer, and all new backing singers, Rossignol sang of love and light and rebirth in her clear glorious voice, touching the hearts of all who heard her. She was strong and vibrant and magnificently alive. She still hung off the microphone stand and smoked like a chimney, though. The crowd loved her. She took three encores, to rapturous applause, and nobody even looked like they were thinking of killing themselves. It's nice when a case has a happy ending.

After the show, I went round the back to her dressing room. To my surprise, the door was being guarded by Dead Boy. He had the grace to look just a little embarrassed.

"So, this is your new case," I said. "No wonder you didn't want to talk about it. Bodyguarding is a bit of a step down for you, isn't it?"

"It's only temporary," he said with great dignity. "Until she and her new management can agree on someone they trust."

"She could have asked me," I said.

"Ah," said Dead Boy. "John, she's trying to forget what happened. You can't blame her, really."

"What happened to the bullet hole in your forehead?" I said, deliberately changing the subject.

"Filled it in with builder's putty," he said briskly. "Once I've grown my hair out a bit, you'll never notice it."

"And the hole in the back?"

"Don't ask."

I knocked on the dressing room door and went in. The room was full of flowers. I would have brought some, but I never think of these things. Rossignol was taking off her make-up in front of the mirror. She didn't seem particularly pleased to see me. She gave me a quick hug, kissed the air near my cheek, and we sat down facing each other. Her face was flushed, and she was still a little breathless from the set.

"Thank you for all your help, John. I do appreciate it, really. I would have phoned, but I've been very busy putting the new set together."

"I was out there," I said. "It went over great."

"It did, didn't it? John . . . don't take this wrong, but, I don't want to see you again."

"There doesn't seem any good way to take it," I said, after a moment. "What brought this on, Ross?"

"You remind me too much of bad times," she said bluntly. "I need to move on, leave it all behind. Now I'm alive again, I see things differently. I live only to sing. It's all I've ever wanted or needed. There's no room for anyone else in my life, right now. And especially not for you, John. I am grateful for everything you've done, but . . . as near as possible, I want to live a normal life now. I'm not staying in the Nightside. It was only ever somewhere to make a start. I'm going places, John."

"Yes," I said.

"I'll write a song about you, someday."

"That would be nice."

She turned away and started removing her make-up again, pulling faces at herself in the mirror. "You never did say—who hired you to look after me?"

"It was your father."

She looked at me sharply. "John, my father's been dead for two years now."

She dug into her bag and found an old photo. It was unmistakably the man who'd come into Strangefellows to hire me. So—a ghost. Not all that unusual, for the Nightside. Rossignol was touched.

"He always was very protective."

"Well," I said, "I guess I don't get paid for this case, either."

I gave Rossignol a good-bye kiss, wished her all the luck in the world, and left her dressing room. Humming the blues.